Other titles available in the Savannah Stories:

Blast From the Past

Payback

First Comes Love

Tainted Love

Walking On Broken Glass

Angel Unaware

Blood Lust

Other titles by J.L. Lemon

Second Chances

The Savannah Stories

Revelations

The Savannah Stories

Revelations

J.L. Lemon

ISBN-13: 978-0-9796117-8-0
ISBN-10: 0-9796117-8-4

Published 2011

To my precious Mom and Dad

We will fight and prevail Savannah-Style

I love you both so very much

"The only Thing that should surprise us is that there are still some things that can surprise us."

Francois De La Rochefoucauld

1

Savannah stood naked and bound spreadeagled, her body drenched in sweat. In front of her: Jeffrey Holland, his powerful body poured into only a white t-shirt and worn jeans. In a bizarre twist of fate, the former doctor strongly favored a TV doctor – McSteamy, if she remembered right. Only instead of alleviating pain, Holland enjoyed inflicting it.

He reached toward her, his icy touch glided down the valley between her breasts. A predatory smile curved his lips when she shivered in the restraints. "You know what's next, don't you?" he asked.

Yes, she knew. She remembered the victim's bodies, their breasts sliced away, leaving two bloody circles staring up at her at the crime scenes. Jeffrey removed them with surgical precision, mutilated every part of the victim's femininity and carved a number inches above the excised flesh. The number signified a tally and Savannah's was to be number ten.

He circled one breast then the other until the nipples painfully tightened, "And I'm going to take my time with you." Jeffrey lifted his scalpel, the blade gleaming in the bright room.

Savannah tried once more to pull free of her bonds, willing the chains to break, praying they would. But like Holland's gaze, they held strong. She thrashed now, panic flooding her system.

Her struggle aroused him as evidenced by the thickening bulge in his jeans. He stepped closer, "Keep fighting, Savannah. I love to see a woman struggle. Her skin flushes, her heart pounds," he placed the scalpel beneath her ear, "and when I cut into her, the blood oozes out and it actually feels hot, like it absorbs the panic and fever of her fight."

The instant the blade nestled at her pulse, she froze. The only movement: her lungs heaving for air. She tried to calm down but he stood so close she felt his heat, stared into the dark emptiness in his eyes. Pure evil danced behind them, promising heinous acts and suffering beyond human comprehension.

His other hand touched the hollow of her throat with a feathery graze. She sucked in a sharp breath, holding it as his cold fingers stroked the side of her neck. With any other man, it would feel gentle as a lover's touch but Savannah knew by experience the former doctor used it to gauge her level of fear.

His hand swept up the angle of her jaw and her breath released in the form of a whimper. Her life was literally caged between his two hands. The slightest pressure and the blade would sink in, parting the skin like butter as it opened the carotid artery.

"Don't let me stop you," he said. "Flail, writhe and scream. You'll exhaust yourself and that'll make it easier for me."

She felt the tip of the scalpel prick the skin as he eased it down her throat between her breasts. He pressed the cold edge against her right nipple. She closed her eyes, dreading the impending pain.

"Open your eyes," he demanded softly.

Opening her eyes meant obeying the monster, relinquishing another part of herself to him. Of the few things left in her control, it was that and she refused to give him the satisfaction.

Sheer terror closed around her throat, constricting it until she struggled for breath. It was coming soon.

"Savannah, open your eyes." He grew impatient. "Open them now."

No, she defied silently. *You will not see the fear in me again. You will never get that part of me again.*

The razor sharp edge of the scalpel sank into the flesh beneath her collarbone, unleashing an excruciating tide of pain down her arm and through her chest as Jeffrey sliced a "0" next to the "1" he'd carved months earlier. She was Jeffrey's longed-for goal. She was Number Ten.

Savannah screamed, instinctively strained against the bonds for precious freedom as blood poured from the wound, spilled down her breast.

Jeffrey dipped his finger in the warm, sticky blood, studying it, "You know how much blood a person can lose and still live? The magic number is forty percent. Can you believe it? Forty percent or more is considered the maximum amount of blood an adult can lose before their body cannot compensate." He smeared the blood in a line that traced her carotid, "If I nick that precious artery, how long do you think it will take to lose just twenty percent? Your heart will race and your skin will grow pale, your systolic and diastolic blood pressure will converge, the blood vessels in your arms and legs will contract. Your mind will get fuzzy as confusion sets in." His voice softened to a soothing tone, "When you reach thirty-five percent, your heart beats even faster to catch up like a runner lagging behind in a race. Your blood pressure begins to collapse and that clarity you have now? Completely gone."

His hand fisted her in her hair, pulling her head back, extending her neck. She felt her carotid arteries bounding with each beat of her heart. Her throat lay bare as he placed the scalpel blade beneath her ear at her pulse, the pressure increasing with every second ticking by.

He smiled, "This time you don't walk away. This time you die."

Savannah bolted upright, a scream poised at the back of her throat, her hand pressed to her throat. No fountain of red spurted between her fingers. Only her pounding pulse met her trembling touch.

Her vision darted around the room, searching her surroundings before realizing she was in bed at home – their new home. She was safe.

The cry still fighting for freedom finally died as she noticed Ennis sitting beside her, his hand on her hip, concern etched in his handsome face. He'd been trying to wake her, "You okay?"

Savannah slowly released the deep breath, "Nightmare." A chill sank to her bones. Her skin glistened with sweat and her heart punched against her ribs. The pain was so real, the fear so crippling it would take a while to settle down.

"Jeffrey?"

She nodded, wiped a hand down her face. It was irrational, she told herself, to be afraid of Jeffrey Holland now. He was locked in a place he couldn't reach her or hurt her anymore. The nightmares were merely aftershocks, lingering echoes of the old terror she hoped eventually would fade. But Holland's face still haunted her in the night. He, along with his stepbrother Cole Jordan – who'd been a cop – sent the city spiraling into panic with their spree of sadism and death. The problem now – Cole evaded capture for nearly four months and though Savannah feared Jeffrey the most, Cole Jordan was a rapist and just as determined as Holland to have his way. To have Number Ten.

Forty percent. Jeffrey drummed it into her at the cabin. Forty percent and she was basically dead. Her subconscious wove a tapestry of hellish memories and incorporated them into nightmares she'd hoped were over. The tightness of the restraints. The icy breeze blowing across her flesh. The smell of blood and death. The agonizing pain he inflicted. Forty percent. *And it'll take a long time to reach that forty percent. I'll make sure of it,* he vowed.

Ennis stroked her thigh, "You need to see that doc again?"

Her shoulder ached in remembrance of every painful, horrible moment with the two. She'd gone to a therapist to help heal the mental damage while still trying to recover physically. Besides the injuries, she developed such a crippling paranoia, she insisted she and Ennis sell the old house and move. But as she discovered, simply changing addresses didn't exorcise the demons in her head. She took another deep breath to calm down, "I'll go if it happens again."

O O O

It had to be the nightmares causing it. Savannah dropped to her knees and heaved in the toilet for the third time before leaving for work. The night terrors usually brought bad moods, not puking, she reflected. She didn't feel particularly bad but the throwing up was getting really old. For the past week or so she suffered from one bout or another, making her wonder if she caught a bug somewhere.

Unfortunately her morning didn't improve when she approached the sergeant's desk for an update on Cole. No sightings, no phone calls, no luck at all. Nearly four months and no one cornered him.

The extended time between reports inspired hope that he'd finally run across the wrong woman and she'd killed him. Savannah did her part after escaping Jeffrey and Cole's remote cabin by ventilating him a few times. Maybe he was dead, she thought with a smile. The day began looking brighter with that prospect.

At least until she and Ennis were called to a crime scene. The good mood she fostered for all of half an hour swirled the drain when her husband zipped around the corner in their detective's Taurus. The g-force pushed her against the passenger door while the motion pushed her breakfast up her throat.

"You callin' that therapist?" Ennis asked from the driver's seat.

Busy trying to salvage her "most important meal of the day", she entertained calling her M.D., not her shrink. If Ennis insisted on driving NASCAR style, she'd insist on Dramamine or a new driver. Just as she tried to reply, the car rounded a corner at a speed that tested the safety belt threshold.

"I'll call if I have more nightmares," she reminded then braced one hand on the dash, the other on her stomach. Deep breaths. Deep,

deep breaths, she told herself.

Ennis was going to slow down – he just didn't know it yet. The light ahead of them blinked red and she automatically checked the intersection. Cars heading east and west proceeded forward as their light turned green. Since the Taurus currently headed north, something needed to give. "Slow down, Ennis. Traffic's starting up and this car isn't equipped for a demolition derby. It about to have a nervous breakdown." *And so am I.*

She braced, closed her eyes and heard screeching tires all around. The Taurus came to an abrupt halt. She waited for the jarring crash that never materialized. Instead, horns honked to the left and right of them. Savannah chanced opening her eyes then released a long held breath. Cars stopped a few feet from the passenger and driver doors, just enough for Ennis to blast through. At that rate, the nightmares wouldn't prompt another visit with the shrink – her husband's driving would, right after she shoved her heart back down her throat into her chest again. "The guy at the aquarium is dead. He isn't getting any deader if we're a few minutes late. *We* on the other hand..." Savannah's complaint trailed into silence as she grabbed the door handle – not just for support but for something to squeeze besides Ennis's throat. With her husband and partner playing Traffic Tetris, it challenged not only her sanity but her breakfast.

Between his driving and their late-night hours trying to finish moving, it was a miracle she found any semblance of reason to start each day. Winter and spring had been hellacious. First her breast cancer surgery and radiation treatments then Jeffrey Holland and Cole Jordan came along. The last few weeks of packing their belongings and hiring a moving company sapped her energy and tested her good nature. Finally after the moving men placed the furniture, she asked them to please assemble the bed. Ennis wanted the TV, she wanted the bed. Now, holding on for dear life in their detective's car, she wondered why she hadn't heeded her boss's advice and scheduled more time off. She really needed the rest and her husband needed a refresher course on safe driving.

As the gray Taurus sedan rounded corners and bucked through intersections, she struggled to prevent what coffee she drank from making a return trip. "Ennis, I swear," she held a hand to her stomach. "You are the amusement park ride from hell. What part of 'slow down' is not connecting with your brain? I know Mathis beat us to the scene but he was *two blocks away* when it was called in. We had to drive from the station. At Warp Speed, I might add." They approached the Atlanta Aquarium – their destination – and she instinctively braced her hand on the dash. Sure enough he applied the brakes with the same teenage finesse he operated the accelerator.

"Sorry, sugar. I'll try to do better." He opened the door and got out.

She'd heard Ennis promise to ease up on the accelerator since they met. He meant it at the time but never quite managed to follow through. He'd drive sanely back to the station but like the next rising of the sun, his Richard Petty style driving would return full force.

Savannah attempted to unclench her gut while prying her death grip from the door handle. She got out and as the sweltering heat sank in, so did a brief wave of nausea. "He said he'd do better," she whispered to her stomach.

It was a good thing she didn't puke. Surveying the crowds outside the aquarium, she not only would have been photographed but televised tossing her cookies. News crews and bystanders crowded the sidewalks to the yellow crime scene tape.

Cameras swung in their direction and reporters converged, all jockeying for prime positions. Without words, the two detectives picked up the pace in hopes of avoiding questions. Both knew the effort was futile because the faster they walked, the more organized the reporters grew. They crowded together, creating a blockade until half a dozen mikes were shoved under the detective's chins. Questions ranging from the victim's identity to how it happened to doubts of the aquarium's safety were tossed at them, all answered with the same, "No comment."

She'd be grateful to get indoors with air conditioning. Summer ushered in an unusual and brutal heatwave that made citizens hot, sweaty and angry as evidenced by the reporters' and the detectives' short tempers.

She and Ennis dressed as cool as possible for the weather, she in a beige pantsuit and sleeveless violet pullover, her dark tresses bound in a ponytail. Ennis got the short end since he had to wear a full suit – a fact he mentioned every so often.

The pair flashed their badges at the uniform officer standing guard at the door. He nodded with the clever observation, "Hell of a thing. Place ain't been open a year and this happens. Bet we'll be on the national news by noon."

Savannah felt the familiar pang of a headache beginning. The cop was right. Besides the publicity surrounding the grand opening, this would be the crowning glory of all. She could already feel the mayor breaking a bigger sweat than all the media assembled at the scene. The city touted the new aquarium as the newest, biggest, and most modern attraction in the nation. Perhaps even the world. Tourism was up drastically in those few months since the opening. Positioned in the middle of downtown, the place looked like a giant blue rolling wave from the air, from the street and probably from inside too. It housed over ninety thousand animals representing four hundred species from the ocean exhibit to fresh water to a "one of a kind tropical diving experience". They built the aquarium in an underwater tunnel style so visitors walked "through" the ocean and fresh water exhibits surrounded by aquatic life. Water, water everywhere and Savannah couldn't swim.

She and Ennis passed another horde of people inside – witnesses she assumed, they joined John Mathis in the "tunnel". John had a knack for looking disheveled but that day the forty-six year-old heavyset detective looked particularly out of sorts. With his brown suit coat slung over his arm, it revealed sweat stains on his chest, under his arms and on his back. The sight made her dread the upcoming conversation. Mathis and heat did not mix well.

Unfortunately, the air conditioning she looked forward to seemed to be shut off. Not good for traumatized witnesses, overworked detectives or a newly expired individual. Adding to the lack of cool air was a new dilemma. The enclosed tunnel caused her claustrophobia to kick in. This was getting tedious already.

She watched the sharks swim by, mere feet from her, separated only by a few inches of plastic. They stared as they passed, seemingly trained on her. Was she the only one feeling eyeballed as an afternoon snack?

"Big boys, ain't they?" Mathis motioned to the fish.

Yes, evidently she was the only one feeling like a human McNugget for the beasts swimming by.

Mathis continued, "Curator said there's six million gallons of salt water in there."

"Along with one very dead man," she added. About that time, another fish swam by and nibbled at the body, causing her to flinch, "If forensics doesn't hurry, there won't be a body left."

"Yeah, but I got some pictures of the victim when I got here. The employees are trying to round up the fish first."

Staring up into the enormous fish tank, Savannah asked Mathis, "How many people saw this happen?"

He consulted his notes, "About twenty, twenty-five. Mostly tourists."

She flinched at the thought. The visitors would go home with a hell of a Kodak moment and the Georgia Bureau of Tourism wouldn't appreciate the publicity of the morning's events either. "Anyone get photos of it when it happened?" she asked.

Mathis shook his head, "Outta luck there. Already checked."

"Well, it was worth a shot." She surveyed the crowd standing behind the crime scene tape. Moms and dads held their children close, shock still registering on their faces. She hated to ask the next question, "How many kids saw it?"

"Luckily, only three."

"That's three too many." She touched her forehead to rid herself of the growing perspiration. If she thought it was hot and muggy outside she gained a new respect for misery upon entering the balmy aquarium. She removed her jacket, slung it over her arm, "It's hotter than the hinges in Hell."

Mathis mopped the back of his neck with a handkerchief, "Yeah and I got thirty minutes baking time ahead of you. I'm shedding pounds by the tons. One of the workers said the air should be on in an hour."

She sure hoped so. The sauna wasn't good for people or fish. Now she focused on the children, counting them. Unless her eyes deceived her or she hadn't paid attention in math class, she counted approximately ten kids, not three. Still, ten was a far cry from the dozens she expected, "Where were all the other kids? This place is crawling with them this time of day."

Mathis wiped his brow then referred back to his notes. Savannah knew him well enough to realize he hated retracing his steps *and* his notes for anyone. His pudgy face, along with his stance revealed his annoyance. On the tip of his nose sat reading glasses that he purposefully glanced over, "They were at the 'Finding Nemo' exhibit on the other side of the building." He pocketed the small notepad to prevent further inquiries from his female colleague.

Another fish swam past, nibbled at the body. More blood oozed into the already cloudy water. It was a disaster for the victim and the fish, Savannah reflected. The former for obvious reasons, the latter because their world was now completely contaminated.

Ennis hastily stepped back as a huge, stocky brown fish swam by them. By Savannah's estimate, its length was probably around three and half feet long and over a foot and a half tall. It had two long spiney dorsal fins and when it opened its mouth, she too stepped back. The teeth lining its jaws were long and sharp as needles.

"What the hell is that thing?" Ennis asked, shrugging out of his gray suit jacket and loosening his tie.

"It's called a Cubera Snapper," a new voice answered from behind. "That one's about sixty pounds."

"Probably closer to sixty-five or seventy by now, dontcha think?" Mathis pointed to his colleagues respectively, "Detectives Prince and Rutherford," then to the man, "Harold Gerard, caretaker of this charming exhibit."

Savannah and her partner turned to see a man, early fifties, dressed in navy blue Atlanta Aquarium overalls. A ring of gray hair wrapped around his head like a Roman wreath, crowning his pleasant features. Pleasant, that was, until Mathis opened his mouth. Savannah got the distinct impression the two exchanged more than details about the events that morning. And unfortunately for Mathis, he had the personality to alienate people quickly.

By the time Harold finished reviewing what he'd seen and heard,

Savannah concluded he'd not seen much and heard even less except the screaming of the now traumatized tourists.

"Who has access to the tanks?" she asked.

"Just employees," Harold replied and stared into the tank. "I don't readily recognize that fella but he could be a new hire."

"We'll need an employee list. Circle the names who work this particular tank too."

He nodded, "It'll take me a little while."

"How do employees get up there anyway?" she pointed above her. "What kind of security is there to prevent the public from entering?"

The man described the way up, adding, "Gotta have a passkey to get in."

"We'll need a list of anyone with a passkey too. That includes employees, security, managers and any extraneous maintenance people. Anyone who's ever had access to this facility." She looked around, "Are there security cameras at the doors?"

"Yeah. With this kind of setup, the aquarium wants to protect their investment as thoroughly as possible."

Mathis chuckled, "Didn't cover all their bases, did they?"

Ennis whispered to him to shut up. Savannah tried to ease the frown shadowing Harold's face, "Thank you for rounding up everything for us."

The caretaker sneered directly at Mathis before addressing her in a more genial manner, "No problem. When I get 'em, mind if I search you out instead of him?"

Savannah handed him her card listing her name and number on

it, "Not at all."

Ennis leaned in, "We'll need to talk to the head of security too."

"I'll get him for you," the man replied.

"Mathis," she called in an exaggerated southern belle accent, "would you be a sweetheart and take that interview?"

He grumbled under his breath then, "Sure, Mom. Anything else?"

Harold, eager to leave, directed his next statement to Savannah and Ennis, "If you need me, my office is upstairs, turn right, the last door at the end of the hall." Harold headed off in the direction of his office.

She turned to Mathis, "He's supposed to be helping us, John. Mouthing off doesn't promote that giving feeling."

"Hey," he shrugged, "everyone's a suspect. Didn't they teach you that in detective school?"

"Yes, but they also highlighted finessing a witness to cooperate, not having them dummy up or loathe us."

Ennis changed the subject, "You took witness statements, right? What did they say?"

Mathis sighed once more, incensed that his notes were required again. He thumbed a few pages, "Besides the big sploosh, thrashing of the victim and his resulting death, a few noted someone was with him just before he took a header. General consensus says it was a dark haired woman but a few malcontents claim it was a man. All say dark hair. And with that, I say we can all safely adjourn for lunch."

Sometimes the urge to pop Mathis in the chops loomed closer to the surface than it should. Savannah felt the blood rise in her cheeks. Ennis touched her wrist as a sign to calm down, "After you interview security, right? Here," he reached in his jacket. Handing his notepad to Mathis, he offered a trade, "Take mine and I'll take yours. That should relieve further angst of referring back to actual detective work."

A half-smile curved the rotund detective's mouth as he switched notepads, "See, Prince? You just gotta speak the right language for me to understand."

Savannah rolled her eyes. Sometimes Mathis was a master at delegating work, not participating in it unless absolutely necessary – and the heat dictated his eagerness level. She craned her neck to gain a better look at the floating body above her, "Can't even tell if the guy was married."

Ennis joined her in an identical stance. The body, besides being minus several chunks of flesh, was also minus most of his left hand and foot. "Nope," he agreed. "Somebody had an afternoon snack."

Mathis chuckled again, "Who wants to hang around to see which one poops it out?"

Both Savannah and Ennis slanted him irritated frowns. "Mathis," she said, "your folks should have invested in a shrink for you. The fish will be lucky to survive this."

Mathis elbowed Ennis, "Well, we know *she* won't be gutting any of the unfortunates." He waited a moment then groaned, "Oh, hell. Gimme back my notes."

"What for? Feeling guilty for ditching us already?" Savannah jibed.

"Nah. I figured talking to live people is better than what you and Rutherford signed up to do. You two can deal with Bait Boy."

O O O

After pulling on latex gloves, she and Ennis followed Harold's instructions, climbing up to the feeding and maintenance area. The stairway was wide enough for two people to pass each other but her claustrophobia didn't see it that way. The frantic beating in her chest tried to blossom into an unmerciful hammering but she managed to contain it. Ennis thankfully realized the depth of her fear and tried to help her cope as best as possible. Even now, she felt his touch on her back as they ascended the stairs.

At the top of the stairway was a door with a sizeable white placard with bold black letters "Employees Only". A passkey reader was installed next to it.

The door to the feeding area, normally closed, now stood wide open. Savannah and Ennis rounded the doorway to find two uniform officers standing sentry, arms crossed and waiting impatiently. "You guys gonna be here a while?" one asked her.

"You late for a date?" Savannah volleyed back. "You know the drill. After the next shift arrives, you can go."

One gave her a look describing his displeasure of waiting all day at the hot, balmy crime scene. The other swallowed, his cheeks pale, "Ma'am, it's just that I'm kinda squeamish around blood."

Both Savannah and Ennis stopped in mid-search. They angled a glance at each other then at the cop. Ennis spoke first, "And you're a cop?"

He shrugged, looking greener by the second, "Thought it was better than an EMT."

"Not by much," Savannah replied. "How long have you been on the job?" Not long, she knew but getting his mind off the bloody mess floating in the tank was paramount.

He chanced a look at the body, pressed his hand to his mouth and dry heaved, "Three weeks."

She felt for him, she really did. Sickness plagued every rookie and every veteran cop occasionally. But, "There's an easy remedy for your problem, at least today."

"What's that?"

"Don't look at the body."

The mere reference to the deceased caused guttural noises to percolate from the rookie's depths. She saw him about to surrender to the urge and shooed him toward the door, "Go, go, go before you complicate things."

Ennis stepped aside to allow the officer a speedy exit. Savannah already bent down to inspect the floor. A small red streak caught her attention. Blood. "Looks like our victim or suspect was cut."

The distinct sound of heaving drifted up the stairway. Savannah and Ennis winced.

Footsteps replaced the vomiting and groaning from below. She heard muted mumbling and whispers as people ascended the stairway.

She rose to confront them – and oust them – if they weren't authorized to be there.

Two men rounded the corner, their apparel casual in khakis and blue polo shirts. They wore black duty vests over their shirts, on the upper right breast was an embroidered badge with "CRIME SCENE" embroidered below. Today Hartley and Brown drew the lucky number. Damien Hartley, a man in his mid-twenties with a perpetual slyness about his features, loved bantering with her at crime scenes and telling jokes.

He sat his tool case down with a half-grin, "There's a cop downstairs heaving his toenails in a trash can."

"And that's exactly where we want him," Savannah replied.

He allowed the grin to spread, "That's what I like about you, Detective. Your empathy."

"Mathis is probably rubbing off on me. We've worked together for so long."

Hartley stated, "I've heard if you work together long enough, you start lookin' like each other too."

"That's marriage, not the job, and if I ever begin favoring John Mathis in any respect, I demand someone shoot me."

Damien cocked a brow, "I would but they still refuse to assign me a weapon for some reason."

The two shared a laugh. As long as the joking didn't cross over certain lines, she'd indulge, but Hartley had a way of twisting a regular joke into the macabre.

Being the senior crime scene tech, Hartley adapted an almost sadistic arrogance when training a newbie. Today Brown, whoever he was, became the recipient, "Take the stairway then the exits. When you're done, check the Dumpsters for anything out of place."

Shell-shocked, Brown muttered, "Dumpsters?"

"People throw murder weapons in Dumpsters all the time. Be sure to check inside thoroughly."

"B-but shouldn't we start in here?"

Hartley tossed Savannah a devilish grin while snapping on latex gloves, "That's my job. Get movin', we're burnin' daylight."

Decidedly unhappy and disgusted with his assigned task, the young man stepped out, tool case in hand.

Savannah put her hands on her hips, "Hartley, that's mean. Makin' that kid do a garbage pull by himself."

"I'll call in more hands after a while," he assured quietly. "Don't get your panties in a bunch. He's got to learn that police work is not always a pretty business, unless he's working with you." His vision flicked toward Ennis, "No offense, Detective."

Now Ennis's hands plopped on his hips. It took time for him to adjust to Hartley's personality. If she thought Ennis was protective *before* the nuptials, she quickly discovered it to be minor league compared to now. But this time Ennis merely sighed, "None taken. We found what we think is blood right there." He pointed to the spot on the floor. "You also might look for a knife or something like it."

"And we need the door handles and railing dusted for prints," Savannah added.

Hartley peered over said railing into the massive tank, "I suppose you want me to reel in our catch for the day."

Her brow sank in response. *Use discretion, Hartley. You never know who can hear you.* And lately the department took a few hits for their lack of tact.

Hartley shook his head, feigning disgust, "I do all the work and you guys get all the credit." Damien did a double-take back to the tank then squatted for a closer look in the cloudy water, "I don't think fly fishing will work –"

"Hartley, give it a rest," she warned. Private jokes aside, continual ones set her temper on edge, probably because she'd seen the devastation death caused families. She had to notify the loved ones, not Damien Hartley.

"Not in a joking mood, eh?" Hartley sighed then conceded, "Since we're being painfully professional here, I could use your help." He pointed into the tank, "I see the guy's wallet down there."

Savannah joined him at the railing, her vision following his pointing finger. Sure enough, upon closer inspection, a brown wallet lay atop a rock similar in color.

Hartley retrieved two nearby nets and handed her one, "Position yours in front of the rock and I'll flip the wallet into your net."

She gently eased the net into the water to prevent dislodging the wallet prematurely. She leaned down trying to look through the murky water to correctly place the net.

Hartley dipped his net carefully then nudged the wallet aside, sending it safely into Savannah's. She retrieved the net and opened the wallet. "Barry Vaughn," she announced, along with his address. "Ennis, call Walsh and have him run Barry's background and financials for us. Maybe by the time we get to the station, he'll have some info for us. Of course, he'll have to hurry if *you're* driving."

2

No arrests, no warrants, no parking or speeding tickets. According to the law, Barry Vaughn was an upstanding citizen. His bank account turned out to have a few thousand dollars with no previous large deposits or withdrawals. Out of six credit cards only one showed promise with several purchases of flowers over the past few months. Barry chose one florist in particular – Petal Pushers – and the amount of each purchase astounded Savannah but her opinion of him plummeted upon seeing his membership to, "Hotlanta? Oh, that's classy." Hotlanta, a sex and swinger joint, opened downtown a few years back. The times Savannah drove past on her way to Georgia's, the parking lot brimmed to overflowing. Evidently, unabashed fornication never went out of style.

Her stomach soured at the thought of entering such a den of iniquity. She imagined people flailing around like wild pagans, doing things that should have been outlawed – and probably were in most states including their own.

"This could be our acorn," her husband said, ever the optimist.

Somehow she failed to see the silver lining of his statement. People who frequented such establishments didn't just shy away from the cops, they ran like their feet were on fire and their asses were catching. If a cop managed to grab anyone in charge, they demanded court orders and lawyers. She sighed, "I hate these jackpots. Why can't people just be normal? Now we have to go in there and… and…" she searched for a palatable term but found none.

"There, there," Ennis assured. "At least we don't have to buy a membership to talk to them."

She held a hand to her stomach at the mere suggestion, "I'll try to disguise my contempt and intolerance before we walk in. Let's hit the flower shop first though." In that time she'd try to steel herself before crossing the threshold of Hell. She examined the credit card statements again, "Three orders of flowers from Petal Pushers in one day."

"Vaughn was a busy man. Hope he kept their names and addresses straight because getting 'em wrong *would* be grounds for justifiable homicide."

O O O

With a name like Petal Pushers, Savannah expected a small, family owned business tucked away in an older, more established part of Atlanta. What she got was a warehouse-size assembly line reminding her of the clothing district in New York. At least stepping inside the building provided respite from the stifling heat, unlike the aquarium earlier in the day.

Weaving through dozens of busy workers became a chore, especially when one carried an enormous arrangement the size of Stone Mountain. "Comin' through," one employee warned before barreling his way past the detectives.

The delicate fragrance of flowers inspired images of Georgia. Savannah's older sister loved working in her flowerbeds and babied her plants like newborns. If Georgia ever saw Petal Pushers, she'd likely disappear in the warehouse of flora for days then emerge holding an arrangement capable of sinking a battleship.

Several work tables sat throughout the large building, all with one sort of bouquet or another. Large built-in refrigerators lined three of four walls, their glass doors revealing literally thousands of flowers to be chosen for sprays or vases. Savannah counted every color of the rainbow as they passed by the refrigerators. Roses, carnations, lilies, daisies, chrysanthemums, orchids and hyacinths were only a sampling of flowers available. She even spied ivies and other green plants across the room. "This place is seriously big and organized," she mumbled.

"Comin' through!" another voice yelled, forcing the two to yield the right-of-way to a huge spray of yellow roses.

"Hey," Savannah called, displaying her shield. "Where's the owner?"

The woman sighed impatiently at the interruption then nodded her head to the left, "Over there. Guy in the burgundy shirt and black slacks. Name's Jerry. Now if you'll excuse me…" She darted toward an open door where a man loaded a delivery truck, "One more!"

These people need to try decaf, she thought. Ennis glanced both ways like a child crossing a busy street, took his wife by the arm and guided her through the mass of humanity for being trampled by a stampede of carnations.

Jerry seemed personable enough from a distance. That gave her hope. He laughed with a customer who finished relaying an obviously humorous story. Bidding the fellow good-bye, Jerry turned his attention to Savannah and Ennis, "How can I help you folks?" He focused on Savannah, visually sizing her up, "You're more iris or lily. Lemme guess. Blue. No, wait…" He stared until she felt herself flush. Then, "You like purple, don't you?" He reached beneath the counter for a pamphlet that he opened for Ennis, "I've got just the thing for your lady."

Savannah would have been more impressed with Jerry's psychic abilities if she hadn't been wearing a violet blouse with her beige slacks and jacket. She opened her mouth to speak when Jerry's enthusiasm leapt in with, "Listen, I can have this very arrangement ready for you in less than twenty minutes guaranteed." He tossed a wide, bright smile at Savannah, "Or it's free *and* the lady can choose an additional arrangement for delivery at a later date."

He sounded like a pizza commercial. And as lovely as his offer was, they were there for business. She showed him her badge, "Actually, we're here to ask about other deliveries you made."

The sight of the badge not only closed Jerry's mouth but pursed his lips as well. Ennis took over, "We need your records on a customer named Barry Vaughn. He placed three orders for flowers three days ago."

"Listen," Jerry leaned onto the counter, his voice so subdued they had to lean closer to hear, "I'm all for helping the police but these are my customers you're messing with. I mean, Barry's one of my best. When he orders, he orders the Rolls Royce, if you get my drift."

Savannah understood protecting a client's privacy. But in case he missed the memo, "Barry Vaughn was found dead this morning, Jerry, and we need your help to find out why he's dead. We'd appreciate your cooperation with those names and addresses."

She literally watched the blood drain from Jerry's features. His mouth worked but no words emerged. Then, "You mean, the guy on the noon news was Barry? The fella in the aquarium?"

"The names," she said then added a pleasant smile, "please..."

Still stunned at the news, Jerry headed toward a smaller room. He was gone a few minutes and returned holding a computer printout, "I can't believe he's dead. You think one of these women did it?"

Ennis took the printout, answering, "Dunno. That's why we look at anyone who knew him."

"How about you, Jerry?" Savannah inquired, mostly to ruffle him. "Where were you this morning?"

His eyes rounded as though she reached for her gun, "Me? Here all morning. My employees can vouch for that."

Savannah winked, "Just checking."

3

It was bound to happen. As sure as snakes slithered and cockroaches scattered from daylight, one could bet money on Mayor Franklin O'Neill scurrying to the nearest TV camera. His ability to sniff out the media rivaled a bloodhound tracking a scent. With his lofty promises and unreasonable expectations, he'd weaseled his way into the mayor's office a few months earlier, defeating Savannah's choice for the job. She figured the fact that O'Neill favored Winston Churchill swayed the voting public to elect him and the guarantee of change cinched it.

Harry Worthington was Savannah's vote. An ex-cop with an exemplary record, Harry promised an earnest effort to improve the city's safety. His downfall: He presented his plan in true law enforcement manner, addressing the people like cadets – frank and at times brusque and hadn't played well with the voting public. With crime headed up instead of down and a few rogue officers giving the department a black eye, the voters decided against putting one of "them" in charge of the city.

Instead, the votes went to O'Neill, the man in the Armani suit who'd yapped his way to the mayor's office with promises of a kinder, smarter, more efficient police force. A police department he would see held responsible for bad conduct while doing a better job of protecting citizens. With all of O'Neill's changes in policy, it felt like the *police* wore the handcuffs instead of the criminals.

As if Franklin wasn't pestilence enough, there was his son Rusty. The carrot-topped thirty year-old stood consistently at his father's side, ever present at fundraisers or TV appearances and looked more like a comedic sidekick than an offspring.

Standing alongside Franklin at the news conference about Barry Vaughn, she wondered if the whole O'Neill clan evolved from stumps or hammers because only an idiot made impossible promises on behalf of the police department. The biggest: finding Vaughn's murderer before week's end. She, Ennis and Mathis served as sacrificial lambs if the killer slipped free. The ones no one would remember if the killer was found and imprisoned because O'Neill would claim the credit.

Mayor O'Neill's press conference probably played well with the citizens but Savannah knew the truth. While promising the killer's apprehension, Mr. Mayor also unveiled a recent change in department policy. He eliminated overtime and halted all raises until "crime was under control in his city."

As a result of his frugal nature, the homicide closure rates declined. Without the hours, investigations ground to a crawl and adding to her woes – without overtime, paying off their new home took a big backseat.

While the mayor yammered, she whispered to Ennis, "You owe me twenty bucks."

"I never accepted the bet," he reminded.

"Yes, you did. I bet you twenty bucks O'Neill would be groping for cameras before day's end."

He leaned closer, "I shrugged. Shrugging doesn't constitute accepting a bet. Now be quiet or he'll hear you."

O'Neill proceeded to inform the public that the police had tangible leads in the case, which Savannah knew were anything *but* tangible. The mayor guaranteed that he himself would assure every available cop would be assigned to the case until the killer was apprehended. Savannah surveyed the sea of faces listening in rapt silence. There had to be a special place in hell for politicians, she thought. Along with flies and lawyers, they served no real purpose except to make people's lives miserable.

Amid the TV cameras, the mayor's lies and general din of noise, Savannah and Ennis struggled to look pleasant and confident. Once the press conference concluded, she exercised her jaw, rubbed her cheeks to release the smile frozen on her face, "I feel much safer knowing Mayor Franklin O'Neill is in charge," she quipped sarcastically. "He's much more convincing and qualified than Worthington."

"Savannah," Ennis drew his finger across his throat in a slicing motion.

She ignored it, "Seriously. To hear him, we live in Mayberry. Safe and secure."

"Shush already," Ennis cut his vision behind her.

After the dog and pony show, she needed to vent. She stood properly quiet as O'Neill babbled on then listened in mute shock as the police chief green lighted every one of the mayor's orders. Between O'Neill, his son and the police chief, it was the holy trinity of stupidity.

The closest O'Neill came to police procedure was paying for parking tickets. He had no clue how hard or long they worked an investigation. And why couldn't she speak her mind anyway, she was about to ask when, "Is there a problem, Detective – what was it again?"

You gotta be kidding... He not only stole the office from a more capable candidate, now he conveniently failed to remember his "hard-working" detective's names. It figured.

Ennis made a silent appeal to be nice – an appeal she tried to abide by. "Prince," she corrected in a more courteous tone than she expected. "Detective Prince, and there's no problem if you really approve overtime for us and actually assign more detectives to the Vaughn case." Then she added the obligatory "sir".

O'Neill's face pinched into an angry pug frown, "I don't expect you to understand this but there are certain budgets to maintain. The last mayor was a spendthrift. I ran on the promise of tightening the city's belt. We all must sacrifice, Detective. That means the police department will run leaner with less overtime and, perhaps, fewer officers."

"You just promised your constituents all resources would be assigned to the Vaughn case. Three detectives are far short of all resources." She felt Ennis tugging at her arm as a sign to shut up. What he forgot – she truly hated liars, particularly stuffy, arrogant ones that thought they knew everything, including the duties of a police detective. It wasn't exactly a Caribbean vacation anyway but stripping them of extra help was unconscionable.

"Back off," her husband whispered.

The mayor's vision narrowed, "Three detectives is a sufficient number if those detectives are doing their jobs and doing them well. Can I assume you do your job well, Detective Prince?"

Savannah bristled, shook Ennis's hand from her arm. She planned to explain in vivid detail what she did well, not only her job but busting chops and other body parts when necessary. The little girl raised with an iron fist and plenty of dates with Mr. Hickory Stick, grew up with a steel backbone and no one, not even Jeffrey Holland, succeeded in breaking it. Some pipsqueak mayor didn't stand a chance.

The two visually squared off – him anticipating a scathing reply and Savannah yearning to give him one.

Ennis gave up trying to neutralize the confrontation. He settled for standing behind her, probably ready to pull her off the mayor if she pounced.

"I *am* good at my job," she said, surprisingly calm.

"Wonderful," he said with exaggerated delight. "Then there's no problem. I will expect regular progress reports from your senior officer." And with that, Mayor Franklin O'Neill waddled away. She never hated Winston Churchill, she reflected with a sneer. Not until now.

Ennis blew out a breath, "Are you crazy? You can't declare war on the mayor and win."

"I fought cancer and won. The mayor's nothing," Savannah emphasized the last word because to her, he was nothing.

Ennis rounded her front until their vision met, "Savannah, you're *still fighting* the cancer and you are winning. The battle isn't over. You can't tackle two powerful opponents at once. No one can."

She bowed up to argue but he pressed a finger to her lips, "You can't and you won't. Let's forget about him and solve this case if we can."

"He's right, Prince." John Mathis stepped into the conversation. "You got bigger battles to fight. Stick to those."

From the corner of her eye, she saw the media loading their cameras into their vans. No one paid attention to the scene unfolding between the detectives. No one paid attention unless it fell out of the mayor's mouth. She shook her head. Eventually the voters would learn what a lying idiot they elected to run their city. And when they did, it would probably be too late.

4

This can't be right, Savannah thought while counting back, back, back on the calendar. Every week lacked one important mark. The beginning of her period. She'd been so busy lately, had she forgotten to note it at some point? The truth dawned replacing the confusion with alarm. Busy, yes. Mostly forgetful. Thinking back, she skipped her birth control while recovering from Jeffrey's cruelty. Not necessarily a problem until they sold the house.

She referred back another month, mentally counting the weeks, "This is when the house sold and…" Automatically her heart sank. "Ennis and I made love that night," she groaned. "Twice."

Savannah hid her face in her hands and cringed. *I'm probably pregnant.* It explained the mysterious puking and why she struggled to button her blouses. The latter she blamed on her two pound weight gain but didn't realize the poundage migrated to her boobs.

She made a mental note to pick up a pregnancy test on her way home. A baby, she thought. A baby *right now.* With medical bills, house payments, not to mention questions about her health and the breast cancer. Plus she was still coming to terms with Jeffrey and Cole. Shaking her head, she remembered her mother's saying – God sure has a sense of humor.

"What's wrong?" Ennis asked as he walked in her office.

Quickly she diverted her attention from the betraying calendar to Barry's background check. "Just looking at Vaughn's life. He was a massage therapist so what was he doing in the maintenance area of an aquarium?"

He shrugged, "Dunno but he had to have a passkey or know someone with one."

"None of the names on the employee list corresponds with him, at least not yet. Maybe the passkey list will help. Harold was having trouble getting that list together. Mathis said he'd pick it up for us. I hope he can hold his tongue long enough to get the list without inciting a riot."

"Until we get that, why don't we look at the Hotlanta site?"

She leaned back, incredulous, "You think the key to this case is a porn site?"

He toned down his enthusiasm, she assumed, to sell the idea to her, "We have to work all angles of the investigation."

"You still said that with a bit too much zeal." She turned to her computer and typed in the website. Before the page loaded, Ennis rushed to her side, eyes darting to each picture that loaded. Expecting it to explain everything, she sighed, "Men."

In fiery block letters, the internet ad read, "Hotlanta – A hot date for all seasons, a hot date for all reasons."

Savannah and Ennis watched as the letters seemingly melted into the midnight black background then rose from their cyber ashes to reignite again. Photos of semi-nude women in compromising positions graced their vision, making her squirm in her seat. She hated for Ennis to see the beautiful women, their long, shapely legs draped over men who clearly should have been taken to the woodshed in their youth.

Ennis's attention seemed strangely riveted to the screen as the pictures faded only to be replaced with more revealing, sometimes pornographic ones. Savannah closed the webpage, breaking his trance. "Why'd you do that?" he asked. "It might give us a lead on the case."

Swiveling her head, she peeked over her reading glasses. He normally didn't salivate over naked women – except her. The man next to her stood mesmerized at the screen. If the last several months hadn't been so tough on her, she'd have waved off his curiosity but she'd had breast surgery that left a scar and Jeffrey added plenty more to her body. Savannah was never physically perfect in the first place but now she felt those flaws and her insecurities rearing up in earnest.

She replied, "The only thing it'll give us is the urgent desire for a decontamination shower. We already know it costs fifty bucks to join – try getting approval for that – and we already know Barry was a member in good standing." Reaching in her desk drawer, she grabbed the Tums and popped two in her mouth. Sometimes the job reminded her why cops dropped dead of coronaries at an early age.

"We should at least print out the questionnaire. If you're uncomfortable with reading it, I'll do it."

Had he completely lost his mind? She wasn't about to let him run rampant through a bunch of naked females, in real life or trolling cyberspace. Especially on the premise of reading some trashy questionnaire that served no purpose. Sometimes her husband reminded her of a teenage boy and today he really needed to reel in his hormones before she helped him with that task. "Uncomfortable? Ennis, here's the definition of uncomfortable. You stop at a roadside restroom to take a pee. In the midst of doing your business, you see a note scrawled on the wall that reads, 'For a good time meet me here at 5:00'. You look at your watch and notice it's 4:59 and you're not done peeing yet. *That's* uncomfortable. This," she pointed to the screen, "makes me hurl – and it won't help us find the killer."

A knock at the door suspended the conversation and upon seeing Mathis, she gave silent thanks for his arrival because her constitution couldn't take much more. She asked Mathis, "What did security say?"

"If I was a fish in that tank, I'd hire a bodyguard. Their security guys are one step above Jello in the brains department. They couldn't tell me who was assigned to the passkey used. You're lucky they located the 'print' button on the printer. Here's your key list, courtesy of Mr. Personality Harold Gerard." He tossed a small ream of paper onto Savannah's desk.

The resounding thud nearly inspired her to the visit the Mylanta, "Gee, thanks." She removed her glasses, pinched the bridge of her nose. If they ever mined their way out of the paperwork, they might find the killer before they collected their pensions.

The rotund detective plopped into a nearby chair, peered over his own set of reading specs, "You want me to look through the list?"

A ray of hope brightened her features. She much preferred interviews to wading through mountains of papers any day, "Sure. We can handle the interviews."

"You want me to go rattle their cages at Hotlanta too? Save you and Rutherford the trouble. I heard you mention peeing and hurling and that combination ain't conducive to prying info from anyone."

Relief slackened her shoulders with the offer and she sighed. At least one of her wishes came true that day. Jumping off a cliff sounded better than going to a swinger joint for any reason. She thanked Mathis for the offer.

Mathis shrugged, "No prob. I'll save your delicate psyche this time."

Ennis frowned, "What about *my* delicate psyche?"

Mathis chuckled, "I'm doing this for Prince. If she turned you loose in that joint, she'd probably never see you again."

And with that, Savannah threw back another Tums with hopes Mathis, for once, was completely wrong.

5

When they walked into the autopsy suite, Savannah felt Ennis's squeamish nature rising to the surface. He literally despised the autopsy room – not that she enjoyed it but someone had to brave it or fake their courage. She opted for the latter. Ever since her encounter with Jeffrey and Cole, sharp stainless steel instruments took on a new, more terrifying significance. She planned to keep her distance from the scalpel for two reasons. One was pretty evident. The other was Francis "Frank" Griffin. While being an excellent medical examiner, he also possessed a penchant for macabre drama. He used instruments and theatrics to make his point. Showing his theory of how a victim died was his specialty and it gave detectives pause when forced into his presence. She dreaded the little show but knew if she didn't try to participate, Griffin would give her "the look" everyone adopted since Jeffrey's attack. The one that without words asked, "Are you okay?" For months, she'd struggled to show she was, indeed, okay. Today would prove whether that was true.

The sounds of metal against metal grated like fingernails on a blackboard. The lingering odor of formalin simply made her ill, more today than ever. Scales eerily familiar to the ones found at Krogers hung from the ceiling, only these weighed livers and hearts, not bananas and apples. Death was never rosy but judging by the meat puzzle on Griffin's autopsy table, Barry Vaughn's death went beyond the call of duty.

Dressed in heavy duty apron, latex gloves and plastic hood, Griffin leaned over Vaughn's remains like he might be welding Barry back together again.

Tall, lanky and in his late forties, Griffin personified the reason people shied from the morgue with his wicked demeanor and as R.J. might say, a face that could stop a clock. Creepier still was the fact Griffin truly enjoyed his work – sometimes a little too much. He reminded Savannah of Hannibal Lector when he hummed while cutting people open or smiled too eagerly at a poor unfortunate's liver.

Frank glanced up as they approached, then smiled behind the blood spattered shield, "I was just finishing up."

Savannah heard her husband make a mild gagging noise. She gently reminded, "I told you I can do this. You're gonna puke if you're not careful."

Ennis raised a hand to indicate he'd suffer through it. He closed his eyes and swallowed, "I'm fine." Then he leaned closer to whisper, "I'm not leaving you alone with him."

Griffin, scalpel in hand, used it to point across the room, "Wastebasket by my desk. It's had a lot of use from rookies."

Instinctively she focused on the scalpel until he sat it down. Stop staring, she told herself. It's Griffin, not Jeffrey.

Ennis flared at Frank's remark, "I'm not a rookie. I just have a sensitive stomach."

"He does, actually," she concurred. "What did you find besides bite marks on what's left of this guy?"

She and the doctor looked over the remains that resembled raw ground beef in places. Thanks to the hungry fish nibbling on him, chunks of his body were missing, leaving gaps in his arms and legs and a few from his torso. At that instant she felt grateful for their placid goldfish. At least, they wouldn't feast on her and Ennis if their bowl broke.

Frank bobbed his brow, "You mean the McNuggets?" He waited for laughter. When his joke fell dead, he sobered, "He didn't even have time to drown. Whoever shoved him basically dumped a giant piece of bait into the tank. You can imagine the feeding going on."

"Yes and so can my stomach so let's not get too graphic," Savannah requested.

The doctor slanted her a curious glance, "Never expected you to be squeamish."

"Only in certain cases," she lied. "What else?"

With a gloved finger he pointed to an area a few inches below Barry's left nipple. She noted a horizontal slit about an inch long. "Stabbed between the ribs."

"Right and it's a surprisingly clean stab wound. Usually there would be some tearing where the victim twisted or fought. This one," he shrugged, "in and out. It's not a hunting knife or ordinary kitchen knife."

"A dagger?" she suggested.

"The blade measures three and a half to four inches long so if it's a small dagger it's possible." He pointed around Barry's mouth. The skin showed signs of bruising around the lips, the shape faintly appearing like a palm and fingers. "Looks like the killer covered his mouth before sticking him." He motioned to an empty autopsy table, "Stand near the edge of the table for me."

"We don't need a visual," Ennis said tersely. His brow sank at Savannah. Without words, he tried to discourage her from participating. In his own thoughtful way, he attempted to shield her from all potentially upsetting encounters. Today, however, she'd try to recapture a shred of her routine with Frank.

Frank stripped off his hood, gloves and apron then stepped to the sink to wash his hands.

Ennis took that opportunity to whisper to her, "You don't have to do this. He'll understand and if he doesn't, I'll make him understand."

"Let me try." She patted his arm only to see his jaw clench.

Savannah watched Griffin pick up his pen then motioned in a circle for her to turn around. She did so, taking a deep breath to brace herself. *I can do this. I can be normal again. I can…*

From the corner of her eye, she saw Frank fist the black pen. She braced herself, trying to prepare herself for whatever was about to happen.

"No peeking, Detective," he scolded good-naturedly. "You'll ruin the whole show." He positioned himself five feet behind her, "The attacker came from behind while the victim stood near the aquarium's railing." He took three quick strides until Savannah felt his immediate presence and caught the faint hint of his Old Spice. She began turning on her heel when cold fingers covered her mouth. For a brief instant, she regressed several weeks when a stranger's cold touch meant to kill her.

The doctor's other hand swung the ink pen with a swiftness that made Ennis cringe. Savannah twisted in his grasp, the demonstration suddenly becoming too realistic to her. He held steady, clearly believing her effort was an act, and brought the pen's tip to rest against her side.

By then Ennis looked ready to maim. His vision remained on her, his nostrils flared and voice exact, "But our victim was stabbed in the chest."

Savannah rolled her eyes. *Thanks, Ennis.* By pointing out the discrepancy, he'd inadvertently given Frank another crack at her.

Indeed, after a critical frown, Griffin waved his hand with a flair indicative of a director telling his actress to take her place. She blew out a breath, partly annoyed that Ennis signed her up for this, partly because she really wanted to chicken out. Jeffrey's image tapped at her consciousness, threatening to wreck her efforts toward a normal existence. She had to take control, she told herself, and chickening out wasn't an option in her profession.

Savannah positioned herself accordingly, tamping down the rising nausea and memories threatening to surface. If she wasn't careful, *she'd* be hurling in Griffin's wastebasket, not Ennis.

"*You don't need her to play the victim,*" Ennis emphasized a little too loudly. "Just tell us what happened."

"Won't take but a sec," Griffin assured.

Just like my heart attack, she wanted to say. Despite the pounding in her chest, she resumed her position by the table again, waiting for Frank to approach. A hand covered her mouth and she forced herself to stand still. *It's Griffin, not Jeffrey. You're safe.*

An arm came into view and the pen came to rest below her left breast between her ribs. "I stab you, pull the knife and," the hand on her back doubled her over the table, "I push you into the aquarium."

Ennis clamped his hands to his hips, "Who in their right mind is gonna let someone stab 'em and shove 'em in a carnivorous fish tank?"

Savannah straightened as the answer replaced Jeffrey's smiling face in her mind. She knew by her experience with Holland and Jordan, "They wouldn't unless they were drugged or incapacitated somehow."

"We have a winner," Frank's cheered with a wicked smile. He pointed for her to stay put with him still behind her, "If I simply wanted to kill you, I'd cover your mouth," he did so without warning which made her tense.

Her hands automatically fisted and her heart recommenced its relentless race as adrenaline flooded her system. She struggled not to react because Ennis appeared close to detonating.

Griffin continued, "Then I'd take my knife," he pulled her head back against his shoulder until her throat lay bare. He rested the tip of his Mont Blanc beneath her ear.

Memories flashed in her rioting brain, one of Jeffrey's scalpel positioned in exactly the same place. She frantically grabbed for Frank's arm, trying to free herself. Like Jeffrey Holland months earlier, Griffin's hold remained solid, "And I'd cut your throat from ear to ear."

Savannah shivered as the cold metal trailed across her throat. Her heart slammed against her ribs and she struggled for air as she pulled free.

She refused to look at Ennis, not until she regained her composure. In the meantime, Griffin, oblivious to her inner turmoil, seemed pleased with himself, "You couldn't scream at that point, you'd just die. I wouldn't have to push you in the water. The only show I'd see would be a spectacular spray of arterial blood. Barry's killer wanted a public display of flailing and splashing about while Vaughn was eaten alive."

Savannah released a tremulous breath and gathered a modicum of courage to face Ennis. When she did, his expression demanded to know her current state of mind. She nodded despite teetering on the precipice of bidding sayonara to her breakfast.

Griffin proceeded, "Doesn't exactly narrow the suspect list but I do have an offer of good tiding."

Ennis hinted, "And you waited to tell us after your drama because…"

"I like to recreate the victim's last moments if possible and Detective Prince is always such a good sport."

She managed a half-smile. Her good sport status was like Elvis Presley. It had officially left the building forever.

Ennis sternly advised their colleague, "You can put the pen down." It certainly wasn't a request. Savannah read the threat in his tone despite it sounding benign enough.

His protective nature dictated that he protect her from all threats, including imaginary assaults from a Mont Blanc.

Taken aback by Ennis's abruptness, Frank slowly and purposefully laid the pen aside. He lifted his hands as if to show they were empty while leaning toward Savannah, whispering, "What's wrong with him?"

"He's more protective of me lately," she replied with a hand to her stomach. The churning ebbed slightly, giving her hope the Cocoa Puffs she ate might stay down.

As if she'd explained the situation in great detail, Frank's expression drained of color, "Oh, I forgot. Sorry if I made you uncomfortable. It wasn't my intention." He quickly changed topics, "On to less adverse subjects, I found a couple of surprises for you two. The first one is rhubarb."

"Huh?" Now *she* was lost.

"When you said he might have been drugged, you weren't far off." He waved them toward a large jar sitting on a cabinet. The contents needed no introduction. Savannah gently pushed Ennis aside, knowing his queasy nature rose fast at the sight. The doctor pointed to bits settling close to the bottom, "He'd eaten raw rhubarb leaves. In early China, Tibet and Mongolia, they used rhubarb medicinally to induce vomiting and supposedly cure certain illnesses. But you should never, *never* eat rhubarb leaves, cooked or raw. They contain the toxin oxalate acid and eating the leaves can cause poisoning. He was too sick to fight back. That's why the stabbing was so clean. In. Out."

Ennis meandered back. He pointedly ignored the jar and its

contents, "Why would someone poison a guy then decide shoving him in a fish tank would work better?"

Savannah leaned against the cabinet with the realization, "Great. We might be looking for more than one suspect –"

"Or two, maybe three," Frank suggested. "*Or* perhaps one very sadistic, very thorough killer. The lab also confirmed traces of rodenticide in his system. He must have been poisoned sometime within the last few days."

"Then why wasn't he dead already?" Ennis asked. "Rat poison kills pretty quick I thought."

"Some do but this is anticoagulant rat poison. Takes a while for the victim to bleed to death internally. Unless he began having nose bleeds or bloody urine or stools, he may not have known it was a serious problem. A shame, really. Vitamin K works relatively well to counteract anticoagulant poisoning."

All three stared at Barry Vaughn's remains. Griffin shrugged again, "This guy was universally hated." He patted Savannah on the shoulder, "That's why I'm glad I deal with the dead. They come to me, I don't have to search them out, chase them down and arrest them."

She tried to smile but couldn't bring herself to. The case erupted into chaos with national coverage, the mayor's posturing and now they probably had more than one person trying to complicate an already convoluted case.

Ennis checked his watch, "The phone dump should be back by now. Let's check it out." The declaration rang of desperation. Ennis would do or say anything to leave the autopsy room, especially today, according to his sour expression.

She had to admit it sounded like a damn fine idea. "And while we're at it, we'll see if Hartley's crew found a knife at the scene." She turned back to Griffin, "Do us a favor, okay? Don't find anymore potential killers for us. We've got enough on our plates."

"At least it's not rhubarb on your plates," he said then winked, "or rat poison."

6

Mathis slapped a folder onto Savannah's desk. It was labeled Hotlanta Member List. "You'da thought I was a lion running after a pack of deer," he griped.

She leaned back in her chair waiting for the punch line. Mathis didn't waste a minute, "I walk into the joint and automatically everyone scatters like mice. It's like they could smell I was a cop. I mean, do I look like a cop?"

She wondered if that was a joke. Playing it safe, she didn't laugh. Mathis dressed like a cop, talked like a cop and carried himself like a cop. His attitude boiled down to "everyone's a liar until proven otherwise".

While Savannah kept silent with the exception of a shrug, Ennis ignored the ridiculous question, "What's your take on the owner?"

"Let's just say I know why some people fake their real identities online." He tapped his temple, "Kinda comes off as a whack job then you realize she'd need a software upgrade for that." He shrugged, "I dunno. It's surprising she can keep a business running but then sex ain't exactly hard to sell."

Savannah scooped up the folder. Slipping on her glasses, she opened the rather substantial file. At that rate, it was going to be a longer day than she originally thought.

Mathis pointed to the folder, "I expect you and him to remember this favor for a long time. I waded through that den of iniquity for that list. A list, by the way, that's around thirteen hundred people long."

The information slackened Ennis's jaw and compelled a groan from Savannah. Giving the file an informal thumb-through, she formed a conclusion that might save a few days of trolling through every name, "We've got Barry's phone records and credit card receipts. We know he either called or was called by at least three women he sent flowers to." She shuffled a separate stack of papers, these far less cumbersome. She skimmed down the list of names, "So far Ennis and I have narrowed it down to these women. Tracy Martin, Lucy Driscoll, and Danielle Callahan."

John's brow lifted, impressed, "Wow. And I thought you two just wanted to nap while I did the legwork."

Savannah glanced up to see him smile and wink. She heaved the laborious file back at him, "Just for that, take this heap and see if you can find those names in it."

O O O

On the way to Barry's workplace "Impressions", Savannah thought out loud, "Rhubarb poisoning isn't common knowledge, is it? I mean, unless you cook with it. I called Georgia before we left and she knew about it. But me, I'd be a victim and not even realize it."

Ennis shrugged, "I expect Georgia'd know plenty about food.

She cooks enough and tries different recipes all the time."

"So one of the suspects is educated in food preparation but none of the three women is a professional chef. She must just enjoy cooking like Georgia does."

"What about the rat poison? Did the killer switch horses and decide it was quicker to slip Rid A Rat into the food?"

The next possibility made her head hurt, "There could be more than one killer. I mean, from what we've learned the man *was* shameless about his conquests. Places like Hotlanta don't exactly promote monogamy."

Ennis dodged a giant pothole before pulling the Ford into the business's angle parking, "Maintenance. A lost art around these parts."

True, she agreed. The parking lot lacked serious upkeep, leaving a driver evading holes the size of basketballs. And upon seeing the building, it explained why the word "good" wasn't included in the title "Impressions". Unlike the new building Petal Pushers resided in, Impressions showed its age and signs of neglect. Savannah puzzled over the concept. A person needing a massage daring into an area requiring everything from car alarms to police escorts to ensure safe passage. Nope, not computing. Not unless Barry Vaughn provided other, off the book type services.

The exterior paint peeled in places showing evidence the building once sported pink and white. "Barry Vaughn" and "Patrick Hess" were painted in fancy white lettering on the plate glass window, followed by the business hours.

Ennis wrinkled his nose, "What kind of massages you reckon they give?" He reached for the door with black iron bars bolted on the front.

Savannah pointed to the window, "According to this, deep tissue massages." She slanted him a dubious grin, "The question is what tissue and how deep? From what I gather, Barry liked to give women a thorough servicing."

"And none of it revolved around reflexology." He pulled on the door. Above them, a bell jingled their arrival and within seconds a tall, angular man appeared from deep within the bowels of the building. With boyish blue eyes and blond wavy hair draping past his collar, he looked more like a teenager masquerading as a massage therapist. She assumed the man to be Patrick Hess. When he smiled he seemed to ramp up the charm. He wiped his hands on a towel, "Welcome to Impressions. You scheduled with Barry? If you are, it'll be quite a wait."

Try forever, Savannah thought. The two presented their badges while Ennis spoke, "Actually we're here to talk to his colleagues and look around his office."

Patrick's wide blue eyes rounded, "Whoa. Look guys, I'd love to help but this ain't Russia and you ain't the KGB. Barry isn't here right now and I'm backed up with my clients and his. God, I'll be glad when he gets back."

"You'll be waiting a long time unless you believe in reincarnation then there are still no guarantees," Savannah answered. "Barry Vaughn was found dead this morning."

"Wha?" Patrick's jaw slackened, his eyes widened enough to nearly fall out. "Dead? Are you sure?"

She hated it when people asked that. She reached in her suit jacket, retrieved a photo of Barry's ashen face on the autopsy table. The fish managed to make hors d'oeuvres out of his nose and parts of his ears but for the most part, Vaughn remained recognizable. She displayed the photo long enough for the gravity of it to hit, "No Photoshop here. It's as real as that yawning hole in your parking lot."

"About that tour of his office..." Ennis hinted.

"Down the hall," Hess pointed, "last door on the left."

Savannah opted to take the office while Ennis questioned Patrick. Slipping on a pair of latex gloves, she followed Patrick's directions, padding over plush cream carpet until reaching the end of the hall. She noticed the place didn't look terribly clinical but it instilled enough heebies that she expected a nurse to pop out of any closed door she passed.

Barry Vaughn's office proved to be a dichotomy from the bright, nearly blinding atmosphere at the front desk. Pushing the door open revealed a dark cave of a place with the lights switched off and closed Venetian blinds. Savannah flipped on the light. There were two bookshelves, one against the far wall, the other behind a large executive oak desk. The desktop remained as meticulous as Georgia's room when they were growing up. The militaristic fanaticism drove Savannah nuts. One sweater out of place and Georgia went gunning for her.

A brass nameplate bearing Mr. Vaughn's name framed the front of the desk. Three files stacked together lined the desk's edge. On the other side sat a daily planner opened to the fifteenth, the previous day's date. Surprisingly, the desk lacked the one object she expected to see. A computer. Years ago a desk devoid of a machine seemed normal. Now it raised a flag with her. How, besides his planner did he manage to organize his life and business?

She pulled her phone out and dialed Mathis, "The guy's got no computer in his office. I'll bet he keeps it at home."

"I'll give the place a goin' over when I get there," he answered.

She placed the phone back on her belt, opened the top right desk drawer. The inside stood pristinely empty as did the bottom drawer and the bottom left drawer. The top left had pens, pencils and a pad of paper inside. She lifted the pad and angled it toward the light to see any impressions from previous notes. To the naked eye, no obvious impressions appeared. She sat it on the desk for later analysis. Concentrating on the planner now, she noticed his schedule for the previous day was filled with appointments. Flipping back a page or two, she saw nothing except appointments scheduled for the past several days. Looking further back, the name Danielle Callahan appeared every Monday until the last week. Her name had been not only marked through but vehemently scratched out.

Savannah jotted it down in her notepad. She turned to leave when something caught her attention. A small private refrigerator sat neatly tucked behind his desk, hidden beneath a wall of built-in shelves. Bending down, she opened it, seeing half a dozen Diet Pepsis and a salad.

Turning on her heel, she spied a wastebasket next to Barry's desk. She leaned down to see several wadded pieces of paper. Opening one revealed his penchant for high dollar champagne. He'd ordered two bottles from a local store. Another note cancelled an upcoming conference in Detroit. After flattening out the third lump of paper, she considered it a little nugget of gold. "Tracy M. at 8:00 p.m. on the 15th – Majestic Restaurant."

She quickly made a note, called forensics and gave instructions on what items needed to be analyzed upon their arrival, including the notepad and refrigerator contents.

Stepping from the office, Savannah heard Ennis and Patrick still conversing. "He called in sick this morning," Patrick was saying. "Said he caught a bug. I told him to go see a doctor. I think it's stress from all the women he dates."

"All the women?"

Savannah stopped. In her brief absence, Ennis developed a rapport with Mr. Hess. She wanted Patrick totally at ease and when two guys chatted about another's conquests, they didn't need a woman intruding.

"Oh yeah," Patrick zealously emphasized. He sounded upset but mostly envious, "He always had a new woman on his arm or in his bed. I'm surprised he stayed with them long enough to learn their names. And lemme tell ya, no one was immune."

"What do you mean?" Ennis asked. Savannah loved the way he fell into character at a moment's notice. Depending on the person or situation, her husband donned one of a dozen hats. He sounded more interested in learning Vaughn's romantic style rather than a cop trolling for answers. Ennis finished, "He had that much charm that the women just fell at his feet?"

"Hell, yes. Pissed me off too. There's this girl working here. I was interested in her and Barry found out. He had an arrangement the size of Central Park delivered then my allergies kicked in which shot my chances with her. No one likes someone sneezing at 'em."

"What's this girl's name? We'll need to speak with her since she knew and worked with him."

"Tracy Martin. She called in sick too."

Curiouser and curiouser, Savannah thought as she walked in the room. Patrick was busy writing something a piece of paper. She and Ennis exchanged a look, silently agreeing that she'd remain quiet and let him continue taking the lead.

Patrick glanced up, acknowledged her then handed the paper off to Ennis who remarked, "You know Tracy's address from memory."

"Told you I liked her but Barry got to her first. She won't even look at me."

"We'll need his client list. Can you grab that for us?"

Patrick nodded, "Hang on. I'll be right back." He took two steps then paused to address Savannah, "Now I remember."

She and Ennis looked at him, hoping he recalled a vital piece of information regarding the case. He grinned, pointed at her, "Anyone tell you that you look like Rita Hayworth?"

The corners of her mouth curled into a tiny smile as she nudged Ennis, "Not often enough."

Patrick chuckled then disappeared to the back. Savannah showed Ennis the note she'd made about Barry's dinner date the night before. "Tracy M. for dinner at Majestic," he read with a whisper. "Reckon that's our Tracy?"

"I'd bet money on it."

"They coulda got food poisoning there since they both called in sick."

"Suppose so. If that's the case, she should be at home or in the hospital, depending on the severity of the poisoning."

O O O

"Yeah, I know him, the belly crawlin' bastard." The first words out of Tracy Martin's mouth besides "who are you" rendered both detectives temporarily speechless. The severity of the poisoning hadn't affected her resentment toward Barry Vaughn, nor had it facilitated a good vibe of being innocent of any charges, say, like murder.

The more vocal people tended to be, the less Savannah trusted their abilities of self control. On the other hand, the quiet ones had their moments too. Or people who answered their questions with such chilling composure that Savannah wondered if they weren't members of Sociopaths Anonymous. No, if Tracy Martin was the killer, she was going out with foot to the pedal, balls out and damn proud of it.

With an attitude and personality like Tracy's, it surprised Savannah that she fell for a womanizer like Barry Vaughn. Taken aback by the woman's abruptness, Savannah blinked, "Tell us about him."

The short-haired brunette shooed them inside while giving the neighborhood a quick peruse, "Get in here before everyone sees you. They'll think I'm a felon or something."

Well, you're certainly not sick like you told Patrick Hess, the female detective thought but held her tongue.

Since she didn't invite them to sit, they settled for standing in the modest sunlit entry, two against one – or at least it seemed that way. Tracy Martin had a chip on her shoulder about life in general, Savannah supposed. It showed in her posture and frank nature.

"He's a real gem," Tracy resumed. "Comes on to me at work, I agree to go out with him. First few dates are fine. Know what the bastard does on our fourth date?" Expecting any number of different answers, both detectives were surprised to hear, "He feeds me strawberries."

Ennis looked to Savannah for the punch line but she shrugged. Tracy sighed with frustration, "Hel-*lo*, I'm allergic to strawberries."

"Did he know this?" the female detective ventured.

She looked at Savannah like she was two bricks short, "*Of course* he knew it. I told him the night we met because he ordered chocolate covered strawberries. Bastard blindfolded me and fed 'em to me four days later. He watches me swell up and break into hives with me beggin' him to take me to the hospital. Would he? Hell no. He laughs. *Laughs.* Says I look like a Halloween costume. I beg him for help and before my throat completely closes, he calls an ambulance. Do you know how much that costs? My insurance company is still screamin' at me, you know, like I eat strawberries for thrills or something."

Savannah saw Ennis rub the back of his neck. She wasn't sure if the spiel annoyed him or he curbed a laugh. Either way, the interview suddenly swung to her lap, "So when was the last time you saw Barry?"

"A week ago at Hotlanta."

"Is that where you met originally?"

"We met on the Hotlanta website then met for a date. His profile neglected to include that he's a twisted, sadistic bastard. Had he been up front, I sure as hell wouldn't have dated him *or* accepted his job offer."

Savannah's confusion mounted, "Why did you continue working for him after the strawberry incident?"

"He and Patrick pay off like slot machines. I wasn't giving up that plum job."

Savannah's mouth opened to respond but hung slack in dismay instead. It wouldn't have taken her two shakes of a sheep's tail to leave Impressions and flip burgers until finding a more suitable job for her taste – at least one where the boss wasn't a vicious asshole. But Tracy stayed for the money, realizing Barry was a certified, card-carrying jerk. Savannah did a mental eye roll. Go figure.

She returned to the topic of Tracy and Barry's last meeting at Hotlanta. The mention of it steamed the woman all over again, "The bastard strolls up to me like we're still dating. Could… not… believe it."

"What did he say?"

"After copping a feel? He wanted to get back together for some crazy reason. I told him I'd rather be tarred and feathered."

"How'd he take that?"

Tracy waved it off, "Detective, he's like a dog. He usually goes from one bitch to another but that night he kept following me around the club until I yelled at him to leave me alone or I'd kill him." She spoke the last three words with a significant degree of delight. Shoulders straightened, chin up, she finished proudly, "The remainder of my evening was quite pleasant."

"How many people heard you threaten to kill him?"

"I dunno, ten, fifteen. Why?"

"Because he's dead," Ennis blurted. Savannah noticed him stewing through most of Tracy's chatter. He obviously held back as long as he could.

The news stripped a few gears according to Tracy's expression. The implication dawned close behind, "Hey, I didn't do it."

"Then why are you lying to us?" Savannah asked. "Number one, you lied about the last time you saw him. According to his planner, you had dinner with him last night at Majestic and that's easy enough to verify. Number two, you lied about being sick to your boss because lookin' at you right now, you appear rather healthy."

For each lie, Ennis made a show of counting them on his fingers, "That's two strikes. Wanna try for three?"

Tracy sighed, shook her head. "I did see Barry a week ago at the club. He wouldn't leave me alone so I agreed to have dinner with him. Any restaurant I wanted, he said. I chose Majestic because they have killer calamari –" As though realizing her blunder, she apologized. "I like the food."

"His phone records indicate you called him last night at," Savananh referred to her notes, "10:15. What was that about?"

"Well, we went out to dinner and me – stupid like – thought he'd changed. He said he was sorry about the strawberries. I thought he was sincere until he stuck me with the bill. The bastard. I called to bitch him out about it. You know how much the food is at Majestic? Insanely expensive. I'll have to cancel my spa membership to pay that bill."

Heaven forbid, Savannah wanted to say. "What did Barry order for supper?" "What else? A salad and dessert. The dork never strayed from his routine."

"Where were you this morning around eleven?"

"I was at the gym on Highland Avenue. You can check if you want."

Savannah smiled, "Oh, don't worry. We will."

7

Savannah loved the new house. It sat back from the street and had a long driveway that comfortably accommodated her Camaro and Ennis's Dodge Ram. Unlike their previous home, large mature oaks and pines stretched wide to shade the house and most of the front and back yards. The house itself looked charming sitting beneath the yawning boughs.

The moment she stepped inside, Savannah fell in love for the second time in her life. For such a large place, it felt warm and comfortable, like it invited visitors to relax and stay a while.

The square footage equaled a small country compared to their old house. It had three bedrooms, not two and the spacious kitchen had marble counters and a kitchen island, things she'd wanted for ages. And she and Ennis could finally occupy a bathroom together – the new house had two instead of one – without climbing over each other. The place looked and felt like *home*.

For all the glowing attributes of their new house, the only drawbacks resided in the neighborhood and its inhabitants. Savannah missed the familiarity of the old neighborhood, the friendly neighbors who waved or meandered over to chat whenever they saw her out. The old neighborhood had elderly couples, newlyweds and in-betweens that rarely gave her trouble and most always had a smile. It also had its share of barking dogs and stray cats that, if she had extra tuna would set it out, hoping to encourage the kitties to patrol her place for mice. The new neighborhood lacked the cacophony of barking and meowing to the point the silence nearly kept her awake.

As for the neighbors, they presented a hodgepodge of absolute weird and downright spooky. The house across the street was occupied as evidenced by the newer model Chrysler in the drive, the lights that flicked on at night – and the fact the curtains shifted a few inches when Savannah went to introduce herself. No one came to the door.

Then there was the Collins family residing next door. A bright white picket fence framed a perfectly manicured lush lawn and flowerbeds. That, in turn, framed a freakishly maintained bright white single story house.

Savannah suspected a problem when she initially met the mid-thirties Martha Stewart and her young son. They hadn't met Martha's husband yet but their son brought Savannah flowers the day they moved in. She was impressed with the boy's gesture and his junior GQ attire. He presented the flowers in a flawless, mannerly way that reminded Savannah of the Old South.

Then the boy's mother appeared. Dressed in her own upscale style, Mrs. Katherine Collins introduced herself with a slight tilt of her head and wide, genial smile curving her lips. A mane of wavy red hair flowed past her shoulders but her eyes gave her away. The green pools seemed to size Savannah up. One brow lifted as a sign the detective wasn't received very well at all. Mrs. Collins glanced down to see the yellow flowers Savannah held. Savannah thanked the boy again which brought his mother's vision to the boy then over to her meticulously manicured flower garden. Savannah saw her brow dip to a momentary frown then bob up again with another smile on her face. She patted her son's back, "How sweet. He picked them fresh from my garden. Well, nothing's too good for the new neighbors. Not even Mommy's prized daylilies."

Her family had lived there ten years, Katherine said, adding the neighborhood was quiet for the most part. Then Katherine began her own unique interrogation. Were they car enthusiasts because she hadn't seen a Camaro "that age" since the last charity car show. But it was in good shape, she finished.

"I try," Savannah replied, not sure how far to take the response.

Katherine noticed no little ones at the Rutherford house. Were they planning on having children? If so, the informative Mrs. Collins possessed a list of the best schools around. What did they do for a living? Oh, how *delightful*, she'd said at Savannah's response, giving the detective the feeling it was anything but delightful. Mrs. Collins followed up by saying the neighborhood would feel unconditionally safe having police officers living nearby.

She had the savoir-faire to mention the "unfortunate incident" with Jeffrey Holland and Cole Jordan. "It's a relief to know one of them is in jail. Has there been any word on," she struggled to remember then, "who was it again?"

"Cole Jordan and no, there's no word on his whereabouts but –

pardon my blunt
nature – we're hoping some nice young lady gutted him and left him for dead."

O O O

The early dawn cast a soft glow through treetops and across lawns, illuminating the grass just enough to locate the paper. Savannah shrugged on her comfortable blue robe – "comfortable" translating to old but not quite threadbare – to retrieve the day's news. To make herself halfway presentable, she brushed a hand through her unruly hair hoping to prevent a wild, disheveled appearance – and to prevent a bird from mistaking it as a nest.

She padded across the lawn to retrieve what she knew was a paper filled with the mayor's well articulated verbal manure. Then fate struck.

"Good morning, neighbor."

Startled at the unexpected voice, Savannah jerked rod straight then groaned when her back argued its displeasure. If the voice hadn't the decency to be female *and* a neighbor, she'd have screamed for Ennis. Just because they moved didn't mean her uneasiness waned one whit. With little effort, Cole Jordan could easily find her because despite what she told Katherine, in her heart she believed Cole still lived and breathed close by.

Turning toward Katherine Collins, one thought entered her weary mind. People shouldn't be out at such an ungodly hour, not unless national security was involved.

Her neighbor seemed to get secret pleasure from surprising her, "Sorry, dear. Didn't know you were so jumpy."

Savannah squinted into the dusky morning to see her industrious neighbor busying herself watering flowerbeds. Did the woman have no shame? Not only did she possess the audacity to rise with the chickens but she dressed to the nines just to water plants. With perfectly pressed dark slacks and light blue blouse, Katherine waved the garden hose across her prized flowers, giving them a gentle shower. It was then that Savannah decided Katherine was more exhausting than Georgia. Her sister at least slept normal hours and had good sense to wear a robe until the sun came up. Savannah forced a smile, "Good morning, Katherine. I didn't expect to see you out so early." *I didn't expect to* be *seen either, at least not by anything short of wildlife...*

The neighbor's smile was more genial, "Early bird gets the worm."

Savannah couldn't help it. She chuckled, "But the second mouse gets the cheese."

They both shared a more relaxed laugh. Katherine switched off the water, laid the hose aside, "Actually, my azaleas needed a good bath and since you're here, I wanted to ask if you'd considered joining the homeowners association."

It was too early to talk to people, much less talk business. Savannah shrugged, "We're still receiving the other family's mail and not getting all of ours. Once we're better settled, we'll look into it." *Plus, I need to find out if I'm pregnant or not.* She'd intended to use the pregnancy test while Ennis showered but since the neighborhood night owl caught her, she'd have to wait.

And Katherine's continued enthusiasm grated on her. The woman had to be on some really happy dope to be excited about a homeowners association. "I can't wait to fill you in on the perks of membership," Katherine said. "I'll make my grandmother's coffee cake with refreshments. Bring your husband too and he and Edward can talk football while you and I chat. You really won't regret joining and if I can't convince you then my grandmother's coffee cake is sure to." The cheerful lilt in her voice didn't prevent her from visually appraising Savannah's attire. One finely arched brow lifted.

Oh boy, Savannah grumbled. The one morning I look like a train wreck…

Pulling the robe tighter around her, she resisted the urge to say anything past, "Soon as I can, I'll gussy up and be over." She added as an afterthought, "And I'll talk to Ennis about coming along." *This oughta be a laugh since you don't approve of my family, our vehicles or our profession.* But she expected *not* inviting the new neighbors to join the homeowners association was an unconditional sin somewhere in the universe. No need to tilt the galaxy on its ass, Savannah guessed. After all, there was power in numbers and what better way to ambush the next new family than with a thousand members of the "homeowners association"? Especially when its leader came conveniently armed with a Stepford smile and Grandma's coffee cake?

"Come to think of it," Katherine continued her visual perusal of

Savannah's general state, "we don't have any police detectives on the membership rolls."

Finding the conversation humorous now, Savannah inquired, "And you know this how?"

"I'm on the Board of Directors. Didn't I tell you?"

Oh, for shit's sake. That certainly explained the narrow glances and cocked brows regarding the lawn – and the Camaro and Dodge Ram. Savannah suddenly felt ill. She knew it hadn't slipped her mind. Katherine waited for the "appropriate time" to drop that bomb. It just happened to arrive the day Savannah looked and felt like a dung heap. The detective's memory might slip occasionally but the knowledge they sat a few feet from a Board of Directors member wasn't one of those times.

Katherine patted her arm the way Savannah's aunt did Grandma Prince when she couldn't recall something. "Poor thing, she's at *that age*," the aunt would say. Katherine's pat suggested it wasn't age but probably something more… genetic. "Don't worry about it, dear," the neighbor assured. "You have a stressful job. I'm surprised you can remember anything. I'm just glad to know you're keeping our city and neighborhood safe."

Savannah tried to smile back. The condescending compliment and tone landed like a fist. She expected Ennis to search her out by now. He'd rolled out of bed shortly after her. Their house, however, remained quiet which told her the chances of being rescued were minimal at best.

From the corner of her eye, Savannah saw a light blink on in the house across the way. The sign of life intrigued her, "What's the story with the neighbors across the way? I tried to introduce myself shortly after you and I met." The situation turned rather spooky for her too. After rapping on the door, no one answered. The newer model Chrysler in the drive gave the impression someone was at home, but not as much as the curtain parting three inches. Savannah hadn't seen a face but whoever saw her standing on the porch clearly had no use for visitors.

Katherine sadly shook her head, "That's Tonya Harris. Poor, poor dear. Had a brute for a husband. He beat her and cut her so badly she spent two days in the hospital. She had to have reconstructive surgery so she's self-conscious about herself and about meeting new people."

Not long ago Savannah reacted the same way to exiting her home, afraid of a man capable of unspeakable brutality. Despite the move, she still double-checked her locks and peered under beds and into closets before removing her holster – just to be sure.

"Does she know we're cops?" Savannah asked. "We're normally harmless people."

"Oh, I've told her and despite her actions it helped knowing the police were right across the way. She'll warm up to you."

Savannah glanced across the street. The light blinked off, leaving the house dark again. "Tell her to call if she needs us for anything. Do you have our –"

"Phone number? Oh yes, I looked you up."

Savannah figured so but, "Did you happen to get my cell number too?"

The two neighbors shared another chuckle, ending with Katherine admitting she hadn't. At least the earlier awkwardness faded with their conversation, Savannah noticed. Katherine didn't seem to care about her new neighbor's appearance or the car she drove and surprisingly, Savannah didn't care that Katherine rose with the chickens to water her flowers or fancied herself a member of the hoity-toity. Savannah said, "I'll get the number to you before we leave this morning." Then she pointed to the vibrant blue and red flowers behind Katherine, "By the way, nice flowers."

8

While Ennis drove, Savannah scoured the client list Barry Vaughn's partner Patrick Hess gave them. Sliding her finger down the names, she stopped at one, "Danielle Callahan is the only name coinciding with the flower deliveries. Lucy Driscoll isn't listed."

"We'll interview Danielle. By then, maybe Mathis will have something new," he veered onto the entrance ramp to the freeway, causing Savannah to brace herself. Her husband enjoyed speed and she knew once he hit the highway, they would pass cars at a blinding pace. Sure enough, at the top of the ramp Ennis punched the accelerator, the force of the action shoving her back against the seat. Instead of merging with traffic, he opted for scaring commuters out of his way. His driving didn't play well with motorists as they shook their fists and offered other, more expressive, hand gestures to the passing Ford.

Ennis pushed the Taurus to its limits and some day she figured it would voice its discontent by dying from exhaustion. The only question was whether it occurred before or after she puked on the dash…

She reached in her pocket and popped a Dramamine in her mouth. Ennis saw it, "You sick?"

"I will be if you don't slow down. You see the speedometer?

Contrary to what you think, the number on the right isn't a goal you should reach."

Ennis slowed the car, giving Savannah's stomach a chance to recover. She put a hand to her belly and an image of a baby flashed in her mind. If she was pregnant, decisions had to be made – ones she'd planned on making much later. They'd discussed having kids but only after so many clear reports from the doctor. If her cancer returned, how would it affect the pregnancy? The stress of all the unknowns and what ifs riled her stomach again. She didn't have time to be pregnant. The job, the bills, the house, her breast cancer checkups…

Her phone rang, drawing her from thoughts of babies, two a.m. feedings and the possibility of raising a hellion like she'd been. If Georgia hadn't told her R.J. was a raging drunk from the beginning, Savannah would have assumed she drove her father to the bottle. Not that she admitted to being a bad child. Just difficult or "trying" as her mother once put it.

"There's no cell phone," Mathis complained. "Who don't have a cell phone when they run a business?"

She rubbed her forehead, feeling a slight ache beginning. Babies and murders. The two just didn't mix. Having a kid meant desk duty – a most loathed assignment – and possibly even retiring from the job after the baby's birth. They couldn't afford a nanny and even if they could, Savannah refused to let a stranger raise her kids. *Stop thinking about kids, damn it. You don't even know if you're knocked up.* "I think forensics pulled a cell phone out of the aquarium but chances are slim they'll retrieve anything. You still at Vaughn's house?"

"It's a cesspool. There's more fluids in this place than on a hotel bed. If I could wear one giant rubber glove I'd feel safer."

Savannah smiled at the image, "For now, why don't you search for a computer and his bills? There's gotta be a bill for his cell service, whether it's mailed or paid via electronic banking."

"From what I can tell, this guy was more about Happy Hour than keeping his financials up to date on this machine. Hey, here's a pile of mail."

She heard him thumbing through the bills then, "We have a winner. Atlanta Cellular. I'll call 'em for the records. You and Rutherford still interviewing the harem?"

"We're leaving Lucy Driscoll until after lunch. We're headed to Danielle Callahan's now."

"We shoulda flipped for who got this job, Prince. I got conned into doing the Hotlanta thing. You shoulda volunteered for house-cleaning."

She could almost see the curl in John's lip as he spoke. He wasn't a germ-a-phobe per sé but certain filth turned his gut. Evidently Vaughn's abode wreaked of rampant sex. Savannah could only imagine what the place looked like. Barry Vaughn was the Energizer Bunny of fornication.

She was about to answer when Mathis said, "Hey, I found a photo album. You should see the women in here. He musta had a new lay every night or something. There's a different face in each picture." He paused then, "Except one. She shows up more than a few times."

"We'll take a look at it when we get back. Maybe by then you'll have the cell records too."

"Yeah, until then I'll walk down memory lane with Barry…"

They said their goodbyes and Savannah updated Ennis on John's discoveries. "This case already has long hours written on it," Ennis lamented. "Sure you're up to it?"

She assumed he referred to her run-in with Holland and Jordan. She'd used most of her vacation to recover so bowing out of the investigation not only showed weakness but stupidity since their mortgage needed paying. Since she was neither weak nor stupid, she answered, "I'm fine."

A quick glance in Ennis's direction revealed a most unattractive frown darkening his handsome features. "That's not what I meant," he said.

She patted his hand, "Ennis, I *know* what you meant and I'm fine. But thank you for asking."

He nodded, the Gloomy Gus face replaced by a bashful grin. He resembled a little boy at those times. The words "adorable" and "cute" came to mind but she'd never say it out loud since those terms didn't gee and haw with the male ego.

Ennis returned to the original topic, "I wonder about that rhubarb. Tracy seemed genuinely surprised to learn of Barry's death but how'd that stuff get in his system?"

"Maybe the restaurant? I want to question the kitchen staff at Majestic."

Ennis's foot came off the accelerator. The protective husband replaced the bashful boy and he looked at her as though she'd grown another head, "Are you nuts? That place is rife with Atlanta's richest people. Even the mayor frequents the place."

By lifting one brow, Savannah asked a question Ennis recognized and answered, "I read the entertainment section of the Sunday paper, not just the headlines and sports like you. If we go into that restaurant and accuse the staff of attempted murder, they'll hang our asses on spits for supper."

"I did a little digging on the place. They've been cited by the health department a couple of times for some serious violations. Serious like mice and roaches."

Ennis found it hard to believe, "A place like that?"

"A place like that. Just because it costs a fortune to eat there doesn't mean the restaurant is any cleaner or more careful with their food. I want to take time to question the staff."

He gripped the steering wheel as if to brace himself to the idea, "You sure there's no history of crazy in your family?"

Little did he realize how much crazy existed between the Prince and Culberson sides. And the two together? R.J. and Charlene probably praised God none of their kids started talking to themselves or sprouting multiple personalities. Savannah chuckled at her husband's sincere question. Was there a history of crazy in her gene pool? "Honestly, Ennis. Would I tell you if there was?"

O O O

Contrary to Tracy Martin, Danielle Callahan lived in a swanky two story home, complete with a pool in the backyard. Not one of those cheap plastic jobs but the real dig-a-big-hole type that Savannah found gaudy. She always hated the one at home in Augusta, mostly because she couldn't swim.

The Callahan home sported a semi-circle drive guarded by iron gates which currently stood open. Neatly trimmed hedges lined the drive all the way to the front of the house.

"Why would a woman who has *this* party with a lowlife like Barry?" she asked Ennis.

"Love does strange things."

"You mean lust. From what we know about Barry, he made his feelings quite clear to every female he encountered. They're good for sex, nothing more."

Ennis inched the car along the driveway, seemingly as awed as she. He gawked at the sheer size of the McMansion, "His brain must have sunk to his shorts because dumping a woman who's loaded is stupid. Even if all he wanted was a roll in the hay, he coulda led her on and married the girl for her money."

She turned in the seat, joking, "You *do* realize how that sounds to your wife, right?" Savannah waved off his deer in the headlights shock. Evidently no, he had no clue how it sounded to her – but did now.

His reaction inspired a smile from her, "By the way, the word you're searching for is 'prenup'. If she's got that much money, she's got a damn good lawyer helping her keep it."

Few things impressed Savannah, much less intimidated her, but a spread the size of Connecticut prickled her. "We're not getting a thing out of her," she mumbled. "Even if she's guilty she's got fifteen lawyers ready to flay us alive."

Ennis sounded surprised, "It's not like you to knuckle under so quick. I mean, you're the one wanting to stir the hornet's nest at Majestic."

"I'm not knuckling under." She hitched her thumb at the mansion, "Look at it. Does that say 'I have to cooperate with the police'?" Before he answered, she opened the door, "But you let some kid jump her fence and we'll be summoned in a heartbeat and criticized when we don't shoot him on sight."

They made their way past the huge manicured lawn and up the cobblestone walk. They passed a vast, patchwork quilt of a flower garden. By the time they reached the front door, they stood, flanked by two ball-shaped topiaries standing nearly eye level. Savannah sneered at the opulent flaunting of wealth. Rich people really got on her nerves. Evidently ignoring the spectacle, Ennis thumbed the doorbell. He leaned closer, whispering the assurance, "I didn't marry you for your money."

"Good, 'cause there's less of it now than ever." She nudged him, "For heaven's sake, Ennis, I *know* you didn't so calm down."

The door cracked open a few inches. Expecting a butler, Savannah already had badge in hand and displayed it for Jeeves. Surprisingly, a woman peeked around the door, one dark, finely arched eyebrow lifted, "Yes?"

"Danielle Callahan?" Savannah mentally backpedaled, floored by the fact Danielle herself greeted her guests instead of hiring a butler. They received a nod in response. Savannah pointed to herself then Ennis, "Detectives Prince and Rutherford, Atlanta Police. We have a few questions about Barry Vaughn."

The door swung wider, revealing the fact Danielle looked ready for a dinner party or some other swanky event. A white silk blouse framed her petite form along with black slacks hugging her hips. Danielle gave the neighborhood a quick glance for snooping neighbors, "Then I suppose you should come in."

The detectives stepped inside the spacious foyer. Off to the right stood a sweeping staircase that offered an open view of the entry from the landing. The huge crystal chandelier suspended above them reminded Savannah of the "War of the Roses" because for a house that size with imported furniture and pricey knickknacks, someone somewhere was bound to kill for it.

They followed Danielle through the marble tiled entry into a massive living room with equally expensive furnishings.

The floral-patterned couch sitting in the middle of the room bore no signs of actual use. An elaborately carved coffee table sat between it and two beige wingback chairs. Danielle gestured toward the couch, "Please sit down. Would you like some tea? I was about to pour myself some."

Ennis was in the process of declining when Danielle said, "I'll be right back. Sugar for anyone?"

"No, thank you," Savannah replied to the woman's back.

Danielle made tracks quicker than a rabbit, she thought.

Ennis joined the sentiment of no sugar then leaned in to hear his partner whisper, "She's nervous."

Danielle returned with a silver tray holding an intricately designed china teapot with hand-painted violets and matching cups and saucers.

Their hostess poured the tea into their respective cups and Savannah thanked her, picked hers up. She cut her vision to Ennis. To him, drinking hot tea rated as high as drinking motor oil. He leaned onto his knees, raked a hand through his hair. She wasn't sure if it was the tea or teacup he hated worst of all. His large fingers always fumbled with the tiny, delicate handles until finally capitulating and cradling his palm beneath the cup to steady it.

Ennis grumbled his thanks, his dark eyes focusing on the upcoming challenge of holding the teacup.

Danielle eased into a wingback chair, her cup and saucer in hand. In the motions of serving tea, she'd settled down and recouped her composure, "What about Barry?"

"According to his records, you were one of his clients," Savannah said.

The cup rattled on the saucer, the nervous reaction not lost on either detective. Danielle now struggled to stop her hand from trembling, "Yes, I was."

"How did you meet?" From the corner of her eye, she saw Ennis cogitating on whether to attempt picking up the dainty cup or not. He reluctantly reached forward.

Danielle explained, "I needed a massage therapist and someone from the club recommended him."

Someone, she said. Savannah found it difficult to believe a friend would recommend Vaughn. "How long had you been seeing him?" She asked.

"About a year."

"Was he any good?" Ennis asked, frowning at the tiny handle. He curled his finger around the handle, tested the hole. He sighed.

Danielle didn't seem to notice his quandary, "I've had better but he wasn't bad."

"Did your relationship ever venture beyond a working one?" Savannah inquired. "Records show he sent you an expensive flower arrangement. Massage therapists don't usually do that."

Danielle sipped her tea. Savannah guessed the frown wasn't due to insufficient sugar. "Did we sleep together, is that what you're asking?"

"I'm afraid it is," Savannah phrased it as benignly as possible after seeing the light beam off a diamond ring on her left hand. They all assumed Danielle was single or divorced but the sparkling marble-sized rock telegraphed the depth of poo they'd stumbled into.

Danielle hesitated while Ennis gave up being proper and graceful and, as usual, held a hand underneath to steady it. He looked at their hostess, "Ma'am, we realize we're puttin' you on the spot but we will be discrete with the information."

His assurance failed to assuage her concern, "So you're saying whatever I tell you will be in strictest confidence?"

"Yes, ma'am," his partner concurred, "as long as you tell us the truth. If you withhold information or lie, it's out of our hands and our boss takes over. He's not one of those forgiving types."

Danielle cast a searching glance over each shoulder then returned the tea to the tray. Elbows on knees, she spoke quietly, "Barry and I did have an affair – a brief one. My husband is married to his job and that bitch gets all the attention. I'm not making excuses for myself but a woman has needs. You understand."

The last two words were directed at Savannah and no, personally she didn't understand. Ennis kept her so worn out that *needing* sex never entered the equation. Of course if the little test turned blue, there would be no sex at all once she swelled to the size of Dallas.

Danielle proceeded, "I got lonely for companionship and Barry showed interest. At the time I didn't realize what a jerk he was. I slept with him a few times but by the second tryst, he was daring into darker places."

Savannah figured she meant kink and not caves. Danielle fidgeted with her wedding ring now. Savannah sipped her tea and tried not to react, "By your tone you didn't approve of the lifestyle."

The woman's back stiffened, "You use the term rather loosely, don't you think? Lifestyle isn't what I'd call it and no, I didn't approve. I broke it off when he took me to some den of iniquity called Hotlanta."

"When was the last time you saw Barry and in what capacity?" Savannah asked.

She brought the teacup to her lips while surveying her guests.

Savannah had the feeling she was sizing them up, trying to determine if bluffing them might actually succeed. After indulging in a leisurely sip, Danielle replied, "Two weeks ago and it was professional. I told him we were through in all respects and not to contact me again."

That could explain her name being scratched out on Barry's appointment book, Savannah thought.

"What about the flowers? Did you approach him about those?" Savannah felt their hostess closing down with every passing second. At those times, without any evidence proving the woman killed Barry, it was best to wrap things up and leave…

"I did not. I immediately tossed them in the trash."

Ennis gave one last swallow and returned the cup to the tray. He was more than happy to rid himself of the unwieldy object, "Where were you yesterday morning around eleven?"

"Having my manicure. I get one every week at that time. I assume you'd like my manicurist's name and number to verify I was there."

Savannah finished off her tea then nodded, "Yes, please."

A noise at the back of the kitchen alerted Savannah that someone entered the house. Danielle straightened slightly in her chair, her hand smoothed her hair in time for a paunchy, well tanned gentleman in his mid-forties to sidle up behind her and kiss her cheek, "You didn't tell me we had guests."

Savannah noted the white shorts glared against his bronzed skin. His bare chest sported more dark hair than gray as did the wealth of meticulously styled hair on his head. He looked like a young version of the football coach Jimmy Johnson.

"They're with the police," Danielle stated with such ease it made Savannah wonder how well she could lie. Then she wondered how the woman might explain their presence to him.

Both detectives rose, extended their hands and introduced themselves. Beauregard Callahan's handshake belied his upscale name. Despite the two band-aids ringing his fingers, he squeezed hard enough Savannah winced. Such handshakes indicated fear or anger and Savannah put her money on the latter. In that brief time, she recalled Beauregard Callahan was a considerable contributor to the mayor's campaign. The perfectly styled hair jogged another memory – one from TV. He incessantly bombarded the unwitting public with his Callahan's Castles commercials like the Nazi blitz on London. He left no channel unscathed, ensuring to assault every viewer with his diatribe. Mr. Callahan made his fortune building McMansions like his own. *Oh brother*, she thought. *Just when the pasture had enough turds.*

"Why are the police here?" he asked his wife.

Savannah waited and when Ennis opened his mouth to answer, she nudged him into silence.

Danielle sipped her tea and in the meantime, gathered her aplomb to reply dismissively, "Oh, they're here about Barry Vaughn. You remember him. My ex-massage therapist."

The emphasis on "ex" couldn't have been missed by either a blind or deaf individual. She'd said it not merely with her voice but a facial expression that needed no further details. Her husband wandered behind the couch, his hands settling on his wife's shoulders to gently rub them, "Forgive me, detectives, but I'm incapable of assembling even the remotest shred of sympathy for the bastard. After what he did to Dani, I support whoever killed him. They deserve a medal, not incarceration."

Beauregard's statement roused Savannah's curiosity, "What did Barry Vaughn do to her?"

His nostrils flared and lips pursed. Danielle's façade showed signs of cracking. With his wife's widening eyes, Savannah sensed she wanted the interview to end before their stories didn't mesh and more invasive, personal questions were asked. The female detective sat back as did Ennis, a sign neither planned to leave anytime soon.

Beauregard's chubby cheeks flushed, "The bastard tried to take advantage of her at his workplace. Should have been arrested for assault because I'm sure some poor woman got raped."

Savannah saw Ennis writing notes. She furthered the topic, directing her question to Danielle who looked ready to faint, "How long were you a client again?"

"Eight months," the woman begrudgingly corrected.

"Mr. Callahan, when did you learn of Vaughn's sexual advances?"

Ennis kept jotting as the conversation continued. Beauregard lifted one hand, "I don't like your tone, Detective. Nor do I approve of what you're leading up to. Dani was basically a victim of sexual assault and yes, I wanted to cure Barry Vaughn of his deplorable behavior but Dani pleaded with me not to. I obliged her. Instead, I hired a personal massage therapist. A woman."

Savannah heard her husband's pen scribbling hard and fast then, without looking up he said, "If I learned some jerk was coming on to my wife, I'd want to skin him alive."

Savannah knew he meant it too. There were times when Ennis's protective nature came on a little too strong. He'd let his facial expressions or inflection do the talking.

Beau's jaw clenched then as if he mentally reminded himself to relax, he spoke calmly, "As would any devoted husband *however* I meant to *sue* him out of existence."

Watching his hands slide into his shorts pockets and curl into fists, somehow Savannah doubted that. Having a much younger wife as pretty as Danielle and seeing his jealous demeanor rise to the surface, she suspected Beauregard Callahan was a force to be reckoned with.

He reinforced the fact by nodding to the door, "My wife has answered your questions. Now you can leave."

Savannah read between the lines. Leave or be escorted out by the seats of their pants, probably by a team of lawyers...

She rose to her feet, thanked them for their time. Beauregard marched to the door and opened it without a word. His stance warned of dire consequences if they lingered a moment longer or uttered another word. So Savannah waited until she stepped over the threshold to finish, "If we have more questions, we'll be back."

9

She and Ennis headed down the hall toward her office but when they approached his, the sweet smell of home-baked cookies wafted past. Earlier in the week, Georgia promised to make chocolate chip cookies and Savannah couldn't wait to sink her teeth into them. The cookies, soft through and through, were coveted by any soul fortunate enough to score some. The lucky individual – if wise – promptly stashed the rich, chewy treasure in a safe place until they could shamlessly consume them in private, preferably with a tall glass of milk.

Savannah peered in her husband's office to find a bowl sitting on his desk. She greedily rubbed her hands together, made a beeline toward them, "Georgia made the cookies."

Ennis wrapped his fingers around her elbow, stopping her, "Those are mine. Dig out of yours."

She appraised the grasp on her elbow, "My, aren't we stingy. Glad I'm not on a deserted island with you."

"Georgia don't bake those often. Plus, I recall you growling the last time I reached for one of yours."

She wanted to say that her *stomach* growled at him but chose not to. She knew her sister left her a bowl too so she headed to her office to stash them before word of their presence spread.

When she and Ennis entered her office, they found a man sitting at her desk. He was faced away from the door, studying the few family photos lining the cabinet behind the desk. He sported short blazing red hair and looked as willowy as the little tree trying to take root in their back yard.

Savannah cleared her throat. He spun to face the two, his face as red as his hair. Her stomach instantly dropped. Oh my God, it couldn't be, she thought. Her day started so well for it to circle the drain because of this moron. He appeared thinner than the image on TV but that fiery red hair became a blaring beacon for stupidity and not just because he made the mistake of sitting at her desk.

The man busied himself chewing something and by his blissful expression, he liked what he tasted. Her vision drifted down and caught sight of Georgia's cookies, the once brimming bowl currently scavenged down to half. He'd been munching on them without her knowledge or permission. Far beyond irritation, Savannah struggled to hold back unadulterated anger, "When I look in a mirror, you are *not* who I see." She pointed to her nameplate, "So since you're name isn't Detective Savannah Prince, get outta that chair."

The man bolted to a standing position, "Sorry, Detective. I was told to wait in your office until you returned."

"Were you told to sit at my desk too?" She approached him and judging by his swift departure from her chair, he read her expression correctly. Move or be moved.

He ran the back of his hand across his mouth, sweeping away any crumbs, "Sorry."

After appraising what was left of Georgia's cookies, Savannah fired a withering scowl at their presumptuous guest. She opened the desk drawer and with great ceremony, placed the bowl inside then slammed it. She made a show of removing a key from her slacks and locking the drawer.

The man took the hint, repeating, "Sorry."

"Have you been introduced?" a new voice inquired. It belonged to their captain, Josh Hunter.

Savannah glanced up to see his broad shoulders and muscular physique standing in the doorway. Her boss, nearly forty, showed signs of being older with beginning wrinkles at his eyes and salt and pepper hair. In their time working together, she'd most likely given Josh Hunter most of his gray hair and a few of those wrinkles between his brows. Today, his hesitant demeanor threw her temporarily but not enough to curb her anger.

Keeping her eye on the newbie, she replied, "Yeah, we're homicide detectives and he's Cookie Monster." She frowned at Josh who also finished off a rather large, tasty cookie courtesy of her sister.

Seeing her rising ire, Josh defended himself, "Georgia brought me a bowl. You, me, Ennis and Mathis."

Hands on her hips, she aimed an accusing tone at the redhead, "How many did you eat?"

"Three. I thought you left them there for people to eat."

"I'm not that nice."

He stared at the drawer, "They're really good."

His eagerness to confess, paired with his sated but embarrassed smile, didn't help his cause. "I know that," she carefully enunciated. "My sister made them and gave them to *me* to eat. I've been looking forward to those cookies all week then I walk in and find you pilfering them."

Josh cleared his throat. Savannah shifted her vision to him in an attempt to inform him her annoyance hadn't quite bled out yet. In turn, his vision shifted to their guest, "Rusty, this is Detectives Savannah Prince and Ennis Rutherford. They're the lead detectives on the Vaughn case." His voice adopted a nervousness she caught immediately, "Savannah, Ennis, meet Rusty O'Neill."

Fate sure knew how to screw with her, she lamented silently. As if having Georgia's delicious culinary efforts plundered wasn't enough... Rusty O'Neill. The name literally hurt to think about, like hearing fingernails on a blackboard. Or salt in a wound. Rusty O'Neill, she harrumphed. More like *Rusty O. Nail.*

And for some odd reason, Savannah sensed she overlooked the meaning of Josh's pointed introduction. If Rusty expected pomp and circumstance, he should hit the road and search it out 'cause the police department wanted to throw him and his daddy on a plane marked "Return To Sender" which meant somewhere "up yonder way" as her mother said. Technically it meant New Jersey. What she wouldn't give to send the doity woim back to The Mosquito State.

It was Ennis who spoke the evil truth and practically swallowed his tongue while doing it, "The mayor's son?"

Josh forced a smile, "He's here to observe the Vaughn investigation."

Savannah braced her hands on her desk and spoke directly to Rusty, "We not movin' fast enough for our city leader?"

"Detective," Josh followed up with a pleading look. He reacted as if she'd slapped *him* with the words instead of the mayor's son. After a brief shake of his head, their captain looked to Ennis, no doubt asking him to control her.

"I assure you, Detective Prince," O'Neill finally spoke apologetically. "I'm not here to interfere or pressure or look over anyone's shoulder."

"You're not gettin' another cookie no matter how you sweet-talk me."

She meant every word but he smiled all the same, "I'm basically trying to keep my father off your backs. I know he can be overbearing and grouchy so I offered to follow the investigation and keep him informed."

Savannah looked at her boss, "And you agreed to this?"

"I had a choice?" Hunter chanced entering the room, "Look, you got off to a bad start. Shake hands, go to your corners," he glanced at O'Neill, "and leave her cookies alone."

"Mine too," Ennis warned. "I maim thieves."

Rusty thrust his hand to Ennis who, with his left hand on his hip, shook the offered hand with his right. Savannah saw the "dead rat" handshake he gave the mayor's son. She felt equally as enthusiastic. She and her husband were now carnies. They had to juggle their high profile investigation while keeping "baby" from poking a fork in a socket. Yippee.

O'Neill eagerly offered to shake her hand. Both hands currently gripped her desk with wishes it was the mayor's balls. Savannah slanted her husband a look before sliding her hand into Rusty's and giving it a single solid handshake.

"The pleasure's all mine, Detective," he said a little too jubilantly.

"It sure is because I find no joy in this," was all she said.

Ignoring the comment, Rusty clapped his hands together, "Okay, where do we start?"

"We?" Ennis inquired grimly.

Savannah joined in, "Where's your badge, Junior?"

Rusty's shoulders slumped from their eager, confident posture. He shook his head, "I understand you consider me a threat."

"No," Ennis corrected, "we consider you a third thumb. You'll make it harder to investigate this case because we'll be stepping around and over you."

"I don't intend to make this harder on you."

"You're O'Neill's son," Savannah replied. "You can't help yourself."

Behind Rusty was Mathis, bobbing his head this way and that, trying to find a way around their new redheaded obstacle. "Hey you, move your keister. People gotta work here."

Emphasizing John's warning, Savannah motioned Rusty aside

then addressed their colleague, "Have you met our chaperone on the Vaughn case?"

"Don't have to," he glowered over his reading glasses at Rusty. "I'll just stumble over him from now on." John's knack for putting people in their place without uttering a syllable was well known throughout the station. His disdainful glare sent Rusty back another step. It seemed to please Mathis.

It certainly pleased Savannah. She noticed papers in her colleague's hand, "What'd you find out?"

"Nothing on the computer. Just porn sites and movies. But I did get phone records." John patted his ample stomach, "I finished those cookies your sister sent. Those were good."

Ugh. More salt in the wound. Everyone enjoyed a brimming bowl of the scrumptious delicacies except her…

Ennis's jaw dropped, "You ate them all?"

Mathis shrugged, "She only sent one bowl and I was hungry." He plopped into a chair across from Savannah's desk, leaned back and fanned out his treasure.

Savannah settled behind her desk, leaving Ennis to sit in the chair beside Mathis. The trio effectively shut Rusty out. Their positions forced him to stand behind the chubby detective and peer over his shoulder. If O'Neill realized how John Mathis detested the move, he'd have backed off.

Glasses perched on the end of his nose, John's narrowed vision shifted to the side. Then, as if accepting their guest's obnoxious behavior, he sighed.

Savannah took the opportunity to unlock the drawer containing Georgia's cookies. She passed the bowl to Ennis then Mathis. Both eagerly partook of the offering. She grabbed two then secured them back inside the drawer. She noticed Rusty craning his neck, hoping to be included in the handout. Savannah shook her head at him, reached for her own reading glasses, "Tell us about the phone records."

"Vaughn was a busy boy. When he wasn't moving and shaking, he was dialing women, probably lining them up like cattle."

She sank her teeth into the velvety richness and, for an instant, her tension melted away like the soft, sweet cookie in her mouth. Georgia was nothing short of a culinary genius. In the kitchen, her talents equaled their mother's. One bite of the chocolate chip rapture took her back to the days when they arrived home from school and Charlene met her daughters with a plate of cookies and a tall, cold glass of milk.

Now Savannah was double mad at Rusty for swiping the goodies. Stealing someone's cookies should have been against the law, not just rude, especially when the filching encroached on memories of her mother.

Looking over the phone records, she noted calls to Tracy and Lucy and a few to Danielle. Something else caught her attention, "All three women called him too."

Ennis asked, "What's up with that? If Barry was such a louse, why bother contacting him at all?"

"Uh-oh," she swallowed the next bite nearly whole. "Look

halfway down the page. The 0641 number is Beauregard Callahan's. He called Barry a few hours before he died."

Rusty cleared his throat. She glared at him, "Hush up back there. Your excessive noise is interfering with my concentration."

He shook his head, "Detective, I honestly dislike upsetting you but my father specifically asked that you leave Beauregard Callahan alone."

She credited Georgia's delicious cookies for half the satisfied smile brightening her features. The other half she credited with irritating Mayor O'Neill.

Ennis flashed a warning – a warning she ignored, "Does he now? Why is that? Because Callahan bought your daddy's way into the mayor's office?"

Mathis blew out a breath, "Jeez, Prince," then leaned closer, "if you like your job, shut up."

Ennis's frown deepened. He was saying the same thing without words. Savannah backed down a degree, "Callahan's got a lot of money, Rusty. People with that luxury have been known to ask for favors from people they've given money to."

Rusty's tone never reflected the insult she'd hurled at him moments earlier, "I realize that, Detective. Callahan's Castles built my house. And when –"

"Whoa," Mathis interrupted. "You sayin' what I think you're sayin?" He directed his question to Savannah. "Beauregard is Danielle's husband?"

Ennis nodded, "And he's *very* protective of her."

Savannah appraised Rusty's mood. If the mayor's son boiled, he did so beneath the surface.

Mathis glanced over his Ben Franklin glasses at O'Neill, "She's got a point, kid. If Beau found out about Barry, and he likely did, he's a viable suspect. And he's probably using your father as a shield." John winked at Savannah, "Your father probably don't even know Callahan's a suspect."

And the moon was made of green cheese. Rusty's smarts might have been as scarce as bird crap in a cuckoo clock but Daddy wasn't so stupid. He specifically sent Junior to corral the cops, a fact Rusty basically admitted to, "Look, guys, Daddy doesn't want Beau's name brought up."

Savannah bowed up, "Then Beau shouldn't have called Barry Vaughn on the day he died. Clam up, Junior, and let us do our job. Your daddy doesn't want to be associated with a murderer, does he?"

The mention of it had Rusty loosening his tie and unbuttoning his collar, "Of course not."

She finished, "Then let us work behind the scenes and if Beau is just a blowhard, no problem."

Flushed with total frustration, Rusty argued, "But if Beau called Vaughn, you have to question Beau about it. Do that and Callahan tells Daddy then Daddy rips on me *and* you."

Mathis rubbed the back of his neck, "Reminds me of two kids. O'Neill, we're doing our job, that's that. Back to business, Vaughn got a call while I was at the house from a woman named," he referred to his notes, "Nancy. Don't know how she fits into his harem but we'll probably find out. I found this photo album in his bedroom."

The album Mathis held measured approximately three inches thick. Savannah felt her jaw – and hopes – drop.

When Mathis sat it down, a solid thunk echoed in the office and all the detectives passed the others a weary gaze.

She opened the book to the first page and saw a dozen pictures of various women, thankfully dressed and not engaging in sexual activities as Savannah feared. The next page, however, revealed Vaughn in all his naked and arrogantly proud glory. The image drew her up short, "Oh, Lord. Mathis, why didn't you warn me?"

He chuckled, "Wanted to see your reaction. I was right. Priceless."

After stealing a gander, Ennis snorted, "Thank God for good genetics."

"You braggin', Rutherford?" Mathis inquired.

"That's what he's doing," Savannah covered the picture with her hand. The day needn't test her stomach entirely, she thought.

Ennis pointed to his crotch, "Let's just say if we were at war, my battleship would sink his tugboat any day."

Mathis bounced an inquisitive, even expectant, look Savannah's way. She smiled and blushed.

Rusty leaned forward to peek at the photos. Savannah slammed the book shut, inadvertently smashing her hand. She cringed at Rusty, "Need me to define the word interfere?"

O'Neill's eyes rounded, his first sign of fear emerging. He

stammered, "Just seeing if Beau was in any of the pictures."

"What are you?" she wanted to know. "An observer or Callahan's mouthpiece? Sit down and be quiet or I'll jerk a knot in ya."

Her dressing down eased him back in his seat. She opened the book again, not recognizing any of the women with Barry. The couples cozied up in a way that probably misled each woman to believe she was Barry's one and only. Barry Vaughn's smile and embrace fooled dozens of women judging by the size of the book. As she turned pages, Savannah searched for anyone capable of murdering a ten-timing asshole then she stopped searching with the knowledge *anyone* would be a murderer in that case.

Every page revealed a different woman, every page a testament to Vaughn's numerous conquests. The sheer volume of estrogen between the pages gave Savannah a stomach ache. They might as well write off seeing their new home again – or taking a much needed pregnancy test – for a while if they had to track down and interview every woman…

"I'm part of this team, like it or not," a temperamental Rusty complained. "You know, I might actually have a few decent ideas now and again."

Mathis shook his head, while Savannah put words with her colleague's reaction, "No, you won't and you are *not* part of our team. You've already proven you're biased because of your father and Beau Callahan."

"Beau's not the killer," Rusty insisted.

Savannah finally hit the roof, "Don't you ever get tired of

running on that wheel? All the other little hamsters take a breather once in a while."

"Detective Prince," her captain's voice scolded from the hallway. "See me, please."

Mathis ducked like she aimed to hit the closest target. She stepped around her desk and as she passed, she heard Ennis whisper, "I told you to ease up."

She didn't dignify it with a response. Instead she chose to march out with chin held high. Yes, Ennis warned her to tone it down with Rusty but frankly, she couldn't see why she should. The little punk was an intentional road block, a barricade for the mayor's good friends and golf buddies.

By the time Savannah reached the hallway, Josh Hunter had retreated into his office, his arms crossed and vision trained straight at her. He crooked a finger at her.

She marched in, lips pursed. Josh motioned for her to close the door. Uh-oh… A lecture with a closed door meant bad things were about to happen and he didn't want witnesses. She lost count of the times she'd been in this position – in his office, door closed and facing that stern frown he'd perfected over the years.

"He's an asshole, I know that," he admitted. "The only one who doesn't is his father who's a bigger asshole than Rusty. But like a cold, he's here to stay until he runs his course so find a way to get along. There's no getting rid of him, no matter how much you bully, humiliate or berate him."

"He says he's an observer but the moment we mentioned Beau

Callahan, Rusty started acting like his lawyer. How can we work this case with him directing who we can and cannot list as suspects?" She was proud of her calm. The words sounded considerably less angry than she felt. Images of popping Rusty's head like a festered zit eased it temporarily. She'd endured worse, her shoulder reminded. Rusty posed no real threat unlike Cole Jordan or Jeffrey Holland. So chill out…

Hunter seemed almost amused at her composure. He probably realized it was forced and barely restrained. "You update me on your progress and I'll decide what Mr. Personality hears."

Savannah sighed as the tension melted from her posture, "*You* need to run this department. We could actually get something done."

"No thanks. I've got enough gray hair." He looked past her toward her office. Puzzlement crossed his already frazzled features, "Is that Seth?"

Savannah glanced over her shoulder to see what amounted to a refugee from the old west. The sight brought her to her feet, "It could be," but honestly she wasn't too sure. The man who seemed to resemble her brother from a distance, was dressed like a Confederate general complete with a red waist sash and sword.

"Are we done here?" she inquired, unsure whether to approach the peculiar looking visitor. After all, lately she and new visitors didn't exactly gee and haw.

Josh nodded, "If it's not Seth, let me know. Whoever it is can't be very stable dressed like that."

Josh was right. Considering her last encounter with a visitor, she'd best approach with caution before venturing ahead too quickly. Rusty didn't have a lethal weapon strapped to his waist. This one did.

She headed toward her office, appraising the fellow in gray slacks, a long gray coat and a Confederate hat in his hand. A bush of a mustache sat on his upper lip and the beginning of a beard shadowed his jaw.

His fingers traced the brim of the hat while waiting outside her office. Why, she wondered, did the nutcases flock to her? Did she have a sign on her door reading "Pit Stop for Crazies"?

When the man faced her, all doubt of his identity was erased. With the new thick mustache, her brother struck a familiar image of Tom Selleck during his Magnum P.I. days. Seth smiled, "Hey sis, how's it going?"

"Truthfully? I'd rather be hit by a bus." Appraised his attire, she lifted a brow, "Just passing through on your way back to Lonesome Dove?"

Tiny wrinkles appeared at the corners of his eyes as the grin broadened, "That's my Van. Optimistic *and* foolhardy in the same breath. Ennis has his hands full with you today." He plopped the hat on his head to model it for her, "I grew the 'stache for Lindsey's theater play. Since I play General Lee, I wanted authenticity. What do you think? Ruggedly handsome?"

"Indeed. I like you with whiskers. Does Leah?"

"Hates it and she forbade me to grow a beard." He rubbed his palm against his jaw, "I just haven't shaved yet. She wants me to shave the 'stache after the play." He stroked the brush and winked, "I'm gonna try and wheedle her into letting me keep it. I've had some real compliments on it."

Despite the fact the mustache enhanced his good looks, she could see Leah's gripe. If Ennis grew one, kissing him might take on a different appeal. She wanted to kiss her husband, not a hairball.

Tucking the hat under his arm, Seth mentioned he drove by their new house, "Swanky part of town. Maybe I can drop in later this week and see inside. Lindsey loves it. She's calling it her vacation house."

"She likes it because it's new to her."

"But Dunwoody?" He leaned closer, teasing, "Sure you're not on the take?"

Savannah took it in stride, "I told you the story behind the house."

"Yeah, I remember. You mercifully took it off a woman's hands. I'd only advise you to be careful of the neighbors to the north. Their house and lawn look too perfect."

If you think that's spooky, you should meet the residents of that perfect house. Just the other day Savannah caught Katherine primping the flowerbed. Numerous garden tools lay within easy reach as she meticulously tended the azaleas and hydrangeas. It gave Savannah the idea maybe a tool belt might come in handy. Instead of hammers, nails and pliers, the woman could stuff trowels, seeds and a bottle of Miracle Grow in it.

"I think they're obsessive compulsive," Savannah answered.

"Well, be careful. People like that are either fanatics or serial killers." Then, as if realizing what he'd said, he apologized for the serial killer remark. Everyone's tiptoeing grew wearisome. Yes, she had nightmares and her mind still occasionally trolled the depths of the painful memories. But hearing the term "serial killer" didn't cause some traumatic knee-jerk reaction the masses feared. Hearing their *names* did.

Seth reached in the back pocket of his slacks. Out of it came two tickets, "Lindsey instructed me to deliver them today. Aunt Savannah gets priority over everyone, even Aunt Georgia but don't tell her that. I can't stand it when Georgia gets her feelings hurt."

"Your secret is safe with me, Gramps," she joked.

The tiny lines at his eyes deepened as he smiled. He really did favor Tom Selleck with the mustache... "There's still room for extras in the play," he hinted. "As wounded soldiers. Interested?"

She shook her head, "I can't act."

Seth smiled so big, his teeth gleamed from beneath the brush, "Call me Gramps again and you won't have to." He glanced at his watch, "I gotta go. We're rehearsing and I was late last time."

Savannah hugged him, "It doesn't look good if General Lee is late to the Civil War. Thanks for the tickets. We'll be there."

He kissed her cheek and she ruffled his thick curly hair, "You look like Magnum P.I., you know that?"

Seth considered her statement then winked, "I see why Lindsey favors you."

The two said their goodbyes and Savannah returned to her office. Inside, she found not only Ennis, Mathis and Rusty waiting for her but a wisp of a woman sitting in the chair recently vacated by Ennis. Ennis introduced the woman, finishing, “She’s Barry Vaughn’s sister.”

10

"My brother had numerous girlfriends," Nancy Eliot said, dabbing tears then twisting the tissue between her hands. "But he was so handsome, the girls naturally flocked to him."

Savannah wisely kept her mouth shut. She believed in honesty but not brutal honesty. Yes, Barry had a tremendous number of females notched on his belt but that wasn't to say the women didn't yearn to notch his noggin with a hatchet. And to an extent, Savannah gave Barry credit for being good-looking though he wasn't anywhere near her type. She appreciated men who were big and strappin', gentle and kind, not afraid of her temper and yes, attractive but didn't parade around like they knew it. Plus they had to be from Texas and have the name Ennis Rutherford.

Dressed in beige slacks and green v-neck blouse, Nancy appeared refined and stoic, until her brother's name came up then the stoic façade cracked. She dabbed another tear threatening to fall. She and Barry favored enough people recognized their familial connection. Tawny colored hair, green eyes and slim noses. Distinguishing them as brother and sister proved easier than establishing Georgia and Savannah's genetic connection to Seth. The older he got, their brother transformed to R.J.'s mirror image. Georgia took the other route to become Charlene's spitting image and Savannah fell somewhere in the middle. Nearly everyone who saw her and Georgia together remarked how alike they looked and when Savannah felt lowest, she revisited those compliments.

Nancy continued, "When I dropped by, I figured Barry might be home. I was surprised to see the police cars." She struggled to retain her composure, "They told me to come here and talk to you."

Savannah tried to lessen the anxiety by chit-chatting about his girlfriends. It would divert Nancy's attention away from how Barry died and maybe give them a lead or two on the case. "I know this is hard, Ms. Eliot, and we appreciate your help. Did Barry mention a current girlfriend or any new dates lately? We're concentrating on the last week or two for now."

His sister thought a long moment then, "No. He only mentioned a meeting with someone at ten thirty yesterday. He never mentioned a name."

"Any indication of the person's gender?"

She shook her head, "Sorry. But I recall he didn't sound happy about the meeting though."

They were getting nowhere fast. Savannah glanced balefully at the photo album on her desk. Mathis kept groping for the nudie filled book to speed things along. It forced Savannah to play a role she really wasn't prepared for. Parent. Stop it, she wanted to tell him. Stop reaching for this ugly testament to her brother's moral backsliding.

"He was a good brother. He helped me pay bills when I fell

behind. He didn't necessarily like it though. He had a bad temper and when he thought I was screwing up, he told me about it."

"Something about brothers," Savannah replied. "Mine does the same thing."

What was it about older brothers, she wondered. They felt obliged to advise or lecture and occasionally seize control of the younger sibling's life. If the advice and lecture failed, Seth always got angry with her. Blisteringly so and that sparked her temper which always ended in chaotic, terrible arguments that sent innocents running for cover. Only the past few years had she and Seth grown closer. Upon leaving the army, he and Leah moved back to Atlanta which gave them the opportunity to build a real relationship. She credited Leah for that. No one accused Seth of being warm and cuddly but then no army ranger was, she supposed. His wife became an intermediary between the two because invariably, one or the other took offense at the other's actions or comments. Leah coached, persuaded and sometimes outright lied to ease the tension between brother and sister. When Lindsey was born, her brother softened considerably, and Savannah guessed she did too. Still, as difficult as their journey had been, she couldn't imagine losing him the way Nancy lost Barry.

"How about past girlfriends? Did you meet any of them?" Savannah asked.

"Oh sure," she dabbed more tears, "I met most all of them at one time or another."

Then you stayed very busy… Mathis reached for the book once more and Savannah tilted her head with an unspoken warning to back off. She returned to Nancy, "Any of them disappointing to you?"

Nancy nodded, "I told Barry about certain women." Her voice quavered, "He never listened."

Savannah couldn't say the same. When she was eight, she tattled to Seth that she saw Tammy Wilson in the backseat of some guy's car. They were fogging the windows, she told her seventeen year-old brother at the time. Then Tammy's naked butt pressed against the window, the lily white cheeks staring back at Savannah like two alien eyeballs. To that day she could still see the two half-moons pressed in the middle of the steamed window. The next day Seth broke up with Tammy, leaving her crying on the sidewalk. Sometimes there was justice, though she thought Seth let the girl off easy.

Mercifully pulling herself from the memory, she forged on, "Do you happen to recall any of the girls you warned him about?"

"Not their names, no."

Mathis pointed to Savannah's desk, "We got a book from Barry's place that has pictures in it. You can identify them that way."

Savannah leveled an incinerating glare at him. Leave it alone, she wanted to say. Most of it was lewd anyway and no sister wanted to see her brother in his birthday suit.

If they'd had time to remove the vulgar pictures, Savannah would have agreed sooner. But Mathis insisted so she pushed the heavy book toward him, "Since it was your idea..."

Mathis lugged the thing into his grasp and as he did, Savannah felt obligated to warn their guest, "Ms. Eliot, there are a few nude photos in the album."

"Naked women don't bother me."

Savannah cleared her throat uneasily, "They are of your brother, I'm afraid. Just thought you should be forewarned." She aimed the comment at Mathis.

Nancy hefted the album into her lap. All three detectives watched in silence as she skimmed the pages. Savannah remembered where Tracy, Danielle and Lucy were located – right in the middle of Barry's nudies. She squirmed uncomfortably, waiting for Nancy to stumble across them. If Vaughn's sister suddenly belted out an earsplitting scream, Savannah planned on pointing straight at Mathis when the whole station rushed into her office. His fault, she'd say. He made the woman look at her brother's naughty parts...

Nancy flipped page after page and once at the book's middle section, still hadn't reacted to what Savannah knew was there. That left Savannah cold. Hell, *she'd* nearly suffered a stroke when she came across them and his own sister breezed past them like they were family reunion material.

Rusty scooted to the edge of his seat, peeked over Nancy's shoulder. Savannah waved him back, "Rusty, fetch Ms. Eliot that refreshment." The woman initially declined the offer but she'd settled down now, plus it would busy their resident pest. Savannah inquired, "What would you like to drink, ma'am?"

Without looking up, Nancy answered, "Coffee's fine, thank you. Two sugars."

Rusty sighed, disgruntled with being volunteered. Savannah

leaned back, satisfied, "Stir it real good now. Those cubes can be stubborn."

Rusty grumbled as he walked out. It turned out to be perfect timing as Nancy flipped another page, announcing, "I remember warning him about her." She pointed to Danielle Callahan. "She's married."

"Where do you know her from?" Savannah asked.

"I work as a server at this restaurant in Duluth. I saw her with an older man. He looked like Jimmy Johnson, you know, the football coach. Anyway, I overheard him talking. I remember it because he was so red in the face when he reminded her about their prenup. When I found out Barry was dating her, I warned him to break it off and why."

Savannah slipped on her glasses, jotted a few notes, "Did you hear anything else of the couple's conversation?"

"Only that he found out she was stepping out on him. He told her if she didn't terminate the relationship, he would. He was creepy. He was so cold and composed when he threatened her, it gave me the shivers. I tried to make Barry listen. Do you think that man killed my brother?"

Savannah kept her suspicions to herself, answering instead, "We're following other leads in the case too. The more information we have, the faster we hope to find the person responsible for your brother's death."

Rusty rounded the corner, stopped and eyed the group. Savannah casually motioned for him to hand off the coffee. "Did I miss anything?" he asked in a manner suggesting he missed the winning touchdown and knew it.

Conveniently ignoring the inquiry, Savannah pointed to the book, "Ms. Eliot, do you recognize any other women?"

Barry's sister examined the photos with painstaking concentration. With a raised brow, Rusty looked at each detective, anticipating an answer to his question. No one obliged or pretended to try.

Nancy tapped one picture, "Her. I recognize her. I dropped by one evening and interrupted things, I guess."

Savannah peered across her desk. Nancy pointed to Lucy Driscoll. "What gave you that idea?" the detective inquired.

The woman blushed, "Barry got upset because I showed up."

Savannah wrote that down, "Did the woman appear upset with you?"

"No, no. She acted upset with Barry. He got mad because I interrupted them. *She* seemed upset with him. I must've interrupted an argument. When I asked Barry about it later, he said she was a drama queen. Said she was sick or something because she took a lot of medication. I don't know. She was quiet and unassuming to me."

Ennis asked, "Did he say anything else?"

"Only that he was glad to be rid of her."

"How about any others there?" Savannah motioned to the book.

Taking her time, she studied each page. She came across the photos of her and Barry. Tears glistened in her eyes when she spoke, "He might not have been a model boyfriend, but he was a great brother." Defeated, she closed the book, "I don't recognize the others. I'm sorry. I thought I met all his girlfriends. Clearly I hadn't. I'm afraid I'm not much help."

"Actually," Savannah assured with a sympathetic smile, "you've helped more than you know."

11

A few phone calls produced Beau Callahan's location. In typical affluent style, Mr. McMansion spent the hot humid afternoon playing golf. Prying that information from his secretary became a game of chess until Savannah threatened to send a building inspector to every Callahan construction site in town.

"He's in the middle of his round at Pine Meadows," the woman begrudgingly confessed. "Can't this wait until he's finished?"

Savannah assured her it could not. So she rounded up Ennis and they headed out to the golf course. They drove and drove until the number of buildings grew sparse and the so did the traffic. Savannah took the opportunity to kick off her shoes and lean back in the passenger seat to stretch her aching back. Might as well relax before doing battle.

Thirty minutes later they still hadn't found the entrance to the posh course surrounded by luxuriously constructed homes. Savannah had heard of Pine Meadows but only in reference to bored, wealthy people who needed something new to throw their money at. A brand spanking new house the size of a mini-mall sounded just right to them, evidently. They could park their Rolls-Royce inside their air conditioned garage, call their next door neighbor for a meeting to decide what direction to take the city economy. Lovely.

Forty-five minutes into the drive, a sign for Pine Meadows graced their presence. Ennis exited the freeway and veered right, following the arrow on the sign.

Savannah sat up straighter in her seat, slid her loafers on, "Finally. We've been driving for nearly an hour."

"Driving long distances ain't no big deal to me. It takes thirty minutes to get from our ranch to Amarillo."

The Texas Panhandle was a nice place, she agreed. Big wide open spaces as far as the eye could see. Breathtaking sunsets that disappeared behind the horizon. Cows, horses, pigs and people shared the land without neighbors griping or calling animal control on the dapple gray horse trotting down the road with a cowboy on its back. Savannah liked the openness of the plains, mostly because the crippling claustrophobia never reared its ugly head when she visited. There were downsides to the place though. She'd seen snow before but not in such voluminous amounts. And when it rained, sometimes the sky opened until the roads washed out. The biggest surprise of all: she quickly discovered just how hard the wind could blow on Planet Earth. The Panhandle winds could uproot fully mature trees, flip semi trucks and practically yank a girl bald headed in minutes. The best remedy as she found out was to stay inside during those times or risk having her hair yanked out by what Ennis called "The Panhandle Breeze".

Ennis was right. It did take thirty minutes to travel from the ranch to Amarillo but, "No offense, babe," she said, "but there ain't much to look at on the way to Amarillo either. Cows and tumbleweeds mostly. I'm used to lots of angry drivers, trees hugging the roads and buildings that dwarf me."

"No offense taken," he said, signaling for a turn.

Another difference between here and there, she mused. Thoughtful cowboys signaled their intent to turn. Atlantans just plowed their way through traffic with the attitude *I know where I'm going so why don't you?* Ennis's courtesy probably confused the other drivers, making them wonder *what the hell is that stupid blinking light?*

They approached the entrance to Pine Meadows and pulled onto the road leading to the golf course's main office. She saw Jaguars, Beemers, a Mercedes, and even a Bentley parked in the lot. Ennis wheeled their plain but trusty Ford beside the Bentley, giving Savannah a momentary swell of joy. *That'll make 'em wonder who's breached the fortress...*

She glanced beyond the main building. Stretching for miles was a beautifully maintained golf course. Golfers drove their carts down the narrow cart path lined with a variety of blooming flowers. She closed her eyes, imagining the greens, the fairway and the challenge of scoring under par like she did in high school. Sadness settled over Savannah when she saw golf carts puttering along in the distance. She longed for the days when the warm sun, chirping songbirds and smell of fresh cut grass meant preparing for the upcoming tournament season. In her youth she spent hours at the driving range, playing practice rounds, enjoying time away from troubles at home and her biggest concern was whether to use the three or four iron.

With all but R.J. encouraging her to play, she sharpened her skills to win two Georgia Junior Championships before age eighteen and three high school state championships. At the time, the Augusta Chronicle lauded local talent and she began appearing on the sports page with her newly minted nickname "Augusta's Stealth Bomber".

Her success garnered choice scholarship offers from the universities of Georgia and Tennessee and Alabama. She'd been seriously entertaining which school to attend when fate struck a cruel blow. Her mother was diagnosed with breast cancer. Depression and anger drove Savannah to her father's coping mechanism. She drank her way through her senior year, the fog of bourbon failing to numb the pain of her mother's loss. She drank her way through tournaments and discovered local fame as fleeting and fickle as life. She drank her way from State Junior Champion to just another high school golfer trying to score under par on the course. In later years, her failures simply hurt too much to reflect upon. She packed her trophies away, stashed her old golf clubs into the back of a closet and along with it, the memories of her once promising career.

A pang of guilt made her wince. Wasted youth. Bad choices and judgment. Drinking had been her ruination once. She vowed never again and with Ennis by her side, his love and devotion helped keep her buoyed from the bottle.

"You okay?" Ennis asked from the driver's seat.

Emerging from the memory, she nodded, "Just remembering."

"If you feel up to it, play a round sometime. You got those new clubs Duke Shelton gave you."

She seriously considered that. A most unlikely source provided her with renewed hope of her dream. New golf clubs, fitted to her height and swing. The man who gave them to her insisted she try to rekindle the passion for the game. She promised she would – but then no one successfully said no to Duke Shelton. His money and influence verged on scary but Savannah learned that Shelton, despite his weird lifestyle, truly had a heart.

Her gaze passed across the first fairway, the little thrill from long ago surprisingly appeared. Her heart skipped a beat at the thought of holding her driver and swinging for the green. Augusta's Stealth Bomber may have grown older but she still had the passion. Savannah smiled, "I might do it."

She recognized Beau Callahan's silver Jaguar and motioned for Ennis to park next to it, "We'll see if Beau's expensive import develops hives from our humble Ford."

Ennis parked, cut the engine, "Savannah, let's use kid gloves with Beau. If the mayor finds out we're poking around –"

"I'm not planning to accuse him of murder. I only want him to account for his whereabouts the day Vaughn died. He wormed out of it at the house by pushing us out the door."

"Still," he scratched his head. Savannah got the idea he searched for a palatable way to present his thought so she waited.

After a moment he gave up, "Be cool with him or let me handle it okay?"

She batted her eyelashes, "Afraid I'll offend?" Then she smiled,

"Tell you what. I'll start the interview and if you believe I'm too rough, take over. Just do it in a nice way." She extended her hand, "Deal?"

He finally cracked a smile of his own, shook her hand, "Deal."

Ennis resembled a boy when he grinned. It was one of many reasons she fell in love with him. He had such a boyish charm, no woman in her right mind could resist him. Too bad the staff at the country club found it easy to dismiss his charisma. When they walked inside, the climate chilled from the balmy summertime temperatures – and not due to the air conditioning. They turned positively icy when badges were flashed. Ennis introduced them and proceeded to inquire about Beau's location on the course.

The man behind the counter looked more suited to receiving guests at a five star hotel than sunburned golfers. His baleful frown pleased her. Rich people needed to get a clue. Like the middle class and poor, they burped and farted and had to flush toilets after doing their business. The only difference: the middle class and poor didn't flush golden toilets.

Mr. Five Star hemmed and hawed about "releasing that information" until Savannah displayed her badge again, "See where it says 'police'? That translates into cooperation – from you."

Apparently her message fell short of hitting its mark when he asked, "Is it an emergency?"

"For him or you? Because the longer you stall, the madder I get." She leaned across the counter, "Tell us Beau Callahan's approximate location then provide us with one of those snappy golf carts. Otherwise, we have to use our Ford to traverse the front *and* back nine to find him."

O O O

"Don't these things go any faster? Come on," Ennis pressed his foot to the floorboard of the golf cart, verbally willing it to speed up.

They were traveling at a decent clip in her opinion. Especially for an open vehicle that provided no roll bar or helmet for protection. "No and I'm grateful they don't. Not with you behind the wheel." She held on tight as her husband inadvertently veered off the cart path and into the bumpy rough. Tall grass scraped the undercarriage of their meager transportation which encouraged her to ask, "Want me to drive?"

He jerked the wheel, whipping the cart back onto the path. He floored the accelerator again, "I just wish we'd get there before Christmas."

His impatience amused her. Finally, a vehicle that refused to be bullied by his lead foot. A grin crossed her face despite her growing nausea, "Ennis, golf is a slow game. It wouldn't make sense giving the players an Indy car to drive to each hole."

He looked at her, his frustration mounting, "I had a soapbox racer that went faster than this contraption."

"The road," she reached for the wheel. "Watch the road."

The golf cart swerved off the pavement into another patch of grass, bounced and rumbled along and barely missed a row of pink azaleas. He steered back on the smooth pavement, complaining, "And these damn little sidewalks..."

Cart paths, she silently corrected. Not little sidewalks. Savannah braced herself with one hand on the dash with hopes of convincing him, “Again, a slow game that, to some degree, is supposed to be relaxing. No need for speed or superhighways.”

Ennis harrumphed but kept a vigilant eye to the narrow road. She shook her head. In a moment of folly, she imagined Ennis joining her in a game of golf. Her husband never claimed to be a patient – or composed – man when dealing with games. Football taught her that early on. He shouted and shook his fist at the TV as if the Cowboys and their coaches could hear him. He stormed from the room when the other team scored. He literally boycotted the team, but only for a day she noticed. Then his blood ran royal blue and silver all over again in anticipation of the next week’s game. So putting a nine iron in his hand and telling him to aim for a four inch hole wasn’t going to work.

The golf cart lurched to the left, jerked back right and Ennis instructed, “You’re driving back. Maybe I can catch a nap during the ride.”

Yes, her husband, the patient one. Right… She glanced up to spy a shocking white object in the near distance. “Is that Beau?” An overly tanned physique in white shirt and shorts waddled from his golf bag with a club. If Beau’s goal was the Bronzed Adonis look, he fell far short, settling more for Burnt Toast. “It is Beau,” she sighed with relief. The frightful ride was finally over.

Ennis slowed to stop as Savannah watched Beau remove something from his pocket then bend toward the tee. From her golfing days, she recognized the object he held, "A golfing knife."

Ennis sounded confused, "They have knives in golf?"

"It's like a Swiss Army knife only it has a divot repair tool, a tee punch and a groove cleaner for the club heads. But guess what else it has?"

"I assume by the name it has a knife."

"And it measures about four inches long, around the length that killed Vaughn."

Impressed, Ennis nodded, "Then let's have a word with Mr. Swiss Army."

Still holding to the roof and dash, she refused to let go until Ennis killed the engine. Beau swiveled to see their visitors. His three golfing buddies did the same. The only difference: Beau's smile evaporated upon recognizing the two detectives heading toward him.

"This is beginning to look like stalking or harassment," Beau said, leaning on his seven iron.

Savannah chuckled under her breath, "Thinks a lot of himself, doesn't he? Only people who'd stalk him would be women asking for the brand of his hairspray."

Ennis only smiled at the observation then answered Beau's statement, "Need to ask you a few more questions for our investigation."

As they neared, Savannah recognized his golfing buddies as city councilmen. He stabbed the tee punch into the ground then drew back, curses spilling from his lips. He stomped back to the golf bag, slinging his hand as he went.

"Problem?" Savannah inquired.

"Besides you? You made me cut myself. Why didn't you schedule an appointment for this anyway? It's embarrassing to have you nipping at my heels in front of my friends."

Savannah crossed her arms, "Seems as though your planner is so full your secretary couldn't squeeze in a twenty minute sit down for us." Actually, the secretary left the impression Beau absconded to some tropical paradise – on another planet – and no one short of God Himself would be allowed to contact him. So suspending Mr. Callahan's golf game took on a new, cheery meaning for her. "It's only a few questions. Don't worry," she waved the others to proceed with their game then finished, "we won't interrupt very much."

Beau's chubby cheeks flushed. He wrapped a Band Aid around the cut, continued muttering to himself. Savannah noticed two of his other fingers bandaged the same way, She pointed to them, "Had a few accidents lately?"

"He's a disaster on the golf course," a councilman joked. "It's a tossup whether he uses more balls or Band Aids every round."

Beau's mood blackened further at the insult. He jerked his thumb behind him and called Savannah and Ennis like dogs, "You two. Ask your questions over here."

They followed him several paces behind the tee box. He leaned on his seven iron as Savannah bulled right in, "We have a witness that remembers a particular conversation between you and your wife. It's in regards to your prenup forbidding adultery, at least on her part."

He rolled his eyes, "That's all you've got? It's my right to converse with my wife, is it not?"

"Seems odd this conversation took place around the time Barry Vaughn was seeing Danielle in more than a therapeutic way."

"Sometimes," Beau's vision flicked to Ennis, "we must remind the women in our lives of their place. In my case, it's a legal and binding contract that she stay monogamous to her husband. If she fails, I have every right to divorce her."

"But you didn't," Ennis said. "Why?"

"She took care of the problem." His narrowed vision returned to Savannah, "As I instructed her to do."

She calmly stated, "You called Vaughn the morning he died. What was that about?"

"I reinforced what my wife told him. It's over so move on." He turned and began his trek back to his friends.

His arrogance stoked Savannah's temper, "Where were you at eleven o'clock the morning Vaughn was killed?"

Beau stopped in mid-stride and when he swiveled to face her, the hairs on the back of her neck prickled. He marched back, gripping the club in his fist. She half expected him to take a swing at her but he kept it at his side. He replied harshly, "I was at a hotel in Columbia, South Carolina, trying to line up investors for a new subdivision here. Does that satisfy you, Detective?"

Not even close. "What hotel was that?"

Beau's nostrils flared, "I don't remember, either the Marriott or Sheraton. Ask my secretary."

"I'm asking you," she nudged.

Beau flushed beet red beneath the tan. He retrieved the golf knife from his pocket, opened it to the groove cleaner. The metal point scraped through each groove with far too much force. "I'm gone more than I'm home so it's difficult to recall every detail."

"Think real hard," she prompted. "It's important and you don't want to be wrong. If you stayed at a hotel a few days ago, the name should be easy to recall."

He closed his eyes, gripped the club and knife with a ferocity that nearly unnerved her. "The Marriot," he squeezed through clenched teeth. He pocketed the knife and pointed the club toward his buddies, "May I?"

"Surely," she stepped aside to let him pass. The rich businessman grunted as he did so. He managed four steps before she said, "Just one more quick question."

Beau swiveled back to her, sighing, "It's never quick with you. What is it now?"

"Do you use that fancy golf knife for anything other than golf?"

"What the hell is that supposed to mean?"

"If we test it for blood, are we going to find yours and perhaps Barry Vaughn's blood on it too?"

Beau's complexion paled unlike his temper, "How desperate are you? I may be clumsy but I'm not a killer. Last I looked, it's hard to drown someone with a knife."

Savannah stepped closer, "That's just it, Mr. Callahan. Vaughn was stabbed then tossed in the tank. You've got motive, a dodgy alibi and a possible murder weapon in your pocket."

"I've also got lawyers who'll break you like a pony if you push this any further. Now, I'm going to finish this round in time to call them. That way, you can direct any further 'quick' questions to them." He stomped toward his buddies, grumbling the whole way.

"A pony, huh?" she harrumphed.

Ennis's hand settled on her arm, "Don't take that threat lightly, babe. He's rich enough to do it."

He could try, she thought. Lots of people had and they all failed. But she'd promised herself she'd try to listen more to Ennis, the voice of reason. Her Libra loved harmony in his life which continually made her question his choice for a wife. Not that her inner Gemini hated harmony. The sign of the twins just promoted havoc, she supposed, at least in her.

As Beau approached the tee box and evaluated the upcoming shot, it surprised Savannah that he stayed with the seven iron.

His club choice told her was a conservative. Judging by the distance and water hazard surrounding the front and sides of the green, she'd have gone with the six iron. Granted, if the shot was off, the ball would plunk into the back bunker but if she hit it just right, she'd make the green with the shot. The way Beau played the hole, he'd be lucky to par it out instead of possibly scoring a birdie.

Beau placed the ball on the tee and stepped into his stance. He took a few practice swings. Savannah cleared her throat. Beau's shoulders slumped, "What's wrong now? Can't you find the exit?"

"Sure can but I notice you need serious help with your swing."

She leaned closer to Ennis, whispering, "It has more issues than National Geographic."

Ennis pursed his lips. Libra's harmony circled the drain because Gemini had a point to make. Her husband nervously drew his hand down his face, "Be careful. He's boilin' right now and it ain't because of that sunburn."

Unlike Ennis, his buddies chuckled at the simple observation regarding Beau's swing. Beau, as Ennis poetically mentioned, boiled in his designer shorts and polo. He was too angry to speak.

If she felt cheeky enough, she'd have dragged out the six iron and taken a whack at the ball just to show Mr. Callahan how golf was meant to be played – full throttle and aggressive. She didn't collect all those trophies by settling for par. She went for the green almost every time but she also knew when to finesse the ball. Savannah attempted to *finesse* her explanation, "Your head is too low and you're flexing your knees too much. Plus, the way you swing, it'll hook right into the water." Okay, she thought. Two-thirds of it qualified as tactful. The last part, hell, she just wanted to say it.

"You're a golf expert now?" Beau chided.

"Two time Georgia Junior Champion and three time state champion in high school," she proudly stated.

Beau laughed, "A high school golfer's analysis of my swing. A high school golfer who chose police work over college or, perhaps, even turning pro."

Now that was low, even for the rich bastard. She cringed as

memories of full athletic scholarships floated to the surface. The hot afternoons she walked the fairways in a haze of alcohol, haphazardly swinging the irons, missing tap-ins on the greens. All the tainted memories that went along with being a recovering drunk came flooding back in an instant.

Savannah shored up her wounded dignity. True, she wasn't swinging golf clubs as a pro but she *did* wield a mean gold badge, a gun and a suh-weet set of handcuffs that she'd dearly love to fit around Callahan's affluent wrists. "That's true but here's a free tip. The six iron is the right postage for that zip code." She smiled at the other men, "Good day, gentleman," then began walking off.

Beau released something akin to a growl, lined up his shot. Savannah turned to watch. He retained his usual slack stance, swung back and struck the ball. It sailed toward the sky then veered sharply to the left. He uttered an expletive as his ball splashed directly into the water. The shot was short and wet, just like she'd said.

His buddies turned to Savannah. Beau refused to acknowledge her presence. She just shrugged, "I told you so. But I'm merely a high school golfer who chose police work over turning pro." She felt Ennis tugging at her arm but she couldn't resist one last comment, "Look on the bright side. There's no damage to the fairway with that shot."

Ennis grasp tightened in a way that refused argument, "Let's get in our pedal car and skedaddle before he uses that club on your head."

12

When Savannah and Ennis returned to the station, he veered off to Josh Hunter's office to update him. She went to her office to begin the arduous task of calling hotels in Columbia. A feeling nettled her that it was a futile effort that would waste a good amount of her remaining shift. Beau Callahan found a way to weasel out of his problems, it said and lying was just one tool in his arsenal. Lawyers were another. And before she forgot, he had the mayor's undying support as well. In some cases money evidently *could* buy friends.

Savannah stopped outside her office upon sight of another visitor. Funny how she regarded guests with trepidation now. After the Rusty fiasco, everyone was suspect. This guy was much heavier than Rusty, sported burred off black hair and judging from his profile had a baby face that made his gray Georgia Department of Corrections uniform seem implausible, like a kid dressed for Halloween. He studied a plaque on her wall then turned his attention to her commendations that Georgia insisted she display.

She watched him, wondering why a prison guard might roost in her office. Usually they stayed away from police stations unless they had their own dilemmas. If that were the case, he'd either be at the sergeant's desk or some other detective's office – unless he had information regarding Barry Vaughn.

Hopeful that was the case, Savannah stepped inside and greeted her guest. The man she guessed to be around twenty-three turned to face her. His youthful face unfurled a dimpled grin, "Boy, he wasn't kidding. You are pretty."

She smiled despite herself, extended her hand, "That's an interesting ice breaker. Savannah Prince and you are..."

He gave her hand a solid shake, "Mike Baldwin. I'm a guard at the prison."

That could have meant one of two places. Atlanta had Hamilton, a newer level three women's facility and Norcross, a brand new level five maximum security for men. She motioned to the seat beside him, "Which one? Hamilton or Norcross?"

"Norcross, ma'am. That's a fancy place, all sorts of cameras and security gizmos to it. We hardly have to leave our stations. Everything's basically run by computer. You seen the place?"

"Never had occasion to but I've heard it's a fortress. What brings you here, Mike?"

He sat down, crossed his legs, "Well, there's a fella inside that says you know each other. Seems like a nice enough guy, even helped diagnose my sister's gall stones just with me tellin' him the symptoms."

This wasn't about Barry Vaughn, her gut warned. Baldwin was here about an entirely more sinister subject. One she'd tried to cope with and forget. As her stomach knotted, she reminded herself to calm down. "Is this *fella's* name Jeffrey?"

"Yes ma'am, it is. Jeffrey Holland. He wanted me to pass along a message to you and seein' as how he did me a favor, I couldn't rightly refuse."

Then you're either crazy or new to town. Considering Jeffrey and Cole's brutality had been front page news not long ago, she bet on the latter, "Are you new to Atlanta, Mike?"

"Yes, ma'am. Moved here last month from Kentucky. Wife got transferred –"

"Then you don't know the background between Holland and myself." She swallowed the bile rising in her throat. Images she scarcely managed to tuck away now roared back, clawing open old wounds, "He and his stepbrother Cole Jordan raped, tortured and killed nearly a dozen women here in Atlanta. They abducted my sister and myself and we barely survived." A stabbing pain above her breast vividly reminded her how close they came to death. She rubbed the old scar, trying to ease the ache, "So yes, I know Jeffrey Holland but I have no interest in anything he would say to me either in person or via a messenger." She made her way to the door and stood, waiting for Baldwin to take a hint.

The blood rushed to Mike's face in shame, "Sorry, ma'am. You're right. I didn't know the particulars of the situation but he seemed to think the information would interest you. It concerns this Cole Jordan's whereabouts. He says he can help you find him."

Savannah's jaw set so hard her head hurt, "Look, you seem like a nice guy and I'm sorry he dragged you into our drama but I wouldn't believe a word he said."

Mike stood, his shoulders slumped in defeat, his face showing the embarrassment she'd hoped for. "I'll just pass it along anyway. He said if you're interested in finding Cole, come see him."

"Tell him I decline."

Mike's hands buried in his pockets as he smiled apologetically, "Sorry, ma'am. I'll be going now."

She waited until he stepped out of view to take a deep shaky breath. Jeffrey was back in her life. Or *trying* to get back in it. He was never going away, not in her mind, not in real life. He would haunt her forever.

Savannah bolted from her office, down the hall and around the corner to the restroom. She dashed into the nearest stall, bent, and heaved. Tears welled in her eyes at the thought of Jeffrey Holland insinuating himself in her life. The scar above her breast hurt in earnest now. The scars on her back joined the chorus, reminding her how every strike of Jeffrey's cane split the skin and how each wound wept with blood. She groaned, trying to rid herself of the pain and the memories.

Another terrifying thought emerged from the misery as she stared into the toilet. If she was pregnant, how could she protect her baby from the evil of Jeffrey and Cole? They had to find Cole and put him behind bars. It was as paramount as keeping Holland locked away at Norcross, his every move and breath monitored on camera.

"Detective? Are you okay?" a voice called.

When the female officer spoke, Savannah jumped as if Jeffrey uttered the words. She assumed she was alone in the restroom. She'd bulled in with no regard to others, intent on expelling the distress from her body. Now she realized that her hip braced the stall door open for all to see her mortification and sickness.

Facing the new rookie would have to wait. Savannah didn't trust herself to successfully hide her fear and mask it with her usual banter and forced smile. Instead, she sniffed back the tears, wiped away the ones that fell and tried for a steady voice, "I'm fine, thanks. Must have eaten something that didn't agree."

"Did you eat at that Mexican place down the street?"

The officer clearly couldn't take a hint. There seemed to be an epidemic of it. "Yeah," she lied. "I won't be eating there anymore. Thanks again." She listened for the door to close before rising to her feet. Stepping from the stall revealed the restroom was empty now and Savannah took the opportunity to straighten her face and steel herself. But when she looked in the mirror, the pale reflection stopped her. Tired eyes stared back, haunted by memories of Jeffrey. She saw the shaken confidence and wondered if everyone could. She'd changed so much in four months, aged more than she should have. She'd become more cautious, paranoid and scared. All because of Jeffrey and Cole.

She headed back to her office and breathed a sigh of relief when seeing it devoid of people. It gave her the chance to solidly bolster her façade when Ennis happened to return. She needed to busy herself and the hotels in Columbia needed to be contacted. Work helped ebb the tide of panic so she sat down to begin the arduous task of refuting Beau's alibi.

She exhausted all the five-star upscale hotels in the city then called everything in between until only the fleabag half-star wannabes were left. Might as well be thorough, she figured, but each phone call met with the same results. None of them listed a Beauregard Callahan.

Between calls, the desk sergeant tossed a note on her desk with a stern, "I may only be a sergeant but I ain't no secretary. From now on, answer your own phone."

Hard to do when you're always using it, she wanted to say but chose to smile demurely, thank him then secretly mumble an x-rated name for him as he walked out. Judging by his handwriting, he told the truth. He certainly wasn't a secretary because no one this side of the medical profession could decipher the message. Waiting another minute on hold awarded her the time to analyze the chicken scratch, "Call Patrick Hess. Says it's important." Beside it the sergeant scrawled out a phone number. This he clearly wrote to preclude any confusion and keep her from asking for clarification.

Hanging up from another no-tell motel, she prayed Barry's business partner might shine a ray of hope on her case. She dialed the number on the note, "Patrick? Detective Prince. You called earlier?"

"Rita," he gushed, "thanks for calling me back. Once it calmed down around here I remembered an incident a couple of weeks ago. It involved one of Barry's clients. Rich, uppity woman. She was a regular Monday appointment."

Rich and uppity. No-brainer, "Danielle Callahan?"

"Callahan, yeah, that sounds right. Anyway, this dude stormed in and let Barry have it. Told him to stay away from her and mad as he was, the words 'or else' didn't have to be said."

"Can you describe the guy?"

Once again Patrick's voice turned buttery, "Only for you. Guy had gray hair, looked kinda cooked from a tanning bed. Got the perfect hair going though. Musta taken him a whole can of spray to get that hold."

And that would be, "Her husband."

He gulped, "That was her *husband*? I thought it was her father. His tone and behavior sounded like a daddy minus the shotgun."

"When did this happen?"

"Two weeks ago Monday, I believe."

"Thanks, Patrick. If you remember anything else – I mean anything, please call me."

"Sure will, Rita." He paused a moment, making her wonder if he remembered another detail from the incident. She waited for him to continue. When he spoke again, he sounded tentative and shy, "While I got you, how about dinner or drinks sometime? Interested?"

A flattering invitation, she thought as her thumb stroked her ring finger, but, "'Fraid I'm spoken for but thanks for the offer." They said their goodbyes, leaving Savannah with images of hers and Ennis's wedding. The warm sun, the crowd of friends and family gathered to celebrate and Ennis standing at the alter, his smile proud and earnest as his love for her.

"I hope that smile is for me."

She looked up to see Ennis leaned against the doorframe. "As a matter of fact, it is," she said. She noticed he kept staring at her. "What?

You don't believe me?" she asked.

His curiosity finally got the best of him, "Some rookie stopped me in the hall and said you were sick."

For shit's sake. Did the rookie use a bullhorn to announce the whole incident? Now Ennis would worry all day – out loud, no less. To quell his concern and his impending interrogation, she merely replied, "She's overreacting. I just had an upset stomach."

"She mentioned you eating at a Mexican joint. I don't remember that."

"Ennis, she's wound tighter than an eight day clock. All rookies are." She lowered her voice to a whisper, "I had to tell her something to back her off. I'm fine, really."

He nodded but she recognized the beginnings of the Inquisition assembling behind his handsome brown eyes. Unless she changed the subject, he'd dog her and she'd fly off the handle at him. If she told him about Baldwin's visit, he'd hit the roof like he always did whenever Jeffrey or Cole were mentioned. The fewer fireworks, the better, she told herself long ago. "I called all the hotels in Columbia. Like we suspected, no one has a record of Beau staying there. *And* that was Patrick Hess on the phone. According to him, Beau stormed into the business about two weeks ago and threatened Barry with more than a lawsuit."

Ennis hiked his left brow higher, "Did he threaten to use his nine iron to hook a couple of different balls into the water?"

"I'd bet money on it." She focused on the contents of his hands. "Whatcha got?"

"You wanted phone records, baby, you got 'em." He tossed a few sheets of paper on her desk, "I'll dispense with calling Beau a hypocrite but his wife needs a premarital agreement for him too."

One look at the phone records and she recognized why Beau hedged on his whereabouts. "Miss Alexa's Escort Service, Atlanta."

Ennis said, "I used my charm to wheedle the fact he signed up for a whole morning's worth of carnal gratification. I didn't want details. Thought I'd spare my stomach."

How lovely. Beau got his bean waxed at the same time Barry died. "Well, we're back to square one."

"Afraid so," Ennis agreed.

"Incredible. He'd rather be considered a murder suspect than proved a cheating husband." But it didn't dismiss the possibility that, "Maybe he hired it done. Who knows? I'm not giving up on getting Callahan that reserved spot at the bail bondsman." Savannah rubbed her temples, "But I do say let's table this until after we interview Lucy Driscoll."

The phone rang and she reached to answer it, thinking perhaps it was Patrick Hess with more information. His compliments hit her ego just right despite the fact she realized it was mere flattery. Still, comparisons to Rita Hayworth were damn fine flattery.

When she answered the phone, the caller's voice sounded familiar though it wasn't Patrick Hess. The man's tone left no doubt of its intent. Pay attention. "Detective Prince, do you enjoy your job? Let me rephrase that. Do you enjoy receiving a paycheck?"

What the... Exactly what asshole felt brave enough to rake her over the coals without serious consequences? "Who is this?" she demanded.

"Mayor Franklin J. O'Neill. Answer my question."

Oh… *That* asshole. Instantly Savannah's mouth went dry which was more favorable than swallowing her tongue. She replied "yes", ending it with the obligatory "sir". To a degree, people could prepare for war. Getting ready for an ambush was impossible and that's what O'Neill loved to do. Ambush. She tried hard to remember the last time she stepped into a pile of shit that deep. Her first visit to Texas, she thought, when she found the only fresh pile of horse dung in a two thousand square foot radius.

"Are you an idiot?" O'Neill wanted to know.

"No sir, I'm not."

"Are you mentally challenged in any way?"

"No," she left off the "sir" this time because his inflection indicated if brains were dynamite, she couldn't blow her nose.

"So you are knowingly and willingly ignoring my order, is that correct?"

If his intent was to push her buttons, he succeeded. Rusty was laughing somewhere in the metro city limits – laughing at *her*, she fumed. Franklin's Mini-Me better head for the hills when he popped out of his hole. She'd be there with a giant mallet and whack that rat so hard he'd end up in China.

"Do I need to speak louder, Detective Prince?" The mayor shouted into the phone.

Wincing, she yanked the receiver from her ear, saw Ennis glare at it. *Who is that,* he mouthed to her. She jotted a note, "Mein Führer." Into the phone, she replied, "I can hear you fine, Mayor."

"Good, because I will only say this once. If I hear you've harassed Beauregard Callahan one more time, that shiny gold badge will turn silver again and you'll be walking a foot patrol. Are you hearing that?"

Loud and clear. She acknowledged as much, "With all due respect, Mayor, we're trying to solve a murder, and we have several avenues to –"

"I promise you," he cut her off, "if you cross me again, it will be the worst mistake of your life."

She wavered between anger and uneasiness. He sounded furious to the point of exploding. She erred on the side of caution, "I'll do my best not to."

"Good day, Detective Prince." He immediately hung up.

She dropped the receiver into the cradle, feeling like the dog that peed on his shoes. "Remember Beau's reference to breaking me like a pony?"

Ennis flinched, probably foreseeing what came next. She sighed, "Someone called the trainer."

13

After work she dropped by the market for catfish. After their day, she and Ennis deserved more than a hamburger for supper. She trekked down aisles for cornmeal and onion for the hush puppies. They would help fill not only the Southern food pyramid but also her ravenous appetite.

She tried resisting the cereal aisle. Mothers with kids clogged it from front to back and her Cocoa Puffs sat right in the damn middle of the fracas. She weaved a pathway through the labyrinth and proudly emerged with a large box of cereal. With the security of that night's supper and the next morning's breakfast safely in her basket, she headed to the checkout.

When she got home, the mail provided a bright spot. Sifting through the bills, Savannah ran across a small envelope with the return address 4885 Tilly Mill Road. Tonya Harris, the woman across the street. Inside was a card with a drawing of a Monarch butterfly. Savannah opened it, "Welcome to the neighborhood." Below it Tonya added a thanks for the phone number and a promise to meet soon.

The card prompted a smile from Savannah and she headed off to prepare supper with renewed hope for their move. So far the neighbors leveled off to a certain degree of weird but nothing they couldn't live with.

While Ennis showered, she cut up the catfish, marveling at the quick adept, manner in which she wielded a knife. By the time he emerged from the shower, she'd already finished cooking the hush puppies and begun frying the catfish. As though struck by the food equivalent of gold fever, Ennis's eyes brightened and he greedily rubbed his hands together, "We're eating good tonight."

Savannah smiled. She only cooked like this on the weekends or on days off. But he was always good to compliment whatever meal she strung together on workdays. Today, however, she knew she hit the jackpot with him. Her husband's food repertoire revolved around basic meals – hamburgers, steaks, beans with fried potatoes and cornbread. But catfish, as she discovered early on, brought out a whole new Ennis. The one who lingered by her shoulder watching her fry the fish like an eager hungry child.

"We deserve this," she said. "I know it's strange to see me in the kitchen on a work night but a hamburger just doesn't say 'here's your reward for being dumped on'."

Ennis sidled up behind her, brushed her hair aside, pressed a kiss to her nape, "I've got another reward for you, if you're interested later."

"It's a date. But for now…" She offered him a hush puppy which he consumed directly from her grasp.

Returning the favor, he slipped one in her mouth, "Good to see you with an appetite again. How's your weight doing?"

"I would say it was back up to one thirty-five but I'm two pounds heavier. You can stop worrying."

"Can't help it. You were too scrawny at one twenty." He kissed her cheek, gave her bottom a playful swat, "I'm glad you've got those extra pounds."

She was happy to see a relaxed smile on his face. He'd worried himself to pieces over her weight. Truthfully she wasn't too excited about the weight loss either but after Jeffrey's incarceration and her trips to the therapist, the pounds returned. And then some.

The doorbell rang as she scooped the first batch of catfish from the frying pan and transferred them to a nearby plate. She placed the second batch of fish in to cook, her smile and good spirits dissolved temporarily, "Y'know, I'm really tired of being 'welcomed' to the neighborhood. Would you mind answering the door this time?"

"Nope, but first I require payment for the favor." He swiped another hush puppy then headed to the door.

She was *more* than tired of the welcoming committee – frankly she was exhausted from it. Two other neighbors hiked down the street the night before to introduce themselves. She hadn't wanted to invite them in because their living room still looked like a storm blew through. Tonya Harris had the right idea. Send a card.

"It's for you," Ennis breezed past, pinched off a bite of catfish and blatantly consumed it. He swatted her bottom again, "That's some good grub, woman. You're hired."

"I prefer cash for my paychecks but will also agree to a trip to Lenox Square Mall." She removed the Kiss The Cook apron – a wedding gift from Dane – then slipped it over Ennis's head, "You know how to fry catfish?"

His hands went to her hips and drew her against him, "Turn up the heat and keep poking 'em until they stop wigglin'."

She pecked him on the lips, "I believe that's your strategy for making love, not frying fish." She removed the pan from the stove, sat it aside, "Who's at the door?"

"That little Jack Nicholas kid from next door. He couldn't quite say Rutherford so he used the Cliff Notes version and called you Mrs. Prince."

She made her way to the front door to find James standing with yet another handpicked bouquet of flowers. These were daffodils and Savannah would bet twenty bucks they did *not* come from his mother's prized flowerbed. A quick survey of the nearest yards provided proof. The lady two doors down would be livid to see the yellow daffodils yanked unceremoniously from her display. "Hi James." she greeted, making sure not to commit the cardinal sin of calling him Jim or Jimmy since Katherine detested nicknames. "What can I do for you?"

He extended the bunch of flowers to her roots and all. Savannah smiled while cupping her hand beneath the dirt covered roots. She thanked him and with that, he felt comfortable answering, "Mother wants to know if Georgia would come to her club."

"James," a voice called from somewhere nearby. It was his mother. She and a man Savannah assumed to be her husband padded along the sidewalk, carefully avoiding the lawn that needed a good mowing again.

Up the driveway they came until meeting Savannah at the door. Mrs. Collins, perfectly made up in an expensive pantsuit and meticulous makeup, held a small wicker basket covered with a red and white checked towel. Perfect.

"Savannah, my husband is finally back from his trip and I wanted to properly introduce you. This is my husband Edward. Edward, this is our new neighbor, Savannah Rutherford. Isn't she positively delightful?"

There it was again. The word. And as before, Savannah had the feeling Katherine didn't mean it in a nice way. Dressed in a crisp black suit, Edward gave the impression of a lawyer or IBM executive. His features were pleasant when he smiled, and when he extended his hand, Savannah pegged him as henpecked. His limp handshake surprised her but figured living with Katherine would make anyone wilt.

After the "nice to meet you", he tried conversing on for size, "So you and your husband are cops."

"For heaven's sake, Edward," Katherine scolded as though he'd called their new neighbors trailer trash. She enunciated carefully, "They're *detectives.*"

It occurred to Savannah that her fight or flight reflexes were in the process of shaking off their cobwebs for the first time in a couple of days. The eerie couple caused a nasty prickle along the back of her neck, one that usually surfaced when faced with a gun or Jeffrey's name was mentioned. She fought the sensation by reminding herself it wasn't *polite* to shiver in front of the neighbors and it was considered uncouth to slam the door on them no matter how many heebies they gave her.

Katherine continued, "Edward wanted to bring wine. I told him it's tacky if you don't know whether the person drinks or not. So many people have problems with alcohol and we'd be horrified if we insulted so I brought you a banana nut loaf and blueberry muffins. There's hardly any sugar so diabetics can indulge too."

"Thank you for the goodies," she retrieved the offered basket, praising God that Georgia wasn't that fanatical. In the middle of praising the Lord, aromas from the bread and muffins drifted from the still warm basket. Fresh from the oven and perfectly presented. *I mean, seriously?* If she needed any more proof they'd moved onto Stepford Lane, she wasn't sure what it would be. So the only proper thing to do was offer, "Do you need the basket back –"

"For heaven's sake, no. Keep it," Katherine waved it off with a smile. "Consider it a bonus."

Savannah tried her friendliest smile, "Will do. I'd invite you in but –"

"Oh, I can smell it from here!" The neighbor cast an enthusiastic glance past Savannah's shoulder. Only an idiot missed the unspoken question – May I come inside?

Savannah hated to tell the woman but the answer was unequivocally *no.* She fought the innate urge to step back and slam the door to reinforce it too. Even if Katherine fell to her knees pleading to cross the threshold, Savannah refused to allow entrance. She trembled to think how the woman might react to moving boxes being used as impromptu shelves and tables.

Mrs. Collins continued, "Haven't had catfish in ages. Do you bake yours?"

Katherine's elation literally took her aback. The Collins family usually refrained from such behavior and to see it in action unnerved any unsuspecting witness. Plus, no one except Ennis ever went nuts over Savannah's cooking. Of course no one else usually had occasion to sample her culinary efforts either. "I pan fry like my mama did," Savannah replied.

Complete silence inside the house caught her attention. Men and kids always busied themselves making noises of some sort and when the house fell quiet, that meant men and kids were up to something. She wondered if Ennis helped himself to the fish or really did try to cook what was left. She hoped the latter wasn't the case. He was great at a lot of things – even some cooking, but nothing more complex than scrambled eggs.

Their neighbor found a new – and annoying – interest. Talking. "I have the most delectable recipe for catfish. You add some oregano, paprika and after it's baked, voilà! Add a lemon wedge and parsley – instant hit!"

Her fish was just fine, thank you, without the oregano, paprika, big top clowns, ringmaster and the rest of the circus. Her mother believed in simplicity, not tossing in everything short of the kitchen sink. "Thanks, I'll give it a try," she lied. With the house still awkwardly quiet, she rounded up her husband, "Ennis, come meet the neighbors."

Edward's expression brightened with recognition, "You're the detectives working that aquarium drowning. I knew you looked familiar."

"That's us. Long hours and little pay. *Ennis*, the neighbors," she reminded. Finally she heard a noise in the kitchen. Mere seconds passed when Ennis sidled up behind her wiping his hands on the Kiss the Cook apron. He was chewing – a fact not lost on Savannah. There was no telling how much her husband consumed while she endured the neighbor's visit. She hoped he saved some for her since she was ravenous.

He extended his hand to Edward, "Ennis Rutherford," then shook Katherine's hand with a smile. His vision migrated to the basket of muffins Savannah held, "Hey, dessert! Thanks, guys." He thrust his hand out a bit too eagerly in Savannah's opinion. He'd been eating or his mood would've been as sour as hers. After the customary introductions, she intended to excuse herself for the sole purpose of scavenging whatever Ennis left her. "Did you leave me any supper?" she wanted to know.

He winked, "I only snuck one. It's your fault for being such a good cook."

Her confidence level regarding cooking rated in the mediocre range. Sure, her mama taught her to cook and cook pretty well, but if the way to a man's heart was through his stomach, she'd feared her cooking abilities would take the longest detour in history. It hadn't but she was quite certain Ennis hadn't married her for her casseroles.

Having a sister that rivaled Julia Child didn't exactly help either. If meals were music, Georgia's classified as a symphony. The older sister could hold her own against any top ranked chef, Savannah was sure of it.

Katherine beamed, "This is a treat having another cook living next door."

"She's an excellent cook." Ennis's bragging brought a blush to her cheeks. He winked at her, "When I can get her in the kitchen, that is." He bent down to the basket of muffins and bread. He inhaled long and deep, "This smells as good as Georgia's muffins."

His declaration sounded positively dreamy. Meanwhile, Savannah's ego fell flat on its keister. She realized her culinary talent lagged behind her sister's but to hear him gush over the neighbor's fare? Okay, so she suffered from jealousy *and* starvation, "Thanks for everything, guys. We appreciate it."

"Anytime," Katherine smiled. "Next time I make a German Chocolate Cake, I'll save a little back for you two. I use imported chocolate from Germany for more authenticity."

And vanilla from Madagascar and for the frosting: coconuts from Brazil. Savannah's stomach growled as the aroma of the catfish and hush puppies drifted past. She practically wrote off eating supper as Katherine leaned closer, laid her hand across Savannah's wrist. Savannah wondered if the woman meant to confiscate the muffins and banana nut loaf. After all, emotion wasn't exactly a plus in the new neighborhood and Ennis just violated that law in spades. If repossessing the goodies was her goal, he'd fight her tooth and nail for them. He loved dessert of any kind and since she hated bananas, Savannah only hoped she got a blueberry muffin before he wolfed them all down.

Katherine kept her hands off the basket, thankfully, and lowered her voice to a whisper, "Pardon my presumptuous nature but did I see

Georgia Prince drop by the other night?"

Savannah did a mental eye roll. She wondered how long it might take. James's reference to Georgia finally found the light of day as Katherine basically salivated over Georgia's name. Georgia was a well known face around town and because her newest book hit the New York Times bestseller list the last week, Savannah expected her sister to garner much more attention in the near future. She already scheduled interviews with local morning shows and radio shows. The other morning she called Savannah, crowing about the networks wanting to arrange interviews with her.

The neighbor seemed to detect Savannah's hesitation, "I noticed the family resemblance and remembered your maiden name or I certainly wouldn't have mentioned it."

Yeah, right... "She's my sister," she answered. "And yes, that was her." Now she realized the reason for the breads. A bribe. Yay.

Katherine clapped her hands together with the same annoying exuberance, "I told Edward you were sisters but he dismissed me as usual." She addressed her husband in a condescending tone, "I *told* you we have a veritable celebrity on the block."

"I'm just a cop, not a celebrity." Savannah gently reminded. *The celebrity lives across town.*

Oblivious to her gaffe – or blatantly ignoring it – Mrs. Collins continued, "I would just hate to impose on you since we're new neighbors but do you think Georgia might attend my book club meeting and sign a few copies of her newest release?"

It wasn't exactly a question. *You have my muffins so give up your sister.* "She's really busy right now but I'll ask," was all she said.

"Do, please. 'Killer Instinct' is a classic in the making." Katherine leaned closer, "I meant to tell you, I've heard therapy can do wonders for your condition."

Confused, Savannah inquired, "What condition?" Then it occurred to her Katherine might have meant residual effects from Jeffrey's abuse.

Instead she was surprised to hear her neighbor say, "Your acrophobia. From what I read, it's severe enough to require therapy."

"I don't have acrophobia." Claustrophobia, yes. That other thing, no.

Ennis interjected, "She really doesn't. That's Georgia's imagination at work."

Embarrassment reddened Katherine's face, "My apologies. I assumed since Georgia based Summer Pearson on you that you suffered from a fear of heights."

I'm not Summer Pearson, Savannah thought then stated, "Georgia knows better than to base a character on me, unless she's forgotten the definition of 'grievous bodily harm'."

"But there are so many similarities." Katherine's vision felt practically intrusive as it swept up her body, "Your height, your eyes and hair, your profession, and you drive an older sports car. The initials of your name – Summer Pearson, Savannah Prince."

Okay, enough was enough. She was *not* Summer and to prove it, "So her partner is a six foot two attractive Texan with a penchant for brown beans and fried potatoes?"

"Oh," Katherine exclaimed, "so you *have* read the book."

14

Icy fingers skimmed over the broken, bleeding skin of her back, making her shudder against the restraints. The wounds were long and deep. The chill from Jeffrey's hand slowly receded. Replacing it - the sting of salt from his touch. Savannah writhed in the bonds, praying for the throbbing and stinging to ease. Instead, another slashing sound sliced the air. The cane was coming again, to strike her flesh with the force of a hammer, its bite razor sharp.

A split second of pressure registered before the excruciating pain wrenched a scream from her depths. It traveled throughout her body in fiery shockwaves. She recoiled against the unbearable agony as a wave of nausea swelled in her throat. The all encompassing misery was repeated and endless. The throbbing of one strike of his cane reverberated for what seemed like minutes, inching its way into her bloodstream to her fingertips and toes. This, *this* pain illustrated why victims begged their tormenters to simply kill them. To end the pain.

But Jeffrey Holland thrived on pain. A woman's screams of agony gave him the pleasure that most men found in lovemaking. He approached her from behind, stood close enough she felt heat pouring from him, felt the rough denim jeans scraping her raw skin. Felt his arousal pressing against her bottom. She cried out when he rubbed against the wounds, the sound trailing to uncontrollable weeping. Please, she wanted to beg, please stop. But if she uttered those simple words, it fueled his sadistic behavior.

Savannah clenched her jaw, pursed her lips. There would be no plea. Nothing except a muted groan escaped. And this, she discovered, also excited him. Her instinctive response to pain caused him to step back once again with cane in hand. She looked up and prayed to God again to please stop this man. *Please save me from this cruel beast. Please...*

She bolted awake, a scream poised on her lips. Her heart pounded wildly against her ribs as if trying to burst free. She held the breath while she reoriented herself. The room was dark, not vividly bright as moments before. Her body, rigid and trembling, did not feel alive with fire. Her vision darted around the moonlit room to realize she was at home in bed with Ennis. Somehow he snoozed through her nightmare and she was surprised and grateful she hadn't roused him.

Slowly, she released the pent-up breath. She shivered from a sudden chill and realized sweat drenched her nightshirt. The nightmare – the same one haunting her for months – came back with a ferocity she hadn't expected. Jeffrey was behind bars. She was safe from him. But Cole. There was always Cole to worry about.

She sat up in bed, unable to return to any semblance of restful sleep. The clock read four thirty in the morning. Ennis would be up in another hour or so. Since sleep was out of the question, she slipped into a new nightshirt and shrugged into her pink fluffy robe, hugging it close with hopes of getting warm.

She waited until she stepped in the kitchen to switch on a light. Ennis knew nightmares still plagued her but he would wonder why it reappeared in the middle of the Vaughn case. She refused to tell him about Mike Baldwin and Jeffrey. Jeffrey was her monster to slay, not his. Baldwin made a huge mistake being Jeffrey's puppet. If he made the same mistake again, she'd alert the warden and let him straighten the guard out.

But for now she just wanted caffeine, anything to help shake off the residual fear. She brewed the coffee for her own taste which, in Ennis's words, meant strong enough to float a pistol.

Her hands continued to tremble as she scooped the coffee into the filter, poured the water and pressed the on button. She had to calm down, she told herself. It was only a nightmare.

For many people nightmares represented inner fears of what could be. Savannah's exemplified horrific reminders of what actually happened. Each night she prayed that they stayed locked away in a shadowed corner of her mind and most nights she successfully steered clear of that corner. But thanks to Mike Baldwin, he not only shoved her into it but shattered the carefully crafted box containing the terrible memories.

She didn't wait for the coffee to finish brewing before pouring a cup. She wrapped her hands around the cup for warmth, hoping to rid herself of the shakes. But the pain remained vivid in her mind, the beating, the blood, Jeffrey's taunts, his touch.

Savannah unlocked and opened the window over the kitchen sink. Perhaps the warm night air would help. It was the first time she welcomed the uncomfortably balmy breeze to embrace her.

The gentle wind wafted in and on it she smelled humidity and Georgia pine from the nearby trees. Crickets rasped and chirped their rhythmic song, enthusiastically serenading anyone silly enough to be awake at four thirty in the morning.

Savannah felt herself relax a bit. The breeze and the coffee helped warm and calm her. She closed the window then stepped over to the kitchen cabinet.

She thumbed through a small caddy sitting next to the day's mail. The caddy contained a phone number she kept tucked away, save for emergencies. She didn't have the phone number in her phone for personal reasons because she didn't want anyone to see it.

She flipped through a few business cards when she finally came across the one she wanted. Dr. Lisa Coates. She saw Dr. Coates for several weeks after Jeffrey and Cole's abuse. Ennis called her "the doc" but she was more than an average run-of-the-mill shrink. She was Savannah's safety net for sanity. Coates helped her reclaim her life from Jeffrey and Cole. She worked with her until the nightmares lessened and the fear faded enough Savannah could breathe again. Dr. Lisa was her crutch when she felt dangerously close to slipping into the black abyss known as Jeffrey Holland.

She stared at the name, debated over calling her later for an appointment. After a few minutes, she placed the card back in the caddy and closed the lid. For now she'd wait. Baldwin got the message and hopefully Jeffrey did too. Hopefully…

O O O

Restful sleep eluded her even after returning to bed. This time, however, Katherine Collins was the culprit of her nightmares, not Jeffrey. Savannah spent the remainder of the night being buried alive in blueberry muffins. She ate her way out only to see a smiling Katherine Collins holding another giant basket full of muffins that she dumped on top of her. No amount of clawing or climbing liberated her from the food hell. And Ennis certainly hadn't helped by extolling glowing compliments on the baked goods *and* comparing them to Georgia's. She awoke with an upset stomach and a new intrinsic hatred for blueberries.

Pressing a hand to her belly, she watched as Ennis drummed his fingers on the steering wheel. They were on their way to interview Lucy Driscoll that morning but Savannah's mind kept wandering back to last night's supper. The catfish, she admitted proudly, tasted reminiscent of her mother's. It hit the spot with her and Ennis and even Edward seemed impressed. The one person who didn't: Katherine.

Ennis hinted and badgered until Savannah broke the cardinal rule of allowing anyone except family past the doorway. To her credit, Katherine kept mum on the house's general disheveled condition, but couldn't quite muzzle the criticism of the food. "That dash of oregano would put some zing into it," she'd said. Clearly attuned to the sensitive nature of Southern women's egos about cooking, both men paused in mid-chew and glanced at Savannah. To *her* credit, she'd taken the snub well but not without thinking *Lady, I have a gun so be careful...*

"Does my catfish need zing?" she asked Ennis.

"Zing?" He repeated as if she spoke a foreign language. He made a turn and then evidently deduced the problem, "You're not letting Katherine Collins bother you."

Bother her? Not exactly. Consume her was more like it.

"You're a fine cook, sugar," he assured, "and your catfish far outshines anything of hers. You and Georgia fix suppers men wolf down. Katherine fixes what the country club élite choke down. Did you see how much catfish Edward ate? He even complimented your sweet tea."

He had, hadn't he? He devoured two fillets, four hush puppies (yes, she counted them) and drank two glasses of her "forty weight" sweet tea, as Ennis called it. And Mr. Collins voraciously scarfed it all down. Now that Savannah reflected on the previous night, Edward showered her with genuine compliments about her cooking. So much that Katherine squirmed in her seat. Maybe Mrs. Flawless Collins had an Achilles' heel after all.

Savannah leaned across the seat, kissed Ennis on the cheek, "Thank you."

"Her muffins aren't bad though."

A vivid flashback struck at that instant. One of basketball-sized muffins pounding her on the head. "I wouldn't know. You and Edward ate them all."

Ennis winced then apologized. He followed it with, "You can

have the banana nut bread."

As if he didn't know, "I hate bananas."

He drove another block then, "Has something happened lately?"

The hairs on the back of her neck stood on end. Oh great. His sixth sense chose that moment to kick in. Did he suspect she was pregnant? Or had he heard about Mike Baldwin's visit? Either way she refused to make eye contact, "Why?"

"You haven't been yourself."

"Then who have I been?" She didn't intend to get surly but discussing the morning's events required more than a short drive. Getting her nerve up required hours and lots of aspirin and maybe a bubble bath.

"Do you think the cancer's back? Your next appointment's coming up."

"No, I don't think the cancer's back."

"Is it Jeffrey? You had nightmares last night."

She skipped the reference to Jeffrey, grousing, "Yes, I had nightmares of two-ton blueberry muffins trying to squash me flat."

He chuckled, "Muffins?"

"Yes, Katherine dumped a load of giant muffins on me. It hurt. That was my nightmare." She watched his shoulders slacken. Maybe she'd assuaged his fear because she couldn't endure his mother hen routine so early in the morning.

"But that's not why you've been sick. At the station, and last night around one o'clock."

Well, crap. She'd hoped he was asleep when the urge hit. Clearly he'd been wide awake. Savannah scrambled to answer, "Ennis, I'm eating too much. I've gained two pounds already. This move has been hell on my appetite."

"Then why won't you eat my eggs anymore?"

The mere mention curdled her stomach. Eggs. The one breakfast she dearly loved and now the smell turned her gut. He'd scrambled a couple for himself that morning, leaving her struggling to hold down the two bowls of Cocoa Puffs she consumed. To prevent an embarrassing scene from unfolding, she excused herself to the bathroom and took time for the E.P.T. which literally spelled it out for her. *Pregnant.*

Now what did she do? She was pregnant and their debt continually increased. Mortgage, car payments, insurance, medical bills, utilities. Add to that diapers, car seat, bassinet, clothes, the list went on and on. Then there was the job. She dreaded it when Ennis jumped on that bandwagon. Once he learned about the baby, he'd harp about desk duty then maternity leave which would no doubt lead to retirement talk.

She needed the job, not just the money but the routine of going to work. Babies changed all that. Babies were more than a day job. Babies were 24/7. For eighteen years…

Savannah rubbed her forehead. She *really* needed to talk to Georgia before her brain exploded.

"I mean, you love eggs." In that time Ennis had stopped at a red light. He turned to her, expecting an answer. Instead, her hand raced to her mouth. Lord knows she tried to stay calm but her face felt hot and sweaty and her gut volcanic, "I do love them, Ennis. I'm just craving chocolate right now. It will pass with time." About nine month's worth.

That seemed to ease his concern somewhat, "It's that time of the month?"

"Yep." At least it should've been. Instead she got a baby and a feral craving for chocolate and a new hatred of eggs. Hmmph. She might as well have been buried by a dump truck loaded with those stupid muffins. It would've been more merciful.

They pulled onto Lucy's street that sat in a nicer part of the city. Not the high dollar houses like Beau Callahan but plenty of cute two and three bedroom abodes perfect for middle class folks. Limbs from old, established trees arched over yards and sidewalks to shade the street, something Savannah was grateful for considering the unrelenting heat. From what she could see, Lucy's yard had one of those trees shading the street. Finally, she thought. Their luck was changing.

As they drove down the street, kids played along the sidewalks and in yards while mothers or babysitters watched over them. It was funny, Savannah thought. The difference in people's reactions to police cars, even unmarked detective's cars which really were more conspicuous than their name implied. In particular parts of the city, people headed for the confines of their homes to discourage police from bothering them. Others stood outside basically daring cops to interact with them. Thankfully those parts of the city were located outside Savannah's precinct or "zone". While she and Ennis worked in a decent area, they were far from the plum districts like Beau Callahan's neighborhood.

Lucy's neighbors fell into the ordinary category: just curious enough to hang around. With the exception of a few mothers shooing their children inside, most decided the lawn needed a little extra watering with the garden hose. The inquisitive neighbors. Savannah wondered if they too packed baskets of muffins for newbies on the block.

Ennis consulted the note with Lucy's address. He angled the car to the curb – right under the shade of the towering oak. "Let's hope she's not got an overprotective husband stashed somewhere."

Savannah nearly laughed at the irony. He redefined the term "overprotective husband."

Lucy Driscoll lived in a modest home sandwiched between a family with two kids and another house, this one lacking the upkeep of hers.

They made their way up the cobblestone walkway and approached the quaint little cream colored house with red and pink roses blooming beside the porch. Ennis gave the door a solid three knocks and they both retrieved their badges.

The door opened to reveal a woman dressed in gray Georgia Tech sweats. Lucy Driscoll stood about Savannah's height with a trim waist, her dark hair tied into a ponytail. The broad shoulders and strong jaw gave her an intimidating appearance but it was her voice that convinced Savannah to let her partner introduce them.

Lucy's quiet, reserved tone combined with avoidance of eye contact signaled Savannah to back off. The woman required a softer touch with an interview, not a gruff, take-no-prisoners approach like hers. Ennis, being his genteel, courteous self, could probably finesse every detail from her without trying.

Lucy stepped aside, "Come in."

Guiding them to a small living room, Lucy grabbed the TV remote and switched off the TV. Then, it seemed, she wasn't sure what to do. She settled for placing the remote on a nearby table. She offered them a seat and they opted for the sofa across from the TV.

"Can I get you anything to drink?" she asked, focusing on Ennis. "I have coffee. It's flavored though."

Savannah strained to hear the hushed offer. Ennis shook his head – clearly he had no problems hearing the woman, "No, thank you. Ms. Driscoll, tell us about Barry Vaughn. Where you met him, how well you knew him."

For her physique, it surprised Savannah when Lucy basically glided to her seat. It took practice to have grace with her size. All her life Savannah felt like a stork with her long arms and legs. She sure never considered herself graceful.

According to Lucy, she'd met Barry at Kroger when she bought fixings for a casserole. He'd stopped by after work for butter and romaine lettuce. "He loved salads," Lucy continued. "He made his own but sometimes liked to drop by," she hesitated, trying to remember then, "Majestic Restaurant. He loved their salads and desserts."

Savannah wanted Majestic to be their next stop. The restaurant kept popping up in the investigation and when that happened, it usually led to something. She'd run the idea by their captain once the results of the food analysis returned. If Josh Hunter agreed, she and Ennis would go stir up the nouveau-riche of Atlanta and perhaps steam more than their clams.

Ennis looked around, "He sent you an arrangement of flowers a few days ago. I don't see them."

The silence in the wake of the question caught Savannah's attention. Lucy fidgeted with her hands then clasped them together, "You won't. I gave them to a nursing home. I wanted nothing to do with Barry or his flowers."

"Why not?"

Savannah noticed Lucy was quiet and careful with her answers. While Ennis listened closely to her replies and tone, she concentrated more on Lucy's body language than the words. Her arms and legs crossed, she still refused to look directly at either detective for more than a few seconds. Her general evasiveness put Savannah on edge but it really nettled her when Lucy decided to disregard the question entirely.

"I need coffee. Sure you don't want a cup?" She rose from her seat, leaving the two exchanging questioning glances.

Ennis opened his mouth to refuse – Savannah knew this about her husband. Unless it was guaranteed good old-fashioned coffee brewed from a can from Kroger, he'd likely refuse. But she wanted answers and what better way than to partake of an offered beverage, even if you had to choke down some sugared motor oil with a French moniker?

"I'll take one," Savannah answered to her husband's surprise. No, the weird smell posing as coffee hadn't inspired her to experiment. Lucy's nervousness had. Ennis declined the offer as expected. Clearly he decided it wasn't worth the gamble.

Lucy left the room, leaving Savannah to raise an eyebrow, "She's hiding something."

Ennis agreed with her whispered observation. She visually breezed over the living room, seeing framed photos lining the fireplace mantel. The silver frames showed an older couple – Lucy's parents, she assumed. Some were of children, probably nieces and nephews since the house showed no signs of kids.

Savannah stood up, stretched, then meandered to an antique drop-front desk serving as a mail sorter. The flat top had minimal scarring and was in good shape for its age. Bills sat to one side, catalogs and magazines to the other, all neatly stacked with a letter opener on top. The magazine pile consisted of current issues of Maximum PC, CPU and MacLife. Interesting. She figured Lucy's reading material fell into most Southern women's repertoire. Most, including herself, received their monthly fix of Southern Living and Southern Lady like all traditional Georgia females in good standing. It was handed down generation to generation and Savannah just assumed it worked its way into the Steel Magnolia DNA.

Looking closer at the collections of magazines she noticed the recipient listed "Luke Drury". At least it made more sense to her. Guys and their electronics. She took another look around for sign of a male presence in the house. Like the kids, she saw no evidence of a man anywhere so who was Luke Drury?

A small cluster of prescription bottles sat nestled in the corner of the open desk. She leaned closer to investigate. The stash reminded her of Nancy Eliot's statement regarding Lucy, "Barry said she was sick or something because she took a lot of medication."

Reading the small type became a challenge so she slid her glasses on. Dr. Justin Sheffield prescribed Cipro and an allergy medication. A different label from another pharmacy sat between them. Dr. Alan Burch prescribed estrogen for Lucy.

Without straightening, Savannah turned back to Ennis, hitched her thumbs at the desk. May not be anything, she thought, but it didn't hurt to take notes. What seemed innocuous oftentimes proved important later. She filed the names of the doctors and drugs away until having a chance to scribble them down. She hated to spook Lucy Driscoll into silence by blatantly taking notes.

Turning back to the desk, a small drawer sat ajar. Before Lucy returned, she leaned down to peer inside. A photo caught her attention. Without removing it, she saw it was a five by seven of a dark-haired young man around twenty years old. The resemblance said it was Lucy's brother. Why would she have a picture of her brother in a drawer instead of on the mantel with the other family?

"Do you like cream or sugar?"

Lucy's nearness startled Savannah. When the detective made eye contact, she expected Lucy's expression to be in the vicinity of offended or upset. She was neither. The fact Savannah prowled around the desk had no obvious effect on their hostess.

Savannah retained her composure, "Cream with a touch of sugar, please. How old is this desk? It's beautiful." She knew it was an antique but only thanks to Georgia. She'd gone shopping with her sister several years back when Georgia searched for a hand carved drop-front desk. Savannah's limited knowledge and inquisitiveness hopefully eased any concern Lucy had about finding a police detective nosing into her things.

"Late eighteen hundreds is what the saleslady told me," Lucy said, returning to the kitchen. "Doesn't really look that old, does it?"

Savannah agreed it didn't. When she swiveled, Ennis waved his hand in a desperate attempt to lure her back to the sofa. She'd overstepped her bounds, in his opinion, and feared Lucy might close off all communication with them.

But sometimes a cop learned more by casual roaming than firing questions. She opted to take the former approach while leaving Ennis the latter.

Lucy returned with a lime green cup filled with creamed coffee, handed it to Savannah. The female detective thanked her then motioned to a bandage around Lucy's hand, "What happened?"

Lucy shrugged it off, "Grabbed a hot pan on the stove. Not a good day."

Savannah cringed. Every woman who ventured toward a stove eventually fell victim to a burn and the pain sank all the way to the female ego. She noticed Ennis gearing up for his question and answer session. Before they headed back into that Q & A, Savannah said, "I couldn't help but notice the photo in the drawer. The two of you really favor each other."

Until then, Lucy's icy demeanor thawed considerably. Now, however, she reached around Savannah with the polite "excuse me" and pushed the drawer shut.

Ennis frowned the "I told you so" frown, telling Savannah she'd screwed up. Okay, maybe so but how else did they get answers? And since when did inquiring about photos cause such an uproar? It wasn't exactly like the Barry Vaughn Naked Bible of Conquests.

Lucy's uneasiness emerged in her eyes. Besides focusing on the drawer, the two wide pools blinked a Morse code that told Savannah the picture held quite a story.

Finally she said, "Luke is on vacation and it's just as well. He and I don't see eye to eye on most things."

"That speaks for most brothers and sisters, I think. Where'd he go for his vacation?"

"I don't know. I'm just supposed to keep his mail."

The statement bothered Savannah. According to the magazines' mailing labels, they lived at the same address so of course she'd keep his mail. Another thing nettling her – if Lucy and her brother unsuccessfully coexisted, how did they live together without killing each other? If she and Seth shared the same space, someone would be maimed or dead by week's end.

Ennis cleared his throat. Savannah heard the impatience in the simple act. She delayed far too long in his opinion but she'd gleaned a decent amount of information from her snooping.

She and Lucy returned to the living room. Savannah winked at her husband then sat down, playing her assigned role, "A little girl talk isn't a sin."

Ennis ignored the comment and turned to Lucy, "About Barry

Vaughn. What was he like?"

Lucy squirmed, looked away. "He was very bold and outgoing."

Savannah took the opportunity to write down the prescriptions she found while Ennis inquired, "Did the two of you take it past supper and drinks?"

"He wanted to but he was too aggressive for my taste."

"Can you elaborate on that? What do you mean he was aggressive?"

Savannah watched her focus on the fitness magazine on the coffee table. She'd seen the look – the attempt to detach – in plenty of women including herself. Lucy Driscoll was about to announce Barry made unwanted sexual advances toward her. The question was had he forced those advances too far?

Lucy leaned forward, closed her eyes, "On our third date Barry took me to dinner and Guys & Dolls at the Fox Theatre. When we got back, I thanked him and told him goodnight." Tears welled as she spoke, "He pushed his way inside. He said he deserved more than gratitude for the date." She plucked a tissue from the Kleenex box and dabbed the tears.

Ennis gently urged, "What happened when he pushed his way inside?"

"He grabbed me…"

Savannah heard Lucy's one thread of control unraveling. Reliving the event brought back horrific memories the woman thought long concealed. Now she cruelly discovered they were alive and festering beneath the surface. Lucy wiped more tears, "I fought back. He was so angry and strong. I hit him and kept hitting him until he left."

Ennis eased away from the touchy subject, "Ma'am, where were you day before yesterday around eleven a.m.?"

Lucy appeared grateful for the change in topic, "Here. I was cleaning the house."

The doorbell chimed and Lucy quickly excused herself, visibly relieved for the interruption.

Savannah fell back with a sigh, "Being attacked is a good motive for murder."

"Indeed," Ennis said. "And it's easy to understand why she would have done it." He lowered his voice, "But last I looked *you* didn't toss Toby Jackson in a carnivorous fish tank because of his actions."

"I was never given the opportunity."

He frowned, "You found a way to cope, you didn't resort to murder."

"I found you, Ennis, that's what helped me cope. She has no one. Even her brother left her high and dry."

A male voice boomed from the front door, "Why are you crying? The cops did this to you?"

Lucy's was next, "Kurt, calm down. They're just asking questions–"

Savannah and Ennis rose from the couch in unison. It never failed. The presence of cops just invited trouble, generally with family members "protecting" their own. Most times it escalated to harsh words, nothing physical. She'd been in her share of physical altercations with people's family but once they saw the handcuffs, they calmed down. Family or not, the voice at the front door raged with anger so hot, Savannah put a hand to her gun, just in case. Facing a weapon usually extinguished tempers. Usually.

Ennis glanced down and upon seeing where her hand rested, he reached back for his weapon.

"Kurt, don't!" Lucy panicked.

From around the corner emerged a short tub of a man dressed in worn jeans and a white tank top. Upon first glance, he didn't look particularly intelligent. Then he proved it by charging the two detectives, his fists pumping and breaths coming in short bursts like a stampeding bull. His face flushed beet red and what little hair on his head flared out like a baby bird's feathers. He almost appeared comical except his girth rivaled a Mack truck. "Why are you harassing her?" he yelled. "She ain't done nothin' wrong!"

"Sir, stop where you are," Savannah warned. It was her first confrontation since Jeffrey Holland. She'd won that fight using a golf club and fully intended to win this one also – if her chest didn't explode from the intense pounding. She wasn't just protecting Ennis and herself. She had to shield their child from the world's crazies and she'd damn well do it, golf club or not.

Her grip tightened on the .38. She saw Ennis in the same position – ready to draw at a moment's notice. For a brief instant, Holland's face appeared on the beast bulling toward them.

"Take a flying hike, ya fascist bastards!" Kurt yelled.

Savannah exchanged a look with Ennis. We've got a real winner, it said. During her career, she'd been called a number of things, some more colorful than others but fascist?

"Mister, you'd best stop right there," Ennis ordered. Typically, suspects stopped upon sight of Ennis Rutherford. His height combined with broad shoulders and muscular physique demanded compliance. And usually, suspects heeded his tone of voice. They might fight Savannah or run from her because she was female but Ennis, when provoked, presented a commanding appearance and stance that stopped most people cold. But not this time.

As the bruiser headed toward them, Ennis nodded once at her and they pulled their weapons in unison.

Another flashback clawed its way to her consciousness but Savannah tried to push it away. She was not easy prey as Holland claimed. She was a woman in control of her world – finally. Well, most of it anyway…

In the few seconds that Kurt closed the space between them, her brother's training took over. She reared back to punch Kurt in his doughy stomach. Her size ten foot sank deep into his gut, right below the sweat stain on his tank top, and left a perfect outline of her loafer.

Sheer surprise twisted Kurt's face, his rage instantly vanished as he reversed direction and stumbled back, slamming against the wall. His impact rattled pictures hanging above him, leaving them askew. A groan eked out as he slumped, cradling his middle.

With that, Jeffrey Holland's face faded from Kurt's massive form, especially when Ennis retrieved his handcuffs. "Good shot," he praised.

She leveled her gun squarely at their attacker but her hand shook from stress and fear. Her voice, however, remained solid and confident, "Don't think I won't spend a bullet on you. You sit there nice and still or my finger might slip."

Kurt's fleshy hand rubbed his stomach. "Fascist bitch," he snapped.

"Jail or the emergency room. Your choice. Keep jawing and *I'll* decide." She tried to steady her trembling hands. She couldn't hide them from Ennis who zeroed in on them. He knew, she berated herself. He knew exactly what haunted her in those few seconds.

His expression asked one specific question that she answered with a nod. Yes, she was okay – now.

Lucy stood by, still wiping her tears, apologizing for Kurt's behavior, "He's very protective of me but I never expected him to attack the police."

Frankly, neither did Savannah. She'd had her share of ambushes during her career and contrary to popular opinion, practice did not make perfect. Good reflexes and keen instincts helped but nothing prepared a cop for a surprise attack.

But judging from Ennis's expression, she'd spend the trip to the station assuring him all her marbles were accounted for. The last thing she intended to do was field questions about her abilities or preparedness about returning to work. So far she prevailed over cancer, survived two torture killers and not only visited her own shrink but the department shrink, as per her captain's orders. With all that she *still* received guarded glances from officers or she walked by conversations only to have them cease the instant she strode by.

Once the incident with Kurt traveled the grapevine, the looks would return. She fully expected her boss to question her actions but she refused to apologize for defending Ennis and herself. She would, again, have to reassure someone that she was really okay, that punting a man into a wall didn't set well with her but neither did getting annihilated by a nutcase.

Even as Ennis loaded Kurt into the back seat, he slanted her another of the "looks". Savannah fought to retain her composure. "I'm fine, Ennis. I'm really okay."

Her husband nodded once, temporarily satisfied with the answer. As if her husband's concern wasn't enough to try her patience, the drive to the station practically sent her temper soaring.

Thanks to Kurt, the car smelled of sweat and beer. It perfumed the interior to the point her gag reflexes kicked in and she rolled down the window. She sighed then propped her elbow on it, grateful for the flow of fresh air.

"False arrest!" he cried repeatedly to the open window. If he expected the unassuming public to rescue him, his hopes were unequivocally dashed when they all began laughing as the car passed by.

Savannah couldn't help herself, "They're laughing at you, dumbshit. Shut up."

Kurt continued his verbal assault, bellowing his chant as they traveled down the busy street. She coped decently well until he began a campaign of kicking the car windows.

That does it… "Pull over and pop the trunk," she told Ennis. No doubt by his expression, her husband detected the exact degree of her homicidal mood. He didn't argue with her. He just followed directions. He eased the Taurus to the curb and thumbed the trunk release. Savannah flung the door open, deciding the car wouldn't file abuse charges unlike their annoying passenger.

The fact they stopped on a busy street seemed to sober Kurt, "What's going on? What's she doing?"

As she passed the back seat window, Savannah glared at Kurt. She made no effort to curtail her anger, at least when it involved facial expression or scrounging around in a trunk. She shoved things, tossed others aside and created enough clatter to catch Kurt's attention. After spelunking a while longer, she unearthed the item she searched for.

Kurt repeated his question to Ennis who answered, "I try not to interfere or question her when she's in that mood but it sounds like she's rearranging the trunk."

"She's stuffing me in the trunk?" The first sign of panic emerged.

She rounded the back of the car with another glare warning him to behave. He was still prone in the seat, his legs coiled to kick at the window – until witnessing her fierce look. His legs eased down to the seat. "You're stuffing me in the trunk?" he asked, his voice muffled behind the glass.

When she jerked the door open, the motion rocked the car, "Don't tempt me. First, it's against department policy. Second, our trunk isn't that big but, hey, if you insist, I'll try."

"Bitch!" he shouted. His legs recoiled and kicked. Two feet

raced toward her, forcing her to quickly step back to barely avoid the blow. The hobble in her hand seemed to beg to wrap around Kurt's neck, not his ankles. She resisted the urge to strangle him with it, but again, just barely.

Ennis scrambled from the driver's seat after witnessing the attack. He nudged her aside, his jaw set as he focused on Kurt, "You son of a bitch..." Ennis's large hands encircled Kurt's ankles and he literally hauled him to the edge of the seat. When he secured one arm around Kurt's knees, he reminded Savannah of a cowboy in a calf-roping contest. Ennis reached back to her, "Gimme that hobble. I'll make sure he turns blue before we get there."

"I'll handle it. Remember, he has to walk into the station," she then addressed Kurt, "because we're not carrying your miserable ass." She looped the belt over his ankles and cinched it down. Ennis held the hobble strap tight as they slammed the door on it. Kurt had no room to wiggle, much less kick at the windows. They got back in the car only to be greeted by, "Fascist assholes."

"That's right," Savannah replied with lethal calm, "and these fascist assholes also have a gag in the trunk. It's only got a few bite marks from our last suspect. Wanna try it on for size?"

Ennis did a doubletake at her remark. No, they didn't have a gag but Kurt didn't know it and all she wanted was a few minutes of peace before they arrived at the station. Ennis evidently understood her intent and joined in, "Be glad she just hobbled your legs."

"What else is there?" Kurt wanted to know.

Savannah gifted Ennis with a conspiratorial wink then flashed a wicked smile at the rearview mirror, "I get inventive when situations call for it. One more word outta your mouth and you'll find out how creative this bitch can be."

O O O

From the street, their station house resembled a large, red brick house trimmed in white, however a number of things set it apart from that image. One, an antique street lamp sat sentry at the sidewalk, the precinct number painted on the globe. Two, several patrol units and a couple of detective's cars were parked outside the building and three, a handcuffed and hobbled Kurt Graham yelling police brutality as Savannah and Ennis struggled to drag him toward the entrance. His outburst drew attention from passers-by, visitors and cops alike. Savannah's demands to pipe down only added fuel to Kurt's tantrum.

Hot and sweaty from his raving, Kurt yanked free from both detectives. Where did he think he was going, she wondered. His feet were safely restrained so the simple act of walking turned into a nightmare for both him and the detectives. She watched in disbelief as Kurt shuffled a few feet down the sidewalk. At that rate, he'd arrive at the street corner in about an hour. "Seriously?" she asked. "You think you can outrun us like that?"

He answered by shouting police brutality. Shaking her head, she told Ennis, "Let's round him up before we're the stars on tonight's news."

A couple of long strides later and Kurt Graham was back in their custody, Savannah wrapping her fist in his moist shirt while Ennis guided him by one arm.

Kurt's massive weight and wild flailing strained at the scar above her breast, the discomfort threatening to derail her composure. Jeffrey's handiwork kept giving and giving, she mused darkly.

She flinched as a thick wad of spit splattered across her cheek. Kurt followed it with a vicious but colorful epithet. She'd heard the name during her career but usually from uncivilized males or rednecks with limited vocabulary regarding the female anatomy. The name bothered her but not as much as the slimy grime on her face.

Both the spew and rude moniker enraged Ennis and he spun Kurt, no doubt to show him some manners. Savannah wheeled Kurt back to her, wiped the spit from her face and made a show of depositing it on Kurt's already wet shirt. She leveled the warning like a brick, "You really want a beating, don't you?" She grabbed the bottom of his tank top and yanked it over his head, "Spit on me now, moron."

Appraising Ennis's mood took no genius. He wanted to hurt the guy but there were too many witnesses. Her husband's jaw clenched and released, unlike his hand on Kurt's arm. "I'm telling 'em to book you for child molestation."

They towed Kurt into the police station past more gaping citizens and chuckling cops. By then, Kurt found other more descriptive terms for his escorts, causing a nearby mother to cover her young child's ears.

A small relief washed over Savannah upon sight of the booking officer. *Let's see Einstein spit loogies at this cop…* This particular officer refused to tolerate misbehavior from anyone, least of all suspects. Like any cop on the job for twenty years, Sergeant Newlon had graying hair and had seen a lot and rarely found his job entertaining. The instant he caught sight of the shirt stretched over Kurt's head, his brow sank, "A spitter, huh?"

"That ain't all," she replied, yanking Kurt to the forefront. "This gifted mastermind won the lottery today. Charged us like a bull."

The officer appraised the sweaty suspect, "What's that on his gut?"

Her vision centered on the red imprint of her size ten, "I didn't have a Taser."

"Gotcha. Dumbo enjoys beating up lady cops." He rounded the counter then abruptly stopped, his nose twitching. Savannah assumed he got a whiff of their walking gym sock. Indeed, Sergeant Newlon back-stepped, "I hope that stench doesn't cause brain damage." He cringed at the odor, calling, "Douglas, come book this one before I pass out." He leaned closer to Ennis and Savannah, "He's got allergies so bad he'll never notice the stink."

Smells that bad razed buildings, Savannah wanted to say, so Douglas stood no chance of escaping it. She handed off Kurt's personal effects to the sergeant. The bag contained loose change, a pocket knife and five dollars.

A fresh-faced cop emerged from another room with eagerness only found in a newbie, "Whatcha deed, Sgt. Dewlon?"

Newlon smiled, "See what I mean?" He addressed his officer, "Book this one for assault on a cop."

"Whoa, wait a minute!" Kurt argued, "She hit me! I never touched the bitch!"

Newlon's voice deepened to a growl, "Spitting on a police officer is assault and you're lucky you're here and not in the hospital."

Kurt's head swiveled side to side beneath the shirt. The comical scene brought momentary joy to her until another wave of aromatic terrorism wafted past. She backed off, fanning herself for fresher air.

Kurt finally spied her through the thin fabric, "I'm getting a lawyer to sue you for police brutality, bitch. You injured me. I think you broke a rib."

"Oh, cry me a river," she shot back. "If you find a lawyer dense enough to defend the likes of you, I'd make sure he actually passed the bar exam." She turned to Ennis, "We'll go see the boss after I wash this halfwit's slobber off my face."

O O O

Savannah hated rumors. Most were bogus and the one that weren't took on their own life. By the time they traveled the grapevine, people embellished them more than Elvis' jumpsuits. Today, she *really* hated rumors. Officers whispered as they passed by her office, others smiled and chuckled. In one short morning, she'd managed to become the topic of conversation at their precinct.

Josh Hunter strode into her office without knocking, "Do you need to contact a union rep? You should keep them on speed dial since they know you by your first name and your shield number."

Her boss could really give a pep talk. "This about Kurt Graham?" she asked.

Hunter took a seat next to Ennis, "Unless there's another incident you've neglected to inform me of."

Ennis snorted, "She saved us from being steamrolled by that whack job."

Josh ignored Ennis's attempt at helping, "Word has it you kicked him and now he's screaming for a lawyer."

Savannah removed her glasses, addressed her boss, "Be glad I didn't have a Taser or he'd have motor skill issues right now. Look, I defended us. That's all. The bastard's as big as a Brahma bull. I had to do something. At least I didn't shoot him."

"There is that," Josh agreed. "But he's also claiming you threatened to lock him in the trunk of your car. That true too?"

"No. He assumed I was going to," she referred to Ennis who nodded.

Hunter finally relaxed. "So the hobble was justifiable?"

Ennis's frustration sprouted, "If we wanted the windows and our heads to remain intact, yes."

Mathis popped in, gave Savannah a thumbs up, "I hear those big dogs of yours came in handy. Way to go, kid."

"I do what I can," she said with considerably less enthusiasm. Once Mathis went on his way, she reached in her pocket for an antacid and found the note she'd written earlier. With the Vaughn case going south, she needed to reschedule her appointment with Dr. Wyatt. No one would be happy with her, and she'd likely get lectured to death but juggling wasn't her strong suit. When she tried, something inevitably fell through the cracks and with her luck it would be her job. Plus, she had the baby to consider. Dr. Wyatt's appointment took on a different meaning now. It wasn't just checking for cancer – she needed to be sure the next seven or so months went smoothly. That meant an *additional* appointment for Dr. Boulton, her OB-Gyn, and lengthy discussions on how to prevent her breast issues from conflicting with her pregnancy.

Captain Hunter consulted a page from his desk, "Well, since you're not headed to Internal Affairs, I'll update you on the Vaughn case. The salad from the takeout container had rhubarb leaves in it."

"From Majestic?" Ennis asked.

Josh nodded, "So if you still want to talk to the staff, do it. From what you've learned, is anyone looking good for this jackpot yet? O'Neill wants an update."

Savannah answered first, "Will I get slapped if I say Beau Callahan? Because he still could've hired the hit."

"I won't slap you but O'Neill might," Hunter said, "Other than Beau, who's a candidate?"

She replied, "Right now, until his alibi checks out, Kurt is highest on our list. He's got an abnormal obsession with Lucy, he's got the motive and certainly the temper to kill. Problem is, he'd need access to the aquarium and he's not the sharpest knife in the drawer. He's the type that needs Post-It notes on his underwear to remind him which end they go on. I'm leanin' toward Lucy. She's pretty quiet."

"The quiet ones always bother you," Ennis mildly accused. "You think they're hiding something."

"Nine times out of ten they are," she defended.

"Some people are just quiet," he reminded.

"Shyness is one thing, Ennis. Lucy Driscoll isn't shy, she *is* hiding something."

"For what it's worth," her husband changed the subject, "my money's on Tracy Martin. She was mad enough to kill. Didn't mind telling Barry she would either. That's our contribution unless Mathis found a better suspect."

Josh shook his head, "Nothing concrete yet."

Their captain never nagged them for answers. His easygoing disposition left them to their own devices until they specifically came to him with information. Josh's sudden eagerness told Savannah one thing. The mayor didn't want an update – he demanded one. The old fart couldn't wait to start his re-election campaign. If he rode every detective to their grave to win, so be it. "Tell Mr. Mayor these things take time. Perps normally don't walk in and confess but that's why he pays us the big bucks – to beat the confessions out of them." She ended her lecture with a wink.

Josh returned it with a smile, "Keep me posted and keep the beatings to a minimum. All that bad publicity might impede the mayor's re-election hopes."

15

Majestic Restaurant sat on the perimeter of Atlanta's newer and more upscale suburbs. Driving to the eatery, they passed a McDonalds, Wendys and Dairy Queen. Savannah knew they were close when Jaguar and Hummer dealerships came into view. When a lowly Ford breached the fortress of luxury, a person knew they made a wrong turn.

Ennis kept driving until small manicured mini-parks flanked the road. In the distance they saw two story homes surrounded by acreage and iron fences, an area christened Manchester Estates. Savannah just called it Moneyland. Three miles past Moneyland sat Majestic, a ritzy five star restaurant serving dishes that would cost her a day's pay – or more. She literally hated dealing with rich people. Besides sticking their noses in the air when cops arrived, they always, *always* acted affronted by the simplest question as though their ancestry was in question. The worst part – they possessed a knack for putting a person down for the smallest faux pas… "I gave Mathis the list of kitchen employees on duty the night Tracy and Vaughn met. Nearly had to threaten the manager with SWAT before he let go of the names. I told John to start with *Executive Chef* Emily Gant." She ensured to place proper emphasis on "Executive Chef" since the restaurant manager corrected her on the phone. She made the critical mistake of saying "cook". Evidently "cook" meant something entirely different in the restaurant world. To her it was semantics. Kind of like being a *little* pregnant, she mused darkly.

The manager informed her that Majestic did not employ a *cook* but an *executive chef* as well as a *sous chef* by the name Robin Cameron. He driveled on about an expediter and chef de partie or something to that effect, all of which confused her and generally pissed her off more. She'd called Georgia for definitions of all the hoity-toity titles.

"The executive chef is pretty self-explanatory. They're in charge of menu creations, business aspects and staff management. They're the head honcho. The sous chef is second in command…" At that point, Savannah questioned whether this was food or war they discussed. Georgia found the reference humorous, "In a way it is war, I guess. The restaurant kitchen can get tenuous with orders and all those people in one hot, cramped area. The sous chef can fill in for the executive chef and can also schedule staff then the expediter basically takes orders from the patrons and hands them off to the chef. The chef de partie is in charge of a particular area such as the fish chef, grill chef, sauté chef, things like that."

Savannah rubbed her temples. Rich people… She'd settle for drive-in cuisine at reasonable prices over a plate of unpronounceable and exorbitantly priced grub any day.

Ennis pulled the Ford into the parking lot and switched off the engine. They exited the plain looking Taurus and she tried real hard not to notice the Mercedes they parked next to or the Porsche two spaces down. It was the Ferrari parked closest to the establishment's door that sparked her temper. The wealthy had nothing better to do than blow money on big houses and little cars. While the homeless starved, the well-off hopped in their new Carrera and drove to Majestic to eat raw squid. Amazing.

The sun's relentless rays beat down on them and the pavement shimmered like water. The weather seemed stuck on broil for the past few weeks. Not a pleasant situation for expectant mothers. Savannah dabbed the growing shine from her forehead as they headed to the restaurant entrance. At least it would be cool inside. Rich folk abhorred sweating as much as mingling with the common folk.

To her surprise, the aromas drifting from the restaurant actually smelled appetizing. Savannah smelled steak and onions mixed with a vast array of other delicious foods – and the rumble in her belly wasn't just the baby. She was *hungry*. The grumble in her gut grew louder so she did the next best with her mouth besides eat. She kept talking, "God, I feel dumb. My sister knows more about this than I do."

"That's because she cooks more."

Savannah frowned at him, "You trying to make points with me? 'Cause you're not." Looking around at the opulent eatery, it reminded her of Katherine Collins, the perfect wife, mother, and all-around female, "I can't believe Katherine reads Georgia's books."

Ennis seemed equally puzzled, "Yeah, I thought she was busy reading cookbooks or gardening magazines."

"She probably writes them, not reads them. Now I'm supposed to wheedle Georgia into attending her book club meeting. What is

Georgia supposed to do there anyway?"

"I dunno, but she's more of a social butterfly than you are. She'll probably love it."

Savannah lifted a brow, half-teasing, "Keep talking and I'll show you antisocial. I'm pretty sure you're wanting sex again this century so I'd hush if I were you."

They approached the entrance where a middle-aged man stood sentry. He wore white gloves and a burgundy doorman's uniform with the name Majestic embroidered in gold across the breast pocket. He pulled the door open for them, "Detectives, welcome to Majestic Restaurant."

She and Ennis gave each other a cursory glance from head to toe. Were they that obvious? Maybe if they'd driven up in an official cruiser but a plain Ford sedan?

The doorman eased their concern, "My dad was on the job. I recognized the car."

Ah, that helped. Now she wouldn't enter the gates of Hell wondering if the discount tags still dangled from her clothes.

One step inside the establishment clarified just how far out of place they were. Gold sconces and landscape paintings adorned dark paneled walls, giving the room an air of elegance. Centered in the room was an ornate marble fireplace. Savannah stood, amused at the sight. A fireplace casting a nice warm glow across the crowded dining room – in the summertime.

No one manned the reservation desk. They searched around until Ennis suggested they make their way to the kitchen by themselves.

"You want to give the staff a stroke?" she asked, standing on tiptoe to peruse for staff members. "They'll show up. They don't want cops lingering around and I'm sure that doorman has alerted the manager we're here."

"The doorman seemed okay with us."

"Maybe so but we're bad for business. No one wants the cops around unless they called 'em."

By that time, the maître d' appeared. A slight built man with slicked back hair and anemic mustache swooped in like a hawk on a mouse to intercept them.

His narrowed vision appraised their attire, then he wrinkled his nose. "May I help you?" he asked, clearly suggesting he'd prefer to *help* them right back out the door.

With great joy and enthusiasm, Savannah displayed her badge and ID, "We need to speak with your chefs." She enunciated the last word clearly, ensuring the guy understood the depth of *her* annoyance.

He angled himself in an attempt to strategically block their presence from the diners, "May I ask which chef you are referring to?"

She nodded, "You may and the answer is every last one of them." She pointed behind them, "Is the kitchen this way? We can find it ourselves while you tend to your reservation book. You might want to delay or cancel a few of 'em 'cause this may take a while."

Her statement instilled sincere panic. His complexion paled and he pressed his hand to his heart suggesting a heart attack might be imminent, "Heavens, no. The executive chef cannot be disturbed. She's very busy."

"Do you think we're here to swap recipes?" she deadpanned.

"It's imperative we stay on schedule."

"There's a coincidence. We have that same goal. Now if you'll excuse us, we're going to talk with the chefs."

"For pity's sake, there's no reason to bother them. They're quite busy."

As if they weren't. "This is an ongoing investigation. Unless you enjoy sharing a cell with men considerably larger than you that answer to Bubba, Brick and Toothless, you'd best step aside. Interfering with a police investigation is a cardinal no-no."

"I'd never interfere but please," he begged, "can't you just talk to the sous chef?"

"We will talk to *all* of them. There's one word I'll say out loud to this lovely gathering of diners if you don't move. That word is 'ptomaine'. That oughta free up all the chefs for quite a while."

The maître d' verged on outrage. "For pity's sake," he repeated. "Come with me." He waved his hand dismissively at them, "Just try not to look so déclassé."

For the second time in minutes, Savannah eyeballed Ennis's attire then her own. Ennis looked confused. Knowing the word's meaning, she tried to hold her tongue but failed, "One more crack like that and you'll see what our illustrious dé *slammer* looks like from the inside." The nerdy little twit. For two cents and three seconds, she'd twist the guy's mustache in a knot.

They wove their way between several tables seated with

businessmen. All conversation ceased when they passed by. A few noses tilted further into the air while other diners appraised the two detectives and their Average Joe attire or as Snidely Whiplash so kindly labeled them: déclassé.

They stopped at a doorway tucked in the back of the establishment. Snidely stepped aside, "This is the kitchen. Try not to take too long."

Ennis clapped him on the shoulder when he passed by, "We'll try *real* hard."

Savannah watched as the maître d' rubbed his shoulder, cringing as if considering crying police brutality. She'd scarcely held her temper with Kurt's continual caterwauling so she couldn't promise the same restraint with Snidely.

Ennis gave her a sidelong glance of utter disbelief, "Ptomaine? I bet you drove your folks nuts with those kinds of wisecracks."

She half-shrugged, "Probably. I once heard Daddy tell Mama if I'd been twins, it would've amounted to an everlasting riot and if I'd been triplets, it would've been an insurrection." She thought back with a frown, "Come to think of it, Mama agreed."

By the conclusion of her statement, her hand had migrated to her stomach. *Someday you'll have the daughter you deserve.* Her mother's words seemed to haunt her now, reminding her of the hellion she'd been. Savannah prayed their child would take after Ennis in that respect. Calm, sedate, thoughtful. No problem.

Ennis chuckled, "Ma called me a holy terror."

Well, that settled it. *We're doomed. As parents, we are officially toast.* With that cheery thought, she followed Ennis into the spacious kitchen to see people swarming like bees between rows of gleaming stainless steel cabinets. They fussed, crossed paths holding plates, scarcely missing each other by inches. They fussed some more while squeezing past others to their destination then resumed work. If Savannah worked traffic control in the large kitchen, she'd have either been mowed down a dozen times or popping Valium like aspirins. She hadn't seen so much chaos since the Olympics came to town.

The clatter of utensils and plates occasionally outnumbered and drowned out voices. At the same time, aromas mixed together in a hodgepodge, making it difficult to discern one from another. Grilled chicken mingled with sautéed vegetables and other meats could only be detected by a discriminating soul – or a hungry one. The heat in the room rivaled a sauna. Hot and steamy air hung heavy with the variety of foods, making Savannah glad she didn't work in a kitchen most of the day.

Oblivious to either smells, heat or humidity, Ennis tried in a subtle way to gain the busy crowd's attention. He called Emily Gant's name but no one seemed to notice. He tried again. Nothing.

Savannah thrust her badge for all to see, "Executive Chef Emily Gant. We need a moment of your time."

Even with the rather loud summons, the flurry of activity barely slowed. With the exception of one woman, everyone else continued their frenetic activity.

A tall willowy female, Emily Gant possessed the air of royalty as she approached. Savannah wondered if she expected the detectives to bow and courtesy. The chef wiped her hands on a pristine white towel then tossed it into a bin meant for laundry.

Ennis beat her to the punch and held out his hand, "Detectives Rutherford and Prince, Atlanta Police. You worked the night of the fifteenth, right?"

Subtle, Savannah thought. She got the feeling her husband felt as uncomfortable with the hoity-toity joint as she did.

Ms. Gant nodded and with that her vision darted past the detectives and zeroed in on someone behind them. "Stop," she practically shouted. "I specifically showed you how I want this arranged," she concluded with a scowl. Then as if regrouping her temper, she sighed to her guests, "Can we talk while I work on this?"

Ennis agreed – something Savannah probably wouldn't have done, at least that quickly. Make the chef sweat, so to speak, despite the fact her porcelain skin showed no signs of flushing or perspiration. The female detective curbed a sneer. Ice water must have run in Gant's veins to battle not only the summer heat but the furnace they currently occupied. The brief time she stood in the sultry kitchen, moisture crept to the surface of Savannah's already reddened complexion. No wonder Gant's temper fired so fast, she thought. The kitchen was blistering.

She watched Emily fuss over a patron's entrée with delicate but adept speed. She rearranged asparagus, added a mystery sauce to something Savannah would only eat if she won serious money for doing it, then Gant carefully wiped the plate's edge with a towel. "Now," the chef handed the plate back to her disheartened underling, "it's perfect."

That was a matter of opinion, Savannah thought. The dish probably cost a hundred bucks and it only contained maybe five bucks of food. Plus it was drizzled in that sauce resembling muddy water. "You check everything that leaves the kitchen?" Savannah inquired.

A proud nod and "yes" followed. "And you hired all these people?" was the next question.

Emily wiped her brow – Savannah assumed for effect – and the executive chef nodded again, saying that was part of her job. The detective continued, "Familiarize us with the staff. Who does what?"

She pointed to one woman, "That's our roast chef," then she pointed to a middle aged woman with short dark hair, "the pastry chef and next to her is the grill chef."

Emily craned her neck and pointed to a lanky middle-aged black man trying to look busy in the cold-room, "That's our pantry chef."

Ennis and Savannah exchanged a dubious look. Both found the term ridiculous but had the sense not to say so. Ennis spoke first, "Explain the pantry chef's job."

Emily sighed, rolled her eyes, "He's responsible for preparing cold foods, including pâtés, appetizers, salads and other charcuterie items."

"Now there's a word you don't hear often," Savannah said, hoping Gant caught her sarcasm. "What's your pantry guy's name?"

"Theo Marshall. Why? Is he in trouble?"

"What kind of salads did he prepare a couple of nights ago on the fifteenth?"

Realizing an answer to her question wasn't forthcoming, Emily replied, "I had him prepare a new special salad. It got rave reviews according to the maître d'."

By that time, Savannah removed her pen and notepad from her jacket. She jotted down Theo's name and job. Pantry Chef still had a funky ring to it. She wondered how Theo fit into the Vaughn case if at all. Had they missed an important clue or connection that put the salad chef in the big juicy middle of Barry's murder? "What ingredients went into the new salad?"

Emily recoiled as if Savannah threatened to slap her, "At the risk of sounding cliché, a chef never reveals ingredients of their personal recipes. The competition would find out and use it."

"Don't worry about clichés but you'd better list those ingredients for us." The detective assured, "We do know the meaning of discretion."

Emily passed a glance over the kitchen. Chefs busied themselves with frying, sautéing, and preparing pastries. In a secretive voice, she rattled off the ingredients which, conveniently, did not include rhubarb leaves.

Savannah excused herself and allowed Ennis to resume the questioning. She meandered toward Theo who continued to busy himself in the storeroom. Around six feet tall, the willowy black man wore an apron over his green polo shirt and beige slacks. He resembled a slim tree bending in the wind when he reached down.

As if sensing her presence, he peered over his shoulder, the owl-eyed expression telling her Mr. Theo Marshall feared cops. Now she needed to find out why.

Savannah displayed her badge and called his name in a reasonable tone. Theo winced as though she'd shouted it. She introduced herself then, "I need to ask you a couple of questions."

"Yes, Officer," he drawled. "I'm busy now but I'll do my best."

She casually perused the storeroom and open dry goods pantry beside it. "I understand you prepare the salads for the restaurant."

"Yes, Officer," was all he said.

"Mr. Marshall, quit scrounging and talk to me."

He stood, put a hand to his back as he straightened and turned to her. Apprehension flickered in his eyes when they darted across the room, searching for unsolicited interest or prying ears. She took a wild guess at why Theo avoided her but wanted verbal confirmation, "Why are you avoiding me?"

"Don't mean to, Officer. It's just that, well…" he peeked over her shoulder then checked behind him, "I've got a record. If my bosses find me talking to you, they liable to think I'm in trouble again."

"Have you done something to get in trouble?"

He shook his head vehemently, "No, Officer, not at all."

She held up Barry Vaughn's driver's license photo, "Recognize him?"

Another shake of his head, "No, Officer. Should I?"

Without answering, she continued, "What ingredients were in the salads you served on the fifteenth? And don't leave anything out."

He closed his eyes, thought a moment. Theo named off a list of ingredients, none of them including rhubarb leaves. She nodded toward Emily, "Did Ms. Gant ask you to make a special salad for someone?"

He thought real hard about that one then, "No, Officer, she didn't."

She leaned closer, "Y'know, Theo, if she did it's okay to tell me. You're not gonna get into trouble for it. Did she ask you to spice one up for a particular customer?"

A spark of resentment flared, "She don't *ask* me to do anything. She tells me. But she didn't tell me to spice nothing. Am I in trouble, Officer? I hope not 'cause I can't afford it."

"So far, no." It was at that moment that among the flour and sugar, salt and other seasonings, she spied another box, this one with more punch than the jalapenos on her hamburger that afternoon. "Do you always store the rat poison with the dry goods?"

Theo's eyes widened again, "No, Officer, never."

She pointed to a shelf behind him, "Then how'd that get there? This place got a special Decon Chef too, reserved only for the worst patrons? The health department's gonna love this." She reached for her cell phone.

Theo's thin hand reached toward hers then thought better of it, "Don't, please, Officer. I don't know how the poison got there. I only know it wasn't me who done it."

"Mr. Marshall, besides rats and roaches, this is the mother of all health violations. Remember all the people who could die if that stuff falls into the flour and sugar." With that, a flashback of Vaughn's autopsy appeared. Vaughn had rat poison in his system…

"Let me move it," Theo begged. "The health department will

shut us down. I need this job. I got child support to pay."

"You also have an obligation to the public. Y'know, like not killing them off."

Savannah's cell phone rang. It was Mathis who sounded rather pleased with himself, "You still at Majestic?"

"Yes. Did you find something?"

"Your executive chef Emily Gant? She's Tracy Martin's sister. I'll expect a gratuity in the form of your sister's cookies 'cause I just iced this cake."

"Thanks for the info," she clicked off, wondering if food always consumed John's thoughts. Of course lately it consumed nearly all her time too…

Approaching Emily again, she narrowed her vision, "Does that salad normally come with rhubarb leaves in it or do you save those for your special clients? You know, like the ones your sister brings to supper? Especially the ones that got a kick out of watching her strawberry allergy in action?"

The revelation temporarily stunned the chef. She waved to the sous chef to take over. "I didn't lace the salad with rhubarb leaves." The woman shot Theo an accusing glare.

Savannah ignored it, "Ms. Gant, Theo may have prepared the salad but you said you check everything before it's served, before it leaves your kitchen. Didn't take five seconds to spike that salad before you sent it out."

Both Savannah and Ennis lowered their brows. Emily would have to be brain dead to misinterpret the expressions. The executive chef pointed to certificates on the wall, "I have a Culinary Arts diploma from Le Cordon Bleu."

"Which means you're aware that rhubarb leaves aren't safe to eat," Ennis offered.

"I am a member of the American Culinary Federation –"

"And I'm a member of the Fraternal Order of Police," Savannah countered, "but that doesn't mean murderous thoughts don't cross my mind occasionally, especially when I deal with difficult people."

Frustrated now, Gant barked, "Why would I risk losing all this just for revenge?"

Hands on her hips, Savannah replied, "I don't know. Doctors swear to 'do no harm' yet how many physicians are convicted each year of murder or attempted murder?

Ennis's vision shifted to her, no doubt picking up on the reference to Jeffrey Holland. Her intention was to make a point, not dwell on the subject, she'd say after their meeting. But at the current time, she cornered Emily Gant with her own words, "Executive Chefs oversee the dishes leaving their kitchens. You had to either see it done or do it yourself. Guess which one I'm putting my money on?"

Emily squirmed from the scrutiny. Ennis crossed his arms. After another perusal of the kitchen, she admitted, "Okay, I wanted him to suffer but I only put enough leaves in to make him sick, not kill him."

"And when he wanted a salad to take home?"

Shame shadowed Emily's features, "All it should have done was given him the runs, certainly not killed him."

"No," Savannah pointed to the pantry, "rat poisoning had a head start on that and somehow the rodenticide got stored along with the edible foods."

Shock slackened Gant's jaw as she wheeled to the pantry in search of Theo. Savannah capitalized on her frustration, "Did you toss in a dash of rat poison along with the rhubarb leaves? For that extra zing?" Okay, so she filched the word from Katherine Collins. It suited the moment.

Emily's cheeks lost their color, "I'd never poison anyone. The rhubarb leaves, yes but that's different than rat poison. Besides, he was Tracy's date, not mine."

"So you're saying Tracy might've killed him," Ennis assumed.

It was fun, Savannah admitted it. Seeing the once cool and collected executive chef's façade crumble was worth the trip whether the woman was guilty or not.

"Not in a million years," Emily finally replied.

Savannah played off Ennis's remark, "You sure? Barry watched her break out with her strawberry allergy and refused to help her. If someone did that to me, I'd want revenge."

Elvis and his "A Little Less Conversation" cranked up on her cell phone. Of all the rotten timing, she fumed. Her ringtone should have been A Few Less Phone Calls Please. Without consulting Caller ID, Savannah answered the call with a gruff, "Prince here."

Their captain overlooked her crotchety greeting, "Would you and Ennis happen to be at Majestic Restaurant?"

"Wouldn't happen to be, we actually are. Why?"

"I received a rather heated call from the mayor. He evidently got a call from the restaurant's manager saying my detectives are harassing the chefs."

"Just asking questions is all."

"Well, get outta there now. The mayor says you're wasting your time."

Savannah turned away from Emily and Ennis who were still exchanging choice words. The detective spoke quietly but contempt dripped from her tongue, "Oh. Well, if the *mayor* says it –"

"Savannah, my balls are in a vise and quite frankly the mayor squeezes harder than you."

"Does it matter that the head chef is Tracy Martin's sister? She doctored Barry Vaughn's salad in retaliation for how Barry treated Tracy and –"

"Did the rhubarb kill Vaughn?"

"No, but rat poison was conveniently added to his food and guess what I found stored above the flour and sugar? It was rat –"

"Can you prove the executive chef poisoned Vaughn?"

His continued interruptions rankled her, "No, but she admitted to the rhubarb –"

"Mathis got the blood results back from the crime scene. Both are male. Barry's and our mystery killer's. The executive chef is off that specific hook."

"But the rat poison –"

"Savannah, I'm not asking," His impatience mounted, "Get out. O'Neill's eating there in less than thirty minutes and if he finds you there, it's not just *your* job on the line."

So Mayor O'Neill threatened Josh with his employment too. The city leader had no moral or ethical compass. As for Majestic, she marked it off her list along with Beau Callahan. This was getting old, she thought. Just when they might get answers, the mayor slammed the door on them – again. "Then I ask one favor in return." She slowly rotated to face the frowning Emily Gant, "If the mayor turns up with rat poisoning, keep me and Ennis off the case."

16

Most people called it seething. Her mama called it stewin'. At the rate she stewed, someone was gonna pay. The entire journey home she groused about O'Neill until Ennis took all he could, "Simmer down 'fore you get an ulcer. He's the mayor. We're just cops."

Savannah required a certain amount of time to stew. Once she settled down, she approached the problem logically. But blowing off steam was a necessity for her. Ennis accepted things so easily it bothered her. No, it *infuriated* her. His Libra traits shined through at the most inopportune times. Try being a Gemini, she grumbled. The sign of the twins, the one astrologists claimed was flexible and adaptable. *Not me. I'm the hybrid Gemini. The one who hates change, the one who fights it tooth and nail.*

To appease her husband, she folded her arms over her chest and hushed. But she still stewed...

And the second they entered the station, she headed straight for Hunter's office. Ennis's shoulders slumped, "Savannah, please. We didn't get any leads at the restaurant anyway. Just that teaser about Tracy Martin. Let's follow up on that."

She continued without hesitation, a sign she'd closed down

communication for the interim so just sit back and hold tight. She marched into Josh's office and proceeded to read him the riot act. How were they supposed to close the Vaughn case with O'Neill's continual interference? Did he understand a detective's job or was this a game to him?

Josh Hunter shoved a hand through his hair then grabbed the edge of his desk to dissipate his own anger, "I get that you're angry. The whole station heard you vent about O'Neill." He uttered God's name in a not-so-favorable fashion then, "*The whole state of Alabama* heard you vent. Savannah, you forget I'm in the same boat. This precinct's closure rate is at stake which puts my job on the chopping block. I'm trying to balance work with politics and utterly failing. I do *not* need you breathing down my neck too. I'm on your side, remember?"

She tempered her own voice so the whole station didn't hear, "What do we do now? All we have is a loose lead on Tracy Martin that I doubt will pan out. We're still waiting on Kurt's background and I doubt he killed Vaughn either."

Josh reached in his desk drawer for aspirin, found the bottle empty and ceremoniously dropped it in the trash, "Go home."

The word "go" and "home" fought for a connection in her brain. Did he really tell her to go home? "What?"

"You and Ennis find a way to relax for," he peered at his watch, "three hours. That should clear your mind temporarily and that'll give me time to buy some extra strength Tylenol."

"Who's gonna answer to His Highness?"

"The mayor isn't your boss right now, Savannah. I am. Now

go."

So she went. And Ennis followed her, only he decided to go home and nap while she invited Georgia on a shopping trip to Lenox Square Mall. Ennis's birthday was in two months and she really needed to find a few gifts.

Adding to her general misery, the steering wheel branded her the instant she touched it. She jerked her hand back, lamenting the fact she neglected to equip the Camaro with the sun shade. In retrospect, ever since Franklin O'Neill began campaigning for mayor the weather turned wishy-washy. It snowed more that winter than ever – an unprecedented twelve inches during one snow, then a couple of four and five inch storms. Then by March the heat set in to broil the city. They'd had little to no rain that summer and forecasters saw no end to the drought. That settled it, she thought. Lucifer had landed in Atlanta and she'd crossed swords with him.

She placed a few tissues over the blazing hot steering wheel and driven to Georgia's house to pick her up. She needed this trip to the mall. Lord, did she need it in the worst way...

Cold air blasted from the Camaro's vents, bathing her feverish skin in a refreshing wintry reprieve. It, along with the perfectly timed break, was a welcome relief.

Driving to Georgia's house took ten minutes. After a brief wait, her sister dashed from the house to the Camaro, a whirlwind of pink from her shorts to her ball cap. To Savannah, Georgia resembled a walking ad for Pepto Bismol. Then she realized just how far down her mood spiraled. *Thanks ever so, Mayor...*

Another depressing reflection settled over her. Seeing her sister's beaming smile, Savannah realized the mistake she'd made earlier in life. She should have paid more attention in English class. Then, instead of schlepping as a cop, she could've written books like her sister. Instead of wearing stifling slacks and sleeveless pullover – with the suit jacket to complete the sweltering ensemble, she could have been très cool and not on the verge of spontaneous human combustion. Unlike Savannah who'd dabbed perspiration from her forehead during their trip, Georgia didn't even have the common decency to sweat. The younger sister tried not to let her jealousy show.

Savannah took her time driving to the mall. While Georgia chatted about her upcoming interviews, Savannah reflected on different issues that affected *her* life as surely as the interviews and publicity affected Georgia's book sales. Jeffrey came to mind first, followed by Baldwin's visit. O'Neill and his son followed close behind with their malicious antics and topping it all, she'd unintentionally played fast and loose with her birth control and fate gifted her with a baby.

How ironic that God considered her a decent candidate for motherhood, especially after witnessing the crap she put her own mother through. Being responsible for another human life and trying to raise them to be a proper lady or well-mannered gentleman – was God paying attention when she was a kid? She tried not to ruffle R.J.'s feathers because of the obvious repercussions. Her mother, though more patient than he, still found herself wordless and exhausted at her youngest. Savannah tested Charlene beyond her bounds at times, forcing Georgia to step in as surrogate mother and assistant teacher. Of the two girls, Savannah was a veritable hellion. "Do you think I'd be a good mother?" She blurted the question then instantly regretted it.

Her sister gave her a look of utter disbelief, "Are you pregnant?"

Downplaying her blunder, Savannah calmly repeated, "I just asked if you thought I'd make a good mom, that's all."

Georgia began the campaign of staring. Savannah hated Georgia's interrogation methods. Nag and stare. She hated them because they annoyed her but mostly because they friggin' *worked.*

"But you never ask questions like that," Georgia added, eyeing her suspiciously. "In fact, you've only asked that once in your entire life."

"Look, I didn't ask about a trip to Mars. I asked about being a mom."

"Why won't you answer my question?" Georgia asked.

"Because I asked mine first."

She ramped up the intensity of her gaze until Savannah felt herself flush. She pulled into the mall parking lot, searching the multitude of cars for an empty slot capable of accommodating her red beast. In the meantime, Georgia maintained the irritating stare. After finding a parking place near the entrance, she shifted the Camaro into Park and left the engine running. No need to sweat through Georgia's inquisition.

A shrewd smile curved the sister's mouth. Obviously she thought she knew something, "Fair enough. I think you'll make a wonderful mother. At least you have experience with difficult kids, being one yourself, I mean."

Savannah frowned at her. Was that her way of being diplomatic? Georgia rephrased, "You were difficult, not impossible. All kids are. Pushing their limits and their parents and siblings to the brink of insanity–"

"Thank you, now move on before I get difficult again by making you walk home."

"I'd only suggest you make a few changes in your life is all."

"About the job? Georgia, we need the money –"

"It regards your job to some degree. You'd need desk duty again and you hate that but I think you'd make the sacrifice for your baby. My suggestion is more domestic."

Did she really have to use that word? Savannah and domestic didn't mix that well. She'd finally embraced cooking and surprisingly she actually liked it. But other than that she tolerated "domestic" when forced to. "Go on."

"Don't misunderstand me. You'd be a great mom. Your problem will be keeping your police officer mindset under control. You'd always think like a cop when raising your kids."

Why did that sound like an insult? Thinking like a cop sounded pretty reasonable to her. She held a hand to her stomach, "Protecting my baby comes first, whether they're eighteen months old or eighteen years."

Georgia's Rita Hayworth features brightened, her smile spread from ear to ear. She probably sensed her sister's temper rising so she decreased the wattage to explain, "And you *should* protect your baby.

My point is you'll look at things – and people – like a cop. You'll be overprotective, you know, that obnoxious trait you accuse me of having."

Now the guilt surfaced. All over one simple question, "Thanks for making it personal."

"I know you, Savannah. You'll screen your kid's friends and their parents for outstanding warrants and later you'll follow the kids on their dates to make sure they don't get into trouble. If you can strip off that police officer persona, you won't drive yourself and your kids nuts."

"Was that a pep talk because I couldn't tell."

"You're pregnant," Georgia accused. "Why don't you just admit it?"

Savannah began to protest but her sister pointed, "Look where your hand is."

She glanced down to see her palm resting on her belly. No, not technically resting, she had to admit. More like protecting which was, of course, the very point Georgia tried to make.

Evidently sensing Savannah on the ropes, the older sister continued – with a laugh, "Ennis told me you won't eat his eggs anymore. He thinks he can't cook now. That you'd rather horse down two bowls of store-bought cereal instead of a homemade meal."

Horse down? Her frustration mounted a degree, "You two are doing it again. Talking behind my back. I hate that."

"You've never eaten Cocoa Puffs, much less two bowls at once. Have you taken a pregnancy test?"

Savannah pursed her lips. She didn't want to lie. She couldn't really successfully lie to Georgia. Her sister had radar for fibs. So she nodded.

"Did it turn blue?"

She blew out a breath, "No. It said 'pregnant' but you already figured that out."

"How do you feel about kids right now? You said you wanted to wait until next year."

Savannah never expected that question. The customary smothering hugs and congratulations and Georgia's general cheeriness about the subject, yes. The inquiry about Savannah's feelings about sudden pregnancy, no. The upheaval of the last year probably dictated the careful approach. One thing about her sister. She wasn't stupid. "Well, like they say, God has a sense of humor so here I am a year early."

"And you're okay with it?"

Truthfully, she struggled with the idea. During quiet times, her thoughts drifted to what motherhood entailed, the overwhelming responsibility from zero to eighteen – and that was just for starters. Was she ready for two o'clock feedings, potty training, preschools, PTAs, dating, graduations and college? And that was only if the kid *wasn't* an unruly brat – from zero to eighteen.

The baby was a shock. The baby came a whole year early, according to their perfectly planned schedule. The baby would be tremendously challenging while she attempted to retain a rational mind. The daunting task of bringing up baby put the fear of God into her but the alternative of ending the pregnancy didn't fit her upbringing or her conscience. Taking that step meant sleepless nights for other reasons, plus she really loved Ennis and breaking his trust didn't foster warm, fuzzy feelings…

"Savannah? Are you okay with being pregnant?" Now Georgia sounded worried.

Speak, dummy. She's on the verge of panic, "I'm still in shock but the idea is growing on me and *in* me, evidently."

Her sister practically bubbled with delight as she took her hand and squeezed, "Oh, honey, congratulations. I'm so happy for you."

Savannah couldn't help but smile, "Thank you. I don't know whether to feel worse for the kid or us. If he or she inherits my disposition, I'll be on Prozac. One thing, though. *Don't* tell Ennis about the baby. I mean it, Georgia. I'll tell him but I have to find a good time."

Georgia agreed, "Just don't wait too long to tell him. He's already feeling insecure about his eggs."

Her stomach rumbled and not in a good way. With hand to belly, she carefully cautioned, "Rule Number One. Don't tell Ennis before I do. Rule Number Two. Do *not* mention eggs again."

"Then let's go shopping. I have to keep Lady Visa happy." Georgia opened the door to get out.

"Don't forget Master Card either. I trust you brought him too."

Georgia winked, "I never leave home without him."

The second Savannah opened the door a wall of heat slammed against her. She winced against the fiery blast, grabbed her suit jacket, still envious that Georgia could dress for the weather and she couldn't.

At least, she noticed, others looked fed-up with nature's furnace as she was.

She slung the jacket over her arm, intent on leaving it off as long as possible. Like her sister, her hair was pulled back into a ponytail and as the sun beat down on her, it began to roast her neck. She finally decided she couldn't win.

During their trek toward the entrance, Savannah regularly glanced around them. She tried to do this covertly to avoid undue attention but after her sixth glance, Georgia asked, "Something wrong?"

"Just checking around us. Women don't do that enough when they're out."

"We're fine, Savannah. I'm looking too."

It embarrassed her that the paranoia relentlessly persisted. Even with their new home she insisted on dead bolts. Not one but two. Once she'd been satisfied with a simple knob lock and a weapon in her nightstand drawer. But nearly five months ago, Jeffrey Holland and Cole Jordan changed her life and her front door had since acquired the gleaming brass accessories. On more than one occasion, she caught herself staring at the locks suddenly struck by how much she had become like every other victim of violent crime, desperate to barricade her home and shut out the world. She'd inched her way to this level of freedom. One that didn't completely liberate her of fear but one that felt less stifling. Baldwin's visit changed all that. The kneejerk panic returned with sudden noises, people moving too fast or standing too close. Shit, she was a wreck – again thanks to Cole and Jeffrey.

Making matters worse, sudden heavy footfalls pounded the

pavement behind them. Adrenaline flooded her while her brain instinctively surmised Cole was the culprit. This happened before, it reminded. *Remember Piedmont Park when he and Jeffrey ambushed you and Georgia?* The memory forced Savannah's hand to her gun.

A soft touch on her wrist stopped her. She glanced down at Georgia's hand then met her concerned expression. The sisters stood in the sweltering heat staring each other down. Savannah tried to hide the fear but Georgia's intuition bordered on ESP. She hated that Georgia read her so easily. Of course, Savannah never made a habit of randomly shooting people. Sometimes she wanted to, but she restrained the urge. Reaching for her weapon meant she felt threatened, or felt someone else was. That's what Georgia picked up on.

"Has something happened?" Georgia wanted to know. "You haven't been this edgy in a while."

Savannah watched their supposed threat – a young man bent on racing for the entrance – pick up the pace beside them, oblivious to the close call he just escaped. She scanned their immediate surroundings while hemming and hawing about telling Georgia the truth. Her sister was right. She'd been doing much better until her encounter with Frank Griffin, Medical Examiner and Macabre Extraordinaire. Then Baldwin showed up. So why wouldn't Cole join the party?

As if attuned to her sister's thoughts, Georgia frowned, "It's Cole again, isn't it?"

Savannah just shrugged. Hell, her sister figured it out anyway. Half expecting Georgia to crank up with a lecture, she crossed her arms and waited for the onslaught.

Instead Georgia eased her arm around Savannah's waist, brought her close, "Not surprising, I guess. You went through a lot."

"We *both* did."

"Yes, and we're the only ones who truly understand what happened. They'll get Cole eventually. Don't let him consume you." She patted Savannah's stomach, "You've got better things to think about and if you need to talk, I'm here."

A smile softened Savannah's features. She could always count on her sister. Georgia was bossy, nagging, and stiflingly motherly at times but when Savannah needed an ear, she was always there. Savannah embraced her, "I know and thank you. I appreciate you looking out for me."

Georgia snorted good-naturedly, "That's a first."

"Don't spoil the moment," she joked.

They started toward the entrance again as she slipped on her jacket to try and hide the fact she carried a weapon. Lately though she really wasn't entirely discriminatory about who she shot, especially if their name began with "Cole" or "Mayor".

"So, have you thought about baby names?" Georgia asked.

"I just found out I'm carrying more than my .38. I haven't had time to think about names."

Incredulity ruled Georgia's features, "Savannah, you plan everything. Look at us. We're out two months early buying for Ennis's birthday and you haven't given thought to your child's name? Right…"

It was like having two consciences. The one in her head and the one beside her. "Considering we have nine months to play with names – well, probably seven now, I –"

"Spill."

"Pushy today, aren't you? Okay, I've always been fond of Lily for a girl. Maybe Gabriel for a boy." She quickly followed with, "And no laughing either. You asked."

Georgia didn't laugh but nodded proudly, "See? I was right. You have been thinking about it."

Know it all, she wanted to say. Before her sister fired questions about a nursery and what color it would be, she needed to change the subject. "I'm trying to find a unique gift for Ennis. He's got enough clothes. I'm hoping this place stocks Dallas Cowboys memorabilia." She rolled her eyes at the irony, "Five years ago if you'd told me I'd marry a Dallas fanatic, I'd have choked."

"Five years ago, if you said you'd marry *anyone*, *I'd* have choked."

"Speaking of marriage, when are you gonna make an honest man out of Dane Rutherford?" She recognized signs of denial on her sister's face and stopped her short, "And don't bother denying it. Ennis and I both know about those trips you made to Texas. Not to mention all the ones Dane's made here. He practically lives here now. It's a normal progression toward the preacher and you know it."

She waited and waited for her older sister to answer but realized she was too busy blushing. Georgia resembled a young girl with a crush. The sight warmed Savannah's heart. After the divorce, she feared Georgia might close off to relationships altogether. Dane eased into her life and, in the process, Georgia fell in love with the rascal. Savannah began humming the Wedding March, prodding for an answer.

As her pink cheeks deepened to red, Georgia admitted, "Our relationship *is* more emotional now."

"Is that code for falling in love?"

When Georgia stammered without making a bit of sense, Savannah broke into chorus, "Dane and Georgia sittin' in a tree, K-I-S-S-I-N-G…"

Georgia playfully nudged her, "Shut up."

"Miz Prince," a woman called from nearby. "Ooh-hoo, Miz Prince!"

"Gotta be you," Savannah replied. "Only one who calls me Ms. Prince is the kid next door."

The two turned in time to see an older woman – in her early seventies Savannah estimated – waving and trying to flag them down. Dressed in a powder blue blouse and matching slacks, the older woman paddled along as fast as her legs allowed. With the aid of a cane, it took great effort so Georgia and Savannah went to meet her.

The lady, gleefully smiling at the sight of Georgia, offered her hand for a handshake. "I can't believe my luck," the woman gushed in a thick Georgia twang. Immediately after, she rifled an assortment of shopping bags until settling on one. From it she withdrew a book. Savannah recognized it Georgia's latest release Killer Instinct. Savannah hadn't had time to start reading it but the more Katherine Collins pecked at her about it, she'd probably start that night. If what her neighbor said was true – and there was no reason to doubt her – Savannah would have plenty of questions to pose to Georgia.

"Could I beg an autograph?" the pleasant grandmotherly face beamed. "It would mean so much."

In typical fashion, Georgia enthusiastically agreed to sign. Savannah stood in awe at her older sister conversing with the woman like a close friend. She possessed an informal manner that put everyone at ease around her, even stray dogs, finicky cats and fussy children. It positively galled Savannah that their mother's knack settled only with Georgia. Savannah and Seth could, without great effort or intention, scare the Pope from the Vatican with just one look.

When Georgia scrounged her purse for a pen, the older woman magically provided one – from where Savannah couldn't fathom unless she stowed one nearby in her purse or slacks. While her sister signed the book, the lady introduced herself to Savannah who responded in kind.

"Oh, I can tell your sisters, 'deed I can. You're quite a bit taller than Georgia but the resemblance is undeniable. You got good blood and it shows."

Savannah nearly laughed. She hadn't heard that one since Grandma Culberson said those very words twenty or so years ago. Bless her heart, Grandma believed R.J. Prince wasn't so bad, just a little moody. If being staggering drunk most of the time and beating his kids equaled "a little moody", then yes, R.J. qualified. The brief remembrance of her grandmother brought a smile to Savannah's face and to the little lady beaming over a simple autograph, she replied, "Thank you."

The lady checked the progress of her request then asked, "Are you an author too?"

"No, ma'am," Savannah displayed her badge, "I'm a detective."

"A detective you say?" Genuine interest crossed her heavily lined features. A moment passed when her eyes brightened, "Well, I'll be. *You're* the inspiration for Summer Pearson." Her voice dropped to a whisper, "I had a friend who was deathly afraid of the color white. Couldn't eat marshmallows, sugar, rice or drink milk. Even got married in a green weddin' dress. Her phobia got so bad that when it snowed last, she sold her house and moved to Florida. Sweetheart, don't let your acrophobia get that bad."

Oh, for the love of God... This bad déjà vu needed an exorcism. First Katherine, now the sweet little lady politely asking for Georgia's autograph. Worst of all – a smile teased at Georgia's mouth. She considered this funny? Oh, *really...*

Savannah shook her head, "I'm afraid my sister misled the masses. I'm not afraid of heights and I'm not Summer Pearson."

With an elegant flourish, Georgia finished signing the book, "Actually Summer is a lot like Savannah. Two of a kind, actually." She returned the book to the lady who thanked her.

The woman patted Savannah's arm, "You get help for that acrophobia, y'hear?"

Savannah just nodded, watched her walk away. Where the hell was the emergency brake for this train wreck? "Happy with yourself, aren't you?" She harrumphed at Georgia. "You've got the world thinking I'm too scared to climb a damn ladder. How'd she know about the acrophobia anyway? She hadn't read the book yet."

"It's on the book jacket if you'd bother to read it."

"Don't guilt me, Georgia. I've been busy." She patted her stomach, "Not just with a murder investigation but swelling, puking and scarfing down Cocoa Puffs. And why did you base a character on me after I specifically warned you not to?"

Georgia corrected, "I said she's a lot like you, not that she was you. Big difference."

Savannah wasn't buying Georgia's story for a second, "Oh, you want me to build a case on my behalf? Okay, why saddle the character with a phobia?"

"Characters need flaws. They're boring without them. And last I saw, acrophobia and claustrophobia have different definitions. Acrophobia is fear of heights. Claustrophobia is fear of enclosed spaces."

Thanks for the lesson. "Our initials are the same. Summer Pearson, Savannah Prince. Katherine Collins noted a slew of similarities including my height, eyes, hair, even my car."

"Savannah, stop listening to people."

They approached the sports shop and stopped short of the entrance. Savannah continued, "Summer's partner isn't exactly ugly as a mud fence either. According to Katherine, he's six feet tall *and from Texas*, for Heaven's sake. That's Ennis dead out. C'mon, Georgia, tell me the truth."

"All this from your neighbor?"

Georgia's laugh only succeeded in increasing Savannah's annoyance. "*And* Ennis," she defended.

"Have any theories on the grassy knoll too?" With that, Georgia stepped inside the shop, greeted the clerk. Savannah suspected the purpose was to end the conversation prematurely. In retrospect, it didn't matter anyway. The book was written and everyone was reading it and making assumptions she couldn't prevent.

She followed her sister inside and noticed the overwhelming selection of Atlanta based sports. Falcons, Hawks, Braves and Thrashers gear abounded with a few select other teams mixed in for lopsided measure. The walls dripped with Braves jerseys and Falcons attire, since football season lurked close. In a couple of weeks, she and Ennis would once again begin their friendly rivalry, he with his beloved Cowboys and she rooting for her cherished Falcons.

When it came to the Dallas Cowboys, Ennis was a kid at heart. He bled royal blue and silver and if an item sported an authentic autograph, he simply melted in fanatic bliss.

The trick was finding anything Dallas in Atlanta. She'd taken to ordering stuff to satisfy her husband's cravings since the Cowboys were virtually a cuss word in Falcon country.

"How sweet," Georgia gushed.

Savannah turned to see her holding a tiny Falcon t-shirt. Georgia bobbed her brow, "Little Gabriel would look darling in this."

Savannah agreed but, "Ennis would have a conniption if I dressed our baby in that. Unless it's Dallas, it's sacrilege. Besides, what if it's a girl?"

"Have you looked in the mirror? I've seen you in Falcons regalia and rooting as hard as Ennis during the games. Why couldn't Baby Lily wear it?"

She held the small t-shirt, imagining their bundle of joy wearing it. She suddenly felt a wave of pride. A tiny Falcon fan and he or she was all theirs. "You're right. Marriage is about compromise. But I'll wait to get anything until later. Don't want to jinx it, you know?"

Rows and rows of Falcons jerseys, t-shirts and shorts crowded the store. Red on black, black on red. Throwback jerseys. Customized jerserys. All Atlanta. She was screwed. At least to a degree…

What did society do without the internet, she wondered. Dallas memorabilia was as close as her computer and she thanked God for the two month cushion before his birthday.

Display cases across the aisle contained autographed footballs, trading cards and various other gems for collectors. Georgia already migrated to it and Savannah noticed her sister's expression suddenly lit up. "Savannah, look. An autographed helmet."

She nearly groaned at the sight. The full size helmet not only sported Troy Aikman's signature but Emmitt Smith and a few others from Ennis's "Dream Team". Perfect. The first time in months the joint finally had *anything* Cowboys and she and Ennis were mired down in bills. For the sake of argument, she looked at the price anyway. She nearly swallowed her tongue, "That's like buying the Ten Commandments autographed by God. We've got a mortgage to pay, we don't need two – one for the house and one for that thing." She scoured the case for something a little more reasonable. If they had the money, she'd have snapped it up in a heartbeat but if she wagged it home, despite being thrilled, Ennis would still question her sanity. She did, however, have an idea, "Why don't you get that for Dane?"

Georgia found the comment humorous, "Oh, you think because my book is selling, I'm made of gold. Besides if I buy this for Dane, Ennis will be jealous."

Well, at least her sister wasn't dense. If Savannah bought it for Ennis, *Dane* would be jealous. Both brothers pledged their allegiance to the Cowboys – so much that it their cheering evolved to leaping from chairs, stomping the floor or just high fiving each other. Savannah learned early that no one messed with Texans and their football.

Georgia rounded the glass display. Personally Savannah was ready to go. There was only two hours left in her hiatus from hell and she wanted something to show for it. But Georgia's childlike exuberance burst forth once more, "This is *perfect*. A miniature helmet – and autographed."

Savannah braced herself before consulting the price tag. Much better. Plus, the store had just the right quantity. Two. "He can set it on the shelf in the bedroom. You gettin' Dane the other one?"

"He'd love it." She motioned to the clerk, "We want both Dallas minis."

They watched as the salesman removed both miniature helmets, each securely encased in its own clear plastic cube. While he removed them from the display, Georgia whispered to her sister, "We're planning a trip to Tennessee this weekend."

"That's not exactly a hotspot for vacations."

"It is when you rent a cabin in the mountains."

Savannah's brow lifted, her voice had a lilt, "I see. Anything other plans I should be aware of? You know, like the matrimonial kind?"

"Not that I know of. I really wouldn't mind if he asked. I'm not sure he wants to though."

Savannah was sure he probably did. The way Dane and Georgia mooned over each other the past several months verged on embarrassing. Savannah and Ennis kept a running bet the two would be married before long. Savannah's guess was Valentine's Day or possibly a June wedding. Ennis hedged on his bet, saying another full year would pass before Georgia committed to marriage. Savannah happily reminded him that the Rutherford men had a charm that no Prince female could resist for long. Even Lindsey fell into a starry-eyed trance when Dane or Ennis fawned over her.

The salesman cast an evil eye on the innocent little helmets on the counter. His expression could only be interpreted by a native Atlantan. "I nearly sent those things back," he grumbled. "Ain't nobody with sense buys Cowboys junk in Atlanta."

What was it with everyone lately? Biting, pecking or outright leaping on her like a predator on its prey. She'd had quite enough for one day. Not as affable now, she pulled her suit jacket back to casually reveal her badge, "My husband is from Texas, you understand. He may be a Cowboy supporter but being his wife, I have to overlook certain qualities of his and he, like a good husband, reciprocates in kind. You know," she addressed her sister, "he overlooks occasions when an insatiable inclination arises inside me."

Georgia just smiled, played along, "Which inclination is that?"

Savannah pointedly stared at the salesman, "The one tempting me to strangle overtly opinionated people."

He swallowed audibly upon seeing the badge on her belt – and the murder in her voice. "Cowboys might make it to the playoffs this year," he said. "Who knows?"

Savannah beamed back at him, proud he understood, "I think they just might." Digging in her purse, she found the cash to pay with, laid it on the counter just as her phone rang. She expected it to be Ennis checking up on her. It wasn't. "Detective Prince, am I to understand that you called the health department to Majestic following your interview with the Executive Chef?"

Her heart leapt into her throat. The mayor sounded long past annoyed and headed straight to full-fledged livid. She tried to remain calm, "Sir, they stored hazardous material above edible food."

"What the hell gives you authority to basically close down a business?"

His voice grew boisterous enough she knew Georgia and the clerk heard every word. "The public's health gives me authority, sir. To be frank, they stored rat poison above the flour and sugar. The poison was open. Doesn't that warrant a call to the health department?" In the middle of her explanation, she wondered how the mayor found out she called the health department. A quick remembrance appeared of her storming through the station to Josh Hunter's office and demanding answers why the mayor bounced them from the restaurant. That and the distinct recollection she boasted of siccing the health department on

Majestic. *Rusty was sitting in my office. He overheard me and tattled, that little son of a bitch…*

Briefly shifting her vision revealed not only her sister and the clerk were riveted to the conversation but other customers as well.

The mayor continued, "Your authority, Detective Prince, is about to be removed if you do not stop interfering in my life. Majestic is well respected in this town and to accuse them of poisoning their patrons…" he huffed into the phone, making it sound more akin to an obscene phone call than a reaming out.

Savannah imagined his chubby beet red face, his eyes bugging as he raged. He sounded on the verge of a heart attack. *That would finish me off.* "Cop Kills Mayor With Phone Call" the headline would read.

She waited for him to, again, take up his cause since anything she said would have been toast anyway. She wasn't disappointed.

"I just ate brunch there and I feel fine…"

While he blathered about his successful morning outing, she couldn't help but notice his phrasing. Brunch. Rich people partook of "brunch", obviously, while everyone else stuck to the plain "breakfast" or "lunch". No one cared that some bloated, egotistical politician indulged in his brunch at an affluent restaurant. Most of Atlanta couldn't partake of a simple appetizer at Majestic.

"…I won't be the only person demanding recourse if the place is closed because of your meddling. And why the hell aren't you working the Barry Vaughn case, for God's sake? What part of 'high priority' don't you understand?"

Before giving her time to respond, he continued with the blistering dressing down, "Have you seen the papers? We're making national headlines with this thing. *National* headlines. When your captain assigned you to this case, I expected not only to be kept apprised of developments but I expected – no – *insisted* that you *stay on the job* until the person responsible is arrested."

Savannah ducked away from the counter part way through his tirade. She wanted to salvage a semblance of dignity to slink home with. The mayor seemed to sense this and decided to cure that aspiration, "There's a murderer loose in my city, Detective. In *your* city. Don't you think this person should be located and arrested before, God forbid, he or she strikes again?"

Giving her sister and the salesman a quick glance, she hurried outside the quiet store into the chaos of mall noise. "Sir, I apologize. As I understood, you were not authorizing overtime on any case for anyone, even the Vaughn case."

"Authorizing overtime!? You won't even work the case during normal hours – what good would overtime serve? Get back on the job and stay there until this case is solved. And do not, for any damn reason, show your face at Majestic again. If you so much as sneeze wrong while driving past its doors, I'll personally relieve you of that badge."

"I'm headed back to the station, Mayor."

"Make sure to convey my sentiments to your colleague Detective Rutherford as well."

"I'll call him on the way." She made sure the mayor hung up on her – though she expected him to slam the receiver so hard her ears rang.

"Been a while since I've heard someone bring blood on you." Georgia sheepishly broached the subject while exiting the store.

Heat rose in Savannah's cheeks to the point she could fry steaks on them. It was bad enough to get reamed out in private but with witnesses? Shee-yet… "Makes me wonder if he took lessons from Daddy."

Georgia handed her the change from her purchase then a bag containing the gift. Judging by the size, Savannah figured it had plenty of room left to accommodate the meager remains of her ego.

Truthfully, she was surprised Georgia felt comfortable enough to stand so close. With Savannah's luck lately, lightning might have struck.

17

Logic said there was no such thing as a perfect murder and up until now she hadn't entertained trying to commit one. The mob did pretty well at killing people without leaving much evidence but she possessed neither the time or patience to research it. She wanted something fast and easy. Sitting beside Ennis who managed to simultaneously fume and drive, her vision migrated to the holster on her hip. Fast. Easy. *Hmmm...*

"He yelled at you?" Ennis asked for the second time. Once arriving at home, she'd awakened him from a dreaming sleep and now she wondered if he was conscious enough to drive – because he kept repeating the same question to her. Had he not understood her the first time she detailed the humiliating phone call?

"Yes. He. Yelled. At. Me." There. Maybe he got the message. What was it with men lately? They were all driving her nuts. Especially the one perched atop the mayor's pedestal, biting hunks out of his civil servants. Savannah eased her hand to her holster and around the .38's handle, stroking it. She imagined O'Neill's face as she took dead aim on his fat nose.

Ennis snapped around to her with disbelief, "What the hell are you doing?"

Adrift in malicious fantasies, she realized she'd pulled the gun and had been caressing it. All with a smile on her face. Savannah apologized, shoved the weapon back in the holster. Spoilsport.

"If you're planning on going postal, I'm driving you home and tying you to the bed. I don't want you arrested for murder."

Her lethal thoughts screeched to a halt. Lustful images replaced them. She'd like to see Ennis try to fulfill that threat. God knew it sounded more fun than shooting the mayor. "Promises, promises," she smirked.

Ennis flinched, readjusted in his seat, "Don't get me horny. I'm trying to stay mad."

"Hello Pot. Meet Kettle." She shrugged, challenging, "Eh, you couldn't have done it anyway."

Ennis let up on the gas, turned to her. His expression challenged her right back, "Oh really? We'll see about that, sugar. We'll see."

She smiled, waggled her brow, "Gotta catch me first."

Ennis groaned. His hands gripped the steering wheel with a death grip. She'd stop teasing him for now. He looked ready to double back and follow through. She blushed at the image of the whole scene then her mood soured again with new images. These of His Highness O'Neill calling just as naked Ennis climbed atop naked Savannah to make mad passionate love. It was a nice fantasy but she and her hubby did just fine without the dramatics of roping each other down during sex. Plus, if Ennis tried roping her down, he might discover a different side to his wife. The side he wished didn't exist.

After parking the Ram, the two marched inside the station, stormed past the desk sergeant unaware he came loaded for bear too, "The mayor buy you a diamond studded collar for that leash he's got on you?"

Ennis put a hand to her back, a silent plea for her to remain calm and exercise tact. She considered that. No one else exercised tact with her anymore so why should she be so gracious? Then she heard her husband mutter a "please". Ennis really wanted that diplomacy...

Savannah cleared her throat and felt Ennis pat her back to reinforce his request. Okay, she'd give it the good old college try – by not saying anything.

Ennis blew out a breath, prompting Savannah to roll her eyes. She wasn't a complete idiot. Bad temper? Yes. Hopelessly stupid? No. Alienating her colleagues rated rather low on her to-do list in life. O'Neill on the other hand...

"I can't believe O'Neill yelled at you."

Not again. Apparently Ennis still struggled with the concept of a city official breathing fire at her. Why the thought seemed so far-fetched, she hadn't a clue. So, while they made their way to Josh's office, she proceeded to explain the conversation once more, ensuring to emphasize the mayor's indignation. Believe it or not, it really happened, she assured. And she along with Georgia, an unsuspecting clerk and a few bystanders could vouch for the mayor's zealous fit. All over a lousy restaurant that catered to the city's highfalutin palates and because she required a moment of solace. Unable to bridle her anger any longer, she blurted, "He takes the phrase 'War of Northern Aggression' to a new level. He should've stayed in New Jersey and annoyed his own people."

They passed her office which mercifully turned out to be empty of O'Neills. Just as well, she thought. Despite the fact she needed a little vacation, she didn't want the mandatory one called suspension.

Glancing down the hall at Hunter's office, she caught sight of one of the infidels. Her fingers itched to snatch her gun from its holster. She'd try real hard not to shoot the bastard but she dearly yearned to make him pee his pants.

Ennis laid a hand on her arm, "Don't do it or I *will* tie you down." When she didn't respond, his fingers tightened, "I'm serious, Savannah. Don't do anything you'll regret."

Now that was a short list. Things she'd regret doing to Rusty O. Nail. Drawing and quartering. Tar and feathering. Hanging him upside down on the flagpole outside. All these images brought a wicked smile to her weary face. But then an image of Baby appeared. The joyous tiny bundle of soft pink flesh smiled then the little face morphed into a frown. Baby wagged a small chubby finger at her saying *Mama shouldn't do such things because Mama will go to jail and feast on Tofurkey and Nutraloaf with her new roommate Brünhilde – all courtesy of the state.* Brünhilde – German for "armored warrior woman". Savannah – Spanish for "open plain". Not much of a contest, she thought, considering those Germans really perfected the art of battle.

Josh saw her headed to his office and leaned back in his chair. I'll give you latitude, his expression said, but don't expect the whole universe.

Upon sight of Rusty, she stopped abruptly in the doorway,

leaving Ennis to bump into her. She stared daggers at O'Neill's son then addressed Josh, "I hope you got that Tylenol." Then she returned to the redheaded bane of her existence, "You. In my office. Now."

Rusty O'Neill's expression deflated upon sight of her mood. Much like a scolded child, he followed the two detectives past the sergeant's desk where interested peaked in every officer there. Josh followed behind, probably to prevent bloodshed. Savannah and Ennis stalked down the hallway and turned into her small office. The moment the four stepped in, Ennis closed the door behind them, sensing an impending explosion. He was correct.

She rounded on the mayor's son, "Tell me what the definition of 'break' is, you little turd. I'm not talking about what I want to do to your neck. I'm talking about a different definition."

"Turd?" Rusty seemed to be a few steps behind.

She remedied that, "I'll speak slower. The definition I refer to means 'a pause or interval, as from work.' That's what Ennis and I had before you blabbed to Daddy that our asses and elbows weren't in your line of sight. Let me explain what we do. We interview people and we gather evidence. We give that evidence to our lab. In the meantime, we search for more evidence and witnesses. If we hit an impasse it's sometimes temporary. It makes us very sad but we cope and we take a *break.* You know, to rest and refresh our weary minds and bodies. Ever heard of it?"

Rusty's mouth open to respond but she raised her hand, "No, do not speak. Just listen. We must be patient while we wait for the results of our evidence. We must exercise patience throughout the investigation or we lock up the wrong person, Rusty. You don't want that. Daddy doesn't want that either. Give Daddy a message for me. Tell him we're working as hard as we can to solve this case. It takes time *and* patience, the latter being the key word." During the tirade her voice went from low and menacing to loud and menacing. She heard whispers outside the door. No doubt most of the station huddled behind it, hanging on every word. She really didn't care. Rusty O'Neill and his papa were making their lives hell all because Daddy intended to run for reelection.

Rusty cowered under her withering glare, "Wait. He *called* you?"

After seeing her murderous expression, Ennis's hand clamped on her shoulder. Slowly, she turned to him, "Tell me he's not that stupid."

"Yes," Ennis answered for her, "he called her. He forced us back to work."

By that time she'd regrouped, "And he yelled at me. Tell Daddy no amount of yelling at me or making us work from *can to can't* will solve the case quicker."

"I never imagined he'd yell at you –"

"Did you expect he'd send roses? Try something new for a change. Try *thinking* about repercussions to your actions, Junior. I don't mind taking my lumps when they're deserved but they weren't today."

Her anger mounted the more she revisited the verbal reaming out. Edging nearer to Rusty, she continued, "I've fought bigger bullies than your daddy."

Ennis put both hands on her shoulders, urging her back and away from Rusty before she turned loose with more than words. She had more sense than that. Their boss stood directly behind the little shit so why would she flush thirty days of her career by boxing Rusty's ears? She put Rusty on notice instead, "It's called cancer and if I can hold my own against that, I can dig in against your father any day." She purposefully omitted a reference to Jeffrey. Knowing Rusty, she'd have to draw him a picture of what happened anyway.

"Why *did* you call him?" Ennis wanted to know.

Rusty refused to meet their gazes. "He told me to update him frequently and to call when you left for any reason other than business."

She lunged forward but Ennis held true. Maybe slapping Rusty's nose off *was* worth a thirty day suspension. Unfortunately, Ennis's hold remained uncomfortably firm.

After a long moment, confusion wrinkled Rusty's brow, "Can to can't?"

Thanks to her regularly exercising her grandmother's idiomatic habit, Ennis was familiar with the Culbersonism. He gave Rusty the evil eye, "She means from when you *can* see daylight to when you *can't*."

"What do we do now?" Savannah asked Josh. Doing what she wanted was out of the question considering Nutraloaf probably wasn't on prison menus for most pregnant women.

"What were you doing before O'Neill called?"

She put hands to hips which backed Rusty up another step. That helped. "Shopping with my sister."

Ennis's brow dove between his eyes, "I was catching forty winks. I only got twenty."

Josh sighed and rubbed at his temple. In light of recent events – namely Rusty and his daddy – their boss had better invest in aspirin *and* Tylenol stock, she thought. After giving his temple a good kneading, Hunter asked, "Where are you on the case?"

"Waiting on Kurt's background." Ennis clearly didn't trust himself to say much else.

Their captain sensed that fact, "When you get that, interview him then go home." He turned to Rusty, his arms crossed, "And you will not tell your father about it or I'll send you on a ride-along in Zone 3. Believe me when I say your father can write off three votes. Theirs and mine."

"'You're prettier with the rash.'"

Once the shock wore off, Savannah recovered enough to ask, "That's what Barry Vaughn wrote for Tracy Martin's flower arrangement?"

Jerry, the owner of Petal Pushers Flowers, swallowed audibly then, "I read it verbatim, Detective. I'm…" he hesitated, "stunned."

Savannah shouldered the phone to her ear and jotted down the information, "Just imagine if the card were addressed to you. How about Danielle Callahan's card?" That oughta be a doozy.

She heard keys clicking on a computer then Jerry's uneasy voice confirmed, "Danielle Callahan's reads 'You're the best lay I've had in months. Tell Daddy thanks for sharing.'" Jerry's star customer turned out to be a genuine jerk and it seemed he just realized the fact. "And you wanted Lucy Driscoll's card next." He typed a second then, "It says 'Find another sucker, you freak.'"

Savannah heard Jerry release a long breath, no doubt grateful the task was over.

"Not exactly love letters are they?" she asked as she wrote.

Jerry choked out a "no" and she thanked him for his help. The owner tried to muster a smile in his voice, "I've got a new shipment of beautiful purple lilacs that you'd love, Detective. You might drop a hint to your partner…"

Her cheeks warmed with a blush, "Thanks, Jerry, but he's pretty busy keeping me out of trouble instead of in flowers."

The second she hung up, Ennis and Mathis walked in. Her husband overheard the last of the conversation, "Who was that? The guy at Petal Pushers?"

Savannah nodded. Ennis frowned, "He's trying to strong-arm you on the hydrangeas?"

"Lilacs and no, he's trying to strong-arm *you.*"

Ennis stepped closer, whispering, "It's not that obvious we're married."

Mathis unsuccessfully stifled a laugh, "Yeah and it's not obvious I'm fat."

Not appreciating the comment, Ennis plopped down in a chair facing Savannah's desk, "Graham's background here yet?"

She shook her head, "Nope, still waiting for it but I did uncover this interesting tidbit," she handed him her notes.

Mathis peered over Ennis's shoulder to read Barry's Vaughn's not-so-sweet nothings, "This guy's amazing. Women by the bushels despite being deficient below the belt and I don't need no comments from either of ya on that. Vaughn screws 'em then loses them and burns his bridges on the way out."

Ennis blew out a breath, "Surprised half the city wasn't lined up to kill him."

The mere thought of it disheartened her, "Pray they weren't or we'll never get out of purgatory with the mayor. He wants it solved but I don't think he wants the whole city behind bars. Or even half of it."

An officer politely shouldered his way past Mathis to her desk, "Background check you asked for." The clean-cut rookie started out the door then abruptly stopped and offered her a folded note, "Oh, and this is from the desk sergeant."

Taking it, she curiously eyed it, "What's it about?" Written admonishment about taking her calls again? She only had one phone in her office, she'd tell him, and multitasking is hard to achieve with just one.

His shrug reminded her of a young boy's, "Dunno but he said he'd send an update later." He smiled and gave her an impromptu salute, "See ya, Detective."

Youth. It held so much promise – and silliness. During her rookie year, she barely felt comfortable enough to breathe, much less joke with detectives. She slid on her glasses, opened the folder on Kurt's background. The desk sergeant's note would have to wait. If an update was pending, she knew she had time.

One look at the arrest record and she realized, yet again, why daylight should only be mailed to certain prisoners. "Here's someone you don't bring home to Mama. Kurt's been arrested for assault, theft, and aggravated assault."

Ennis took the printout from her, scanned it for himself. "He attacked a guy for supposedly flirting with his girlfriend."

John's jaw dropped, "You mean he's actually had a girlfriend?"

Savannah put in her two cents, "She had to have low intellect and a stealthy nose to tolerate that incompetent, whiffy asshole."

Mathis continued reading the report, "Kurt made a believer out of the poor guy too. Threw bacon grease mixed with lye on him. The lye burns right through and the bacon grease prevents the victim from washing it off." Ennis shuddered at the description as Mathis concluded, "Ain't no gift you ever want."

Savannah agreed, "And if you mess with this guy, don't just search him for guns and knives. Search him for Tupperware." She blew out a breath, "So far we have the three women, two of whom know men with motive for murder. Beau and Kurt could have killed Vaughn, now all we need is a guy tied to Tracy Martin to add to the mix. For that, I would assume a background check on Barry's partner Patrick Hess might be prudent since Barry poached Tracy from him. Beau could've hired someone to kill Barry because he made 'advances' on Danielle but we'll never know because the mayor forbade us to touch Beau." Resting her head in against her hand, the whole sordid, convoluted mess convinced her that world peace was easier to achieve.

Mathis held a hand to his belly as he chuckled, "Since when does that stop you?"

Savannah rewarded him with a half smile. It seemed nicer than an exhaustive description of why she disliked unemployment.

John removed his specs, "Seriously, you've battled the chief of police, handled a few high profile criminals and now you're stymied by some punk who won his position by a hundred lousy votes? You're gettin' soft, Prince."

"I'm getting *older*, John. My pension looks better and better each day. I'd like to collect it at some point because it might come in handy." She perused Kurt's rap sheet once more, knowing one of them had to interview him. Personally, she'd rather be lit on fire than face the linguistically impeded moron again. "So," she closed the folder and prayed for a volunteer, "who's interviewing Graham?"

And like that, the room fell silent. Ennis, who'd begun biting his fingernails moment ago, appeared suddenly engrossed in the task. Mathis volleyed his vision between his colleagues. Settling on Savannah, he decided, "You shouldn't do it. He's already babbling every legal phrase he's seen on Law & Order, plus this time you're liable to kill him."

No argument there. The station saw enough fireworks for the week. She and Mathis referred to Ennis who conveniently continued gnawing his nails. Annoyed by his silence, Mathis finally took the hint, "I'm gettin' the short end every time on this case. First Vaughn's house, now the psycho asshole. You two *really* owe me."

Magically finished with his manicure, Ennis nodded to the note, "What's that about?"

Savannah almost forgot about the desk sergeant's note. She flipped it open and in a handwriting one degree short of chicken scratch, it read, "Possible sighting of Cole Jordan in Rome, GA. Locals are investigating. Will update you later."

She swallowed hard. The sight of Cole's name brought back images of running for her life, dodging bullets, and trying to find Georgia before he and Jeffrey killed her. Rome, Georgia. Less than a hundred miles separated them. Technically seventy or so. Not much breathing room, especially for nearly five months of freedom. Savannah expected – hoped – he'd trekked further than that by now. Like Canada, Greenland but most preferably Hell. She tried to clear the unease from her voice, "Another Cole Jordan sighting."

Ennis tensed in his chair, and before he could ask where, she told him. His jaw clenched and released. "He's getting closer. Two weeks ago it was Chattanooga. This week Rome."

O O O

The interview room was big enough for a single holding cell, a metal table flanked by two chairs and a small cabinet containing legal pads and a few other supplies.

Contrary to the interview room, the observation cubicle lived up to its name – a small compartment no bigger than a broom closet. Once the door closed, the person standing inside only had a one way mirror to visually connect with the outside world. For a claustrophobic, the room might as well have been a knife at their throat. Ennis hated the autopsy suite. It made him literally ill. Savannah despised the observation cubicle for the same reason.

The second she entered the tiny room, her chest constricted, robbing her of breath. The walls seemed to close in, squeezing out the air she so desperately needed. She shut her eyes, told herself the room was fine and she was too. But her mind conjured thoughts of the ceiling and walls crushing her, trapping her in the small space. The pressure in her lungs increased until it felt like a giant fist closing around them. Since childhood she suffered the debilitating claustrophobia. The older she got the worse it became. Concentrate, her brother once told her. Concentrate on slow, deep breaths. In and out. Slowly.

Ennis recognized and understood her reluctance to enter the tiny, stifling room. He'd never witnessed her in full panic mode, when she sweated like a pig, gasped in vain for air and swore her heart was exploding. When her mind reeled and sanity hung by a precarious thread. Luckily she spared him that horror and spared herself the humiliation. But he'd seen her struggle in elevators and small rooms. His usual answer was to kiss her. Strangely it helped. Standing shoulder to shoulder with him in the shoebox of a room, she wished he'd draw her against him and plant a whopper on her.

He did the next best thing. He clasped her hand in his, whispering, "Wait outside, babe. I'll tell you how it goes."

Breathe. In and out. Slowly. She shook her head, not trusting herself to speak.

"You can barely breathe. How's it gonna look if you're passed out with me bent over you? It won't be pleasant for either of us. Mathis will say something tacky."

Savannah felt herself smile a little. That was Ennis. If he couldn't kiss her out of her panic, he'd joke her out of it. She tightened her grasp with a thank you.

He reciprocated by blushing. He waited a minute before asking,

"You okay after getting that note about Jordan?"

In and out. Slowly. Still silently repeating the mantra, she nodded. The pressure in her chest tried to ease but her heart kept bounding against her ribs. As for Cole, she honestly wasn't sure how to interpret the note. If the reports were true, Cole inched his way closer to her. That fact didn't help her current dilemma and she fought harder to control her breathing. "I'm fine," she said. "He's not here, that's all that matters."

The interview room door creaked open and John Mathis stepped in. In his hand he held a manila folder containing Kurt's rap sheet. He loosened his tie, which as a result, now hung askew. He rolled up his sleeves, "Welcome to our humble jail," he told Kurt. "I'm the guy gonna book you for murder."

Once the gravity of John's declaration sank in, Kurt pointed to his shirt, "I didn't kill nobody. That bitch tried to kill *me* though."

Mathis stared over his glasses at Graham, "Oh yeah. Thanks for reminding me." He began jotting notes in the folder. "That's first degree murder *plus* assault on two police officers. Wait, maybe I should try for attempted capital murder on two police officers. Has a better ring to it. You really know how to rack 'em up, don't ya, Kurt?"

"I didn't kill anyone," Kurt maintained, his voice wavering between panic and anger. "Whatever that bitch said, she's lying."

In that time, Savannah calmed down a degree only for her temper to ignite. Being called a bitch had a way of souring a woman's mood. And if the cretin called her that other, more graphic epithet, he'd be digesting his teeth.

She and Ennis jumped as Mathis slammed a fist on the metal table. The resounding echo reverberated hard enough to rattle the one-way mirror.

John's voice thundered through the room, "If you don't refer to my colleague in a respectable manner, I'll twist you in a knot. She only did what came naturally when faced with an asshole like you. Understand?"

Kurt didn't move. He sank in his seat as Mathis rose from his, "You think it's okay to attack cops. That it's acceptable to threaten a woman whether she's in uniform or not. Is that what you think, Kurt?"

"No, but if she's saying I killed someone, it ain't fact, it's suppository."

Oh dear Lord, have mercy on us, she prayed. We are stuck with this gem of society and prying a shred of sense from him is impossible. It was a foregone conclusion that Kurt Graham was a language-challenged weirdo but was he a killer? Did he possess the intelligence to kill? Yes, he'd proven that by disfiguring a person. It proved he not only possessed the knowledge but chose *unique* methods of punishments. If he killed Vaughn, how did he gain access to the aquarium without raising eyebrows, especially with his mental shortcomings and horrendous vapor trail?

Savannah saw perspiration form on Kurt's face. He turned to the mirror, evidently sensing her presence – or thought he did.

Mathis redirected his attention by holding a plastic bag in front of his nose, "She found your jackknife when she searched you."

Kurt remained still and quiet. Mathis couldn't believe it, "You *do* remember it, right? I mean you don't suffer from that attention deficit thing, do you?"

Kurt glared at him, "I remember it."

"Good." The detective swung the bag back and forth in front of him, "Don't want you accusing her of illegal circumcision."

Kurt drew back in the chair at the same time Ennis flinched, "Just the thought of it hurts. Does Graham understand the meaning of search and seizure?"

Savannah's expression questioned his sanity, "Does he look capable of understanding it? We should've booked the moron for assault *and* murdering the English language."

In the interview room, Mathis continued his interrogation, "If we test this knife for blood, are we gonna find any?"

"Mine, yeah."

"Just yours? I'm warning you 'cause our test is foolproof and we already know a guy did the killing. The blood at the scene came back male."

Kurt's face flushed again, "Is she saying I did something? If she did, she's lying."

Mathis lost the semi-warmth in his voice, "I don't like bastards like you. You get a charge outta disfiguring people and you attack cops. There's two strikes already. The third is that the mayor wants the killer found pronto and he's not choosy who I pick. You won the jackpot, Kurt. I don't care what your alibi is, you're guilty. They're gonna pin a medal on me and stick a needle in you. Death penalty, genius. First degree murder." He turned to walk out but Savannah noticed he lingered a beat at the door. His purpose: to give the news time to register with Kurt.

When it did, their suspect shot from his seat, "What murder?"

Mathis crooked a half grin toward the mirror. He knew he hooked Kurt and the guy now dangled from the line, wriggling for freedom. "Sit down," John barked. He unbuttoned his suit coat from his round stomach, removed it, draped it over the back of his chair. He plopped his hands on his hips, "Playing ignorant ain't gonna save you. Judges don't care if you can count to five, they just want to know which vat of oil to boil you in."

"*What murder?*" Kurt's hands shook as he eased into his chair.

Savannah saw his feet shifting and fidgeting beneath the table. "I didn't kill anyone," he repeated.

Mathis bent closer, "Just like to maim 'em, do ya? Well, you went too far with Barry Vaughn. That little fillet job you did on him? I'll bet that got his attention but not as much as being tossed into that fish tank."

Utter shock spread across the bully's expression faster than the rage had, "What?"

Mathis wiped a hand down his face and he headed for the door, "My IQ is sinking just being in the same room with you."

Savannah saw him look at the mirror then give a quick jerk of his head. He wanted to meet in the hallway. She and Ennis stepped into the hall at the same time Mathis did. Their colleague's bluster melted into frazzled annoyance as he rubbed the back of his neck, "I'm not gettin' anywhere, at least not anywhere fast, and the bastard's as dumb as a bag of hammers. They oughta have a telethon for people like him."

Savannah hid a smile. Mathis was anything if not colorful. Give him a suspect and he'd give you a thousand different words describing them, none of them flattering.

Ennis rolled his shirt sleeves much the way Mathis did earlier, only with a snarl, "I'll get him to talk."

Savannah put a hand to his chest. Letting him in the room meant bloodshed. Mutilation of a suspect tended to upset the higher-ups. "Let me try," she said.

He tensed beneath her touch, the muscles tightening in his arms and jaw hardened to rock. Savannah tried to diffuse his anger by batting her eyelashes, "He doesn't respond to your charms like he does mine. Mathis will be in there, don't worry." She sensed Ennis gearing up for a lecture. The one on safety she heard so often and he'd follow up with how "lucky" she was earlier. What he didn't quite understand – her brother trained her for such travails. Yes, a few people got over on her but not many.

Ennis pursed his lips with the "you'll regret this and you know it" stare then blew out a breath, surrendering his lecture. She patted his chest in thanks.

Savannah gestured to Mathis to enter the room first. That gave him time to sit down and Kurt a false sense of security. Because when she walked in, God only knew what hell might break loose.

She straightened her jacket and gave Ennis her version of a pep talk, "Two shakes of a lamb's tail and I'll be out."

Behind the closed door, Kurt rambled a mile a minute, probably pleading his case to John who developed a sudden penchant for saying "shut up".

Savannah opened the door and the pungent stench of body odor clung to every atom in the room. No wonder John's mood went sour, she thought. Odors that stout conquered armies and took over countries.

The second Kurt made eye contact, he shut up and launched from his seat, sending the chair tumbling backwards. His hands raced to his crotch, giving Savannah the notion John's reference to illegal circumcision did more good than she imagined.

"Stay away from me," Kurt warned, his hands creating a fleshy codpiece.

Savannah did just the opposite, closing the space between them, "You've got my colleague thinking you're dumber than dirt but I know the truth."

As she neared, he flattened against the bars of the holding cell. His eyes searched wildly for an escape currently unavailable, "What truth?"

She rounded the metal table and Mathis leaned back, perched his glasses on top of his head. He was enjoying the show. Savannah stepped even closer to Kurt, "You're not stupid, you're just mean and you've seen me in action. I'm the bitch from hell. *Fascist* bitch, if I remember correctly."

Kurt reinforced the shield over his groin, "Leave me alone." He glanced past her to Mathis, "Help me, dude."

"Sorry," Mathis answered. "Her investigation now, not mine. I told ya. You shoulda talked to me when you had the chance."

Savannah pulled the shade on the interview room mirror, leaving the room off limits to prying eyes. She could almost hear Ennis fuming on the other side. He'd have to listen at the door to keep track of the conversation but she knew her husband. His ear would stay glued to the door until she exited safely.

She shrugged from her suit jacket and handed it to Mathis, "That means the fascist bitch is in charge. I need answers, Kurt, and if you don't give 'em up, I've got serious work ahead of me." She turned to John, "We still got that first aid kit in here?"

Playing along, Mathis hitched his thumb at a built-in cabinet in the corner, "Always stocked."

"Even the suture kit? I'll probably need it."

"Got your name on it from your last interrogation."

Kurt's hands never moved from his crotch. He shook his head, "Lady, I don't know nothin'. I didn't kill nobody."

Savannah stepped closer to him, "Let's get something straight first. Do you want out of here, away from me?"

"Hell yes," he said then backtracked, "no offense. And I want to leave with everything I was borned with."

She stood close enough barely a breath of air moved between them. Her nose begged her to back off and her stomach joined the chorus.

Kurt refused eye contact as his whole face broke into a shining sheen of sweat. Savannah stared unblinking at him, crowding him until his breathing quickened and his body stiffened. She took full advantage, "If you want out with your taters and other parts in tact, tell me if you've been to the new aquarium."

He vehemently nodded. She eyed him, "You been upstairs where they feed the fish?"

Again he nodded, "I went with a friend."

"This friend work at the aquarium?"

"He's got a cousin who did but he moved away."

"But the cousin had a passkey to the facility."

Kurt shrugged a shoulder, "I guess. He slid a card in a machine and the door opened."

"And it gave him access to the upstairs feeding area?"

Three fast nods later, he replied, "Yeah. That's how we got up there."

She leaned closer, "Gimme that cousin's name, Kurt."

He pressed back, "Boyd Brown. But he moved to California."

Mathis wrote the name then opened the door and passed it to Ennis. Kurt, meanwhile, squirmed under her scrutiny. "Can you back off a little?" he squeaked.

"We're not finished yet. How well did you know Barry Vaughn?"

"Met him once or twice."

"You like him?"

Kurt shouldered a bead of sweat from his temple but didn't

answer. Savannah prompted, "This is a new blouse, Kurt, and I hate getting blood on new clothes."

"No, I didn't like him. I hated him."

"Enough to hurt him, right? Because he was seeing Lucy and you've got the hots for her. Barry muscled in on your girl and we know what happens to men who cross you. You give 'em a bacon grease and lye bath."

His body went rigid against hers, his hands fisted. His expression darkened to the same hue when he barreled toward her and Ennis earlier.

Her blue eyes narrowed, "Better reconsider those thoughts you're having. Between me and Detective Mathis, we can hog-tie you and while he's fetching the suture kit and rusty knife, I'll be diggin' for taters."

Mortification drained his ire, paled his cheeks, "Barry Vaughn was a rat bastard. He mistreated Lucy."

"How did he mistreat her?"

"He humiliated her. Made her feel second-rate because she wasn't experienced."

"I assume you mean sexually."

"Well, *yeah*," he said in a way suggesting she was dense.

The note from the flower arrangement jogged her memory, "Why would he call her a freak?"

"How should I know? Barry was a dog. Anyone with mortals probably was a freak to him. He couldn't appreciate a plutonic relationship like me and her have."

"Did you show him what happens to men who overstep that

plutonic relationship? Did you push Barry into the fish tank and let the barracudas finish the job?"

Kurt stood, his hands still protecting his privates and looking less than brilliant. There was a reason for the warning label on the bottom of Coke bottles reading "Do not open here." Savannah figured the reason stood directly in front of her. She waited for her accusation to register and when it did, fear passed over his face again.

"Wait a minute!" he wriggled past her, heading for the opposite side of the room. She didn't bother to follow. He was on the ropes and either going to spill the fact he killed Barry or prove his innocence. Or, she thought grimly, charge at me again.

"I didn't kill anyone," he insisted, wiping a hand down his sweaty face. "I was at Big Planet Comics that day, waiting for my order."

Savannah cut her vision to Mathis, put her hands on her hips. This is not going well, she silently conveyed. Mathis shrugged, "Easy enough to check. Where is this place and what order were you waiting for?"

Kurt rattled off the location of Big Planet Comics, finishing with, "I reserved the new Batman comic and waited thirty minutes for the guy to unpack 'em."

Mathis jotted down the information and opened the door to hand it to Ennis. The knowledge Ennis stood sentry outside eased her anxiety about being in a room with Kurt. For all her bluster, the smelly nutjob still set her on edge. While she and Mathis could subdue him, Kurt's sheer size and anger issues promised significant damage during the process.

Savannah backed off a few steps because frankly she needed fresher air. She glanced at Mathis who leaned against the wall. Verifying Kurt's presence wouldn't take long but in that short time his posture evolved to one she'd seen before. One that warned *look out.*

"You're framing me for this, aren't you?" he growled, barreling straight at her.

Her fight or flight instinct kicked in and this time his destination wouldn't be jail but the hospital. "Graham, I'm warning you. Stop right there!"

But he continued bulling toward her, his fists clenched as hard as his jaw. Mathis raced to position himself between the two, his arm nudging her toward the door. "Get out," he ordered. "I ain't letting Rutherford steamroll me 'cause you got hurt."

Before she could open the door, it crashed open and she spun to see Ennis aiming a Taser straight at Kurt. Her husband's tone refused debate, "Graham, back off or I'll use this thing till lightning shoots out your ass."

Kurt suddenly backpedaled at the sight, his glare never straying from Savannah, "Don't put this on me, bitch!"

The three detectives left the room, closed and locked the door behind them. Savannah and Mathis blew out long breaths.

Ennis propped his hands on his hips, the Taser still firmly in his grasp, "What were you thinking by baiting him like that? The guy's already mental."

A uniformed officer walking by stopped long enough to hand

Ennis a note. Savannah saw her husband's hand tremble as he read. The last few moments took their toll on everyone but, "Ennis, I thought perhaps he'd confess with enough prodding. You know, it has been known to happen."

"So has assault on a police officer."

Okay, he was mad at her. He'd get over it. Someday. "Ennis –"

"According to this note," his chilly voice interrupted, "he's not our whack job."

Well, it was a long shot anyway. Kurt could barely tie his own shoes, much less sneak his way into a public place to commit murder.

Ennis sat the Taser aside. Savannah couldn't help but be impressed. He'd barged in wielding the Taser like a .45 Magnum, ready to zap the crap out of Kurt. She had no doubts he'd follow through on his promise. Her husband protected her absolutely any way he could, even if that meant turning Kurt Graham into a Roman Candle. Still her darling overprotective spouse sounded less than pleased with her, "I also got news on Jordan while you were playing Russian Roulette with Chucklehead."

An involuntary shiver raked her spine. If they didn't catch a break on something soon, she'd really need a vacation – preferably on a deserted island. On her salary, she couldn't even afford a week at Rose Austin Psychiatric Hospital, much less a tropical retreat. But her nerves unraveled at an alarming rate, leaving her patience at its end. She nodded at Ennis to proceed.

"It wasn't him," he simply said.

Of course not. Why should something go right that day? She

rubbed her forehead, curious what the going rate at Rose Austin was lately. "Back to Kurt, I'm guessing his alibi is solid."

Savannah could tell by her husband's foul expression that the alibi was as solid as Stone Mountain. Just a typical day in the world of homicide investigation, she groused. Brick walls, stupid suspects, empty leads and an eejit mayor. All in a day's work…

Ennis referred to the note in his hand, "Seems the owner of Big Planet knows Kurt and he was there to pick up the new Batman comic. Has security tape verifying it if we're interested."

"Shee-yet," she groaned. "How about Boyd Brown? Might as well shoot for the trifecta."

"He lives in Los Angeles and turned in his passkey before he left."

She leaned against the wall with a sigh, "Just great. Batman corroborated Kurt's alibi and Mr. Brown is an honest citizen, at least in this case. Now what do we do?" It was at that instant Mayor O'Neill's accusation of her supposed inadequate intellect hit her like a slap in the face. She defended herself, swearing she wasn't mentally deficient. But staring at another lost lead in the case and the fact even Batman was against them, she wondered who's side destiny was on – the village idiot's or the police department's idiot?

19

The note about Cole Jordan bothered Ennis. For weeks, police departments across the country searched for him without success but Ennis knew for a fact the bastard hadn't ventured too far from Atlanta. About once a week Jordan sent a postcard, the postmark from Atlanta or Dunwoody which told him the creep still hung around, waiting, biding his time. The latest postcard arrived a week ago. Ennis chose not to tell her about them or show them to her. The choice was a gamble on his part but showing her served no purpose other than to upset her and see her retreat into the old paranoia again. Hell, she was already on edge for some reason and it wasn't just because of the mayor.

Few things scared Ennis but seeing his wife cower from sudden noises, refuse to venture outside and worse, carry her gun day and night, certainly qualified. He'd lived in fear for months that she'd shoot an innocent bystander she mistook for Cole Jordan. When he hid the guns, he suffered her scalding wrath. She felt safer with the gun, she said, and they argued for days until he capitulated, leaving her gun on the nightstand where she demanded. She lived in seclusion except the days she saw the therapist. Friends and family did what they could to ease her fears and obsessions. A vast improvement occurred when their house sold. After they moved, Savannah's personality returned, the paranoia faded to a mere shadow of itself and Ennis finally relaxed. Now if he could just keep Cole at bay, life would return to normal.

Lying beside her in bed, Ennis checked the baseball game that now had a score resembling a lopsided football game. The Astros were losing to the Braves again and Ennis quickly lost interest. Savannah, on the other hand, busied herself reading Georgia's newest book.

After another minute, Savannah removed her glasses, pinched the bridge of her nose, "Why does everyone think I'm Summer Pearson? I just don't see it."

While not a voracious reader, she normally mowed through a tome in a couple of nights when the plot intrigued her. This time her interest wasn't focused so much on plot as it was the story's characters. Ennis expected she searched for evidence incriminating her sister, not for who bumped off a character in the novel. Georgia, while vague in her promise, said her characters weren't entirely based on family. Ennis already recognized himself in the book and now he waited for Savannah to see herself as well. It was just taking an act of Congress getting there.

Taking stock of her progress, Ennis surmised in about twenty more pages, his wife might change her tune about her sister's bestseller. Instead of claustrophobia, Georgia gifted Summer with a crippling acrophobia. The character's reaction was so reminiscent of Savannah, Ennis halfway feared an explosion or family fight when she ran across that scene. Georgia understood the severity of her sister's condition but he worried about Savannah's reaction to the scene. She might think her sister cashed in on her vulnerability but to Georgia's credit, she handled it in a delicate, tasteful manner. He wasn't sure Savannah would be as gentle or tasteful with her older sibling…

Nearly two more innings passed before she removed her glasses again. She rubbed her eyes, "I talk too much about our cases."

Ennis saw the connection too. For the most part, Georgia cultivated a brilliant story from her own imagination. She accentuated it with tidbits she'd heard them talk about but the story was all hers.

He turned on his side, his fingers stroked her bare thigh, "You gotta admit it's a great book."

"It is, no question, and I can see you plain as day. I still don't believe Summer is based on me."

He took the opportunity to pick up her glasses. He slid them on his nose, "Are these things working right? If you're reading the same book I did, it should be obvious."

She nudged him with her elbow. Despite the uproar about the book, she was in a good mood and he was grateful. "Savannah, there's a reason people like our neighbors – people we hardly know – believe Summer is based on you."

She cocked an eyebrow, "How many times have I warned you – don't drink the Kool-Aid. You're sounding like that guy on History Channel. The one that believes George Washington came from Mars."

Her teasing inspired a smile. One thing about his wife – she was bullheaded beyond belief. He pecked a kiss to her lips, "Denial ain't just a river in Egypt, babe."

With a lighthearted sigh, she reclaimed her glasses then resumed reading, "Maybe I'll see the resemblance soon."

His hand still caressed her thigh, the velvet warmth inviting him to explore higher until easing beneath her nightshirt. He wanted her to read but damn, she made the simplest act look so seductive.

His mind wandered into forbidden fantasies. To make matters worse, his groin joined the chorus. At this rate she'd be lucky to read another paragraph before he jumped her. With her long waves cascading past her shoulders and her glasses perched on her nose, she looked like a sexy librarian. The day she slipped on the new specs, she'd compared herself to a librarian but meant it in an unflattering way. He, on the other hand, took her comment to another level – especially that night.

Consuming him were images of cornering the sexy librarian between the bookshelves and slipping his hand beneath her blouse. Pushing up her skirt and making wild passionate love sent him, literally, to new heights. And when his sexy librarian with her cute reading glasses reached the brink of ecstasy, he'd plant his lips on hers, smothering her cries with his kiss…

Well, he thought, it's my fault. His arousal arrived in historic glory, apparent to anyone with or without glasses. And now his hand migrated to the very spot he'd been fantasizing about. He glanced up to see her focused on his hand, not the book.

"Is this a test of my willpower?" she asked.

Ennis swallowed hard as his arousal grew rather insistent and painful. His brain still swirled with dreams of taking her with such abandon that books tumbled off shelves and the cries and commotion sent patrons fleeing.

She reminded, "I thought you wanted me to read the book." A smile curled the corners of her mouth, "And while I'm decently skilled at multitasking, reading and participating in certain activities are far beyond my capabilities."

An idea struck him. Multitasking. Hmm… "Go ahead and read. I'll busy myself," he said with a wink.

The beginnings of her smile wavered. Confusion creased her brow, "You're sure?"

She thought he wasn't interested in sex. She was about to find out different. "M-hmm."

Outwardly disappointed and clearly a little bit hurt by his snub, Savannah pushed her glasses back onto her nose with a reserved sigh. He waited patiently – unlike his arousal – for her to start reading. Another minute or two passed when he casually eased her legs apart and positioned himself between them. To spur a reaction, he scraped his day old beard against the insides of her thighs.

He felt her muscles tense as a short gasp filled the air. She lowered the book just enough to see him staring up at her. "What are you doing?" she wanted to know.

Ennis shrugged, "If you have to ask…"

According to her expression, she found his antics slightly humorous, "Ennis, I can't read and –"

"Try. I want to see how long you can read that book while I do this." He placed a kiss to the soft, warm flesh of her inner thigh then trekked upward a few inches where it was much softer and warmer.

Her breath caught in her throat and she closed her eyes, "Not very long, I can assure you."

She'd groaned the last three words as he kissed closer to his target. One hand reached to hold him closer but he backed away, "Keep your hands where I can see 'em."

With a good-humored harrumph, she plopped her hand back on the book, "You're getting terribly demanding tonight."

He grinned, "Someone has to keep you in line. Start reading, woman. Aloud."

20

The next morning, Ennis awoke snuggled close to Savannah, his arm draped over her waist. Her wealth of hair splayed across the pillow, tickling his nose and chin. She hadn't read one page in the book before abandoning it for a romp in bed.

Her sexual appetite verged on insatiable lately and he wasn't about to complain. They'd always enjoyed a healthy sex life but the past few weeks had him struggling to keep up.

That night she'd labeled his foreplay "torture" since he teased her "beyond all decency and reason". In turn, he used her own words against her, reminding that she preferred a lengthy prelude. Maybe not *that* lengthy, he mischievously reflected, but it was fun watching her writhe beneath his touch and downright arousing to hear the woman beg.

Ennis proudly smiled at that recollection. It took a while to learn the complexities of such a strong-willed female but he'd memorized her body until he knew it as well as his own.

He indulged in the memory of moving slow and deep inside her, his fingers tangling in her hair, his mouth locked on hers. Then she strained against him, her thighs tightening as her fingers dug into his shoulders. She cried out when she climaxed and Ennis, still kissing her, swallowed the sound. He reveled in the sound of her pleasure and as he found release, he held and kissed her until she relaxed.

As morning dawned he smiled at the sunrise revealing his sleeping beauty beside him. From the outside, Savannah presented herself as hard, straightforward and unyielding. In their bed, she transformed to a soft, playful vixen who thrived on exchanging control but really didn't mind relinquishing it. Savannah was a formidable woman, especially at work. Few people argued with her on the job and the ones who did regretted it. But stepping over the threshold of home changed her. She removed the formidable shell and replaced it with a softer Southern lady that enjoyed cooking, bantering with her husband and sliding between the sheets for a wild, salacious romp.

His hand caressed the warm velvet skin of her belly then moved to her breast. His thumb found the surgery scar from memory. Ennis considered the small blemish a lifesaver. Had the lump not been detected when it was, Savannah's future would have been much different.

Ennis gave her breast a gentle squeeze. She stirred against him but remained asleep. Easing his hand over her hip, he came across the newer scars from Jeffrey's beating. The cane split the skin, ripping it open until the wounds wept with blood. In his travels along her body, Ennis purposefully avoided tracing the marks crisscrossing her back and bottom. They weren't tender to the touch anymore but they still brought her wide awake if he paid too much attention to them. He had to be careful when kissing his way down the line of her back. Lingering too long or getting too close to the painful memories caused her to tense and protest.

Before his anger destroyed the previous night's pleasure, Ennis eased his hand down her belly then kissed her shoulder. "We've got time before work," he hinted, sliding his hand further between her thighs.

Savannah gasped quietly when he stroked her. Awake but her voice still leaden with sleep, she mumbled, "Babe, I'm worn out." The lethargic, slurred words amused him. True, they spent their time productively that night and made love twice. But worn out? Wow, he was either getting better or, "You're gettin' old if that wore you out," he joked while sliding his fingers deeper.

Her hand stopped his journey and her voice gained surprising strength, "By that I'm assuming you're not wanting sex for a very long time."

He couldn't help but laugh. Horny as she was lately, cutting him off from sex seemed rather improbable, "Make you a deal. You gather your strength and I'll make breakfast."

She nodded. Ennis joked with her about her staying power but truthfully he understood her fatigue. After her surgery she'd undergone radiation treatments for several weeks then encountered Cole Jordan and Jeffrey Holland and had to heal from that. Between the three, she lost not only her stamina but her appetite and along with it, nearly twenty pounds or more. For Savannah who stayed trim anyway, the weight loss worried him. For the last couple of weeks though, he noticed she'd gained a bit of weight. During their lovemaking her body felt softer, fuller than it had in months. Even her breasts reaped the benefit of the weight gain and it surprised and certainly pleased Ennis. His wife finally settled down after Jeffrey's brutality, enough that she began eating again. Maybe life gave them a break after all.

Ennis rolled out of bed and slipped into his jeans. Her surgery scar reminded him of her upcoming appointment with the oncologist. He just couldn't remember exactly when it was scheduled. Ennis zipped up, opting to leave the top button undone for comfort. He placed a kiss on her bare hip, "When's your appointment with Dr. Wyatt?"

She mumbled something unintelligible. He moved to her lips and kissed, hoping to stir her awake enough to make sense, "Come again?"

"Ennis, I told you I'm too tired," she groaned.

A humorous smile curved his lips at her meaning. Making love with her floating in a semi-conscious state never really appealed to him. He liked her to be awake for the main event so to ease her mind, he clarified, "I meant when is your appointment? This week, right?"

A silence followed and he thought she drifted off until, "Next week."

The smile faded. No, the appointment was scheduled for that week, not the next. Now frustration set in, "Why'd you postpone it?"

"Too tired to argue. I go next week. Goodnight." To emphasize her point, she threw the sheet over her head. End of conversation. Only for now, he thought. He'd brace her about it at breakfast and she damn well knew it. If she assumed he was her only obstacle, she was foolish. Georgia would hit the roof once she found out.

He made his way to the kitchen. Slamming her about the

appointment after a night of great sex probably wasn't smart. Instead, he decided to ease into the subject, and emphasize the importance of keeping the original appointment. Ennis yawned while grabbing a frying pan from the cabinet. A gourmet chef he wasn't but he knew his way around the kitchen fairly well for a member of the male population. He credited his mother for the ability to prepare a decent meal. All her sons except Dane could whip out an actual edible meal without a major catastrophe like fire or visits by paramedics.

Ennis rummaged the fridge for the eggs he remembered buying only days earlier. Cracking six into a bowl, he whipped them together with a fork then added a splash of milk to them because his mama and Savannah always did. He'd try her again with scrambled eggs. The last three times she'd wrinkled her nose at them. Maybe she was going through a phase. Cereal over eggs. He'd done that too – at seven years old. Something else was going on with Savannah and she wasn't fessing up. He only prayed it didn't involve her health.

Oh well, if she didn't eat the eggs, he would. He tended to take exception too quickly when she rejected his eggs but when she chose Cocoa Puffs instead? That *really* hurt. Who chose two bowls of manufactured chocolate puffballs over a warm, home-cooked meal prepared with love?

By the time Savannah wandered into the kitchen, he'd scrambled the eggs and prepared four pieces of toast – already buttered and slathered with apricot jam.

Ennis noticed she'd combed her hair and just thrown on a robe. The curves of her breasts peeked out from the cleavage, giving his groin high hopes for an encore. Down boy, he told himself. Business needed tending to but he wasn't stupid. She required a certain amount of caffeine before holding a logical conversation so he poured her a fresh steaming hot cup of java. He pecked a kiss to her cheek, "Good morning, sleepyhead."

"Mornin'," she cradled the coffee cup in her hands, closed her eyes and inhaled the aroma. "This smells heavenly." A tentative sip later, her eyes opened, looking brighter than he expected. "Are the eggs for you?"

"Are they supposed to be?" Here it came. Another friggin' rebuff on his eggs.

She ambled to the cabinet for a bowl – a bowl meant for those damn chocolate balls. Sure enough, she loaded the bowl to the brim, "I'm really hungry for cereal if that's okay."

Her apologetic tone failed to warm his heart. He just sighed. Whatever, he thought. But that sentiment didn't hold true for the doctor's appointment. She may have avoided his eggs, but he wouldn't let her duck the discussion about her health.

He was aggravated but certainly not suicidal so he waited a little longer before broaching the subject. Instead he forced a smile, "Whatever sounds good."

After pouring milk in the bowl – Ennis wondered where she found room for it – she joined him at the table. She plunged the spoon into the bowl, dragging up a heaping spoonful. Savannah chased it with a swallow of coffee and moaned similar to the previous night's romping.

Something was definitely wrong. They couldn't be *that* good but she devoured the bowl in just a few minutes and went for a refill.

Ennis expected a little more conversation. The lack of it told him she mulled over the subject of her appointment. It surprised him when she partook of the toast. At least he hadn't lost his touch on that. As she wolfed it down, she complimented his efforts which told him she buttered him up as thick as he'd buttered her toast.

He learned how to deal with the quiet and sullen side of his wife by sheer luck. Best to pretend he didn't notice the silence, let her cogitate on her problem and eventually she'd open up. He just prayed she wasn't concocting some half-ass excuse for postponing Dr. Wyatt.

Two bowls and two pieces of toast later, Savannah dabbed the corners of her mouth with her napkin with a sated sigh, "I rescheduled Dr. Wyatt for two reasons. One, the Vaughn case is taking all our time and it seemed the natural thing to do."

That qualified as a reason but not a valid one and certainly not one he advocated. He and Mathis were perfectly capable of handling the case while she tended to her business. "And the second reason?"

"To be honest, I'm nervous about it this time."

Ennis stopped eating. "What do you mean you're nervous about it? Do you think the cancer's back? It's not even been a year."

"The last test came back clear," she reminded.

"Then why postpone it?"

"Ennis," her voice held a gentle warning. "I told you why I put it off."

"No, you said you were nervous and refuse to say why." He

stabbed his fork into the eggs. He hated cold eggs nearly as much as his wife's lawyerly ways. "Don't tell the whole truth – just what you want people to know" seem to be her philosophy sometimes. Her behavior equaled Russian Roulette. Playing fast and loose with her health was foolish. "So when you tellin' Georgia? She was going with you, remember?"

"The appointment was Wednesday. I'll call her later today."

"And today is…" he not-so-subtly hinted.

He saw her mentally counting the days off then she scrambled from the chair like someone shot at her, "Shit, it's Wednesday." Her eyes darted toward the clock then she slumped against the counter, "I'm too late."

Served her right. First she weaseled out of the appointment then offered a silly excuse for doing it. Let her incur Georgia's wrath and see how intelligent she felt in its wake.

The phone rang as if on cue. Ennis fisted his napkin, slammed it on the table, and headed straight for the phone, "Good luck passing off those lame excuses on your sister." Far past annoyed and headed straight to fuming, Ennis jabbed the answer button then slapped it on speakerphone. In his heart he prayed it was Georgia. Her sister stood the only chance of talking sense to her.

The heavens granted his wish, "Hi, Ennis. Is she around? I need to ask her something."

Ennis figured it was better to let the older sister dole out the anger. After all, he lived with Savannah so he had all day and night to remind her of her idiotic decision. "As a matter of fact, she's right here. Said she has something to tell *you.*"

Savannah fried him with a blistering frown. He shrugged one shoulder in response. Unlike his temper, his eggs were losing their heat, forcing him to heap them into a mound with his fork with hopes of keeping them warm. If she wanted an ally, he wasn't it. To busy himself, he topped off her coffee then sat the carafe out of her reach. As mad as she looked, he didn't put it past her to smash him over the head with it.

"What's up?" Savannah greeted in a surprisingly cheerful manner.

Georgia replied, "I've been trying to schedule interviews and I have one at eleven. That'll still give me time to go to Dr. Wyatt's with you. I'll be by about nine-fifteen. It's a little earlier but is it okay?"

"About that. I rescheduled the appointment so you're off the hook today," Savannah slid the reply and so fast, even Ennis did a double-take. Clever, he thought, but Georgia wasn't an idiot. When it came to Savannah's health, her personality changed. Instead of a sister offering guidance, she instantly donned a parental role, demanding answers and obedience from the little tyke incessantly whining the word *no.* Much as Ennis loved his wife, she tended to take chances she shouldn't and today he wholeheartedly sided with Mama Bear.

"Rescheduled? Why?"

Ennis refused to look at Savannah. He felt her searing him with the intensity of a blowtorch. Still, he gave her credit – she fessed up, "I rescheduled because we're busy with the Vaughn case."

He lifted his cup to take a sip but Georgia's silence halted his intent. Even Savannah's expectant anger hung in limbo as she waited.

"I did *not* just hear that," Georgia grumbled.

Yep, he thought. Mama Bear's about to go on the rampage. Ennis figured Georgia would explode. For seconds, she struggled for something to follow up with. He could only imagine her expression – disbelief mixed with anger.

"Savannah Charlene," Georgia scolded, the anger rising in her voice.

Ennis turned his back to his wife but kept a cautious ear tuned. He wouldn't be entirely surprised if she flung a slice of toast at him – or even the meager remainder of her precious Cocoa Puffs.

"Go ahead and lecture me," she dared Georgia. "But try fitting in a doctor's appointment between interviews, the mayor's interference, the mayor's son and –"

"I get your point," her sister butted in. "When is the new appointment because there'd better be one." On a normal day, Georgia's knack for intimidating a person rated a solid five on a scale of one to ten. That day, though, Ennis gave her sister at ten. The authoritative dressing-down rang reminiscent of a mother's lecture. Georgia meant business.

"There *is,*" Savannah countered. "I'm rushed, not stupid. It's next Tuesday at ten. Georgia, I can't afford to die. Who would the mayor kick around if I did?"

"Savannah, these appointments are important. God forbid the cancer comes back and you postponed that *one* appointment…"

Ennis chanced a look at his wife. She'd taken to rolling her eyes and leaning her head in her hand. All while Georgia stormed, "Let's see what Seth has to say about this. Want me to call him?"

"Do you enjoy breathing?"

Ennis heard the older sister grumble again, "Canceling your appointment, especially in your condition –"

"Next Tuesday, Mein Führer," Savannah unexpectedly snapped. "At ten."

Ennis noticed her entire demeanor unexpectedly transformed. Sat straightened in the chair, her hands curled into fists. Even her expression warned "back off or else". What did Georgia mean *in your condition*? He sensed a secret between the sisters – one involving Savannah's health. He wanted in on this conversation, "Georgia, what did you mean 'in her condition'?"

Meanwhile, Savannah's posture promised an explosion. She glared at the phone hard enough to shatter it.

After a brief hesitation Georgia replied, "I meant with everything she's been through the last year, she'd better stay current with her appointments. Remember when she tried to cancel back in June?"

Yes, but in June she still battled the painful wounds from Jeffrey's abuse and the crippling paranoia. There'd been an actual reason to reschedule because physically *and* emotionally she could barely walk out of the house.

Georgia's secrecy and thrown together excuse nettled him but pushing the matter would only make matters worse. He'd wait until Savannah cooled down before broaching the subject. "I remember. I can go with her next week. I'll call you with the results."

"Thanks, Ennis," she said, relieved, "I know I can depend on you."

Savannah sat her coffee cup down a bit too hard, "I'm not a delinquent or a fool. I promised I'd go and I will but keep ganging up on me and I'll go alone. I'll take your book and read it and find out what my alter ego is doing these days. Forget acrophobia. Thanks to you basing Summer Pearson on me, I've developed a fear of reading books."

"Savannah," her sister drawled in her deep Southern accent, "you act as though I wrote Summer as the killer. I tried to be flattering with my descriptions."

"By having her cower at the sight of stairs and ladders?"

"She doesn't cower. She's reluctant, like you are about small places."

"Is that a compliment because I can't tell." She sighed, "Nevermind. I do want to know how you came up with the sister *and* brother as the killers."

"Just my twisted mind, I guess."

So nothing to do with Jeffrey and his warped step-brother Cole, Ennis questioned silently.

"So you're not too angry about Summer?" Georgia asked timidly.

"No," she sighed once more. "I was at first because it seemed like everyone's private joke. But if you continue Killer Instinct as a series, leave Summer as is. No more phobias or crazy habits. Josh reads your books too and frankly, I need my job."

21

It was exactly ten twenty-two that morning when her phone rang with Mayor O'Neill who somehow formed the notion, "You're not a police officer, are you? You're a demon sent straight from hell to derail my political future."

Immediately she checked Caller ID. Yep, the number matched the mayor's office, however the caller's voice sank to a gravelly growl like a pit bull about to attack. Franklin O'Neill sounded ready to kill.

Savannah sank into her chair before her knees gave out. Times like this deserved a Valium, she thought. But until her first prenatal visit – which now seemed less likely to be scheduled anytime soon – she'd have to limp along on Tums and pretend.

She popped two in her mouth and chewed, managing with perverse luck to also bite her tongue. Simply put, her day really sucked and showed no promise of improving.

"Are you there, Prince? Did you hear me?" The mayor yelled. O'Neill's rage erupted into an uncontrollable storm and her body reacted in a surprising manner. She froze in the chair and even her throbbing tongue seized up. She wasn't sure if the latter was a good or bad thing, she only took it as a sign of unadulterated shock. Anyone else would have labeled it good since her initial reaction to such an attack was to launch a verbal assault at the offender.

The mayor wanted a response and hesitation would anger him further so she forced a calm reply, "Yes, Mayor, I hear you."

"You've crossed the line this time. I'm having your job, do you hear me? You're fired!"

The last two words kicked the paralysis from her body, including the rebellion incapacitating her tongue, "What line did I cross?"

By that time, she'd risen to her feet again, her indignation followed close behind. The surprise of his ambush waned, giving way to her own blossoming temper. Who was he to accuse her of… of… of whatever the hell he was accusing her of? Besides, *he* couldn't fire her, she wanted to say. He didn't have *that* kind of power yet.

"Find a television and turn it to a local station," he barked. "Can you do *that* without pissing me off?"

Oh Lord, it would be an excruciatingly long day at this rate. First the reaming out by Ennis and Georgia and now the mayor wanted his pound of flesh. Before morning's end, the baby would have his or her say by forcing her to kneel at the porcelain throne. Even with all the puking, she'd begun to pack on pounds until she'd eventually weigh roughly the equivalent of a Buick. Life couldn't get any better and if it did, someone needed to lock up the sharp instruments.

Savannah rounded her desk and headed to the public area where the sergeant's kiosk was located. Weaving her way through citizens and officers, she realized everyone stared at the TV in the corner. Usually abuzz with talking and general din of noise, the room stilled to a surreal scene she'd never witnessed before. A few people pointed to the TV, and Savannah glanced up to see a breaking news banner travel across the bottom of the screen. "Majestic Restaurant Poisonings" it read then the image switched from a live shot at Atlanta Medical to a red background announcing "Two more poisonings reported this morning".

Savannah swallowed hard. The last report she'd heard was twenty-two. Now it tipped to twenty-four. Well, at least she now knew the reason for the call.

"Are you seeing this, Prince?" O'Neill's voice blasted from the phone, "See what you've done?"

She covered her phone as a few people glanced back at her. The mayor certainly didn't require a megaphone when reaming people out. The whole station would hear him if she wasn't careful.

Adding insult to injury, the live shot switched from the hospital to the restaurant. Officials with the health department carried containers out the front door of the upscale eatery and loaded them into vans. The shot changed back to the hospital where the newscaster continued her report, "Two more poisonings to report today. According to hospital officials, a woman and her ten year-old son were admitted this morning for symptoms related to rat poisoning. The two had eaten at Majestic yesterday. This makes twenty-four people linked to a rash of poisonings at the restaurant. Majestic's manager and city health officials declined our request for comment."

She rushed back to her office to prevent additional stares when O'Neill reloaded for another attack. "This isn't my fault," she told him as she pushed her office door closed, effectively sealing herself away from prying ears. "They were storing hazardous materials along with the edible foods."

"Prince!" He yelled so loud it rattled the phone *and* her brain, "You've meddled in my affairs once too often!"

That was enough. He was just the mayor, not God, and God thankfully never yelled at her – at least not yet. And why did O'Neill always blame her for everything? "Your affairs?" she nearly shouted. "How is Majestic your business? It's a restaurant."

"It's *my* restaurant, you idiot! I own it! And you weren't content calling the health department, you had to call the press and brag about it."

She tolerated his ranting, every last bitter word of it, with surprising aplomb. But the whole morning began to wear on her, especially when her little gift from God took offense. Or maybe it was just indigestion... "Mayor, I called the health department but I didn't contact the media."

"Don't lie to me. This has your name all over it."

"'Fraid not, Mayor. You find out who called the media and I can promise my name will not be mentioned."

O'Neill grumbled, unconvinced. He hemmed and hawed then, "We'll see about that." He added a final warning, "Don't screw with me anymore, Prince. I *will* have your job if you do."

He hung up, leaving her mouth open to respond. Instead she stared at her phone, "Apology accepted, *sir.*"

O O O

She drove to Krispy Kreme and before exiting her car, she searched for interlopers. No mayors, no sisters, no husbands to wag their fingers, lecture or yell at her. This moment was the essence of ideal, unspoiled by angry phone calls or disappointed faces so she took a moment to breathe, basking in it. The almost deafening peace inside the car calmed her, gave her hope for the remainder of the day.

She snuck away for the pastry tryst and her boss hadn't asked why she needed to leave. Savannah supposed he'd grown used to her unusual ways and she'd refrained from telling him about O'Neill's latest attack. After all, she needed a little dignity to limp around on.

She bought a dozen chocolate donuts then sat in her Camaro, plowing ravenously into the first three to salve her wounds. She bit into the rich, puffy pillow covered in stunningly silky chocolate frosting and let the sweet goodness spread over her tongue and down her throat like a blessed, welcome elixir. No one could steal that from her. Pure sinful joy melting in her mouth. She made little use of a napkin until the gluttonous orgy ended. She chased the delicious trio down with a cup of coffee and took a moment digest the food and quiet.

Sated in chocolate bliss, she took the opportunity to revisit the previous night's frolicking. Ennis took his sweet time teasing her, building sensations only to deny her until he felt good and ready. In public Ennis Rutherford presented himself as a perfect gentleman. In private he could be a ruthless rascal. He used his tongue to make her beg, his teeth to make her gasp. And she'd gladly obeyed because experience told her he'd reward her soon – and he had.

Her ringing cell phone drew her from reliving the previous night's pleasures. Her shoulders slumped. Why not? Reality always found her. The notion of pitching her cell phone in the duck pond at Piedmont Park stole in then faded quickly. No need to annoy the wildlife with her troubles. She answered it with less than an enthusiastic, "Prince."

It was her boss, "I need to see you now."

Josh Hunter rarely demanded anything unless she screwed up. To her knowledge she hadn't but his tone indicated a problem. She asked, "Is something wrong? All I did was –"

"Just make my office your next stop, please," he cut her off. "I'll explain it then."

Something was wrong. Hunter uttered the word *please* as often as Atlanta saw snow so hearing it rang odd to her.

Fifteen minutes later, she eased the Camaro into its parking place then checked her face and clothes for evidence of her shameless chocolate bender before heading into the station.

The instant Savannah walked through the front door, she knew something was wrong. All conversation ceased upon her entrance. The desk sergeant and officers lingering around the sergeant's kiosk instantly fell silent. Some turned away. None looked her in the eye. A knot formed in her stomach and suddenly her munchies threatened to rebel. When cops blatantly ignored another cop, something *really* bad happened.

As she passed, the desk sergeant gave her an unsmiling, awkward nod. She reconsidered that. It looked embarrassed, not just awkward. The one quality Savannah never associated with the desk sergeant was embarrassment. The brusque fellow who griped her out for stupid, inconsequential things actually seemed too uncomfortable to make eye contact. That, along with the others flagrantly snubbing her presence hustled her to Josh's office. Whatever it was, it was bad. Bad enough no one wanted to tell her.

She knocked twice on Hunter's door – she didn't wait for him to summon her inside. "What happened?" she blurted. "What's wrong?" She'd asked Josh the question but looked to Ennis, who sat nearby, for an answer.

"Sit down, Savannah." Josh's tone was too gentle. Not his boss voice, but a friend's voice. The fear soured to nausea. Cops didn't tell people to sit down unless someone they loved either died or was badly injured. She learned that as a rookie – always have the person sit because you're about to destroy their world…

Ennis patted the seat next to him. His face offered no hints, no help of why she was there and why her boss treated her so delicately. "Is Georgia okay?" she asked. "Seth? The kids?"

"Everyone's fine," Josh replied. "That's not why you're here." He reached to his desk and picked up a padded envelope that resided in a plastic evidence bag.

From the corner of her eye, Savannah saw Ennis wipe a hand down his face with a strained sigh. She retrieved her glasses to examine the envelope. It was addressed to the desk sergeant at her precinct. Still, her mind drew a blank even as her vision shifted to the return address. Written in bold block letters it read "A Reminder."

Josh retrieved another evidence bag, this one containing a DVD. Things began clicking into place. The package and DVD, Josh's compassion toward her and the looks – or lack thereof – from fellow officers. Cole sent a video of Jeffrey beating and torturing her, knowing her colleagues and officers would view it. "Oh sweet Lord." When she spoke, she scarcely recognized her own voice. "Did the sergeant…" she swallowed hard, her words trembled with growing emotion, "and the officers…" Tears welled in her eyes and her furiously pounding heart slowed to a dull, painful thud. After a moment she forced the words, "Did they see it?"

Josh glanced at Ennis then back to her, "Only the desk sergeant but he didn't watch much. Said he couldn't bear to."

A swift chill sank to her bones. Flashes appeared of her naked body spreadeagled and straining against the chains binding her. The sound of Jeffrey's cane slicing the air then slamming against her back. The screams tearing her throat until she could barely speak. The bleeding welts on her thighs, the ones on her breasts. *The desk sergeant saw it all…*

The nausea percolated to the surface until she bolted for Hunter's trash can. Two good heaves later, her donut binge was as exposed as her body and horrific agony on the video.

Josh continued, "He also said he watched it in the video room, away from most of the officers. He also said he was sorry, that if he'd known he'd have immediately handed it to me for evidence."

Savannah barely heard him. She gripped his desk for stability because the room spun and her legs went weak. If she thought the mayor was an expert terrorist, she quickly rediscovered – and underestimated – Cole Jordan's potential.

The images on the video from a camera mounted only feet from her would destroy her in the department. Her reputation and self-esteem would cease to exist and she'd struggled for months to reclaim the latter. All destroyed in one brief morning. And the desk sergeant saw it all. Then Josh's words finally registered. *Oh, mother of Jesus,* "*Most* of the officers?" The shrillness of her own voice startled her. She stared at Hunter, shocked by her outburst and overwhelmed by the emotions coursing through her. Alarm. Rage. Helplessness.

And fear. She'd tried suppressing it but with Cole contacting people – people she worked with and God knew who else – fear made perfect sense and it had her locked in its jaws.

Ennis touched her arm, tried to bring her into his embrace, "Only a couple saw it."

She pushed him back, feeling another wave of sickness rising. She leaned over the trash bin and heaved until her stomach had no more to give. Tears slid down her cheeks. "Ennis," she asked, unwilling and unable to meet his gaze, "did you see it?"

He tenderly squeezed her shoulder, "No, babe, I didn't."

The tears threatened to break into a veritable flood. She thanked God he hadn't. She couldn't handle him seeing the brutality, misery and degradation Jeffrey inflicted.

"Take the rest of the day off," Hunter said softly. "Mathis can work the case this afternoon."

Savannah covered her mouth to curb her sickness. Nodding, she muttered her thanks.

"Ennis, go with her. She shouldn't be alone right now."

"No," she countered, slowly gathering her poise, "I'll be fine. He can stay. I'll be okay, really." She intended to leave via the back door to avoid eye contact with any living soul. She doubted she could look the desk sergeant – or any officer for that matter – in the eye again.

Ennis trailed behind, "Babe, we'll handle this, I promise."

"We can't, Ennis," she headed straight for the restroom. Both ends needed relief now and she prayed she could pee without simultaneously puking. "Cole is going to keep doing this until he destroys me. We can't *handle* this." There was only one way to attempt to fix it. The one way she vowed never to take. "He's forcing me to see Jeffrey."

Ennis grasped her arm, the fingers closed firmly enough to stop her, "No. I don't care what Cole does but you're not seeing Holland."

"*I* care, Ennis. That's me on that video, not you. That's not your naked, beaten body that the sergeant saw, those weren't your screams he heard. They're mine." She continued to the restroom while finishing, "Who knows where Cole will send the next one? To the chief, the mayor, the news media? I have to stop this if I can."

22

The parking lot shimmered white-hot under the glaring sun. By the time she climbed into her car, her blouse was soaked with sweat and beads of perspiration formed on her forehead. Her face pulsed with every beat of her heart. She was devastated, humiliated and angry beyond words. Cole sent that video to the sergeant because she'd not "bowed" to Jeffrey's wishes. She "disobeyed" his demands to see him. Now he exacted his revenge the only way he could. By destroying her dignity and her professional life.

An all-encompassing terror suddenly engulfed her. Had Cole sent the video to the chief or the media or even the mayor? She tried to calm down, to think logically. Cole took orders, she reminded herself. She assumed that Jeffrey somehow told him to fire a warning shot. Jeffrey used strategy, enjoyed playing games. He was a chess player, unlike Cole. As stated, the video meant to *remind* her Jeffrey demanded her presence. To ensure she complied, he stored plenty of ammunition for the future. At least, she expected so.

The racking chill began to ebb as the car's interior heat warmed her skin, eased her shaking. Her stomach still cramped and gnawed at her, leaving her teetering on the verge of sickness. Jeffrey may have been methodical but Cole was a wildcard. If one video caused her misery, why wouldn't he toss in another one or two just for good measure? She'd throw herself off a cliff before dialing the mayor or media so she opted for Georgia, praying he hadn't inflicted the horrors on her sister as well.

Georgia picked up on the third ring. "Did you get your mail today?" Savannah asked, trying desperately to settle her voice, to steady it.

"Yes," the older sister replied with considerably more calm. "Why? What's wrong? You sound upset."

"Those videos of the victims. Jeffrey's victims. Remember those?"

Georgia's voice took on the same thread of alarm, "I remember. Savannah, what's happened?"

"Cole sent one to the station," her voice betrayed her, allowing the panic to surface. "The one of me."

The reply came as a whisper, "Oh my God."

"The desk sergeant saw it and so did a few other officers. Georgia," her composure crumbled fast, "what am I going to do? What if he sent that thing to the media?"

"Calm down, hon. Where are you?"

Savannah wiped away more growing tears, "The station." A crushing paranoia swept through her. What if he was watching her? What if Cole Jordan sat nearby laughing at her humiliation? Or what if he acted alone, sending the video to tip her off balance enough to make *his* move? After all, Jeffrey sat behind bars. Cole freely roamed the streets and his stepbrother denied him his pleasure at the cabin. Jeffrey mutilated the women, Cole raped them. Cole never got his chance with her but swore he would someday. She'd underestimated him once – had she done so again? Maybe *A Reminder* was Cole's idea of *reminding* her of that vile promise.

The terror that dominated her entire existence for months suddenly rushed back. It swept over her like a black storm, obliterating everything in sight except Cole's face and his horrifyingly malicious vow.

She searched all around her, her vision darting from one car to another, searching for that familiar face, the one that was supposed to be an ally, a fellow cop. Cole was there somewhere. She sensed his nearness, his contempt, but most of all she felt his insatiable need for revenge.

"...right now. Savannah? Are you still there?" Georgia's panicked voice demanded.

She swallowed back a modicum of the fear racing through her, tried to sound in control, "I'm here."

"Come over right now."

"I can't. I'll put you in danger. If Cole is after me, I'm not putting you at risk. I did that once, I won't do it again."

"That wasn't your fault. If you're not calm enough to drive, I'll come get you."

"Don't," she barked then apologized. "He wants me, Georgia. I couldn't cope if you were in jeopardy. I gotta go."

"Wait. What are you going to do?"

In her heart she knew Cole hadn't the intelligence to act alone.

He needed Jeffrey for instructions and guidance. Savannah closed her eyes, gritted her teeth. She prayed this day would never come. She had to face the monster again – one last time. "I have to stop these videos and there's only one person who can do it."

O O O

Savannah drove for half an hour outside the city to Norcross Maximum Security Prison. She spent the time shoring up her courage, and steeling herself against the evil that awaited.

Of all her duties as a detective, it was visits to the autopsy suite and to prisons she dreaded most. Though she knew she was more uneasy about prisons than her male colleagues, she couldn't afford to reveal any vulnerability, especially inside. Men – whether cops or prisoners – were too good at spotting weaknesses, and they would inevitably aim for those sensitive places with their barbs and insults. She had learned to maintain a stoic front when entering such facilities but this one was different. It housed Jeffrey Holland.

Today she would come face to face with the man who tried to kill her. The scars across her back suddenly tightened when she moved, making her keenly aware of their presence. All the wounds and resulting scars drummed out a dull ache as if sensing where she was.

Savannah gripped the steering wheel, focusing on her goal, not her physical afflictions. Facing Holland again would require all her strength and fortitude.

She hadn't slept well that night. Jeffrey crept back into her dreams, his image becoming all too frequent the last week. And as usual she'd awakened drenched in sweat, her back and shoulder aching from the old wounds. Perhaps it was a premonition of the day's events, her subconscious reminding that she'd never get peace from Jeffrey, especially as long as Cole roamed free.

Sitting in the parking lot, she yearned to turn the car around and drive away, anything to avoid the ordeal that awaited her. She didn't have to be here, she tried to reason, but in her gut she knew she did.

So she threw on her emotional armor and shoved open the car door. Pride kept her walking with grim determination into the building. It propelled her through the security check-in at the outer control desk where she presented her badge and handed in her weapon. As she waited for an escort, she attempted to settle her thundering heart by reading the warnings and dress code posted in the visitor process area: *The following items are not allowed to be worn by any visitor: Any clothing that displays obscene, inflammatory or gang related affiliation. Any clothing similar to that issued to an inmate or uniformed personnel. Drawstring clothing. Easy access clothing. Extremely loose fitting clothing. Winter coats, gloves…*

"Detective Prince, I'm Officer Burke. Come this way."

Savannah turned. Burke fit the description of a professional wrestler. Bulky shoulders, large muscular arms and powerful legs filled out his gray uniform. She estimated his age around thirty-eight with fine lines beginning at his eyes. The job wore people down on all fronts with the grind of the schedule and working with inmates. Prison guards were hard to find these days, at least the ones who made the job a career.

With his crew-cut, rigid posture and pristinely starched pressed uniform, Savannah pegged him as ex-military. She witnessed the same fanatical attention to detail from her brother even now, years after his service.

Burke struck up a friendly conversation as he escorted her through the first locked door and into the pedestrian trap. They discussed the miserable heat then moved on to baseball scores and commiserated about the Braves' lack of wins that season. She wondered if he would be so pleasant had she not been law enforcement.

They approached a small desk with a walkthrough metal detector. He instructed her to remove her shoes, belt, jacket, watch and keys and place them on the table for his examination. Savannah sat her keys down, took off her Timex then proceeded to shrug off her suit jacket. There was something uncomfortably intimate about the process. As she unbuckled her belt and pulled it from the pant loops, she felt Burke staring at her the way a man watches a woman undress. She removed her loafers, sat them down and coolly met Officer Burke's gaze. Only then did he avert his eyes.

She did a mental eye roll. Men. His visual appraisal only enhanced her appreciation for Ennis. From day one he treated her with both professional and personal respect. He never eyed her in a manner that made her uneasy.

Once she turned her pockets inside out and stepped through the metal detector, Burke instructed, "You can put everything back on now."

Norcross had a state-of-the-art computer operated security system and numerous surveillance cameras. Inmates and as well as visitors were constantly being monitored, no matter where they went.

She and Burke stepped through a steel door, down a long hallway and threw another series of barred gates. Savannah was fully aware that every move she made was being watched. With just a few taps on a computer keyboard, guards could lock down every passage, every cell without leaving their control room. The clang of heavy doors closing behind her caused her chest to constrict. Now was not the time for claustrophobia but the deeper they traveled into the bowels of the facility, the tighter her chest felt. The seed of panic would bloom full force if she didn't concentrate on her breathing. Long and slow. In and out. Show no weakness, she repeated to herself.

At the entrance to Cell Block B, a voice on the intercom instructed her to hold up her pass against the window for inspection. The steel gate slid open and they entered Cell Block B's dayroom. The couch and chairs were bolted to the floor and for entertainment there was a ping-pong table and wall-mounted TV set. Several prisoners dressed in bright orange jumpsuits mingled in the common area. A few watched TV while others stood or played ping-pong. As if they sensed Burke's and Savannah's presence, they all simultaneously turned and stared.

In particular, they stared at Savannah, the only woman in the room. For a moment, the only sound was the TV. She gazed straight back at the prisoners, refusing to be intimidated even though she could guess what each man was surely thinking.

As they passed by the cells, Savannah pictured Jeffrey standing behind the bars of his own windowless cage, the opaque door showing only indistinct movement outside the small room. She imagined him lying on the mattress, his eyes closed as he spun fantasies that would appall any normal human being. But they would excite Holland. He would lie sweating, aroused by the screams of women echoing in his head.

A mechanical snap unlocked the door to the visitation room and Savannah stood staring at it. Behind the door sat her personal demon. The one she failed to exorcise from her thoughts during the day, the one that inspired crippling terrors at night. Opening the door meant opening Pandora's Box. People always assumed evil appeared crazy. That it threatened with teeth bared and glowing eyes. People assumed evil was easy to recognize. Savannah knew different. Evil possessed charm, a gentle voice and a disarming smile. Evil's touch could be tender at times, brushing tears from weeping eyes, tracing a path along the skin or softly caressing a woman's breast. She knew by experience evil was not easy to recognize. The proof sat right behind that door…

She urged herself to step toward the door but something held her back. She had no gun, no protection whatsoever. If Jeffrey lunged for her, how would she defend herself?

Officer Burke glanced at her, "You can go in now."

She continued staring at the gateway to the worst and most agonizing memories of her life. Once she entered the lair, there was no turning back. Jeffrey would sense her fear, see it, feel it, smell it. And that too would excite him. That smile – the one that haunted her day and night – would crawl across his face with satisfaction with the knowledge he still held that power over her.

She couldn't afford to let him in her head. Allowing him to control her emotions condemned her to a life of clawing her way back to normal and falling short each time. "He's restrained, right?" she asked just to be sure.

"Handcuffed, yes," Burke replied. As if reading her thoughts, he added, "And there's a guard too. I doubt the prisoner will try anything, Detective."

The prisoner. That's all Jeffrey Holland was to this man. Anonymous. A man among hundreds.

She took a slow deep breath to brace herself then she opened the door.

When she stepped in the small visitation room, her claustrophobia constricted her throat and chest like a fist closing around them. The beginnings of perspiration formed almost instantly. Her heart stampeded in her chest. It was already going awry and if she didn't rein in her terror, Jeffrey won again – this time without saying a word.

The gray room reminded her of a cave. The light, adequate enough for most people, seemed too muted and eerie to her, as though she'd accessed the deepest, darkest recesses of her nightmares and Holland lurked in a dark corner.

Instead of Jeffrey, she was relieved to see the armed guard in the corner, standing right behind the man she came to see.

Jeffrey Holland sat at the square metal table, dressed in his own bright orange jumpsuit. His dark hair had grown to his collar and stubble still shadowed his jaw. With the exception of some weight loss, he looked exactly the same. He still retained the hard muscle she remembered. The strength to overpower and restrain a woman, to physically force her to submit to his will. Sitting there, his hands folded in his lap and a docile – almost friendly – smile would fool most people. He concealed the evil just far enough beneath the surface that it lulled a person to believe they were in the presence of an average, attractive individual. But it didn't lull Savannah. It put her even more on edge. His meek façade was just that. A façade. Jeffrey Holland was still a mighty force. Anyone stupid enough to misjudge the man's strength would find themselves overpowered and dead.

Her vision drifted down his face and chest until stopping at his hands. Handcuffs encircled his wrists which provided a degree of security for her racing, panicked mind. She battled painful memories of those hands slamming a cane against her, of them carving a number into her flesh with a scalpel.

She was safe, she told herself. He couldn't touch her or hurt her. The guard would stop him which he did when Jeffrey began to stand. The guard put a firm hand to Holland's shoulder, preventing it. Jeffrey momentarily closed his eyes, inhaled long and deep, "I love the smell of lavender." He glanced at the guard behind him, "Only woman I've met who smells of lavender even when she sweats." His attention shifted to Savannah, motioned with his hands, "Welcome, Detective. Please have a seat."

Her heart pounded so hard and fast it made her slightly dizzy.

Her lungs refused to cooperate. Firmly seized in the clutches of panic, they compressed smaller and smaller until she nearly bolted back through the door. Stop, she pleaded with herself. Stop falling apart. Stop falling apart in front of *him*. Instead of racing from the room, she pushed herself to calm down, to quietly ease into the chair across from him. *You can do this. You conquered the monster once, you can do it again.*

The last time she saw Holland, he forced his way into her home and tried to kill her – again. She managed to stop him thanks to her golf clubs being nearby. One good swing brought him down with a broken leg. All she needed was one more to kill him – but Ennis had stopped her.

"Savannah," Jeffrey sing-songed. He'd leaned nearer to her while she'd been reliving the horrors she'd endured. When he nudged even closer, she pushed back in her chair to gain needed space between them. Even shackled and caged, Jeffrey exuded a lethal, menacing presence. Like the chill in the air, it was invisible but palpable.

He found her reaction amusing, "Calm down. I don't bite." Then he teased, "Yet."

"I'm fine."

"Savannah," his voice lilted. "You can't lie to me. I can read a person's body, especially yours and no, you're not fine." He tapped the side of his neck, "Your heart is racing. I can see the carotid drumming against your skin." He interlaced his fingers, sat a little straighter, "Tell me, what's causing it? I doubt it's me. I'm handcuffed, there are cameras watching us and this fine fellow behind me will keep me in line. So what is causing Savannah's panic attack?"

"I'm fine," she said, dabbed at the perspiration on her forehead. She said it aloud more for herself than him. She had to get hold of herself before he figured it out. Because Jeffrey Holland was right. He could read her, at least to some degree.

As expected, recognition dawned in his features, "It's the room, isn't it? A small, windowless room. The walls feel as though they're closing in and you feel like you're suffocating." His head tilted a degree, "So *that's* your Achilles' heel. Claustrophobia. Wish I'd known that when we were together. Things would have turned out so much differently."

"I'm fine," she reiterated with stern conviction.

"Breathe through your nose," he did so, "and hold for three seconds then exhale slowly. Repeat until you're calmer. Don't look at me that way, Savannah. I'm trying to help."

Help her? Right. Savannah saw the delight in his eyes, the satisfaction that he'd discovered her one and only true vulnerability. It didn't take a genius to see the wheels churning in his head, conjuring horrific scenarios to break her spirit using that vulnerability. She tried directing the conversation back, "Where is Cole?"

Jeffrey studied her, his gaze too penetrating for comfort. His dark eyes felt invasive the way they wandered over her. Finally his vision swept back up to hers, "You look different. Put on a few pounds." He waited for a reply that never came. He proceeded, "Have you seen your OB-Gyn yet? It's important to see your doctor as soon as you know you're pregnant."

Shock practically dropped her jaw. How could he possibly know? It was too early in the pregnancy for anyone to actually see the signs, wasn't it? Ennis had no clue, *no one* around her had mentioned the possibility of pregnancy. How the hell did Jeffrey notice so soon?

"You're around two months, I'd say. Bad time for you, I imagine. Morning sickness, clothes don't fit and," he nodded to her blouse, "things are getting bigger each day." He waited again but this time he smiled, "Ah, you're surprised I noticed. I told you, it's a doctor's job to read the body. And I know yours best of all."

Savannah squirmed in her seat. She'd come to wring answers from Jeffrey and instead got ambushed by his keen observation. Okay, she told herself. *He knows about my claustrophobia and my baby. That's what makes this trip so imperative. I have to stop him and Cole before I bring a child into the hell called my life.*

"Congratulations," he beamed. "Suppose there's no chance of you naming him Jeffrey if it's a boy, is there?" He gauged her non-reaction then something disturbing replaced his easygoing tone, "Honestly, I think it will be a girl. A baby girl who has Mommy's pretty blue eyes and long dark hair. I hope it's a girl. It will give me another woman to fantasize about. We'll keep it all in the family. How does that sound?"

Sheer black fright swept through her. He'd threatened her unborn child. Savannah's hands fisted as she boldly met his eyes, "*Where is Cole?*"

Evidently disappointed in the lack of banter, he sighed, "Is he causing you problems? Well, he did possess an obsessive streak about you, didn't he? It was difficult but I did prevent him from violating you, didn't I? Not that I'm expecting thanks but you agree I saved you a certain degree of misery, yes?"

The audacity of the man never ceased to amaze her. He beat her within an inch of her life and he wanted credit for stopping Cole? *Give me a break.* "Do you even know where Cole is?"

With smug delight Jeffrey replied, "I'll use your words, Detective. *What do you think?*"

What do you think. Hearing the words brought back memories of when she'd uttered them at the cabin. They unleashed Jeffrey Holland's wrath and in their wake – a savage beating that nearly killed her.

Swallowing back the queasiness, she regrouped her anger at the man across from her, "I think you lured me here with a lie. I also think you'll die in here and it won't bother me in the least."

"Then before you leave, listen. If Cole shared a video of your..." he paused for effect then smirked, "*experience*, I can help you. I may not have an exact address but I know Cole. He won't stray far from his obsession."

"How can you help me?" she challenged. "You have no clue to his whereabouts."

"I'm disappointed. I'd hoped you'd learned not to underestimate me."

"Don't play with me, Jeffrey, I –"

"Detective, you remember how I play and it's not with words. I can help but my information isn't free. In exchange for it, I have a few demands."

Of course he had demands. Jeffrey Holland thrived on them and she refused to hear them. She angrily rose from her seat, headed directly for the door.

"My stepbrother has a mind of his own, Savannah. You know Cole." From the corner of her eye she saw Jeffrey circle his finger around his temple. "*Muy loco.* No telling what he'll do next. Let's be reasonable. Isn't it exhausting to always look over your shoulder, wondering if he's lurking around, waiting to fulfill those malicious vows to sexually assault you? Doesn't it concern you that your *experience* can be viewed by anyone he chooses to send it to? You and your sister share more than your beauty. You both have successful careers. You are both private women and you both have *experiences* that can be shared with the world. I promise he will use your sister's video to hurt you."

Her hand gripped the door handle until the knuckles blanched white. Now the truth came out. Jeffrey threatened not only her but her child and now Georgia. The mere scope of the situation made her head ache. "And you can stop him?" Because if he answered yes, she'd be on her way to the warden's office making demands of her own. Firstly to see the visitors log then she'd interview every guard associated with Jeffrey. After that she'd troll his mail and pick his cell apart with her bare hands to find out how he communicated with Cole.

"No, I can't. But you can – with my help. Just agree to my terms."

This was way too stressful for her, she thought. She needed to get out, away from him before she literally lost her mind. She hadn't bargained on this chess game of his. Not to this extent. "What do you want?"

The question pleased Jeffrey. He leaned back with the same cocky smirk. His gamble paid off, he assumed, the threat of Georgia's video convinced her to capitulate. He lifted his cuffed hands into view, "As you can see, my needs in life have simplified. I only have a few paltry requests."

She watched his hands lift to his shoulder and tap beneath his right collarbone. "First, I want to see my creation," he said.

Paltry? He considered that *paltry*? The scars of brutality he deemed paltry had altered her life forever. It inspired a paranoia that refused to wane. It caused her to be ultra-vigilant about her every move, wary of every noise she heard.

Paltry? *That bastard...* "That's what you want?" she growled. "To see what you did to me?" Georgia's devastated features crept into her mind. If that video saw the light of day, it would not only ruin Georgia's career but her as a person. The cheerful, kindhearted, gentle lady who prided herself on modesty and refinement would be utterly destroyed by the humiliation.

Jeffrey forced a harsh reality on his reluctant guest. Savannah had to consider more than herself now. With the baby, with her sister. It wasn't just about her anymore. What she needed was time. Maybe even a week to start a serious search for Cole Jordan. But to buy that week and her sister's privacy, she had to bend to Jeffrey's will, at least a little.

With shaking hands, she unbuttoned her blouse partway, pulled it and her bra strap aside to reveal the scars he'd left behind. The unmistakable "1" and the faded, light-handed shadow of a "0". "There, Jeffrey," she bit. "There's your *creation.*"

Jeffrey's vision locked onto the scars. It was sharp, unblinking, entranced. His piercing gaze made the scars ache but she stood rigid, her jaw set. *Go ahead and stare, you bastard, 'cause it's all you'll ever get…*

She began buttoning her blouse but he wagged a finger at her, "Not so fast, Savannah. If you're too eager to deny me, I will assume you are uninterested in finding Cole." He motioned to her blouse, "I've waited months for this. Let me enjoy it."

Her hands trembled as they resumed buttoning the blouse. *Let me enjoy it?* The meeting – and her body's reactions – quickly spun out of control. She struggled to reclaim the upper hand and bent toward Jeffrey, "Give me real information."

Undaunted, he too leaned forward, boldly meeting her gaze, "I've given you real information, Detective. Cole has not strayed far from his obsession."

"That could mean anything. He hasn't left Atlanta? The country? Planet Earth?"

"I could easily give my information to the district attorney. I'm sure he'd listen. I'd get perks for it too. Different prison, more privileges, or perhaps a reduced sentence. After all, I've only been convicted of assaulting a law enforcement officer. Not murder."

"Not yet, you mean."

"Savannah, those videos don't show me killing anyone. You

remember. You watched one."

The lingering sickness crept up her throat as images of Leigh Watney, one of the victims was beaten and raped. Jeffrey and Cole forced her to watch Leigh's brutality before beginning her own journey into hell. And no, the video never showed Leigh's death. Only her suffering at the hands of Jeffrey and Cole.

Jeffrey continued, "And those journals the police found are not in my handwriting. That leaves only one person who could have written those deplorable accounts."

The meaning of his words finally registered with her. He planned to blame Cole for the killings. Despite the videos lacking evidence of who murdered the women, Jeffrey deluded himself if he assumed he'd go free.

"There's more evidence against Cole than against me. I'm not foolish enough to believe I won't serve time but I'll bet you a nice steak dinner that I'm out of prison before Cole."

"Not if I can help it."

"Fingerprints will be his downfall, Detective Prince *hyphen* Rutherford."

The insulting inflection he placed on "hyphen" annoyed her. She never officially hyphenated her married name. When she took her vows, she dove into the deep end, only using her maiden name for professional purposes. Her driver's license and her social security card had her married name. Even the IRS knew her as "Savannah Rutherford". So take that, Jeffrey *hyphen* asshole Holland.

"Cole's fingerprints were all over that cabin and barn," he continued. "*His* prints were plastered on the chest freezer where he stored his wife's dead, mutilated body. *His* prints were found on her body. My prints were absent from the cabin, the barn, the freezer and the body. So much evidence against him. So little against me. Let's see how harshly a jury of my peers judges me." Jeffrey still held solid eye contact, "For now, you should worry about those videos. Cole will probably send them to people you know *and* people who control your career. He'll likely publish your sister's video as well and her adoring public will see a new side to their lovely author. Lose your pride, Savannah, and save yourself and your sister. Allow me my time with you and you, not the D.A., will find Cole." He motioned to the chair she vacated, "Let's negotiate, shall we?"

Dealing with the devil. Desperate people did this. Tragic, desperate people who felt boxed in and hopeless. Savannah was all four. To stand a sliver of a chance at peace for herself and Georgia, she had to sit down with Jeffrey and at least pretend to negotiate.

So she eased into the seat with a promise to herself. She refused to barter away her dignity, no matter what the bastard offered. "What else do you want?" What else could possibly interest him besides seeing his *creation*?

He smiled and she cringed. She truly hated his smile. For such a simple act, it held several different meanings. From phony pleasant interaction to a sadistic forewarning of what awaited her. She recognized the nuance of this smile. She saw it frequently at the cabin and it meant one thing – *I'm in control, you're not.*

When his vision settled to hers, a chill raked her. His brown eyes darkened to black holes that threatened to suck the air from the room, the life from her. "I rarely get visitors of substance," he said. "Reporters, yes. And what they claim are lawyers but I question their competency level. My requests are simple. One, I want to see my creation which you've complied with. Two, I want to *touch* my creation before you leave and three, I want you to visit me every week without fail. I would ask for more but," he winked, "I don't want to appear greedy." He rose a few inches from his seat, making Savannah press back in hers. Her reaction seemed to please him as he reached his cuffed hands out for a handshake, "Do we have a deal?"

Savannah stared at the outstretched hands, remembering the pain they inflicted. With a scalpel, he drew pleas from women they never thought possible and promises they knew were useless. She couldn't bring herself to speak or draw her vision away from his flawlessly smooth hands. Nausea climbed her throat at the thought of touching Jeffrey Holland or agreeing to his deal. Holding a hand to her stomach, a sudden image materialized in her mind. The baby. If the situation adversely affected her, she dreaded to think what her child felt. That image shored up her courage. The baby was her first priority. That meant ensuring neither Jeffrey nor Cole could harm her or her family.

Jeffrey waited, measuring her reaction then finally tapped his wrist, "Tick tock, Savannah. My offer expires in twenty seconds. I'm surprised it's taking this long, actually. You seem like a smart girl so think about this logically. You show up and we brainstorm about where

Cole might be. Eventually you get what you want and I get a little of what I want." He kept his hand available to her, obviously expecting her to shake on the twisted deal.

She closed her eyes, tried to concentrate. Between protecting the baby, Georgia and herself, it all seemed so insurmountable. Reason dictated she couldn't protect everyone from everything but her heart said she should try.

A cold touch on her cheek drew her back with a gasp as the guard shoved Jeffrey back in his seat. Holland chuckled, "My, you *are* jumpy these days. That's why my offer should appeal to you. It would give you peace of mind."

Bile rose in her throat, burning like acid. Jeffrey *touched* her. The earlier wave of sickness intensified and she struggled to push it down. The last time she felt his touch was as he drew her head back to slice her throat. The vile, frigid touch caused a tide of memories to flood back.

"Peace of mind is priceless in your condition and your deal is running short of time. Five... four... three..."

She opened her mouth to speak but nothing came out. She struggled between lying to placate him and flat out telling him to shove it. Either way the odds were he'd never disclose Cole's location.

"Two," he continued.

The door to the room slammed open, startling her. She jerked so hard it felt like someone snapped her spine. The figure in the doorway made her cringe the way kids cowered from angry parents. Ennis stood, hands rolled into fists, his expression so furious it pressed her back in the chair. The only good point – he aimed the molten glare at Jeffrey, not her.

Jeffrey's reaction to Ennis's abrupt entrance: nothing. He merely leaned back and folded his hands in his lap as her husband stalked in.

Anger poured off Ennis in waves. She felt the heat from his ire as his dark eyes shifted from Jeffrey to her. The moment she and Ennis locked gazes, she flinched.

"Tell me why you're in the same room with this animal," her husband demanded.

Holland sighed at Ennis, annoyed at the interruption, "Do you mind? This is a private conversation."

Ennis bristled at the sound of Jeffrey's voice. He rounded the table, leaned to Jeffrey's ear. He whispered something inaudible then pounded the table with his fist. The sound echoed through the small room, forcing Savannah to try and remain composed. Her face darkened with resentment and humiliation. She didn't need or want Ennis to fight her battles. She didn't want Ennis there period. If anyone stood a chance of getting information from Jeffrey it was her, not an overprotective husband and partner.

Whatever Ennis said, it failed to ruffle Jeffrey's poise, "How chivalrous of you but in case you forgot, your wife needs no protecting, especially when armed with a golf club."

"I'm the golf club today, asshole," Ennis growled. "And I'll do more than break your friggin' leg."

Savannah clenched her teeth, fought the rising bitterness. The shock of his abrupt entrance gave way to anger. Anger that he barged in, that he tried to protect her. He'd already begun his campaign by threatening Jeffrey. And for what? To salve his own conscience? If memory served her, she hadn't required protecting when she swung that golf club. And if Ennis bothered to remember, *she'd* tried to break more than Jeffrey's leg too. After snapping his leg with her driver, she'd swung back to crush his skull, to end Jeffrey Holland's existence. But then Ennis stopped her. It had taken every bit of his strength, he'd said, to pry the driver from her hands and prevent her from ending Jeffrey's life. At times Savannah resented him for that too. Had he allowed her to finish the bastard off, she wouldn't be standing in a prison bargaining to keep those videos away from the public.

"Savannah and I are in the middle of negotiations," Jeffrey stated. "I believe she was about to accept my offer when you stormed in."

Ennis spun to face her. Now his menacing stare settled on her, "What offer?"

Jeffrey wagged a finger at him, "That, Detective Rutherford, is private as well. Step outside while she and I discuss this."

Ennis's fists curled tighter at his sides, "What offer, Savannah?"

"I'll explain later," was all she said. It was all she felt comfortable saying. Her nerves were shot, her confidence deflated and with it, her hopes of temporarily ending the nightmare of publicized videos. She dreaded telling Georgia. Dreaded admitting failure. If Ennis hadn't interrupted, she stood a chance of at least *delaying* another fiasco. Now she worried whose video came next – hers or Georgia's. Or both, perhaps. Cole was an unpredictable son of a bitch.

In two long strides Ennis was at her side, his fingers closing around her elbow, "I'm taking you home." He tried pulling her up only for her to resist. She yanked at her arm but his fingers constricted, digging between the bones. He dropped the words like stones, "He's playing you and you're letting him."

Savannah trained her vision on Jeffrey who watched intently. He seemed amused at the display – Ennis trying to take control and Savannah trying to retain it. She couldn't allow Holland to sense weakness in her. One crack in her armor and he'd take advantage of it. This wasn't over, despite what Ennis assumed. Swooping in and hauling her out only solidified her determination. Jeffrey would reveal Cole's location, even if she had to bring that trusty driver with her next time.

She answered calmly, "I know what he's doing and I'm not going home."

Ennis physically dragged her to her feet, "*Yes, you are.*"

Jeffrey chuckled at Ennis, "She's a stubborn one, isn't she? And strong too. My leg still aches from that swing she's got." He bent to raise his pant leg, looked at Savannah, "Would you like to see *my* scar? Seems only fair since you allowed me to see yours."

Savannah wilted inside, her heart dropped. Jeffrey's announcement would create a firestorm with Ennis – as he knew it would.

Using her captive arm, Ennis jerked her to face him, "You *what?*" He refused to wait for an answer, evidently, because he headed for the door with her in tow. His hold tightened slightly to counter any debate.

"Still waiting on your answer, Savannah," Jeffrey called. "There's not much time left."

Once outside the room, Ennis waited for the door to shut then his hands clasped her shoulders and hauled her to her tiptoes. Her anger escalated. She'd worked hard to brace herself for this meeting, to develop impenetrable armor against Jeffrey. For the most part it succeeded until Ennis barged in and took over, leaving her empty of answers she so desperately needed. Thanks to him, the whole trip turned out to be futile – and that infuriated her.

Ennis never manhandled her but today he did a pretty convincing job and for a long moment his strength overrode his rage. His hands clutched her in a viselike grasp, the fingertips again sinking into her flesh. It hurt enough she quietly whimpered, wrenching against his unyielding hold.

Her struggle tightened his grip as he pulled her flush against his body, "Stop fightin' me."

She could feel his hot angry breath on her face, the steel hardness of his muscles. "Then let go," she growled back. "It hurts."

Ennis eased up on his hold but fell far short of letting her go, "Have you lost your mind? You're giving him what he wants. He wants to see the damage he caused, the pain you suffered. He's enjoying this."

"You don't understand," she argued. *I'm pregnant and I have to stop this before it affects our child. I won't allow Jeffrey or Cole to be a part of our baby's life. They've destroyed too much as it is.*

"Make me understand. Why would you risk coming here and going through all that misery again."

"Because I have to stop those videos. Because I can't live in fear forever. Because you stopped me from killing him and ending this once and for all." And there it was. It fell out of her mouth before she could stop it. She hadn't wanted to hammer him with it but she had. Now came the repercussions.

Ennis's hands fell from her shoulders. He took a deep breath and looked heavenward as if asking for help. Finally he blew out the breath, "That's what this is about? Me preventing you from committing murder?"

"Don't try to guilt me, Ennis. Not after what he did to me and Georgia and all those women. He deserved to die." The last of her statement flew out with the heated animosity she'd bottled up the past few minutes. *He* didn't suffer in that cabin, *he* didn't shed a drop of blood and *he* hadn't screamed so hard it stripped his voice and made his throat and lungs ache. And because of that he'd never comprehend the depth of her hatred for Jeffrey.

Her vehemence backed him off a step, "He does deserve to die, I'm not arguing that. But I doubt *you're* capable of living with the knowledge you took a man's life, no matter if he deserved it or not."

His feeble consolation fueled her anger, "I wouldn't be here, in this prison, talking to him if you'd let me bash that bastard's head in."

Ennis stared at her in disbelief, "Listen to yourself. You're either out of your mind or something else is driving you. What is going on?"

He'd pointedly asked and Savannah would pointedly avoid it. First, she wasn't willing to sacrifice their child to a psychopath and his crazy step-brother. Second, she wanted to stop hers and Georgia's videos from being splashed over the news, internet and God knew where else. "He wants me to visit him every week and he'll give me Cole's location. Before you lecture me, I know he won't do it but I was trying, *trying* to buy some time. I don't want another video popping up somewhere, like the news media or mayor. Not until I can sort out what to do next."

His hands returned to her shoulders again, this time in a gentler hold, "Then let me help. It'll be a big mistake if you accept that asshole's deal."

Did he honestly believe she was that stupid? "I wasn't going to, Ennis. I was going to lie to him. It would buy me a week. Then if I didn't make any headway on finding Cole, I… Hell, I didn't know what to do next. I didn't get to that point because you walked in. How did you find me anyway?"

"Georgia told me you were probably here."

Great. Little Miss Tattletale. Normally she'd be angry at Georgia's meddling but she was too tired. Between Jeffrey and Ennis, they drained every ounce of her energy. Weariness seeped to her bones. She was so tired of worrying and dealing with Jeffrey and Cole. She feared she'd never be free of them.

A tender touch on her cheek lifted her vision to Ennis. The hardness melted from his warm brown eyes, "Let me help you. Let me start now." He released her but not before giving her a brief but calming kiss. He stepped to the door and opened it, "Whatever you offered, cram it because she's not coming near you again."

23

The picture in his wallet showed a beaming beauty, her arms wrapped around him in a loving embrace. Her radiant expression told the world she adored the man held. Anyone who knew her realized how rare this look was, and how unlikely it was for her to ever wear a wedding dress.

Ennis stared at that photo, remembered back to that day in Texas, friends and family gathered to celebrate his and Savannah's nuptials. He'd never seen his partner so jittery. Normally bold and confident, Savannah looked thoroughly petrified as her brother walked her down the aisle. Ennis saw her nervously scan the crowd until Seth leaned to her, whispering. Then her vision rose to meet her groom's, her beautiful blue eyes brimmed with hope and love as she walked down the aisle.

The instant his fingers closed over hers, her brow smoothed and her face relaxed. A sense of pride broadened his chest. Just his touch melted the tension from her posture, stirred a smile from his lovely bride.

Most people never saw the real Savannah, the one who laughed freely, teased with a witty sense of humor but also possessed a fragile confidence at times. Only family saw those parts of her. Fears and worries were kept carefully guarded, locked away sometimes even from those closest to her.

Holding the photo, he stroked the line of her jaw. Lately she'd changed from that happy newlywed and reverted back to the withdrawn brooding from months earlier. Back then he understood her mood since she battled the aftermath of Jeffrey Holland and Cole Jordan. Lately she'd suffered nausea and vomiting. Initially he figured she caught a bug but the longer it lasted, the more he worried about her health. And rescheduling Dr. Wyatt's appointment sent his temper soaring. She knew better, he told himself. She damn well knew better than that.

And going to see Jeffrey? Ennis rubbed his face, aghast that his wife exposed herself to such grief. He empathized with her, realized she wanted the videos to stop but Cole acted on his own. Prison bars removed Jeffrey's power, leaving him incapable of directing his stepbrother. Bargaining with Holland proved he retained control over her and that infuriated Ennis. It also made him question why she considered agreeing to Jeffrey's deal. One lone word answered it. Fear. She was scared enough to negotiate with the devil but why?

After leaving the prison Savannah withdrew and shied away from him. No mention of DVDs, Cole, Jeffrey, nothing. She barely said one word to him all evening, the one being "goodnight." He admitted to roughhousing her at the prison and apologized for it. Disbelief and confusion fueled his anger. He'd seized her shoulders with such force he'd unintentionally hurt her. He felt like a heel about it too. His thumb sank directly into the scars below her collarbone and she'd twisted, trying to free herself from the pain.

A knock on his office door broke his train of thought. He looked up to see Savannah leaning in, "Hunter wants to see us." She glanced at the picture he held, "What's that?"

"Our wedding picture," he answered, placing it back in his wallet. "Just reliving the moment."

Savannah blushed and gifted him with a rare treasure: the smile in their wedding picture. Whew. No sign of upset in that sunny smile. With any luck, she'd forgiven him for yesterday.

She added a wink, "I do it too."

That's encouraging, he breathed a sigh of relief. He halfway figured she'd torn her copy to bits after the fiasco with Jeffrey. He rose from his seat, "Did Hunter say what he wants?"

She shook her head, relayed Josh's message verbatim, "Just said, 'You and Ennis come see me now.'"

He rounded his desk and met her at the door. His hand settled at the small of her back and saw her smile at the gesture. Things weren't so bad after all, he told himself. Not when she flashed *that* grin at him.

They walked in Hunter's office, offered a greeting. Their boss didn't respond. Instead he forewarned, "You might want to sit down."

Savannah lost the vibrant color in her cheeks, "Another video?"

"No, thankfully not, but you should sit down nonetheless."

Ennis saw her shoulders slacken, a tiny remnant of her smile returning. He, on the other hand, sensed a certain vibe from their boss. *This*, it said, was where the shit hit the fan because Josh Hunter looked ready to maim. Neither he nor Savannah sat down. Hunter's news surely wasn't that bad, was it? Yesterday dropped the mother of all bombs on them, testing their courage and fortitude way beyond their means.

Hunter waited for them to sit then gave up, declaring, "The mayor knows you're married."

Ennis couldn't believe the words falling from his boss's mouth. Beside him, Savannah wilted. The trace of the heart-stopping smile faded into history and, he assumed, their professional partnership followed suit. They'd worked hard to keep their marriage under wraps and some officers knew but Ennis doubted they felt chummy enough with the new mayor to blab about it. But Savannah always said – you never know.

"There's more," Josh warned. He hesitated a few beats as if searching for a palatable way to phrase it.

His silence set Ennis on edge. Department rules stated they both be assigned new partners so what was the big deal? It wasn't like one of 'em got transferred to Siberia.

Hunter continued, "He wants me to transfer one of you to another precinct. Specifically, he wants Savannah transferred to Zone 3."

Siberia suddenly sounded pretty good now. Zone 3 was the highest crime zone in Atlanta, Georgia. The murder rate, rape statistics, cop killings – every crime surpassed the rest of the city. And O'Neill wanted her dumped in the middle of it…

If Ennis got hold of the mayor, he'd tear the massive ego driven windbag apart. O'Neill declared war on the wrong cop, he thought. *I'll kill the son of a bitch.*

Ennis chanced a look at his wife. Before the announcement, she stood rigid, preparing for whatever bad news their superior officer presented. Afterward, her knees slackened and she took advantage of the chair behind her, her hands white-knuckled around the armrests. The postscript of Zone 3 inspired an audible swallow from her, "Guess it's time to break out the Kevlar vest."

Ennis's temper burst forth so fierce it stopped a few passing officers in their tracks, "The son of a bitch wants to get personal? Fine. I'll run him and his little brat through the system –"

"Calm down," Josh patted the air. "You both knew it was a matter of time before your marriage became common knowledge. I don't know how the mayor found out but I suspect he's putting Savannah on notice to back off." Hunter rubbed his temple, "I sure never expected the Zone 3 remark. If I caused it by threatening to send Rusty on a Zone 3 ride-along, I'm sorry. I was frustrated at him too."

"Oh, I'm guessing that was his own vicious nature emerging," Savannah assured. "Nothing to do with you. Plus, I didn't exactly help issues."

Shoving a hand through his hair, Ennis glared at the officers gathered outside the office window. They quickly scattered. Anger throbbed in his voice, "You can't transfer her there. She'll get shot or worse. She's been through enough –"

Josh pointed behind Ennis, telling him, "Take a breath and a seat. Soon as we wrap up here, I'm calling the chief. You won't be partners anymore but maybe I can lobby to keep her here."

Disbelief rang in Savannah's words, "All this because of my big mouth."

Neither bothered to dispute her. Everyone warned her to back off the mayor and his son. She bulled on as usual and ran across a formidable and influential opponent. Ennis feared the bastard would take aim on her and told her as much. Unfortunately he was right. Ennis married her with the knowledge she was brash, temperamental and headstrong. When someone shoved her, she shoved back – sometimes too hard. "Babe, the boss said he'd help."

"If he can," she amended. She leaned back in the chair, shaking her head, "I may have seriously screwed us and I apologize for doing it. Ennis, I'm so sorry."

"Savannah, let's see what the chief says," Hunter's voice softened. "He's not exactly fond of O'Neill."

A half-hearted laugh surfaced, "As I recall, he's not particularly fond of me either. And with O'Neill digging his claws in, it stands to reason I'm less of a threat."

Ennis's hands balled into fists. He'd strangle that pompous piece of shit. He'd drive to City Hall and do the bastard in. "I'll pull O'Neill inside out," he vowed.

Savannah touched his arm. The delicate brush gave him pause but her voice stopped him, "Ennis, I've stirred the hornets enough. It's best you just take cover."

Josh made a shooing motion to someone outside his office. From the corner of his eye, Ennis saw more officers disperse from their eavesdropping. Josh sighed, "This place is a soap opera lately. Rusty and his father have riled everyone." He reached behind him, plucked a folder from his desk, "When O'Neill demanded I transfer Savannah, I told him to shove it – in my most diplomatic way, of course. I explained that you're both excellent detectives and I refuse to lose her competence and experience."

"But..." Savannah hedged, staring at the folder in his hands.

"But since your marriage is now common knowledge, I have no choice but to assign you new partners. That's one regulation I'm obligated to comply with."

Ennis grumbled a protest. He also managed to include an indecipherable expletive or two for good measure. Savannah sighed, waiting.

Their captain shrugged, "Look on the bright side, guys. You can finally wear your rings to work now. On the less sunny side of life, who wants Mathis for their new partner?"

"Ennis," Savannah blurted before Ennis had a chance to say her name. He settled for hitching his thumb at her, "She needs protection. I want her to have a partner she knows and trusts."

Their boss quickly grew impatient, "Since you're so eager to pass John to each other, let me introduce you to our newbie." He opened the folder, displayed an officer's photo while reading, "Benjamin Olson, twenty-six. He's just been promoted to detective. He grew up in Chamblee, joined the academy at eighteen, graduated twenty-second in his class."

Ennis appraised the young man in the photo. The face staring back sounded five alarm warning bells in his gut. Olson, supposedly twenty-six, looked younger than that with his dark hair parted on one side and combed over like a five year-old. The eyes bothered him too. Their bright eagerness screamed "undisciplined" to Ennis. A kid wanting to play cop. At night, he probably sat at home acting out various scenarios with his duty weapon like most children did with cap guns.

The pimply-faced Beaver Cleaver was expected to protect Savannah? He looked more at home thumbing buttons on his Xbox than chasing down murderers. No one on the street would take Olson seriously which meant no one would respect him enough *not* to draw down on Olson or his partner. The whole ugly picture made Ennis sick. Then his brain suddenly screeched to a halt, "*Twenty-second* in his class?" Savannah graduated fourth in a class of thirty-seven or thirty-eight, Ennis couldn't recall the exact number. They both had medals for expert marksmanship. They *knew* they could trust the other to back them up. This… this *kid* clearly had no abilities or suffered a mental disadvantage if he graduated twenty-second. "Is he an expert marksman?" Ennis asked, figuring the answer but demanding confirmation.

Their boss shook his head. He crossed his arms, bracing for the barrage from both his detectives, "Ennis, he qualified with his weapon or he wouldn't be here."

Resigned, Savannah simply asked, "How many were in the class?"

Josh replied, "Twenty-five."

Ennis panicked, "Give her Mathis. They've known each other for years. He'll be a good partner." This was worse than he imagined. Olson graduated at the bottom of his class, for God's sake. Ennis couldn't have an idiot assigned to his wife. He *wouldn't.* "I mean, the *bottom* of his class? The kid didn't earn the shield, he bought it or knows somebody in the department. *Please* assign Mathis to her."

"Whoa, cowboy," she argued. "Mathis is a fast draw. You need a partner like that."

He swiveled in his seat to face her, "You sayin' I'm slow?"

"No, I'm saying I don't want you shot again. A new guy might hesitate, Mathis won't."

"And you think I'll sleep tight knowing some greenhorn is backing up my wife?" He looked to Josh for agreement but their boss remained neutral. Perfect.

Peeved now, Savannah crossed her arms like Hunter had, "I specifically remember a greenhorn from Texas not long ago. He turned out okay."

"That was different. This guy can't even shoot straight, much less protect you."

"And this, children," Hunter's voice sliced through their conversation, "is why they forbid partners from marrying. You are the shining example of why this department needs more training videos on that subject." He reached into his pocket and pulled out a quarter. Nodding to Savannah, he said, "We're letting George choose your partner." He tossed the quarter in the air, "Heads is Mathis, Tails is Olson."

Appropriate, Ennis thought, because Olson certainly looked like an ass.

Light glinted off the quarter as it spun over and over like a bright silver globe. When it landed on his desk they all leaned forward to see the result. Savannah smiled.

Ennis groaned, "Crap. How 'bout two out of three?"

Josh shook his head, "It's official. Olson is her new partner. I'll bring him in later, introduce him and you bring him up to speed on the case."

"You can't be serious," Savannah balked. "Can't he start on the next case? It will put us behind if we have another warm body to update on this one."

Josh shook his head, "He needs to get his feet wet on the job."

"No," Ennis strongly suggested, "he *needs* to visit the firing range and re-qualify before I let him near my wife."

O O O

She wasn't thrilled about breaking in a new partner. With the exception of Ennis, her luck with partners verged on disaster. She'd only had two good ones, Riley Murphy and Ennis. Now the boss saddled her with a young boy – okay, technically around Ennis's age but Olson's boyish features told a different story. A bad one. His academy photo resembled a senior class photo with "Most To Learn" beneath it.

No, her enthusiasm bottomed out on training a new detective but she wanted Ennis partnered with an experienced, dependable cop and Mathis filled the bill. Her husband compared Olson to mousy-haired Beaver Cleaver. True, Ben's hairstyle and adolescent features made him appear much younger than his twenty-six years. But he was hers now and she vowed to make the best of it.

Young Benjamin entered her office behind Josh. After the customary introductions, Ben shook Savannah's hand, his dead fish grip leaving her cold. At least Ennis had given her a solid grasp upon their first meeting. "How do you do, ma'am?" Ben asked.

Oh, for crap's sake... Eight to ten hours a day of hearing "ma'am". Just what she needed. "Savannah's fine. No need for formalities," she said, thanking God Ennis never danced the "ma'am" dance. She was older than both men but her husband maintained a level of respect without causing her to feel ancient.

Savannah appraised Ben's attire. By his choice of clothes he assumed detective work was a casual affair loosely akin to playing the back nine at the golf course. His black polo shirt and beige khakis inspired a healthy frown on her face. Exactly what academy did this guy graduate from, she wanted to know. Her expression asked her boss that very question.

"We've already discussed that," Josh assured. "Suit and tie tomorrow."

Right... This was worse than she thought. Maybe Ennis spoiled her on breaking in younger detectives. He'd shown up in a suit and tie his first day. He'd been careful about his phrasing, his manners. He'd been a gentleman. Something about Ben Olson told her the guy was Ennis's polar opposite.

The biggest surprise was his hair. Instead of the comb-over in his academy photo, the new detective now sported – a mullet. The length surprised her because of department regulations. He wasn't an undercover cop so those flowing locks needed a significant shearing. She pointed to his mane, "You expect people to take you seriously with that hair?"

"Excuse me, ma'am?"

He didn't look stupid so where was the disconnect between his ears and his common sense? If he refused to stop the infernal name-calling, she'd slap him. "Let me rephrase. Do you expect *me* to take you seriously with that hair?"

Ben's young brow wrinkled as he petted his tresses, "I'm trying to stay within department guidelines with it."

"The men's or women's guidelines?" She pried her vision from his hair and marched to the bookshelf behind her desk. From it she removed one book – the regulations manual. She flipped through it until settling on one page, "And I quote. 'For male employees, hair at the sides and back of the head shall present a neat appearance and not touch the collar except for the hair at the back of the neck.'" She closed the book, "Those are rules, not suggestions. My husband's barber could shear that off to a manageable length. You'd be a handsome boy in ten minutes." She emphasized "boy" in retaliation for his habitual and unnecessary use of "ma'am".

For a moment he stood mute and slack-jawed as if she suggested he have his balls trimmed as well. Then he shook his head, "But my girlfriend loves this length."

"Well, your partner doesn't and you'll be spending entirely more time with me than her so get it cut."

Hunter cleared his throat, "She's right, Ben. You need a good trim. Get that done before week's end."

Savannah nodded to him in silent thanks. Once Ennis and Mathis got an eyeful of Benjamin, she'd never live it down. But maybe by next week, he'd look more like a man instead of a leftover from Woodstock. "So, got any family on the job?" she inquired, referring to Ennis's earlier remark. For the kid to act so cavalier, someone in his family wore a badge and probably held a high rank.

Josh frowned behind Ben's shoulder. He realized her reason for asking but she figured she deserved some leeway since being saddled with the newbie. She wanted Ennis back and still smarted over the split-up.

"An uncle, ma'am," he said, either ignoring her earlier request regarding the abhorrent title – or unable to understand it. "He's retired now but he told me when I made detective to ask for this precinct." He bobbed his brow, "Said not much goes on here, and it was a pretty cushy job."

Her first instinct was to laugh then she thought better of it. Thanks to the mayor, Josh already looked harried enough to strangle the first unfortunate that pushed his patience too far. She settled for disbelief, "That's odd. I missed that memo." She happily overlooked her boss's narrow-eyed warning, "But it does remind me, did Captain Hunter offer you the smoked salmon and petite fours when you reported for your shift? We try to keep those on hand at all times for the new officers and detectives. Helps to maintain the cushy working atmosphere."

Josh rolled his eyes. "Sorry. I was fresh out," he said, hinting that she treaded on thin ice.

She waved it off with a smile and wink, "That's okay. Must be part of those cutbacks our new mayor mentioned."

Ben turned to Josh. By now, Hunter's hands planted squarely on his hips, his frown evolving to a scowl aimed straight at her, "She was joking, Ben. Not about the cutbacks but the salmon."

Olsen chuckled, but Savannah got the feeling he missed the joke entirely. "Oh, that's okay," he said. "I've heard a lot about Detective Prince," Ben said as if he was privy to some indecent or private secret.

Problem was, she expected to hear a lot about Ben as well – from Ennis and Mathis. Playing off Ben's statement, she said, "And he still reported for his shift. Ben, you're a brave young man."

Josh gave up, suggesting, "Why don't you bring Ben up to speed on the case?"

Ben's eyes sparkled, "Is it that aquarium thing?"

To her, his enthusiasm verged on perverse. Watching his fingers comb his thick, ridiculously long hair, she affirmed, "Indeed. Looks like you drew the extra lucky card. You got this cushy precinct and caught a murder case the same day. Better go buy a lottery ticket."

His eyes widened as the idea took root, "Whoa. *There's* an idea."

She slanted Josh a look. No wonder he was twenty-second in his class, it said. It surprised her he wasn't dead last. "Tell me, Ben," she said, "who did you vote for in the mayoral election?"

As though she'd asked for a secret password, he eyed her suspiciously. She began to wonder if the question was too hard for him.

He consulted Josh who shrugged. Ben finally replied, "Franklin O'Neill, why?"

That figured, she thought. O'Neill landed in the mayor's office thanks to people like Ben Olson. Being a newly minted detective, Mr. Woodstock soon would learn the error of his ways. No raises, no overtime, no way, no how. "Ben, by the time this case is over, you'll probably change not only your vote in the next election but your whole political affiliation."

24

Her new partnership was barely four hours old. Somehow it felt like two lifetimes. When partnered with Ennis, she expected a challenge on the scale of Job's boils but he'd taken to the job with astonishing effortlessness. Transferring from a mid-sized city such as Amarillo, Texas should've put the fear of God into him upon passing the Atlanta city limits. But, in classic Ennis style, he accepted his role as pupil to her teacher, kicked back and learned while still being useful. She could not say the same for Ben Olson, especially after giving him a tour of the station.

Halfway through the journey he began yawning which sparked a generous amount of annoyance. "Am I boring you?" she wanted to know.

He yawned so wide she nearly saw his tonsils. He added a long, languid stretch, "Nah. Just got to bed late."

They passed by a female officer which seemed to perk him up a bit. The sight inspired a wink from Ben. Irked, the female officer frowned at him then looked at Savannah in disbelief.

Savannah felt obligated to apologize. This new partnership already tested her patience, now it would test her associations at work, especially if she neglected to find a leash short enough to reel in her hormonal cohort.

Earlier, Savannah wondered exactly why Ben Olson became a cop. Now the harsh truth dawned but she asked anyway, "What made you choose law enforcement?"

He turned to watch the female officer stride by, "Oh, the usual. Kick ass, carry a gun and impress women."

Savannah cleared her throat loud enough to break his trance. He turned back to her as she deadpanned, "I'm a woman and you're not impressing me yet."

Ben broke into an unexpected grin, "Yeah, but you're older and married. Not my type."

Savannah's right eye twitched. *Thanks, asshole. I'll bet this old married lady can still kick* your *ass with one hand tied behind my back* and *being pregnant.*

This was her brilliant future staring back at her. The oversexed, half-impaired Beaver Cleaver didn't earn a badge to help people or make the world a slightly nicer place. No, he got one to get laid – and to successfully flatter his archaic married partner into slapping his nose off. Then she'd see how old he thought she was…

The twitch continued in earnest. Savannah rubbed her eye again then gave her temple a massage for good measure, "Boy, the female officers are really gonna love you."

"You think?"

"Sure," she lied. "Try that charm on 'em. See how far you get."

She motioned for him to move along, "Restrooms are around this corner and don't fornicate in there with girls who might succumb to your charm. Remember the boss has a bladder too and he could walk in on something unfortunate. FYI, fornicate means engage in sex."

The lecture flew over him, "Are you the only female detective here? I haven't seen any others…"

That was the last straw. She stopped with full intentions of setting him straight, "Look, Ben, I've tried to be nice but the truth is one of the quickest ways to upset the boss is to start dating a colleague." *Believe me, I know.*

Ben considered that a moment then, "We'll see. Say, know any good restaurants around here?" He hitched his thumb behind them, "I need a place to take that brunette."

"Don't you have a girlfriend?"

He shrugged, "I like to keep my options open."

"Correction. You like to live dangerously. I'm your partner but don't expect me to condone your behavior or pry some unhinged woman off of you 'cause you two-timed her."

"I'm careful, ma'am. I was hoping you knew a good, kinda upscale place around here. In case I get lucky with that brunette."

For heaven's sake, "*That brunette* has a husband. I've seen him and he's a big, strappin' fella like my husband. So unless you like bleeding profusely in dark alleys, you'd best back off that girl, Don Juan."

"Hey, chill out. I don't date married chicks. They're a waste of time. But I need a good restaurant because I intend to land a single chick around here."

And with your smooth talk, she'll body slam you and guess what? Me and the rest of the "chicks" will pile on for Act Two... She held her tongue, only releasing a modicum of annoyance, "Ben, by the end of the month, you'll have perfected the art of speed eating like we all have. You'll never get home on time and when you do get there, you'll be too tired to eat. The absolute last thing on your mind will be restaurants. The fact I do *not* know any good – or bad – restaurants nearby should be a clue."

They breezed into her office and she abruptly stopped upon sight of the Red-Headed One sitting across from her desk. This was simply not a good day at all. She pointed directly toward the exit, making sure to add a stern, "Get out."

Rusty O'Neill held up a bag of Chips Ahoy cookies, "To replace the ones I ate."

That was, categorically, the dumbest thing she'd heard a man say in at least thirty seconds. "Let's put this into perspective, Junior. Georgia's cookies are like driving a Ferrari. It's a life-changing experience few people get and they always want one more. I've driven that Ferrari, Junior. In comparison, what you're offering me is a tricycle. But you know what?" She snatched the bag, tossed it to Ben, "Maybe my *new* partner would like a snack."

"New partner?"

Rusty was living up to his name again. For a moment she mentally played out a scenario in which she used her fist to knock the rust loose and get his wheels moving. Pulling herself from the fantasy, she replied, "Normally playing dumb suits you because I know you're not really playing. This time it's pissing me off, Rusty. *You* are responsible for *him.*" She jerked her thumb at Ben who'd torn into the sack with a child's eagerness, his attention riveted to their exchange as he munched.

"I'm sorry, Detective. I don't follow."

Why didn't that surprise her? Savannah waved Ben from her office and closed the door, "Your father had me and Ennis separated on the job so I hope you're all happy now."

"I have no reason to be happy about that."

"Really? Even after you told him we were married?"

The color drained from Rusty's cheeks, his eyes rounded.

"What's wrong, Rusty?" she asked. "Cat got your tongue or did the hamster finally fall off the wheel?"

The whole subject was a surprise to him, according to his reaction. But now at least he realized how angry she was – and why.

Rusty eased into a chair, his vision refusing to meet hers, "He wanted your backgrounds, where you're from, your department records, anything I could find on the two of you. I never thought that being married would be a problem. If I had, I certainly wouldn't have told him."

A sincere desire to rip her hair out surfaced, replaced quickly by the urge to yank Rusty's out, "What part of 'your daddy don't like me' don't you get, Junior? He uses anything he can against me." She leaned onto her knees to stare eye level at him, "He stepped into my private life, Rusty." She stabbed a finger at him, "*You* stepped into it. You can't imagine the rage I feel for you both. What you *can* do is get out of my office before I do something to get myself suspended or dismissed. Don't bring me any more food, no more glad tidings, no more anything. Tell me you understand."

In the midst of the brief conversation, perspiration formed on his forehead. He pressed back against the chair to gain space between himself and her temper. Rusty's head tilted forward then back in silent acknowledgment.

Savannah whipped the pointing finger from him to the door, "Git." She rarely resorted to her father's special back-woodsy Georgian dialect but the occasion called for it.

Rusty squirmed at her nearness. She used the interrogation technique frequently to squeeze the truth from suspects. Closing in, robbing a person of their space while specifying the smelly creek they were up – with no oar to their name. Today though, she used the technique to scare Rusty. Perhaps enough that he might leave Atlanta and become a Tibetan monk. Those people never caused trouble.

He rose slowly and as he did, Savannah straightened, clamped her hands to her hips.

Taking three tentative steps to the door, he stopped and turned, "I apologize, Detective."

She stood rigid, not trusting herself to speak. Rusty opened the door, taking the opportunity to remind, "I'm still a liaison for my father. You do have to work with me."

Savannah noticed he waited until a safer distance from her before cracking wise. At least she took it as cracking wise. In the end, she bet those monks would've booted him from their midst for being a betraying pinhead.

25

Ben Olson was a Bohemian freak. A total hippie who had no respect for the job or people he worked with. His hair reminded Ennis of Billy Ray Cyrus and his Achy Breaky Fart. Ennis also knew the smarmy hairdo grated on Savannah. She detested long hair on men. Her exception: Ennis. Only when his hair began to curl at his neck did she suggest a visit to the barber. But Ben Olson? She'd pin him down and personally mow the mop down if she could.

Ennis prayed that was the extent of the boy's idiocy but the gravity of the situation hit when he overheard Savannah alone in Hunter's office. Okay, Ennis admitted to snooping but this was his wife's life at stake. If the refugee from the New Wave Age wasn't able or willing to protect his new partner, Ennis would crack his knuckles on the guy's jaw.

"His mother forgot to sign his permission slip for this field trip." Savannah told their boss. "He needs to go home."

That one single comment set Ennis on edge. The kid wasn't up to par. Worse, according to Savannah's tone, he wasn't even close.

"Give him time," Josh suggested. "I admit he's a little raw but –"

"Raw? If he was a steak, he'd still be mooing and grazing. And what's with his hair? I haven't seen the likes of that since 'Achy Breaky Heart'."

"You heard me. I told him to get a trim."

"If you've got a pair of scissors, I could –"

"I'm working on the situation, Savannah. I'm working on it. You know, Ennis wasn't the most experienced detective when he got here either. His hair was regulation but you had to train him too."

Their boss hit below the belt with that one. No, he didn't have a huge amount of experience when he'd transferred. But the difference in Amarillo, Texas and Atlanta, Georgia? C'mon, he wanted to say. Apples and oranges.

"Ennis was fine," she argued. "He wanted to learn, he wanted to be here. He's a *real* cop. At least we got along the first day we met and he wasn't sniffing all the single female officers, if you get my meaning."

Savannah's defense brought a proud smile to his face. His chest broadened to the point his shirt threatened to burst its seams.

Their boss lowered his voice but Ennis heard every word, "No, he just sniffed one of my female detectives and decided to marry her. Savannah, give Ben a chance. He can't be all that bad." Josh then added a hesitant postscript, "He earned his badge."

Ennis saw the knob to the office door twist. Savannah was leaving so he hustled around the corner to the drinking fountain. He bent, pressed the button, pretending to take a drink. Before exiting Josh's presence, she offered one last valid point, "Sure about that? Or should you check the auction websites to be sure?"

"How long you gonna pretend to drink from that thing? 'Cause you look stupid."

John Mathis scared him so bad he shot to a standing position and simultaneously craned his back. "Jeez, Mathis, give a guy some warning," Ennis winced, put a hand to his back, straightening it until feeling something pop.

"Spying on your spouse? I hear that's a good precursor to divorce."

"I wasn't spying on her. I heard her telling the boss about Ben. The kid's not working out, Mathis. He's a reject."

Mathis peered over his glasses at him, "So let's go talk to her about it. It'll be therapeutic for her and entertaining for us." When Ennis scowled at him, he backtracked, "Okay, entertaining for me."

They rounded the corner to Savannah's office and the second Ennis laid eyes on her, he knew. He knew not to push the issue. Mathis, however, forged ahead oblivious to the firestorm he'd unleash.

At least Mathis had the forethought to knock. But before giving her the chance to shoo them away, they stepped inside.

Savannah sat, elbows on desk, her head in her hands. She looked tuckered, frazzled and not up to any jokes. Ennis wondered if she regretted taking the rookie detective as her partner. By her weary posture, the answer was a resounding yes.

"Don't," Ennis whispered to Mathis.

"You're kiddin', right? This is priceless." He glanced at Savannah, "Where'd you stash Opie?"

When she looked up, Ennis wanted to smash Olson's face in.

His wife's appearance was reminiscent of her radiation treatment days. Tired and washed-out.

"Do I look old?" Savannah volleyed the question between the two men.

Ennis exercised good sense by remaining silent and shaking his head. She didn't look old, he would've said, but she did look pushed to her limit.

Not surprisingly, Mathis bulled right in, "You mean today or every day in general?"

Her head sank back into her hands, "Nevermind."

Ennis's blood pressure steadily rose, "Did he call you old?"

"Technically, he used the term *older* but it rings the same to me."

"And he's still calling you 'ma'am'?" Ennis asked. He already knew the answer since he'd heard her repeatedly warn him to ditch the word. He tried alleviating the situation, "Sugar, he might be trying to show you respect. You're a seasoned detective –"

"Thanks for not saying *older*," she mumbled.

"I'm hoping he's respecting your experience," he prayed the word *experience* fell softer on her ears. Savannah took teasing well but not about age. No woman did, he figured. And as for Olson, he hated to believe Ben aggravated her on purpose. If that was the case, Ennis would have a heart to heart with the rookie, speaking as Savannah's spouse, not her colleague.

She blinked wearily, her blue eyes rising to meet his gaze, "I always gave you credit, Ennis. Ask Georgia, she'll tell you. When we partnered up, you always respected me – *without* calling me 'ma'am'."

Ennis wasn't sure what to say. He'd respected Savannah, yes, but he fell instantly in lust with her too. From his horny brain to his tingling toes, he'd reacted to her beauty, sultry voice, her intoxicating lavender scent. His arousal throbbed at the hypnotic sway in her hips. He suffered blue balls during the day and fitful sleepless nights. He was a miserable, pathetic mess until he finally got her into bed.

"And that hair," she lamented, head in hand. "We're gonna look like Cagney and Lacey out there."

The irony of the eighties reference hit Ennis but he again exercised good judgment by staying silent.

"You mean Lucy and Ethel," Mathis joked.

Her vision narrowed at him with a curt, "Thanks *ever* so. I haven't had a hard enough day."

John cleared his throat offered an apology then agreed, "His mop *isn't* within regulations."

"Certainly not *my* regulations but evidently the department is rather lenient on him. I offered the name of Ennis's barber and of course he declined. You know what he said later?"

Ennis trembled to think of Ben's response. It was a doozy according to her expression.

Savannah continued, "He said that pelt on his head 'is my lucky charm and I remember the story of Samuel and Delilah so I don't need any barber'."

Ennis rolled his eyes. Wait for it. Three, two, one…

As if on cue Mathis burst out laughing, "You're kidding, right?

Samuel? The kid's a riot."

Savannah found no humor as she massaged her temple, "The kid was serious. I think he was sent here to test my patience and boy, am I failing miserably. I set him up in the video surveillance room to scan through the aquarium security tapes. The Titanic had a better chance of hitting land than I do of getting that kid to work."

Ennis slid his hands in his pockets to hide his clenched fists. Ben sounded like a blister – he'd show up after the work was done and that did not set well with Ennis, considering the ignoramus was now his wife's partner. While Ennis boiled, Mathis ventured a guess, "What happened? He asked where the 'play' button was?"

"Worse. He asked me why *he* had to do it. I even let him borrow my notes on the case. I hope reading them doesn't strain that muscle between his ears. Evidently, it doesn't get much exercise."

Savannah had had more than enough. In the brief time they'd been separated as partners, the wear and tear showed in her expression, posture and her voice. She spoke in what Ennis interpreted as a defeated whisper, "It's like he expects me to do all the work."

And that clinched it. Before blowing his top in front of her, he headed for the door, promising, "I'll be back."

A thread of panic suddenly laced her voice, "Where are you going?"

"To either talk or beat some sense into that brat. He's your partner and if this is the best he's willing to give you, he won't be here long, I can swear to that."

"Ennis, calm down," she sighed. "I can't potty-train a rookie and corral you at the same time."

Calm down, she said. Well, that wasn't happening anytime soon. "This asshole is supposed to watch your back. Not just work the case but *protect* you. If he ain't workin', he ain't gonna protect you either. I'm not sacrificing my wife because some fat bastard in the mayor's office wants us split up."

"He's got a point," Mathis agreed. "If this kid is a slacker, none of us want him backing us up. And to be honest I've grown sort of fond of you over the years."

Savannah gifted John with a tired smile and thanks.

Ennis fisted his hands again. The past year tested her patience and love for the job. First with the diagnosis, surgery and treatments then Jeffrey. Now she was handed some pantywaist partner she couldn't trust.

He turned to leave with Savannah protesting, "Ennis, don't. If he doesn't change after I talk with him, I'll tell the boss."

He glanced over his shoulder at her. Whatever expression he held pressed her back into the chair and she swallowed hard.

"No offense, sugar," he said, "but the punk ain't listenin' to you but I'll make damn sure he listens to me." He marched down the hall with her pleading for his return and ultimately lamenting the havoc he'd wreak.

Ennis didn't intend to tear kid apart. Yet. His ultimate goal was to set him straight regarding his job. When he leaned in the video surveillance room, it stood empty. That incensed Ennis beyond rational thought. The little bastard jumped ship on her already.

A uniform officer passed by and Ennis stopped him, "Where's Ben Olson?"

"Who?"

"Tall, skinny kid with a mullet."

"*Oh*, he headed to the locker room. He must be takin' personal time since he's leaving early."

Ennis started in that direction. If personal time meant a ride to the emergency room, then yeah, Ben Olson was taking personal time. However long it took to recover from a broken jaw and ribs. By the time Ennis arrived, he was furious. He threw open the door so hard it slammed against the stop.

Ben spun around, wide-eyed, "Dude, be careful."

Ennis put his hands on his hips, "Get your ass back to the video room, Olson. Despite what your uncle said, we work real homicides here."

Ben splashed some cologne in his palms and pressed them to his cheeks. A smirk crossed his face, "Look, I told Prince I'd watch the tapes but I got a date tonight and I'm leaving from here to pick up my girl."

"You mean if you're able to walk."

"What?" Ben turned to close his locker. Ennis wondered when the boy's common sense abandoned ship – at birth or after his promotion. His bravado would get him maimed at best, killed at worst. Turning his back on an enraged man wasn't the smartest move.

Ennis stalked closer, "Let me spell it for you. I'm Savannah's husband. If anything happens to her, I'm holding you responsible.

Before you dismiss that statement, ask anyone around here how protective I am of her."

Ben turned to him, a shadow of annoyance crossed his features, "Did she complain about me? Is that why you're in my face?"

The arrogant tilt of the boy's chin just invited violence. Ennis fought the urge until finally giving over to it. He shoved Ben into the lockers. Metal crashed and rattled as objects inside tumbled off shelves. Ennis trapped him against the lockers, "She hasn't said a word but she doesn't have to. I can smell lazy on you and if you're too lazy to perform a simple task, you're too lazy to protect your partner."

"Because I won't watch those damn tapes? You're nuts."

Various scenarios raced through Ennis's mind. One involved Savannah calling for help while Ben, in the car, gabbed with "his girl" about which Will Ferrell movie to see that night.

Ennis shoved him again and curled his fists in Ben's shirt, "Listen closely. Watch Savannah's back or I'll break yours." He punctuated the following words with a ram into the lockers, "That's… your… job…"

Ben glanced at the door, evidently hoping someone might rescue him. Ennis would gladly tell him no cop wanted a goldbrick in their midst. Fear finally crept into Ben's voice, "Dude, chill out."

"Don't tell me to chill." He tried to inform the kid, "Your partner, gun, common sense and instincts are the things that'll keep you alive on the job. Since you're only equipped with half of 'em, you are unfit to be Savannah's partner. For some reason she's willing to give you a second chance to show her you're not a clown. Don't disappoint her.

Or else."

Ben's back straightened, "Don't threaten me, Rutherford."

Ennis tightened his hold until Olson flinched, "See? There's that bad judgment again. It wasn't a threat. It was a promise you can take to the bank."

Someone behind Ennis cleared their throat. He knew by the voice that someone was Savannah. He glanced behind him. She stood in the doorway, her arms crossed. John Mathis stood behind her, a humorous smile softening his normally gruff features.

Mildly peeved, Savannah soft-balled her question at Ennis, "You done terrorizing and intimidating my partner?"

Ennis released Ben's shirt. He did not apologize. He wouldn't either. Savannah's safety was worth any lecture, heated glare or suspension he endured. She wasn't happy with him but he doubted he'd be sleeping on the couch for his actions either. Outwardly she appeared hot at him however a subtle nuance in her expression revealed appreciation at his aggressive, caveman reaction. Appreciation *and* considerable relief that he drove home his point without beating Olson to a bloody pulp and mopping the floor with his carcass.

Ben chose that moment to stretch his meager machismo, "He doesn't intimidate me."

To that, Ennis elbowed him into the lockers again. A miserable groan spilled from Ben's lips. Savannah temporarily shifted her vision to her new partner, "If you're serious, then you're either reckless or stupid. When he's angry, Ennis can chase demons back to hell." She calmly motioned Ennis to step away from Ben.

He reluctantly did but didn't like doing it. He still had plenty of lessons to teach the boy and plenty of anger left to enforce them.

"Ben," she called, waiting for him to meet her vision. Her new partner made a show of rubbing his side and glaring at Ennis.

Ennis sincerely hoped the pimply-face runt might follow through on the silent threat. He hadn't had a chance to release his rage on Jeffrey Holland or Cole Jordan and his right hook ached for serious exercise.

"Ben," Savannah called with more conviction. The young man broke eye contact with Ennis to look at her. She continued, "Start pulling your weight on this case or I'll tell the boss. He tolerates a number of things from his detectives but laziness isn't one of them." She hitched her thumb at the door, "Go look at those videotapes and let me know what you find. You have two hours." She waved her hand in front of her nose, "But first wash off that tacky aftershave and give your date a call because your plans just got postponed."

26

"Send her in." The mayor dropped the words like stones, their finality striking fear in Savannah's heart. She spent half an hour trying to figure out what she'd done to, again, upset him. She purposefully kept her distance from Rusty to avoid hives and homicidal tendencies. Unless specifically addressed, she remained silent at news conferences to prevent further acrimony.

Now the mayor summoned her to his office "immediately", according to his secretary. Not her, Ennis, and Mathis. Just Detective Prince.

Savannah closed the Golf Digest she'd picked up to give the illusion she was calm. She placed the magazine back on the table, making sure to return it exactly where she found it. Then, with as much dignity as she could muster, she rose, buttoned then smoothed her suit jacket then headed to O'Neill's office. His secretary flashed a tentative smile when she passed by. Savannah swallowed hard, figuring that particular smile couldn't be a good sign.

Savannah tilted the gold lever on the heavy door and stepped into her private hell. O'Neill sat at behind a large mahogany desk, a pair of gold-rimmed reading glasses sat perched on his nose while he perused paperwork. She stood for a minute, waiting for him to acknowledge her but he never looked up, never said a word.

She positioned herself between two chairs facing his desk and continued waiting. She equated the scene to standing before God for judgment. Of course God wasn't a vindictive jerk and she felt pretty sure that O'Neill's power didn't extend to the divine side.

After what seemed an eternity, he motioned to the available chairs, "Have a seat, Detective."

She thanked him and hesitantly eased into one. This would be a long drawn-out ordeal, obviously, when one swift slice of his authority would sever her from her job if he convinced the chief to terminate her employment. Why single her out, she'd wondered during her trip downtown. Three detectives worked the Vaughn case and he'd sent for just her. There was only one answer. She stood before O'Neill so he could personally fire her.

He didn't look up, "You're wondering why I sent for you."

"The thought had crossed my mind, yes."

His vision shifted to her wedding ring, "How's life with your new partner?"

Bastard. It's a train wreck and you know it. She replied, "Interesting."

"You do understand department policy requires the separation of married officers in the department. All I did was enforce the rule already in place."

Her blood boiled at his smirk but she'd promised herself she'd keep her mouth shut during this meeting. He'd try to goad or intimidate her and she felt sufficiently prepared for it. She simply acknowledged his comment with a tense nod.

"I rescinded my order transferring you to Zone 3. Your senior officer convinced me to reconsider. Said you were one of his best detectives."

His phrasing fostered hope she'd keep her job. Savannah took a deep breath. Things were looking up. And thank God Josh Hunter defended her. Zone 3 equaled a battle zone. She didn't think she could survive the transfer, not carrying the baby and constantly worrying about his or her safety. Without realizing it, Josh saved more than her job... "I appreciate his support." Saying anything past that might have riled the natives so she kept it short and sweet.

O'Neill peered over his glasses at her, "Odd as this sounds, Detective, I think this meeting will prove beneficial for you. But first, I knew your name sounded familiar from the outset. You were the detective abducted by Jeffrey Holland not long ago, correct?"

Savannah nearly swallowed her tongue. *Oh boy. Wasn't ready for that one...* Calm, she told herself as her heart shifted into high gear. Be calm. "Jeffrey Holland and Cole Jordan, yes." The names stirred the same old familiar sickness deep inside her. The blood sank to her toes, making her grateful she was sitting down. She assumed she'd prepared for this meeting. She assumed wrong.

"As I recall, you went through quite an ordeal with them."

She nodded in silent acknowledgment, her mind racing for answers to questions he might ask.

He watched her reaction, her every movement and breath that now came a little too quick for her comfort. She willed herself to push the memories back, drive them back to the corners of her mind where they belonged because she sat in the presence of another evil, this one with a different yet equally destructive power over her.

Moments earlier she'd assumed her job was safe. Now she wasn't so sure. She measured his expression, his mannerisms. The man gave nothing away. She supposed he cultivated his stoic poker face for politics. Never let them see the hammer before it whacks them.

But Savannah knew one thing for sure. If he intended to give her a job-ectomy because of her time with Holland and Jordan, she'd fight him to the end. The department shrink cleared her for duty, that was the bottom line, she'd say.

She straightened in her seat, squared her shoulders, tried to gather what composure she had left.

He leaned back, steepled his fingers beneath his chin, "Any residual problems from that experience?"

Her voice sounded stronger than she felt, "I'm fine, sir. Everything's healed."

"But one can't go through something that horrific without emotional repercussions."

His accusation riled her. He had no idea what she went through, and honestly he didn't care unless it served his purpose. "The department psychiatrist cleared me for full duty. I completed all the mandatory sessions with him. My captain also signed off on my returning to full duty."

"So according to them you're fit for duty. Do you agree?"

She answered a solid, "Yes."

He gave a quick nod as if accepting her answer. He referred to an open file in front of him, "Despite the blemishes on your department record and the unfortunate situation with Holland, I find your tenacious personality an asset to this city's police force."

Was that a compliment? She wasn't sure but decided to pretend it was.

He continued, "Many factors came into play for this meeting. One, the fact you protect fellow officers from what you consider outside influence. Two, you chase down any and all leads in a case, and three, you grab on and won't let go until someone cuts your throat – figuratively speaking, of course. All these points tell me you're a dedicated police officer."

He paused, giving her the appropriate opportunity to thank him. She did, although she sensed a "but" lurking in the shadows. *He wants something from me - most likely something illegal or immoral, but I won't like it.*

"We need more officers of your caliber. The good ones, the ones above reproach." He closed the folder on his desk, slid it across to her, "Not cops that take the law into their own hands. I refuse to tolerate that."

For all his flattery, she realized the meeting was a carefully crafted trap. Good cop, huh? Beyond reproach? Yeah, right. Her departmental file contained complaints and a few incidents fitting his "rogue cop" profile. Somehow she didn't think Franklin O'Neill would cut her an ounce of slack for it either.

The mayor nodded to the file, "I feel it's my duty to protect my officers from potential harm when possible, whether physical or career related. Consider this a peace offering, if you will."

Oh no. A peace offering. It was déjà vu all over again. She'd danced the same dance with a man named Duke Shelton not long ago. He'd offered her a "peace offering" as well. It was Cole Jordan's life history and no one wanted the results from that little gift. She was still trying to recover emotionally from it.

The folder he referred to was a personal investigation into someone's life. Probably another cop and meddling in another cop's business meant one thing: the nosy officer acquired a plethora of colorful names while simultaneously losing any and all support from their colleagues. Calls for help went unanswered, leaving the shunned cop to fight for his or her life. Just because O'Neill ordered the background, nothing prevented him from blaming *her* for it and spreading the lie throughout the department.

The instant she touched that folder, her life would change. Again. And personally, she was sick of change. "Does this regard another officer?" she asked.

He nodded. "Read it, Detective. You'll be here a while, so use your time wisely."

"Do it or else" his tone demanded. But images of retribution from fellow cops continued filtering in. She gently suggested, "This is a job for Internal Affairs, not me."

The mayor leaned back, his frustration escalating, "You'd rather Internal Affairs read it? Fine. But do me the courtesy of noticing the name on the file. *Then* I'll notify them."

Savannah reached in her suit coat for her glasses then plucked the folder from his desk. She wanted to refuse to read the name or even look at the folder but O'Neill made it clear. To be dismissed from his presence, she had to. Once the file was in her possession, she watched his smirk broaden to a menacing smile.

Opening the folder, her eyes widened in shock. Upon sight of the name, the earlier nausea plaguing her returned full force. In her hand sat records from a county sheriff's office in Texas. The date: nine years ago. The name on the file: Ennis Daniel Rutherford.

"Still want me to contact Internal Affairs?" he asked.

Savannah shook her head, struggling with how Ennis's records mattered to O'Neill. Normally they wouldn't, she told herself, not unless there was something questionable about them. Why drag her to his office to show her Ennis was squeaky clean? That certainly served no purpose for him.

The mayor propped his feet on his desk, "Take your time reading."

Anger eventually replaced her growing sickness. Anger at yet another invasion of their privacy. First their marriage and personal lives, now he purposefully dug into their professional lives.

However, the longer into the file she read, the anger ebbed to confusion. She read the record from the sheriff's department slowly. At the beginning, it was unremarkable – even dull as dishwater as her mother used to say – until one paragraph highlighted in yellow.

"Let's hope," O'Neill said, "that he treats other pregnant women with more consideration."

Words failed her. Ennis wasn't capable of what the file said. She *knew* Ennis. But, she thought, he never explained why he left Texas and moved halfway across the country. Escaping a past certainly qualified.

She shook her head in denial. These were lies. What her eyes consumed was a load of malicious fiction. It had to be. "This isn't my Ennis," was all she could bring herself to say. It couldn't be. Not sweet, gentle, thoughtful Ennis.

"That is your Ennis," he corrected, "And by your reaction, I assume he never told you about this."

She barely heard him. She was too busy rereading the lengthy report that told of a traffic stop Deputies Regina Gibson and Ennis Rutherford made on a county highway. They initially stopped twenty-five year-old Kelly Roberts for speeding. Before exiting their cruiser, they checked the license plate to find the car had been reported stolen earlier that day. The deputies approached the vehicle with weapons drawn and ordered Roberts out of the car. Instead of complying with their orders, she grew belligerent and reached beneath the seat. According to the report, after she disregarded another warning, Gibson shouted to her partner that she saw a gun. Gibson and Rutherford opened fire on Roberts with one shot hitting her in the side, another in the stomach.

Savannah took a deep breath, removed her glasses. She pinched the bridge of her nose, scarcely resisting the urge to touch her own belly where Ennis's child grew, oblivious to what Mama just read. Shot in the stomach. She couldn't imagine the devastation of feeling a bullet penetrating her flesh and killing their child.

The report stated while Roberts sat in the car bleeding and suffering a miscarriage, both deputies waited *minutes* to call for an ambulance.

It was later learned that Roberts fled her abusive husband in his car and he'd reported it stolen. And the object beneath the seat: her purse. A search of the car failed to turn up a weapon of any kind.

"Quite disturbing, isn't it?" Mayor O'Neill asked with perverse glee.

A whole range of emotion course through Savannah. Shock, confusion, sadness, outrage and betrayal combined into a storm of utter chaos. Yes, it was quite disturbing. Besides the obvious tragedy, it was also highly disturbing that her husband never trusted her enough to explain his past.

She felt O'Neill's harsh frown and for the first time, she squirmed under his scrutiny. She'd underestimated Franklin O'Neill and his desire for control and revenge. The file literally knocked the breath from her, leaving her trust for Ennis teetering on a dangerous precipice.

"I'm guessing," he lifted her department file from his desk, "he knows *your* history."

She gave a slight nod. Oh sure, she spilled her guts to Ennis long ago. All while he strung her along with the "I didn't plan to be a rancher forever" speech, leaving that as his reason for emigrating from Texas.

She hesitated, torn between conflicting emotions. Finally finding her voice, she asked, "If this is true, why wasn't he dismissed from the sheriff's department?"

"Turn the page."

She did. The file stated Deputy Rutherford resigned shortly after the incident. His employment record showed a gap of eight months – she supposed he returned to help with the ranch until he got another job.

"I understand there was a lawsuit," O'Neill mentioned.

"A lawsuit," she sighed, mentally weary and drained from the past several minutes. Of course there was a lawsuit. Why not? What's one more surprise in their marriage?

He continued, "The woman sued the deputies for the shooting and her resulting miscarriage."

Unfortunately, Savannah understood the knee-jerk reaction. When a cop stopped an individual, they demanded that person keep their hands within sight. When those hands disappeared, cops got nervous. They retrieved their weapons. They warned the person repeatedly to show their hands. If the person ignored the warning, it meant one of a hundred things. Even pregnant women pulled guns on officers but officers shouldered the responsibility of balancing the risk, especially in unusual circumstances. Was Roberts angry, moving aggressively, acting erratically? Had she hurriedly reached beneath the seat or alluded to the fact she may be armed?

But shit, she wanted to say. Shooting her in the stomach? Ennis was a better shot than that. She and Ennis repeatedly competed together at the shooting range, aiming for specific places on the paper target – and he was dead on. She never expected to see him associated with shooting a pregnant woman, much less refusing her medical care after they'd subdued her. Still, "Why would the Amarillo P.D. hire him after that?"

"You'd have to ask them," O'Neill replied.

I may do that, Savannah thought, because something doesn't add up here. She knew Ennis moved from the Amarillo P.D. to Atlanta. Amarillo gave Ennis glowing remarks, she remembered that. They weren't apt to speak highly of an officer capable of what the file accused. There was plenty more to it than the file stated, she thought, and only one person could fill in the blanks. "Is there anything else?" she asked the mayor.

Apparently proud of his accomplishment, he shook his head, "I thought you should know. Here," he pushed her department file at her, "I have no use for this. As you can see, once I dedicate myself to a project, I see it to completion. Who's to say this is all I can find on your husband? Or your family, perhaps." The same malicious smile curled his mouth, "Everyone's got secrets, Detective. Even you and your family."

She stared hard at him. Her jaw set like concrete to prevent a single blistering word from escaping. *You can't declare war on the mayor and win.* Ennis's caution repeatedly echoed in her brain. Just leave, she thought. Get the hell out now before you incite something worse.

He leaned back in his chair, "I trust I have your cooperation from now on?"

Again, not really a question. She reached for the folder only for him to pull it away. "Detective Prince," he prodded.

"Yes, cooperation. I understand." She snatched the file from his grasp.

"Detective, that means leave my friends and my restaurant alone."

She nodded, deciding to listen to her husband's advice. She didn't intend to start a publicity war that would engulf the mayor's private life in an inferno of questions. He'd have her ass on a platter – while disclosing every one of hers and Ennis's failings. Frankly, she'd been in the public eye enough lately and she sure couldn't handle another bombshell about Ennis.

He waved her from the office, "Good day, Detective."

Savannah turned to leave, holding a hand to her belly with a thought of the child growing inside her. She glanced down at the file in her hand and felt her heart break. She trusted Ennis with her life. She'd married him and they were having a baby. Now she wondered who Ennis really was and how many secrets he'd kept from her. And most of all, why hadn't he trusted her?

She shored up her resolve, determined to do two things upon arriving home. First – brace Ennis. The second – burn everything she currently held in her hands.

O O O

Climbing into her car, Savannah fought to retain a semblance of calm. Her mind reeled with questions. Her heart ached from the betrayal and lies of omission. Anger rooted deep that Ennis hadn't trusted her with the information.

She slammed the papers to the seat. *By God, I shared everything with him and he doesn't trust me with this?* He knew about her battle with alcohol and why her denial to drink stood for far more than sobriety – it signified a conscious decision not to become her father.

Ennis knew about the accident several years ago when she plowed into a tree *because* she was drunk, and he knew that was the turning point for her, the one that convinced her to abstain from alcohol.

She trusted Ennis with these and other closely guarded secrets. She stared down at the documents again. Surprises kept cropping up everywhere. From Cole, the mayor, but *Ennis*? And the frustrating part: she couldn't control any of them. Couldn't find Cole, couldn't contain O'Neill, and the biggest question – could she truly trust Ennis anymore?

She headed home, determined to wring answers from him. Driving up, she saw his Ram in the driveway. Good. No waiting for him to get home. She parked her car next to his truck, gathered the folders and headed to the door. The second she stepped inside she saw Ennis standing by the entry table, hands on his hips. "Where've you been?" he demanded.

After the last two hours, she nearly laughed at his accusing tone. She dumped her badge, handcuffs and .38 onto the small mahogany table in the entry. Best to disarm herself before charging into battle because she expected this to get messy.

When she added her purse to her other belongings, she noticed a small pile of mail consisting of postcards, "Is that our mail?"

"We need to talk," was all Ennis said.

No shit, she wanted to say, but let a terse nod speak for her.

Ennis pointedly stared at the postcards. She took the hint and picked them up. Each postcard was from a landmark or tourist attraction in Atlanta. The folders in her hand took a temporary back seat and she tucked both under her arm, "Why would someone send us postcards from Atlanta? We live here."

He motioned to them, "Just look."

So she did. The first postcard showed a beautiful scenic view of Piedmont Park. She flipped it over to see the handwritten message – "One of my favorite memories". She gasped upon sight of the signature. It simply read "Cole." It felt like icy fingers gliding up her neck as she shivered. It probably was one of his favorite memories, she thought. Hers consisted of fifty thousand volts coursing through her body like electrified blood. A hand clamping over her mouth, fingers digging into her jaw, the palm shoving the sound of her scream back down her throat. Jeffrey's body pinning hers to the ground followed by the sting of an injection that rendered her unconscious, helpless to rescue her sister while he and Cole carried Georgia to their car.

She shook free of the painful images, shuffled the postcards to the next one postmarked in Dunwoody only yesterday. It displayed a picture of the wooden rollercoaster at Six Flags. The Scream Machine. Cole signed it, "You'll be my favorite ride. See you soon. Cole."

Savannah's blood ran cold at the sight. Holding on to one last ray of hope, she checked her address with hopes it was sent to the old address. In Cole's scrawl it read *4886 Tilly Mill Road.* Her hand instantly opened, dropping them like they were on fire. *Cole knew their new address.* The truth of that fact scared her beyond rational thought. In some crazy fantasy, she'd hoped for a fresh beginning with the new house. That dream vanished upon sight of the mail, "Did these come today?"

"Not exactly."

"That's not an answer, Ennis. Those things," she pointed to them like they were snakes poised to strike, "were postmarked here in Dunwoody, that one as late as yesterday. When did they all arrive?"

Ennis looked away, "They've been coming for weeks now." He shrugged, "I just didn't know how to tell you."

"Try this. 'The man who tried to rape and kill you is sending fan mail.' Sound logical to you?"

"I was trying to protect you. He sent notes to the old address too. Even when we moved, I expected him to find you at some point. Surely you didn't believe you could hide from him."

"No," anger rose in her voice, "I *expected* my husband to alert me of such developments but I repeatedly find you enjoy keeping me in the dark instead." She retrieved his folder and slapped it against his chest.

He glanced at it, frowning, "What's this?"

"Read it then try to dig your way out. And for your information, I do not need protecting –"

"Really? You don't consider the consequences of your actions. You're too impulsive. Look what happened with the mayor. And visiting Jeffrey? What was that about? And remember what happened with Jordan? If you recall, I told you not to go with him when he claimed to be looking for Georgia. But you charged ahead with no regard with what might happen. You do need protecting, Savannah, for your own good."

It took every ounce of restraint not to slap him. He had the audacity to lecture her and tally what he considered her mistakes? And the most unbelievable part – it sounded as if he *blamed* her for hers and Georgia's abductions and resulting injuries and scars. *Oh, the nerve...*

She stood, the shock and indignation darkening to rage, "My sister was in danger. I doubt you'd leave any of your brothers to die without searching for them. I left with the intention of finding and saving her and I do not apologize for it."

"You had suspicions about Jordan. You were investigating him, for God's sake."

"I am *not* having this conversation but for the record, you never offered to help me find Georgia. He offered, I accepted. If I hadn't, we'd never have found her until she was dead."

"*You* nearly died."

Savannah barely curtailed the urge to draw back and crack his jaw. What did it take to get through to him? This was not the man she married. He'd transformed into a tyrannical bully accusing her of being flighty and rash. What's more, he refused to consider her side of the situation. The fact she dearly loved her sister and he expected her to stay home and leave Georgia to die? In her book, *that* was absurd and irrational. "*She* nearly died, Ennis. Georgia... nearly... died. She would have if I hadn't gone with Cole. You can call me stupid for going but I love her and wanted to save her. And for the record, I'd have done the same thing if you were missing."

She felt sure her last statement fell on deaf ears. His closed off posture of crossed arms and tilted chin conveyed authority, not openness, "You should have waited."

The weight of his words slackened her shoulders. How could he say such a deplorable thing, knowing how close she and Georgia were? She merely stood and stared, wondering who this man was and where her kind, compassionate husband went.

"If you'd waited," he continued, "those videos wouldn't show up at the station and wherever else he decides to send them." He waved his hand over the postcards, "If you'd waited, none of this would be here."

"You're right," she quickly conceded. "But neither would Georgia and I'd rather have her safe." *And if he'd been up front about the mail, I wouldn't have been blindsided but Mr. Sanctimonious seems to forget that...*

The inconceivable notion made her heart squeeze painfully in her chest. The fact Ennis secreted not only his past but their mail then blamed *her* for the scars disfiguring her back. "You insensitive ass." She pointed to the folder in his hand, "I honestly don't know you anymore and that proves it."

His penchant for condemnation evolved to flippancy as he stared at the folder in his hand, "What are they, divorce or termination papers?"

Savannah didn't trust herself to speak. She hoped he regretted the crack about divorce after reading the file. Maybe that might sober him, she thought. Pointing to it, she simply said, "Read."

He opened the folder and his face darkened. "What'd you do? Go fishing? Because I wouldn't spill my guts about my past, you trolled it out?"

She literally shook with anger. She wanted to hit something and hard. Hit it so hard that the pain erased his betrayal, his accusations and his arrogance. "Yes, Ennis, that's exactly what I did. And while I was there I got *my* departmental records too," she slapped the other folder against his chest, "just in case I forgot any of my screw-ups. Go ahead and read my file. I bet you won't find any surprises in it. Unlike I found in yours."

His jaw repeatedly clenched and released. By his expression, his reply promised a crushing blow. Instead of continuing his verbal assault, he opened his file again and glanced over it, "Don't judge me, Savannah. I was a young deputy relying on my senior officer for guidance."

"Guidance? According to that you gutshot a pregnant woman then waited to call for medical attention. *In my whole career*, I've never delayed or denied anyone medical attention. I may not have believed they needed it, but I provided it."

He slammed the folder down, "What's the use of explaining? You've read it and formed your own opinion – after mining it out of my past."

"Stop getting high and mighty on me, Ennis. The mayor dropped this bombshell on me. I didn't dig it up. I never would have because I trusted you. That was my mistake." Savannah squared off with him, "Why the hell didn't you tell me?"

"Because I knew you'd react this way. You wouldn't believe me if I told you."

"So that's what our marriage means? Well, thanks for the faith. For the record, I'd believe what you told me, *if* you'd fess up." She honestly couldn't believe he'd refuse medical help to anyone and found it impossible to think he shot a pregnant woman for any reason. She wanted him to explain it for her but he evidently assumed the worst of her. That hurt the most. "Just tell me," she urged.

Ennis scrubbed his jaw, "When you and I were introduced as partners, your ex-boyfriend – a guy who beat women if you recall – had just approached you because his wife was missing. You went through a lot of emotional stuff that really didn't fit in with this part of my past. Fair enough?"

She took a deep breath to calm down. The argument spurred another surge of nausea and she didn't have time to puke. She was too busy fighting for their marriage, "Fair enough, but you've had many opportunities to tell me and you didn't."

"I didn't want to tell you. You wouldn't have married me and you sure would've requested a different partner."

She pressed a hand to her stomach to settle the unrest, "Oh, that's silly –"

"Is it?" Ennis defended, "Look at you. You're staring at me like I'm a monster."

No, I'm trying to keep my lunch down… "Ennis, I'm wondering why you kept the mail and your past from me when they're both very important to us. The mere existence of that," she pointed to his folder, "came as a total shock to me."

"I didn't kill that woman's baby, Savannah. I called for the ambulance. My partner, my *senior* officer, delayed the ambulance call. I had to step away to make the call. I did it without her permission."

She nodded in agreement with hopes he'd elaborate, "Okay, you didn't kill the baby and you called for an ambulance."

Since knowing him, Savannah never saw such an expression crawl across his face. The murderous stare he leveled on her sent a shiver down her spine. She stepped back as he closed in. His jaw clenched again, this time it remained set.

He'd misinterpreted her statement and assumed she'd mocked him. Alarms went off in her brain. Get away from him, they said. If she hadn't been pregnant, she'd have stood her ground and fought it out but protecting her baby came first, far before her pride.

She kept backing away, her hands fisted. Ennis's stance looked too reminiscent of her youth. Her father cornered her the same way and nothing good ever came of it – only bruises. While she'd never feared Ennis, she did now and if he struck her, he'd get an ample taste of her temper too – from a distance.

Ennis's anger not only scared but surprised her. He reacted as if the incident occurred yesterday, not years earlier. There was more to the story than the file said but Ennis refused to clarify the details or refute the claims. In her mind, his reaction validated the file's contents – that he shot Kelly Roberts in the stomach and that, in turn, killed her baby.

"You don't believe me," he accused.

"Ennis, I didn't say that."

He stalked closer, "Kelly Roberts reached under the seat. She ignored our warnings to stop. She never offered an explanation why she disobeyed our commands." He loomed over her, his face within inches of hers, "She just reached. Reggie Gibson yelled *gun* and fired at her and I did too. There." Ennis's coffee brown eyes blazed with rage as they stared into her wide blue ones. His hot breath fanned her face, "Are you happy now? You know my secret. I shot a pregnant woman but," he concluded, his words hard and exact, "I… didn't… kill… her… baby."

Savannah swallowed hard. She hated this Ennis. Despite showing no outward fear, she was terrified inside. Adrenaline pumped through her veins faster than a torrential flood. Every muscle in her body tensed, ready to fight or flee. Her brain's warning finally registered in the fog of fear: Get away from him. Get away before he hurts you or worse, hurts the baby.

Keeping a close eye on him, Savannah tentatively stepped back to put space between them. He didn't follow. She chanced another step then another until she could breathe again. Until out of his reach. "Ennis, I never said you killed the baby. I just wanted you to explain…"

He stalked toward her again and she assessed her position. The dining table and chairs were right beside her. The kitchen cabinet with the phone sat right behind him. No calling for help from there, she thought. She wasn't about to bull forward, not into that attitude. The front door was her only prospect for escape.

Ennis wheeled around which relieved her temporarily. With his back turned, she took the opportunity to try and step around the dining chair.

"I've got the perfect answer right here," Ennis spun back to her, his fist doubled.

The image of a phone clenched in that fist sped at her so fast she failed to dodge it. Pain blasted through her chest as it struck her breastbone and she cried out, more from surprise than actual pain. The force of the impact propelled her backward, her heel clipped the dining chair and she flailed, groping for anything to stop her fall. The old wound in her shoulder pulled and ached from the strain. Everything progressed in slow motion. Her descent, her frantic clutching for stability – and during her efforts, her only thought was of the baby.

Sharp pain sliced through her head and neck when it collided with the seat of a neighboring chair. By the time she hit the ground, she was face up, her arm pinned behind her back. Her shoulder vehemently expressed its discontent as she pulled her arm free.

Tears gathered in her eyes. Not from the aching or the fall itself. She worried their child bore some injury from Ennis's tirade. Getting pregnant rated low on her list that year but God had other plans. She was expecting now and somehow she'd already changed. Instead of levering herself up and joining the fray, she shied away from her husband's anger to protect their child.

She remained still, gauging her body's reaction and trying to feel a twinge or spasm indicating something was wrong. She prayed the baby withstood the trauma because her back and shoulder sure hadn't.

In that brief time, Ennis's rage splintered as he raced toward her. The hand he offered her wasn't curled into a fist this time nor did it hold a phone in its grasp. But Savannah leaned further away, still unsure of his mood. When he spoke, he sounded like the Ennis she'd fallen in love with, not the vicious stranger from seconds earlier, "Babe, I'm sorry. I didn't mean to shove you. I was going to call the sheriff and have him fax the papers to us. That's all."

She needed to get up and leave before his evil twin appeared again. Most of all she needed to ensure the baby was okay. Using her free hand, she pushed his away, refusing his help.

Ennis stood wide-eyed at her sprawled out on the floor, "Are you okay?"

Did she *look* okay? Savannah wisely held her tongue, settling for a grimace. She felt dizzy, her back and shoulder ached and her leg was slung gracelessly across the fallen dining chair. "I'm fine," she finally lied. Fine. Yeah. Sure.

Ennis offered her his hand again, "Let me help you up."

"Leave me alone," Savannah grumbled. Propping onto her elbows, she held a hand to her head to appraise the damage. No blood, but a sizable lump. His unexpected reaction could have knocked an elephant on its ass so she felt rather lucky for the minimal damage. She thanked God the baby seemed alright because forgiving her husband would take a while, but if his temper affected their child, she doubted she'd ever forgive him.

Ennis stepped closer, "But you hit your head. Do you need to go to the hospital?"

She glared up at him, "I *need* you to shut up and back off."

Reluctantly, he backed away. Savannah unhooked her leg from the toppled dining chair and slowly maneuvered to her hands and knees. Once on her feet, her shoulder and head began hurting in earnest. She straightened with a wince, "You know what? I'm sorry you think I interfered in your life and I'm especially sorry the mayor made me read that." New tears sprung to her eyes and she brushed them away, "I'm sorry about everything."

Ennis reached out to her. She stopped, stared warily at his hand. He expressed another apology, "Sugar, I'm sorry. It was an accident. I'd never hit you, you know that."

"I do know that," she agreed although she wasn't too sure of it earlier. And truthfully she still wasn't. His anger boiled over into such a frenzy, she'd wondered who she'd married. The phone mishap was just that. She'd stepped forward to go around the chair and without seeing her he'd stepped forward in some grand gesture with the phone. When he thrust it at her, he'd accidentally struck her, knocking her off balance. But, she reminded, his temper shouldn't have escalated to that point. Not over a damn file.

Savannah sidestepped around him, grabbed her purse and keys.

He panicked, "Where are you going?"

"I don't know." Physically she ached. Emotionally she was shattered. Ennis lashed out at the truth. Since their marriage, she prayed he'd confide in her. He chose to hem and haw and make veiled excuses for why he moved from Texas. The instant the truth revealed itself, he reacted as though she threatened to castrate him.

A hand on her shoulder stopped her. She closed her eyes, "Ennis, please."

"You're coming back soon, right?" he asked with cautious hope.

She let her silence answer. He gently squeezed, "I'm so sorry."

Tears rolled down her cheeks. "Me too."

27

Ennis watched his wife walk to the car, one hand bracing her back, the other fisting her keys. He hung back as she demanded, although his heart begged him to chase after her and fall on his knees, pleading for forgiveness.

Savannah winced as she slid into the Camaro's driver's seat. Their eyes met briefly before she slammed the door. It took a few seconds for her to start the engine. In that time, he stepped off the porch, walked to her car.

She glanced up and immediately her back straightened, both hands gripping the steering wheel in a death grip. Savannah shook her head, revved the engine. Do not come near me, her expression warned. "Come on, babe," he begged. "Let's talk about this. Don't leave."

Savannah backed into the street without acknowledging his plea or presence. He watched her swipe away more tears then shift into drive, easing the car down the street. She was angry and hurt and had every right to be. He'd managed to lie to her and hurt her, two things he vowed never to do. His secrecy cut her to the soul while his fiery reaction physically injured her.

Ennis stood in the driveway as the Camaro's brake lights flashed on and stayed. A glimmer of hope quickened his heart. Had she reconsidered? He uttered a prayer for her to back down the street, wheel into the drive and at least stay and talk. He could fix this, he thought. All she had to do was *stay.*

The few seconds felt like an eternity as her car sat, idling at the stop sign. *I'm still here, waiting.* He implored the Camaro's backup lights to flash on. *Come back, babe. Please come back to me.* The lights never flashed on. Instead, her red beast turned the corner, headed for the main thoroughfare.

Rubbing his knuckles, the lingering twinge prompted memories of them colliding with her breastbone. Besides shock, Ennis saw fear in her eyes just before all hell broke loose. She'd never been frightened of him in her life – until then. Ennis hung his head, ashamed that he allowed his temper to shatter that trust between them. From now on, she'd probably regard him with a jaundiced eye like she did her father, the man she worked so hard to avoid.

Hitting her had been an accident. She'd moved closer to him for whatever reason and when he turned to point the phone at her, his fist connected with hardness of bone. Standing in the driveway, he relived the nasty argument as fragments continued filtering in. Fear suddenly knotted inside him, "Oh my God. Did I really blame her for what happened with Holland and Jordan?" Ennis rubbed his forehead, muttering a curse under his breath. Oh yes. He'd done that and more.

"Everything okay?"

Ennis snapped to attention at the unexpected voice. He turned to see Edward Collins who stood, casually watering his wife's red and pink flowers. He'd witnessed Savannah limping off on the verge of tears. Just great.

Jealousy swiftly overshadowed embarrassment. People like the Collins family evidently kept their squabbles behind closed doors, refusing to show the world they were normal human beings. At that point he realized how sick Edward and Katherine made him.

Considering how Savannah exited the house and his subsequent heartfelt appeal to her, Ennis had to say something alluding to the truth, "Could be better."

Edward nodded once, returned to his task of watering, "You're preaching to the choir, brother." Ennis didn't dwell on the comment long since he needed to find out where his wife went. Chances were good she headed for Georgia's so he went inside to call Savannah's cell phone. Two steps in the door and he groaned. She left it on the entry table. Probably on purpose, knowing he'd try calling her.

He went to the phone, dialed Dane's cell number. His brother answered on the third ring. "Savannah and I had a fight," Ennis said. "I figure she's coming over to talk to Georgia."

"What happened?" Dane wanted to know.

Ennis told him about the file Mayor O'Neill managed to scrape up from Ennis's days at the sheriff's department.

"You'd already told her about it so it wasn't a surprise, right?"

Shame warmed his face. His silence spoke volumes as Dane urged, "You *did* tell her, didn't you?"

After another pause, Ennis's brother uttered a granddaddy of an expletive then scoffed, “And Mama always said you were so smart. She’ll likely change that opinion after this. Does Savannah think you let that baby die?”

“The mayor’s report left her no choice. He had it edited where I shot and killed that woman’s baby. But…” he raked a hand through his hair, “that isn’t the only reason Savannah left.”

“Damn, Ennis, how could you make it worse unless you hit the woman…” Dane’s voice was cold and exact, “If she comes here claimin’ you hit her, I’ll break you in half.”

Oh, for God’s sake, “I did not hit her. We argued. She fell over the dining chair.”

“Ennis, did you shove her?” His brother’s ominous tone brought images of Dane bracing him against the wall then letting fists fly, all while summarizing their father’s lesson on how to treat a woman. Their parents raised them to use a gentle word and hand with the ladies. If Dane presumed he’d hit Savannah, the older brother would gladly readjust his attitude and the effects of Dane’s beltings lasted for weeks.

Ennis opened a veritable can of worms with the phone call. He tried to calm him down, “I did no such –”

“And in her condition? Are you insane or just stupid?” Dane’s anger deepened to an unexpected rage.

Ennis found himself shying from his brother even on the phone, “It was an accident. I turned and she was too close and she fell and hit her head. It was an accident, I swear.” He decided to omit the postcard fiasco. Dane already figured him for an idiot, no sense proving him completely right. And what was this sudden concern about her condition? First Georgia, now Dane. As far as he knew Jeffrey's wounds had long healed, at least the physical ones...

"Did she hurt herself pretty bad?" Dane asked, his concern thankfully shifting from beating Ennis black and blue. "She may need a doctor to check her out."

Ennis wished he knew. She wasn't exactly forthcoming after that fiasco. "I don't know, but she won't talk to me. I'd call Seth, but I already got you threatening to maim me and he wouldn't just maim, he'd kill me and not leave a body. I'll call work and see if she's there. Let me know if she shows up at Georgia's, will you?"

"I'll call."

"I'll contact the sheriff back home and have him fax me everything about that night. She can read the truth if she ever comes home."

"If you're telling me the truth, she'll be back. Give her time to cool off."

Just what he needed. Faith. His brother still sounded skeptical of his story. It does sound lame, he thought. How many times had he heard abused wives blame the bruises on a fall? Now thanks to his brother, Georgia, Seth and probably R.J. would be out for blood...

He'd worry about that later. He had to find Savannah, make sure she was okay. He dialed the station only to learn her office was empty. The only other place he figured she'd go – Piedmont Park. He started for the door, fully intending to look for her but something stopped him. The pain in her eyes – physical and emotional – plus her tears warned she toed a thin line. If she needed time to think, his presence might backfire. She made it clear she wanted to be alone so he'd give her some leeway for a few hours.

By nine o'clock, he called the sheriff to have copies of the files sent to him. Ennis prayed she came home soon. Once she read the report and learned Reggie Gibson's bullet killed the baby and that Reggie lost her job and the lawsuit, maybe she'd be okay. *My shot hit Roberts in the side but only because she leaned forward when I pulled the trigger. I never aimed at her belly or her side.*

He recalled Savannah's vow. *I'll believe what you tell me.* He doubted her mind was truly that open. Of all the people he ever knew, Savannah trusted the least. She trusted Georgia, and she finally trusted him – until he screwed it up. Lies of omission. Marriages fell apart on less and he hoped and prayed theirs survived. They could patch things up, he assured. He'd work till his last breath to do it. If she'd just give him a chance.

O O O

The dim glow of morning filtered through the bedroom curtains. Ennis gradually opened his eyes from the few hours of restless sleep. His head ached and he felt wrung out from the fight and from the beer he'd consumed.

By two in the morning, he hadn't heard from Dane except when his brother called to ask if Savannah had returned. No word from Georgia, Seth, R.J. or anyone at the station. Ennis resorted to calling hospitals, just in case she had an accident or her injuries were worse than she admitted to. In the end, no one knew where Savannah was.

Morning dawned with the reality she never came home. The faxed information from Texas still sat on her pillow, undisturbed.

Ennis sighed. So much for optimism. He rolled out of bed and lumbered bleary-eyed into the living room wearing only his boxers. If he was alone, he might as well act the part.

As he passed the coffee table, he spied three empty beer cans he neglected to pick up the night before. Well, screw it. They could just stay there. His priorities changed overnight and they didn't include picking up after himself.

Rounding the corner of the couch, Ennis stopped cold. The headache eased slightly. Hope bloomed as his heart kicked in his chest. Savannah lay stretched out on the new sectional. She still wore the same clothes she left in. She'd kicked off her shoes and spread her suit jacket across her for a makeshift blanket. The smooth skin of her forehead creased slightly between her brows. Flashes of her falling returned to his aching head, followed by those of her banging her head against the chair then groaning as she rubbed her right shoulder. Well shit, he thought. He'd forgotten about Holland's handiwork and how really sensitive her shoulder still was. She probably strained it during the fall. Just another thing to feel crappy about. Her *condition* as Dane so tactfully put it.

The sight of her on the couch told him one thing. He'd probably destroyed her trust so completely that she refused to share a bed with him. He shook his head. Dear God, what had he done by keeping this from her?

He debated over waking her or not. She'd wake up once he moved around in the kitchen to brew coffee. Ennis decided to face his worst fear without benefit of caffeine or alcohol. Using her big toe, he gently wobbled her foot.

Savannah stirred somewhat then stretched. Pain registered with the movement and after a subdued groan, she lazily blinked awake. Her vision met his, "Hey."

Finally, an encouraging sign. At least they were still on speaking terms. "You up for coffee yet?" he asked.

She nodded, tossed her jacket aside and yawned. She acted reserved but not like he feared. He placed a filter in the coffee pot, scooped extra coffee in. It amazed him how her constitution withstood the abuse. She used jalapenos and Tabasco sauce the way others used pepper or ketchup. And the potency of her coffee could drill holes in concrete. "How are you feeling?" he asked.

Savannah braced her back, stretched until it straightened, "Stiff and sore but I've had worse."

He broached the subject bothering him most, "You didn't come to bed last night."

Savannah closed her eyes, pressed a hand to her stomach. She appeared almost sick for a minute, swallowing hard and releasing a slow breath. He was about to ask about it when she replied, "That folder on my pillow. I don't care about it."

He nearly dropped the coffee can on the floor. She had to be kidding. "It explains everything. It also shows I'm not the bastard

O'Neill led you to believe. It didn't tell you I shot Kelly Roberts in –"

"Ennis, stop."

"I shot her in the side, not the stomach. And –"

"*Please.*"

"She leaned forward when I shot. I didn't kill the baby. Reggie did. That fax has ballistics reports proving it."

Savannah rolled her eyes, "There's no need for me to read it."

Uh-oh. That sounded ominous. "Why not?"

Instead of answering outright, she combed her fingers through her hair, bringing some semblance of order to it then headed to the kitchen. Ennis saw her toss another scoop of coffee in the basket while it brewed. Ennis cringed. The coffee would be stouter than their home's foundation.

"Ennis, I don't have to read some ream of paper to know you didn't kill the baby. And when you told me you called an ambulance, I believed you."

The conversation was headed somewhere but its route baffled him. Unlike her usual blunt approach, Savannah opted to skirt the issue to a degree and she mastered that tact better than a lawyer. Just the idea of a lawyer brought his headache back and he massaged his temple. He worried himself sick – and nearly drunk – during the last twelve hours. He lacked the stamina to tiptoe through that minefield again. Bulling into it like she usually did sounded better to him, "Then why did you leave? I told you the fall was an accident."

She sighed, "I never accused you of pushing me."

"Then *why did you leave*? I was worried out of my mind."

Her hand on his arm gently urged him to face her, "I left because I couldn't accept the lack of trust. You should have trusted me."

"I do trust you."

Savannah placed a finger to his lips to shush him, "You don't or you would have told me about this long ago. Like the dozens of times I asked why you moved from Texas."

He clasped her hand in his, "And you realize from experience there are situations you'd rather not share, whether you are at fault or not. In your case you didn't tell me what your uncle did to you as a child." He felt her stiffen at the reference to the man who tried to molest her when she was younger.

She pulled away from his grasp, her expression questioning his sanity, "At that point we were only partners, not spouses and we were *new* partners and that. No one dumps their skeleton-filled closet on their new partner. That's like telling all your hang-ups and habits on your first date."

"Granted," he agreed, trying to calm her down. Her temper lit at the mention of her Uncle Bryan and in retrospect, it should have. "You're right. I chose a bad example. But you could have told me about Terence LaVeau when we partnered up."

Savannah put hands to hips, "Oh, my psycho ex-partner who I thought was spending twenty years behind bars? The one I didn't realize had escaped? Gosh, Ennis, how thoughtless of me. I should've known Terence was stalking me and planning to kidnap Lindsey. In the future, I'll try polishing my crystal ball better."

Well, that certainly backfired. He scratched his head, realizing her arguments were valid, his were just puny. But how could he explain it so she understood his secrecy – without inviting her to put a dent in his head?

Savannah opened the overhead cabinets. She removed only her coffee cup. She sat the multicolored mug declaring her the "World's Greatest Aunt" in front of the slowly brewing coffee pot. Clearly she wasn't in a mood supporting his "World's Greatest Uncle" mug.

The brewing coffee smelled strong enough to singe his nose hair. He'd have to cut the potency with a shot of water to avoid an instant ulcer.

Her blue eyes fixed on her department folder in his recliner, "I assume you read it?"

Ennis leaned in front of her for his own coffee cup. She wanted to get shitty about it? Fine, "There wasn't much else to do except read. My wife walked out yesterday."

She ignored the gibe, "Learn anything new?"

Ennis helped himself to the first cup of coffee, "You knew I wouldn't."

"Yes, I did." She sighed, waited for him to relinquish the carafe. When she poured hers, it filled only halfway. She slid the carafe back in the coffee pot then slanted him an irritated frown while waiting for the remaining coffee to brew.

Ennis headed straight to the sink. One good squirt of hot water cut the kick and viscosity to barely consumable. As he sipped the now lukewarm coffee, the answer occurred to him, "Your diagnosis. You weren't forthcoming with me about that. It was basically by accident I found out."

She tilted the meager amount of coffee into her cup, spooned in sugar and cream then stirred, "Is this a pissing contest? I wasn't hiding *anything* from you. I wanted to hear the diagnosis first *then* tell you. That's entirely different than hiding it." After a quick sip, she asked, "How the hell could I? You mother hen me worse than Georgia. I can't run to Kroger's without you asking where I'm going and when I'll be back. You really think I could hide breast cancer from you?"

Okay, so he sounded petty. Ridiculous even. He'd accepted that once he mentioned Terence LaVeau. But damn it, he wanted her to understand he hadn't intended to hurt her. The coffee finally finished brewing and he removed the mug from her grasp to fill it. Once he topped off the cup, he spooned a little more sugar and cream and stirred. Savannah thanked him. He nodded then apologized, "I never meant to hurt you with that news back home. I was wrong to keep it from you, but I do trust you, babe. I do."

"Start trusting me more. I'm in this marriage forever, and unless you're wanted for murder, rape or being a general nuisance, I'm sticking with you indefinitely. So if there's anything else you haven't told me, spill it now before the mayor shoves it in my face."

"There's nothing, I swear." He took another swallow of coffee and choked. Even diluted, the coffee practically walked by itself. He cleared the tears from his eyes and added more water to his cup, "Where'd you go yesterday?" He tried some cream to cut the strength then took another sip. Better.

"I went to Seth's."

Ennis nearly spewed. His mother despised hearing the Savior's name used with such inflection but it bounded from his tongue before he could stop it. The outburst surprised Savannah too and she stood, awaiting the rest of his spectacle.

Meanwhile he tried to calm his pounding heart, "Your brother's? Why didn't you just drop by R.J.'s too? Your daddy could hold me down while Seth beats me to death or vice versa."

She looked confused, "What are you talking about?"

"Good God, woman. Seth's gonna kill me 'cause he probably thinks I hit you. Not only that, he probably thinks I've got this whole sordid past I'm keeping from you."

Her smile should've made him so angry he could breathe fire. Bloody images appeared of Seth and R.J. Prince clubbing him to death in some dark, remote alley. Seth's training as an Army Ranger probably gave him hundreds of quick, efficient ways to dispose of an annoying brother-in-law. It wasn't funny but she insisted on smiling. "What's so funny?" he asked. "The idea of me in traction?"

"No. The idea you think I ran to my brother to tattle. I had Leah look at my shoulder and I talked to her about everything. Are you afraid of her too?"

"Won't she tell Seth?"

"I expect so."

He tensed again. The thought of fighting with her brother made him positively nauseous – or perhaps it was the coffee. But holding his own against big ol' Seth Prince would drain whatever strength he had left.

"They've had arguments before," she continued matter-of-factly. "Leah walked out and didn't come back for a week."

She added the last for effect, he hoped. "I'm thankful you returned sooner than that."

She didn't reply. When Savannah's pensive side surfaced, it troubled him. Her vision migrated to her wedding ring. Ennis's stomach cramped. Her expressionless gaze made him worry she regretted wearing it.

Moments passed so painfully he swore he heard his watch ticking each second away, "You have second thoughts about coming home?"

She shook her head but that distant gaze bothered him. He dreaded the answer, "Then what's wrong?"

She shrugged her good shoulder, "Is there a chance an Ennis Jr. will show up with his mother some morning? Maybe you've got a family back home you don't know about – or haven't told me about."

Nice one. Never saw that one coming. She slipped the blade in fast and clean. "What?" he asked. She never got this outrageous or paranoid until today. Hiding an incident on the job hardly equated to secreting an entire family.

After another survey of her ring, she expounded on the notion, "Maybe he'll have inherited your brown eyes, your charming smile and have that same stubborn cowlick you do."

Ennis instinctively smoothed the back of his hair. Where the hell was she going with this preposterous idea? A kid with his eyes and crazy cowlick? "I didn't leave anyone barefoot and pregnant."

The slight tilt of her head and raised brow reminded him of his mother when she caught him in a lie. Only this time he hadn't lied. At least he didn't think so.

With great ceremony, Ennis upended his coffee cup in the sink. If he had to endure the Inquisition, he'd damn well do it with decent coffee.

As if reading his mind, she sidled up to the coffee pot for a refill, "There's nothing wrong with this coffee."

"Any thicker and it'll form tar balls. Unlike you, I can't drink Pennzoil." While going about brewing less calamitous coffee, he explained, "If I knocked anyone up before I left home, they should have come forward when you and I got engaged. You're accusing the wrong brother, Savannah. Dane is the womanizer – or was. Jake isn't far behind. If there's any kids runnin' around with brown eyes, a goofy grin and kicked up hair, it's their doin', not mine."

Savannah shrugged again, "Okay."

No, it wasn't okay. Whether doubt or payback fueled her crusade, he didn't know but before she ascended that golden pedestal, he'd be happy to knock some reality back into her. She had secrets too. It took her forever to confess to her drinking problem. What else had she conveniently forgotten to tell him? "Oh, yeah? What about you?"

She laughed, "I'm pretty sure I haven't fathered any kids here or anywhere else."

The haughty reply spurred his anger, "How many men have you slept with and did you ever get pregnant?" Ennis immediately closed his mouth. The fiery words flying around in his brain found unexpected freedom – and hit their mark like poison arrows. He truly couldn't believe he uttered them.

By Savannah's expression, neither could she. Hurt and outrage clouded her beautiful features. He wanted the words back, every last one of them, particularly the unspoken indictment of abortion. She held strong beliefs in that area and if she'd ever been pregnant, there would have been a little boy or girl biting at his ankles when he met Savannah.

Her eyes narrowed at him in a particularly unbecoming and dangerous glare. He'd seen that expression once since meeting her acquaintance and she'd been semi-drunk at the time, and she'd swung back to slap the snot out of him. Today, she looked ready to finish the job.

Savannah carefully sat her cup down probably so she didn't chuck it at him, "You're grilling me about *my* sex life?" She took a single step toward him. The slow, graceful movement would have turned him on except for the hostility shooting from her blue eyes. He stood his ground, "You started it by accusing me…"

She moved closer, "You want a number of sex partners and, what, *abortions* I've had? That's perfect, Ennis. It shows you know nothing about me. We're married but I'm still a stranger to you."

"That's ridiculous. I know you don't believe in abortion."

"Yet you asked. I've owned up to my mistakes and aired my dirty laundry with you so after yesterday I *should* question your past."

Frustration overwhelmed her, "Why can't you see my side of this situation?"

"Because the air gets thin at that altitude," he shot back with another pang of instant regret. He knew he needed to shut up but something – pride, he assumed – kept his mouth flapping.

A tiny flame lit behind her blue eyes. History warned him to put space between them before her hand tattooed his cheek. She stood trembling with rage for the second time in two days. A hand across his cheek sounded insignificant but with Savannah's strength, it meant a bruise. Ennis remained rooted, waiting for her fury.

Except for their short, angry breaths, the room fell silent. Her face darkened to deep crimson, her muscles taut in preparation to swing back and nail him. Ennis tensed, prepared to seize her hand or fist, whichever she threw. To his surprise she raised neither. Instead she shouldered past him, marched to the bedroom.

He followed behind, baffled by her behavior, "You're walking out on our discussion?"

Usually she hung around to verbally duke it out with her opponent. This time he *wanted* her to stay and hammer out the argument. However, when Savannah rounded on him he rethought that strategy. By the look on her face, he'd rather just let her cool off.

"I'm getting ready for work," she snapped, "and last I saw, this passed the discussion stage a long time ago." She stomped into the bathroom then wheeled back to him again, "Oh, when I get an opportunity, I'll assemble a list of my sexual conquests and an approximation of my total sexual encounters and get it to you." She punctuated the promise by slamming the door in his face.

He stared at the door, stunned that they'd had not one but two vicious fights. How did it spin out of control so fast? And why had he dumped gasoline on an already volatile situation? *And Mama always said you were so smart...* Dane's sarcasm stung like salt in an open wound. Indeed, their mother crowed about Ennis's intellect and common sense. Most of his decisions met with acceptance and sometimes glowing praise. But the last twenty-four hours proved one thing. Mama Rutherford made mistakes too. Her pride and joy, as Dane would point out, was officially an idiot.

The bathroom door unexpectedly flew open. Savannah now stood completely naked, her body flushed head to toe with anger, "For the record, before our marriage the total number of pregnancies was zero. That means I couldn't have had an abortion which I *wouldn't* have done anyway. So there."

The door slammed again, leaving Ennis speechless and stunned. Yep. No doubt about it. He was a genuine, card-carrying idiot.

O O O

Savannah stood, staring in the mirror. Tears formed and she angrily swiped them away. This was not what marriage was supposed to be. Accusations. Surprises. Tempers running so hot that people got physically injured. But her mother had endured it, hadn't she? Charlene lived in a volatile marriage, every day an uncertainty, never knowing if she'd crawl into bed at night with bruises darkening her fair skin. R.J. turned home life into war. Quiet one minute, raging the next.

Touching the knot at the back of her head, she wondered if this was how her parents began married life. One giant tirade, an accidental push and R.J. not only crossed a line but established an all encompassing fear that ran the gamut from his wife to his youngest child.

Her vision drifted to her belly, held her hand there. She refused to allow her child to grow up in that atmosphere. *My child will not grow up in an unsafe environment. I did it and it screwed me up. My baby will have love, security, stability. This child will not fear or resent us. I will not allow it.* She and Ennis needed time to calm down, gather their wits and hopefully their manners along the way. And if he didn't, she'd gladly explain that it helped if the parents acted somewhat older than the baby currently residing in her belly. Their child deserved better than the last twenty-four hours.

She patted her belly, wiped a tear sliding down her cheek. Arguing wasn't fair to the baby. All the fussing and stress. Her mama would shake her finger at her youngest with a stern warning to straighten up. Ladies don't fight, she'd say. Ladies find other avenues to make their point. And ladies don't jeopardize the health of their unborn child by pitching hissy fits, no matter how much the husband deserved it.

I'll try harder, Mama. But she had to have help. Ennis unwittingly found the most infuriating things to say. She sure hoped it was unwittingly. She'd never known him to be intentionally hateful but his inference about abortion unraveled her last nerve. Did he truly believe she'd go against her raising and her moral compass?

She patted her stomach and stepped into the shower, "It's okay, little one. Don't worry. Everything will work out." At least she prayed it did.

28

"Everything okay?" Josh Hunter asked. He specifically asked Savannah and she wished he hadn't. No, everything was not okay. Nothing was okay in her personal life or her professional life. Rather than fessing up or playing nice, her husband cared more about hiding things from her and accusing her of having abortions. And as for her job, she felt more like an underpaid babysitter than a detective.

Her back and shoulder still twinged occasionally just remind her how positively wretched the last day had been. At least the baby seemed alright. She thanked God for that because dealing with the past twenty four hours *and* miscarrying would finish her off. So for that blessing, she replied, "Everything's peachy."

Hunter considered her statement, shifted his vision to Ennis who bowed up at the words. Their boss looked to Ben and Mathis for any hints but both shrugged.

Ben shouldn't look so innocent, she thought. She held him responsible for practically a third of the mayhem since he dodged duties, offered lame excuses for it then absconded with her notes on the Vaughn case. She could only imagine where they were now. Probably floating around in the chaotic universe of Olson's desk, the surface of which hadn't been seen in days. Oh yeah, just peachy…

Hunter hesitantly accepted her answer, "Anything new on the case?"

Ennis's mouth opened to answer. Savannah beat him to it, "Ben and I are going back over the security tapes." She turned to Ben, hoping for an affirmative answer, "Did you look at the passkey list yet?"

Ben swallowed, shook his head. Savannah rolled her eyes. If one more obnoxious male jumped in the mix, she'd scream, "I told you days ago to do that. Get on it now."

"Ma'am, that's a lot of names," the rookie countered.

"You're not three years old, Ben. You should be able to count higher than twenty and cope."

Mathis chuckled, prompting Ennis to nudge him with his elbow. She appreciated the move but didn't welcome Ennis's offer of, "We'll split the list if you–"

"Fine," she blurted, looking to Josh. "I'll give half the list to Mathis and he and his partner can work with it."

Her exclusion of Ennis's name caught everyone's attention. Ennis crossed his arms. If he didn't approve of the term "his partner", too bad.

"Okay," Josh drew the word out, wary of the growing conflict. "Let me know if you find something."

She acknowledged with a stern nod then jerked her head in the direction of the door, "Let's go, Ben. Work to do."

"Yes, ma'am."

She resisted the urge to correct him. She overheard Mathis tell

Ennis, "Boy, am I glad I'm working with you."

"Can it, Mathis," Ennis griped.

"Yeah, right, I'll rephrase. Boss, is there anything I could do until Hatfield and McCoy work out their problems?"

Josh addressed Mathis, "John, you and Ben split up the passkey list. Get busy looking it over." He waved his hand toward the door then stopped his warring detectives from following behind, "You two, front and center. What's the problem?"

Ben and Mathis hurried from the office, closed the door. In that time, Savannah took a deliberate step away from her spouse. This was *not* leaving the confines of their marriage if she had anything to say about it. Their boss was just that. Their boss – not their marriage counselor, not their pastor or priest. They had no business disclosing their problems to him and he definitely did not want to hear them, no matter what he said.

Savannah's lips pursed as an unspoken warning to Ennis who appeared more impatient than earlier. That meant he planned to spill their issues to Josh Hunter, probably in an exhaustively meticulous manner than would embarrass them both.

Sure enough, her husband confessed, "I said something that upset her."

Savannah crossed her arms, still in steadfast refusal to look in his direction, "This is a private matter. Getting our boss involved is inappropriate, not to mention uncomfortable for me."

Hunter settled into his chair to observe his detectives. By his demeanor, he recognized the can of worms he'd pried open.

Furthermore, he seemed to regret it already as he leaned back, ready for a long, drawn-out discussion.

Ennis turned to her, clamped his hands on his hips, "Can't you let it go?"

Ennis wasn't normally a blockhead. Today, however, he did a fine impression of one and that really irritated her, "What part of 'not here, not now' do you not understand?"

Josh finally spoke, "I get it. You're having marital problems. It happens to everyone and we manage to deal with it. But if your quarreling muddies up this case, I will take action. I've fielded enough cannonballs from the mayor I'm not prepared to battle him and my people. What kind of bandage can you patch this with and still work together?"

"Duct tape," Savannah lashed out, "and lots of it. If you catch my meaning." From the corner of her eye she saw Ennis gape open-mouthed at her.

Josh Hunter scrubbed his face with his palms, "Without shedding too much light, what started this argument?"

"Lies of omission," she blurted only to hear Ennis mutter a blistering expletive in response. God hates that word, she quietly berated. And His last name *isn't* dammit.

Josh turned to him while Ennis offered, "That incident in Texas with the pregnant woman. The mayor gave her the report yesterday – a cleverly edited version labeling me a baby killer."

Hunter's eyes widened, "You never told her about it?"

"Why is everyone stoning me?" Ennis growled. "I didn't kill that baby and I'm the only one that called the ambulance."

Josh opened a desk drawer, took out a bottle of aspirin. He shook two in his hand and popped them in his mouth. Savannah cringed as he chewed them up, swallowed then chased them with water. Their boss sighed, "That's not the point, Ennis. Wives like honesty as much as husbands do. If you suddenly found out Savannah had been under investigation nine years ago for the same thing, I'm assuming you'd want to know too."

"As she has repeatedly stressed, I don't have to ask because she's told me everything." He hitched his thumb at Savannah, fuming, "She acts like I tried to cut that woman to pieces."

Savannah rounded on him again, her indignation darkening to chaste fury. Perhaps he'd forgotten what Jeffrey Holland tried to do to *her*. The carvings beneath her collarbone weren't exactly love notes. If her husband needed a refresher course on Jeffrey's brutality, she'd happily provide it, starting with a sharp – and sorely needed – slap across his arrogant face.

Seeing her swift transformation, Josh quickly intervened, "That's not helping, Ennis. Not helping at all, especially after what Savannah went through."

Sudden realization dawned and Ennis covered his face with his hands, sighing. He apologized to her, "It was a figure of speech, babe. You know I didn't mean anything by it."

Two days ago, sure. Today? Not so much. He'd accused her of heinous things that last twelve hours or so, including betrayal, whoring around, and he left the undeclared accusation of abortion on the table. *No, Ennis, I'm not sure what you mean anymore…*

She addressed Josh without breaking eye contact with Ennis, "He won't try to understand my point of view. He'd rather make tacky insinuations about my premarital sexual conduct."

"Okay," Hunter lifted a hand, "a little too much information there. I'd rather –"

"You're the one who started with the mysterious Ennis Jr. showing up," Ennis shot back at her.

"Ennis Jr.?" Hunter questioned.

Like a wildfire, the argument took on a life of its own, its heat and intensity threatening to destroy everything in its path, even their marriage. Savannah determinedly stood her ground, "With all the surprises lately, how can you blame me?"

"Guys," Josh called, "need to know basis and I *don't* need or want to know."

"Tell her I'm not a murderer," Ennis demanded.

"Tell him I'm not a slut," Savannah insisted.

"*Both of you shut up.*" Their captain dropped into his chair again, rubbed his forehead until it was red. He eyed the aspirin, probably debating whether to ingest them all and be done with it.

"But he –" Savannah began only for Hunter to lift one finger, stopping her.

"Not a word, Savannah," he warned, "not from either of you. I obviously can't help you. It's a subject best dealt with at home but I *can* assist you here at work. Savannah, you and Ben work in your office and

Ennis will work with Mathis in his. If you must interact, send your partners to the other office. You're acting like kids so I'll treat you like kids. Go to your corners and stay. Fight at home. Not here. We have a murder to solve so solve it." He grabbed the aspirin bottle, threw back one more and followed it with a swallow of water. "Treat your partners better than you're treating each other." He stabbed a finger at the door, "Dismissed."

Savannah swiveled on her heel to march out. Ennis's outlandish behavior, his insinuations and his secrecy brought her anger to a head once again. As she opened the door, she wheeled back to Ennis, proclaiming, "I'm pregnant. And before you accuse me of anything absurd, it *is* your baby."

Pleased with her announcement and the delivery of it, she wheeled only to run smack into Ben Olson's chest. Perfect, she thought stepping around him. Just perfect.

She heard the grin in Ben's voice, "Congratulations, ma'am."

"Oh, shut up," she snapped. She turned then stalked down the hall in search of a quiet place without a single member of the male population.

O O O

Ennis collapsed in his chair, the shock still setting in. The entire train wreck from the last day vanished as tender, happy images replaced it. They flooded his brain until a blinding smile brightened his face.

Cradling their infant, singing lullabies, reading bedtime stories and playing peek-a-boo. He yearned for this day, counting it as one of his most coveted dreams. The day he learned Savannah was pregnant.

The smile faded a degree. She hurled the revelation at him like slinging mud. If Mama ain't happy, ain't nobody happy. And Mama was livid. The pregnancy came a year too early. They'd planned for the next year and now were prematurely blessed with a baby. But how, for God's sake? They never, never, never – upon threat of bloody violent death – engaged in unprotected sex. Savannah wasn't ready for motherhood, she said. Not yet. She had a favorite phrase she used at such times, one other than "shee-yet". It was "God sure has a sense of humor". No shee-yet, he thought.

Then it slowly dawned. She'd missed her birth control pill. When her wounds from Jeffrey Holland healed, they'd put their old house on the market to sell and they'd frolicked in celebration. Ennis would bet a hundred bucks she forgot to take her pill once or twice during that time. Her emotional state wavered between stable and unstable anyway so remembering birth control probably rated low on her list. Plus preparing to move had been hectic. Cleaning, packing and still showing up for work. If it was hectic for him, it was chaotic for her. If he calculated it correctly, she was around two months pregnant.

The evil eye she skewered him with seemed to lay blame. Mama's *really* not happy, he assumed. Mama's blaming Daddy for having persistent, spirited swimmers. Ennis prayed the idea of motherhood grew on her because as she painfully pointed out, there was no other option for her.

He leaned back, indulging in fantasies of Savannah carrying their young 'un on her hip and rocking their little lamb to sleep. Then he afforded himself the whimsy of two babies. Maybe a boy and a girl. He'd never seriously entertained names but now he began searching out names fitting the faces of these angels, their chubby little cheeks and tiny pink lips grinning back at Daddy.

His smile spread into full bloom. He was destined for Daddyhood in the coming months. *Wait till Ma finds out...*

"Hey," Mathis leaned in with a thumbs up, "I hear congratulations are in order."

"Don't go spreading the news," Ennis cautioned. "She's mad enough to break us all in half."

"Ouch. She not want kids?"

"It's not that. We had a bad argument last night that's hung over till this morning. She does want kids but now the question is – does she want *my* kids?"

Mathis waved it off, "Give her some alone time. Women are like that. My wife disappeared for hours, sometimes days, after we'd fight. Don't take this wrong but until our divorce, those were the best and most peaceful days of my married life."

Ennis wasn't sure what to say. Mathis approached marriage with a different attitude than he did. John got married and had kids but like plenty of law enforcement marriages, it soured into a bitter divorce. Ennis possessed more optimism for his and Savannah's marriage. They were both cops and both understood the pressures of the job. Neither held the other to impossible expectations…

Expectations. The word struck a nerve followed closely by Savannah's plea – *Why can't you see my side of this situation?* All she'd wanted was the truth and he'd never given her that courtesy. Instead he ignored it and when she discovered the truth he'd yelled and accidentally pushed her. *Oh my God…* A knife of panic suddenly sliced through his self pity. The baby. No wonder she'd left in tears and headed straight for Leah's. Seth's wife worked as a trauma nurse at Grady, the only Level 1 trauma hospital in Atlanta. After the fall, Savannah needed assurance the baby was okay and Leah stood the best chance of troubleshooting any problems. Of course Ennis *assumed* she told Leah about the baby. Being such a private person, Savannah may not have but when she left after the fall, she looked terrified. That emotion should have put him on alert but his anger overshadowed everything, even his consideration toward his own wife. If anything happened to Savannah or the baby because of his lousy temper, he'd never forgive himself.

Ennis shook his head, the joy of fatherhood waning to shame. He'd been a real asshole and he needed to apologize in a way she'd listen. His quandary was how. Walking into her office might leave him with a dent in his head. If her throwing arm was as accurate as her aim with a .38, defenselessly waltzing into her lair meant certain doom or at least a trip to the doctor for stitches. No, what he needed was a way to say "I'm Sorry" without risk of injury.

"Hey," Mathis said before turning to leave, "I hope you ain't predisposed to that twin gene. Now *that* might send her racin' for the hills..."

O O O

She'd been visiting the restroom far too often lately. She knew which stalls had iffy locks, which toilets flushed better than others and unfortunately, she'd nearly memorized the nicks and scrapes on the surrounding tile floor. So far that day she hadn't required the services of the porcelain throne, only the solitude of the small, quiet stall. The comfort of solitude overrode her claustrophobia for some reason but she bet it resided mostly in her temper. For a good ten minutes women entered and exited the restroom while Savannah struggled to dial down her anger from volcanic to simmering. Ennis walked on razor thin ice with her. The last twenty-four hours showed her a different side to her husband, one she wasn't sure she could live with. The distrust, the lies, the accusations and goading – none of it belonged to the Ennis she loved. To a degree the drastic change reminded her of her father. Sweet and thoughtful one moment, hateful and menacing the next. She couldn't live with that, not like her mother had.

I'm overreacting, I have to be. Ennis isn't Daddy. Ennis isn't Daddy. She repeated the mantra until the pounding in her chest settled. Ennis was different than R.J., she told herself. He didn't hit her. *But I thought he might.* And where had the accusations come from? And his distrust? What had she done to provoke that?

A knock on the stall door shattered the endless questions. Savannah hung her head. She just wanted time to think. A little peace and quiet. Why couldn't anyone take a damn hint?

"Detective, are you okay? You've been in there a while."

Wonderful. The inquisitive rookie again. Did the woman roost in the bathroom all day? Of course, she couldn't say much since she basically resided there too. "Yes, I'm fine. Thank you." She straightened her face so hopefully she didn't look as pathetic as she felt.

Opening the door, she stepped out to see the rookie officer. With her nicely pressed uniform and her dark hair pulled back in a bun, her features revealed a bright-eyed enthusiasm Savannah once exhibited. The pride in the uniform, the high hopes for the job. It was sad to see it all melt away in their young faces. Give the girl five years on patrol and her face would change. A hardness developed inside a cop, cynicism took over and with it, their optimism of making a difference and changing the world. This girl was too fresh and inexperienced to realize the road she'd chosen to travel.

The rookie's cheery attitude sprung forth the way Georgia's daffodils did after a good rain, "You sure, ma'am? Forgive me for saying this but you don't look good."

That's because I'm tired. Tired of arguing, of trying to right the world's wrongs, of seeing the worst in people, of fighting criminals and trying to keep the evil at bay. Just wait. When you get to my age, see what I've seen, you'll understand. That's why the baby gave her hope for a new beginning. New life. Innocence. A lost concept in Savannah's world. She clung to that new beginning with a vengeance. Regardless of the puking and swelling and such, she *wanted* this baby. She *needed* this baby and, "I needed a little quiet time away from the boys."

The rookie heartily agreed, "You're telling me. They're getting bossier, aren't they? And bolder, especially Detective Olson."

Oh hell. The disaster named Ben Olson struck again. How, she didn't know but regrettably was about to find out. Savannah knew Murphy and his stinkin' law was alive and kicking due to her luck lately. "What did he do?"

"He asked me out earlier. Rumor has it he's got a girlfriend though."

"According to him, he does. Look," she took note of the name on the uniform, "Prescott, you realize if the boss gets wind of another relationship in this stationhouse, he'll have a stroke. Rutherford and I about put him in the hospital when he found out."

Officer Prescott's eyes widened, "I'll decline Ben's offer. I'm a rookie, I can't afford to get into trouble."

"I understand completely. You decline the date and I'll reinforce the rules to Detective Olson." Savannah made her way back to her office. Trouble. It was Ben's middle name. Correction, she thought. Lately, anyone of the male gender was trouble.

She rounded the corner and upon sight of Ben, drew a deep cleansing breath, held, then slowly released it. She'd read about Zen, the meditative state that was supposed to center a person and bring them enlightenment. Years ago she'd tried her hand at it, all the meditation and self contemplation. It soon became clear that she sucked at it. During meditation, she obsessed that the house needed cleaning or the yard required mowing. During self contemplation, she berated herself for meditating instead of busying herself doing the aforementioned work. But one activity sounded rather soothing and irresistible. Strangling Ben Olson until he turned blue. Now *that* sounded very Zen to her.

She ventured into her office where Ben held a plaque from her wall. The saying on it seemed pretty ironic. The Christmas gift from her brother read: *God, grant me the serenity to accept the things I cannot change, the courage to change the things I can, and the wisdom to hide the bodies of the people I had to kill because they annoyed me.* Yes, she reflected while inhaling slowly and deeply. Very Zen indeed.

Ben looked up, smiled at her, "Need help hiding Rutherford's body?"

She snatched the plaque from his hand and returned it to the wall, "Rutherford's not your problem. I am. What did I say about dating female officers?"

"You said don't."

"Precisely. Ben, be honest with me. Do you suffer from selective memory? Because I heard you asked Officer Prescott out."

Ben countered, "I thought after shift I could do anything I want."

"Do you want to rob a bank after shift too? This place is not a dating service, get it?"

He nodded. Good boy, she wanted to say. God knew it must have taken a Herculean effort for him to rub those two brain cells together. Let's try two for two, "Have you looked at the passkey list yet?"

"No, ma'am."

Well, so much for success. Savannah looked at her watch, "You've had twenty-two minutes. What did you do in that time?"

"Hung out. I was waiting for you."

Hands on her hips, she said, "You don't need my permission or presence to investigate a homicide. Feel free to work independently in my absence. I asked you to look at that list days ago and the boss just told you to get with Mathis on it."

"Yes, ma'am. Sorry. I wasn't sure what to do since you and Detective Rutherford are at odds."

She admitted to being hard to work with. Not impossible, just hard. Any veteran cop hated wiping a rookie's ass. Ben wasn't stupid, he was lazy. No veteran cop worth his or her salt overlooked that. Adapting to situations was vital and Ben acted like he needed a dictionary to look the word up. Today, she'd cut him some slack, but only a little, "Detective Rutherford and I have issues to be worked out, that's all. Today is another example of why you should date *outside* this precinct."

Ben bobbed his head in agreement, "I don't want to knock up a coworker. That would be awkward. And pregnant women get so emotional anyway."

She settled behind her desk, her hands flattened against the surface to prevent herself from hitting her new partner, "Wisecrack like that again and I'll get Rutherford and Mathis to help me hide *your* body." She sorted through papers, handed him their copy of the passkey list, "Let's look this over." Savannah slid her glasses on, scanned the column of names, hoping to find a familiar one. She sensed Ben staring at her. She sighed, "What is it?"

"Who are we looking for?"

Patience, she implored to God. *Bless me with an abundance of patience before I go postal on every man I see.* Now she knew how parents of a two year-old felt. "Remember the guy that got shoved into the aquarium? You know, he was eaten alive?" She waited for affirmation. Once she had it, she continued, "We obtained a passkey list from the aquarium to see if someone there might have known him and wanted him dead. Whoever killed him probably had a passkey or knew someone with one. You up to speed yet or need me to speak slower?"

"I'm fine, ma'am." He offered her the page in his hand, "But maybe you should look at the list since you know who you're looking for."

Her palm itched for her .38. Not to shoot him but she seriously considered pistol whipping some sense into the boy. She weighed the consequences of at least a thirty day suspension against the sheer ecstasy the beating might provide. Some things were better than sex. Winning a million dollars, pounding a giant mullet-wearing sloth into oblivion… "I can't tell you who I'm looking for, Ben, because I don't know. We look for people connected to our victim. I told you who we interviewed. Do you remember their names?"

"Vaguely, ma'am."

At the end of her emotional rope, she plucked the page from his grasp, "Boy, your uncle must have some major clout in the department. Even squirrels remember where they buried their nuts." She peered over her reading glasses at him, "If I find something and ask you to hoof it over to John Mathis, you gonna forget where you're going and get lost?"

Ben laughed a little, "No, ma'am. I can find him. He's the fat detective, right?"

"And you're the dead detective if he hears you say that." She opened an upper desk drawer and rummaged the contents. All she found were pens, notepads, a half-empty bottle of Tums and, like her boss, a bottle of aspirin that looked nearly too good to pass up. "Since you're leaving the list with me, bring me my notes."

She recognized the rookie detective's expression. She saw it regularly with her young nephew and niece. The one saying the question was considerably above his intellect. His eyes closed and he retreated into thought until, "What part of them do you want?"

Savannah trapped blistering words behind her clenched teeth, "What am I? Rainman? That's the reason for taking notes, Ben. So you don't have to memorize everything. Get 'em now."

She returned to searching the passkey list. Sliding her finger down the list of names, she searched for anyone remotely related to the case. Sometimes the name jumped out at her, sometimes she relied on her gut instinct to help pinpoint the person.

But Ben's presence distracted her. Her partner stood, hands clasped behind his back, staring at another plaque on the wall. Savannah glanced over her reading glasses again, aiming to express a strict parental gaze instead of a cold homicidal one, "My notes. Now, Ben. That means without further delay. Go."

He lumbered out of the office. She took advantage of the time to breathe again. Looking heavenward, she silently inquired if this was a test. She spent her whole life with a short, fiery temper which lately grew shorter and hotter. God conducted an experiment, she guessed. To see how deep her fingernails sank into sanity. Not very far, she sighed, and they were slipping fast…

He returned sooner than she imagined, handed her the notepad that looked as disheveled as she felt lately. Thumbing the pages revealed every note intact, another miracle she thanked God for.

"Can I head out for lunch?" Ben asked.

Before now, she resigned herself to working alone but why should another male in her life get his way while she mopped up after him? Nope, not again. "No. You can plant your behind in that chair and read those notes to me."

Ben stared as if she'd lost her mind and perhaps she had. All the turmoil in the last several hours probably snapped a vital thread in her overtaxed brain. If so, they were all going down with the ship, "Sit down. Open notes. Read notes aloud. Simple. Start with the coroner's findings."

He eased into the chair facing her desk. Methodically he flipped through the notepad until settling on one page, "Traces of…" He stopped, squinted at the page then held it for her to see, "What's this word? Rhodiola?"

"That word is rhubarb."

He studied it dubiously then began again, "Traces of rhubarb leaves in the stomach contents. Also found: Rat poison that led to internal bleeding. Victim was starved with –"

"Pretty sure that word is stabbed, Ben, not starved."

"Your handwriting is lousy. I can barely read –"

"Everyone else can read it," she replied, offended by the comment, "so it's not my writing. Proceed from the word *stabbed.*"

"*Stabbed* with a blade about four inches long."

"Majestic's executive chef put rhubarb leaves in Vaughn's salad in return for his screwing with her sister's allergy. The rat poison – I'm guessing – came from Majestic since he ate there and a lot of other people keep showing up at hospitals with the same diagnosis. As for the knife, lots of people own knives fitting that description. So far we've found no one having ties to the aquarium yet someone had an all access pass to the place. That's why this passkey list will hopefully shed more light on the situation."

Ben continued in a monotone voice, obviously uninterested in her verbal analysis, "Fingerprints on railings and door handles were too numerous to islato…" He squinted at the notepad again, "Sorry, *isolate* and identify. Blood from two donors was found at the scene, the victim's and another male donor."

Her cell phone rang and Savannah sighed. What was it with everyone? No one felt compelled to leave her alone that day. And so help her, if it was another man… She answered it in a not-so-pleasant tone, "Savannah Prince."

"I'm at the diner down the block from you," Dane announced in a cheery tone. "I've got two slices of peach pie on order and it would be a shame to let 'em ruin. How about joining me? I want to talk a minute."

Okay, this fella she could deal with, especially when plied with peach pie. The brightest spot in her day resided on a saucer at a cozy little diner down the road. How sad, she thought. But she refused to dwell on it long. People drowned their sorrow and stress in various things. Booze, chocolate, Quarter Pounders. Her weakness just happened to be peach pie. And she noticed Dane Rutherford played dirty when he wanted a favor. No doubt Georgia told him the way to Savannah's heart and her instincts said the impromptu meeting revolved around hers and Ennis's falling out. As appealing as the offer sounded, she really couldn't spare the time, "I'm pretty busy right now. I'm doing the work of two detectives."

"Don't make a hungry cowboy eat alone, Peach. That's cruel and unusual. Georgia's busy with interviews and I'd enjoy the company of my lovely sister-in-law." He threw in a dash of guilt for incentive, "I came across town just to see you, darlin'."

Savannah rolled her eyes, a smile playing at the corners of her mouth. Across town? Hardly. Georgia's house was ten to twenty minutes from the station, depending on traffic. "Lemme see what I can wheedle from my boss."

"No need. Georgia's already smoothed the way. Promised your boss a batch of her cookies if he'll let you go."

Using food for bribery. She'd never considered doing that. Probably because none of her cuisine would be accepted as a valid bribe, unlike Georgia's eats. And what the hell prompted this flurry of meetings and cookies anyway? Had Ennis told Dane she'd run off with the circus or demanded a divorce? For Dane to lure her from work while Georgia smoothed the way with Josh, Ennis must have implied lawyers were imminent. She made a note to cajole a few confections for herself since her sister was in a giving mood…

Dane drew a deep breath, "Mmm… This peach pie smells wonderful. Little bit of cinnamon in there. Smells almost as good as Georgia's."

Now *that* was cruel, even for Dane. He pushed every single button of her cravings. She automatically swallowed, embarrassed that her mouth watered. Her stomach growled loud enough Ben noticed, turned to her. "Dane, you rascal," she scolded good-naturedly. "How does my sister tolerate your antics?"

"She ignores most of them."

It was at that time, her vision stumbled on a name on the passkey list. One she'd have noticed immediately if she'd seen the list days earlier. Days before she read Georgia's book, before Ennis's revelation, days before the mayor's personal jihad against her.

"You still there?" Dane asked.

"Dane, you're my good luck charm. I'll be there in a few." She clicked off, grabbed a pen and circled the name. Handing the list to Ben, she said, "Take this to Mathis. Don't get lost and don't, for Heaven's sake, call him fat."

29

Savannah knew the place well. When it opened eleven years ago, the Jolt N' Bolt became a bastion to her precinct house. Hungry cops spent their lunchtime there, swilling down strong coffee, and scarfing down greasy burgers. Over time the place drew tourists, tired and famished from sightseeing, so the owners "classed" up the joint by changing the décor and adding desserts.

These days the interior's chrome, red and black fifties ambiance suited the tourist trap setting. The owners insisted on authenticity from the food to the booths and checkerboard floor, with the only exceptions being two plasma TV sets installed behind the bar. The food lived up to the era with juicy burgers that wouldn't know a diet if they saw one and milkshakes that could drive even the most despondent person to smile. Savannah vouched for that. Before she and Ennis partnered up, she spent enough time in the place, the owner knew her by name – and her usual order.

She circled the block in hopes of a parking space and finally settled for one half a block away. She climbed out of the Camaro and along with the wall of heat came the aroma of burgers, French fries and onions drifting all the way to the street. As if she needed more temptation. The second she opened the door to Jolt N' Bolt, the smell provoked the same response as Thanksgiving dinner. Just hand over the food and no one will get hurt.

Patrons packed the place from stem to stern with no available seats at the bar, at any table or booth. The business thrived during lunch, with workers, tourists or people just wanting a quick meal in a nostalgic atmosphere.

The barrage of delicious aromas had her stomach pitching the idea of sneaking in a quick burger with that peach pie but that indulgence required more than the twenty minutes Josh allowed for the impromptu meeting.

She scanned the crowd and finally spotted Dane sitting in a corner booth dressed in jeans and blue button-down shirt. Locating Dane Rutherford wasn't exactly a challenge. First, the majority of Atlanta's men didn't own a Stetson or pair of boots and second, of the four brothers, Dane and Ennis favored the most.

When she approached, she noticed his attention riveted to the TV over the bar. The noon news was on and she halfway feared her own picture might appear with the mayor using it for target practice.

She glanced at the table. As promised, two pieces of peach pie sat on the table, one sat across from him with a fresh dollop of vanilla ice cream. Topping it off was a tall glass of cold milk. Dane meant serious business. When Georgia went to blabbing about Savannah's favorite dessert and *exactly* how she liked it, something major had transpired.

"Peach pie and ice cream," she said. "This is a serious bribe, Mr.

Rutherford."

Dane turned to her with a languid smile. Rising from his seat, he opened his arms and wrapped her in a bear hug, "How're you doin', darlin'?"

It took practically every inch of reach to embrace a Rutherford. Every brother was tall and built like a Mack truck through the shoulders. When their powerful arms enfolded a girl, they let her know she was definitely being hugged and right now she needed one. "I'm busier than a one-eyed cat watching six mouse holes but other than that I'm okay." She wasn't revealing too much until he explained the mystery meeting. Logic said it revolved around the fight with Ennis but with the Rutherfords, one could never safely assume anything.

He parted from their embrace but gently held her in his arms a moment longer. His dark eyes searched her face, giving Savannah the feeling he looked for more than emotional scars. When he tilted her chin this way and that, she knew. "Ennis told you about our argument," she sighed. So much for keeping their personal lives personal…

Dane's expression said yes, Ennis told him all about it. The older brother motioned for her to sit then slid in across from her, "He did but wouldn't say how serious it got. My brother doesn't readily confide in me because he knows how I feel about fightin' with womenfolk. He did say something about you falling though. Did he push you?"

"I tripped," she assured. "A knot on my head is my reward."

His gaze remained steady on hers, "Did you have help tripping? Did he hit you?"

It was sweet of him to worry but, "No, Dane. It truly was an accident."

His eyes softened and but his posture remained rigid. He should have realized – and probably did – that Ennis wouldn't hit her. Dane hadn't called the meeting for that, his expression said. Something else nagged at him. He picked at the pie with his fork, "Ennis said you found out about his situation back home."

Her first reaction was to vehemently defend herself as she had with Ennis. But Dane's tone made her restrain the impulse and simply say, "I didn't snoop, Dane. I never would–"

Dane lifted a finger, shushing her, "He told me how you got the information. I just assumed he shared the whole thing with you long ago."

The same heartache clawed in from the night before. Ennis hadn't trusted her enough to share his past. The sadness evidently spread to her expression since Dane leaned forward, covered her hand with his. His warm hold reminded her of Ennis's. In those hours alone she'd missed his tenderness, the way his thumb stroked her hand in a loving caress, the kindness in his eyes and the special little smile that spoke volumes without a single word. She missed her husband, not the overbearing bully she'd seen the last day. She wanted the old Ennis back.

The remembrance brought tears to her eyes. She fought them back. She'd cried enough the night before. Seth's wife spent hours assuring her, quieting her worries and wild notions. Savannah refused to break down again, especially in public and in front of Dane. He'd think the worst and even if Ennis hadn't struck her, Dane might have assumed she lied.

"Peach, my brother ain't the genius Ma thinks he is. All us brothers know it. He's not apt to make intelligent decisions if it tarnishes his image with you." The humor left his eyes and his voice, "Savannah, that incident back home nearly destroyed him. Even when ballistics proved Reggie killed the baby, Ennis wasn't the same. It took us all – me, the boys and Ma to pull him out of that depression. We put him to work on the ranch to give him a change of scenery, something new to do. He never wanted to be a rancher. He loved law enforcement and he'd lost his dream because of a senior officer's negligence."

She listened, battling back tears and barely succeeding. Dane tenderly squeezed her hand which only inspired more emotion. She tried to be reasonable and open-minded as Ennis's brother continued, "Kelly Roberts sued both Reggie Gibson and Ennis. Once her lawyer listened to the radio transmissions and saw the patrol car's videotape, she dropped the suit against Ennis. He joined the department to help people and in less than a year, that happened."

Dane spoke so passionately about his brother and his suffering that the growing tears rolled down her cheeks. She swiped them away, "I got upset because he never told me. I accused him of not trusting me."

He gently squeezed her hand, "Darlin', it wasn't a matter of trust. He was afraid of losing you. I mean, shooting a pregnant woman? He harbored tons of guilt over that. He told me the day he met you that he fell in love." Dane leaned closer, lowered his voice, "He'd kill me if he found out I told you but he'd call home and ask advice from Ma or Cal. He was head over heels. So far gone he even got goofy over your voice."

"My voice?" Why did she suddenly feel self conscious about speaking now? Did her voice amuse Ennis? Irritate him? Obsessing over a voice didn't necessarily signify a good thing.

"M-hmm. He compared it to chocolate. Rich, smooth, and addictive. That's when I knew he'd gone cockeyed over you. Peach, don't let on I told you. Ennis'll hit the roof then he'll hit *me*."

Savannah blushed so fiercely she broke a sweat. Her finger drew an imaginary cross over her heart, a silent promise to keep quiet. She realized Ennis was attracted to her from the beginning. He tended to stammer, his cheeks flushed and if she stood too close, his body tensed and occasionally he stuffed his hands in his front pockets to hide the evidence of a hard-on. Being partnered with such a handsome, well-mannered male wasn't a cake walk for her either. She spent evenings staring at the phone, tempted to call her new partner for any reason, a tour of the city, a walk in the park, dinner and a movie. She managed to contain the urge only to suffer sleepless nights. She tossed and turned, consumed with the idea of him touching her, kissing her. How she would feel cradled in his embrace, how soft his lips might feel against hers. When she discovered how safe she felt in his arms and how forcefully those soft lips could kiss her to her knees, it was too late. She'd fought the attraction, resisted his charm and kind demeanor until it exhausted her, until she surrendered to the truth. She loved Ennis.

Dane continued, "Moving to Atlanta meant escaping his past but he also found his future here. When Ma heard the lilt in his voice about you, she told us Ennis was whole again. You didn't just mend his heart, you mended hers."

She wasn't sure what to say. Dane gave her far too much credit. Ennis healed himself by relocating, resuming his dream in another city. And mothers tended to relax when their children seemed happy. Except for being in the right place at the right time, Savannah had nothing to do with it.

Dane's hold tightened slightly, "I sincerely believe if you left him, it would destroy him. He ain't very bright at times but he means well. Give him another chance, Peach. Please."

A tear rolled down her cheek. She quickly thumbed it away. No falling apart in public, she reminded herself as guilt swept over her. She'd accused Ennis of not trusting her when he worried he'd not only lose her trust but her love. During the last twenty four hours they'd hurled terrible, hurtful accusations at each other, pecking at each other to gain the upper hand. She felt ashamed of herself for attacking the man she loved and trusted with not only her life but their baby's as well.

Josh was right. We were acting like brats. "This marriage thing is hard to perfect. No one ever does, I guess. Just try to improve on it is all."

Dane picked up his fork and sliced off a small piece of pie, "I'll put my money on a marriage that can survive everything yours has. Especially when you survived Jenny Lee Crawford. That told me how strong a little Georgia girl could be."

Savannah laughed despite herself. Of course she could *now.* Jenny Lee Crawford. Before Jeffrey Holland, Jenny Lee was the bane of Savannah's existence. The moment Jenny Lee heard Ennis and Savannah were engaged, his high school girlfriend mounted a campaign to win him back. She harangued them to the point Savannah entertained painful yet innovative ways to dissuade Ms. Crawford from pursuing Ennis. Thankfully once the wedding rings were in place, Jenny Lee faded into the background. Normally Savannah hated to gloat but the memory of her rival's forlorn expression was the sweetest thing since the peach pie sitting in front of her. "She was a trial by fire," Savannah admitted then dug into the dessert.

"I never told Ennis but I'd wake up in cold sweats at the prospect of her being my sister-in-law." He suddenly beamed, "You cured those right up."

"Glad I could help." She watched him attack his pie with the same enthusiasm as she had. Dane relaxed since bracing the issue of Ennis's past. Despite their problems, the two brothers were as close as she and her sister were. And speaking of Georgia, "Seems like you and Georgia have something special. Anything new in that department?"

When she first met Dane Rutherford, would she have considered him a suitable candidate for her sister? Not in a million years. The man was brash, overt with his aggravation and a little too sly for her liking. Georgia tended to be more reserved and delicate. Unless provoked, she held her tongue and the extent of her duplicitous ways only emerged when Savannah's health was involved – like shoving "the miracle food" broccoli in a casserole that didn't deserve it. Georgia and Dane were complete opposites. When Georgia's husband Matthew filed for divorce, Dane seemed pretty eager to step in as her friend. It concerned Savannah but no more than Ennis because he knew his brother, he said, and the situation would head for hell faster than a politician's promises. She reconsidered her stance on Dane after hers and Georgia's battle with Jeffrey and Cole. Dane's true character shined through, telling her that like Ennis, he was a gem that only the luckiest girls found.

Today, his eyes sparkled at the mention of Georgia. It delighted Savannah to see them both so happy, especially after the last few difficult months, "C'mon, Dane. You and Georgia are tighter than bark on a tree. I'm surprised you're not with her right now."

He shoveled a large bite in his mouth – Savannah figured he did it on purpose to give him time to think. To his credit, he smiled then winked. She also noticed he took extra time chewing. A lot of extra time.

She leaned back, smiled with a raised brow, "I have ways of making people talk. Ask Georgia."

Dane swallowed, swiped the napkin across his grinning mouth, "Are you any better at keeping secrets than she is?"

"Dane, *teenage girls* are better at keeping secrets than Georgia."

He bent forward with a devilish glint in his eyes, "Did she tell you about the trip to the mountains?"

She nodded. He eyeballed the people around them and lowered his voice to a secretive whisper, "I've got it all planned. We sit down to a nice supper, champagne, candles and music, the works. Then I present the ring to her." Panic suddenly rounded his eyes, "Or should I? Do you think she's ready to get married? If you think she'll say no, tell me. Has she said anything to you?"

Savannah sat, amazed at his transformation. She never quite saw him so excited *and* flustered. His lack of usual swagger spoke volumes about his depth of love for Georgia. The temporary meltdown, while entertaining and somewhat alarming, only endeared him more to her. Before he suffered an anxiety attack or worse, she assured, "She's happier than I've seen her in a long time and she's excited about the trip. You have the ring?"

His passion on the subject returned full force, "I have it locked in my suitcase away from prying eyes. I swear the woman's worse than a squirrel. She gets into everything, especially when she cleans or does laundry."

Welcome to my childhood, Savannah thought. Her sister rooted everything when she cleaned – closets, mattresses, and at one time she saw Georgia upend couches and chairs to vacuum beneath them. The woman was nothing if not thorough. And if she found one item out of place – God help the offender…

Dane scooped up her left hand again. It reminded her of Ennis. Large, strong hands and a deceptively delicate hold.

He angled her ring to the light, "About the same size, I think. Do you think she'll like it?"

Savannah covered his hand with hers, promising, "She'll love it as much as I love mine."

He frowned at his pie, "This whole thing hinges on whether I can fit behind the wheel of the car. At the rate she's feeding me, someone's gonna serve me up for Thanksgiving supper. I've gained five pounds already. And I'm getting finicky about food now. Georgia's cooking has made me picky. Like this pie. It's good, but hers is…" he searched for an appropriate word.

Savannah had the perfect word, "Exceptional." No one this side of their mother made peach pie like Georgia.

Dane covered his face with his hands. He sounded literally distressed, "And I hate to say it but she puts my mama to shame with her brown beans and fried potatoes."

Savannah, busy chewing, began laughing so hard she covered her mouth before she spewed. Her laughter drew the attention of a few customers who glanced their way.

Dane peeked between his fingers, "For the love of God, why are you laughing at me? I'm miserable."

She swallowed and wiped tears from her eyes, "You sound so confused and it's obvious. The sooner you propose, the quicker it will clear up."

A glimmer of hope crossed his features than as quickly changed to caution, "But the insane happiness, it hangs around, right?"

"Yeah," she assured with a gentle laugh, "it hangs around."

Dane leaned back, patted his stomach and sighed, "So, is there anything *you'd* like to fess up to?"

The question caught her off-guard. Why did he ask that? Had Georgia told him about the baby? He patted his stomach again, this time slowly, deliberately.

She rolled her eyes. Dane was right. Her sister sucked at keeping secrets. Savannah felt fortunate it wasn't front page news already. "Does *everyone* know?"

"Probably but just play along when they ask."

She shook her head, "Georgia would be hell on national security."

He broke into another grin, "Like I said. The woman can't keep a secret."

30

The station was abuzz the second Savannah stepped in the door. The commotion centered at the sergeant's desk where several officers gathered. Each one offered their heated two cents into whatever caused the uproar.

She slowed her trek toward Josh's office, trying to catch pieces of the complaints because insinuating herself into the madness didn't appear safe. Not since the mayor's new budget plan had she seen such uproarious animosity in the stationhouse.

"Sarg, tell me I'm not enlisted. I got my kid's soccer game later," one officer complained.

"My wife and I have had this vacation planned for a year. I *need* this vacation," another said.

The desk sergeant caught Savannah's line of sight and shook his head. She stopped, afraid his frustration revolved around her somehow. After the DVD fiasco, she'd never underestimate fate again.

The sergeant wiped a hand down his face in exasperation, "Prince, your buddy the mayor has single-handedly made enemies of us all. In just ten minutes."

The room fell silent. All faces turned to her with murder in their eyes. Her cheeks burned as the anger seemed to transfer from the mayor to her. She stood her ground, zeroed in on the sergeant, "Since when do I break bread with Franklin O'Neill? He's put me through hell this last week. Whatever he's done, I ain't part of it."

To her relief, her reply extinguished their flaming ire. All she needed was the multitudes piling on to finish her off. Judging from the uniforms surrounding the sergeant's kiosk, they meant serious bodily harm to any ally the mayor had. Savannah took that opportunity to abscond to the safety of Josh's office.

She sprinted by her office and suddenly slammed on the brakes. A flash of purple caught her eye as she'd passed and she always stopped for that color as religiously as she stopped for red traffic lights.

Backing up three steps revealed a large arrangement of purple lisianthus and iris on her desk. It beckoned to her and like any woman in her right mind, she rushed to see them up close – and search for a card from the sender. A small envelope was pinned to a lilac ribbon from, strangely enough, Petal Pushers. She removed the card and automatically a smile curved her lips. Ennis struck while she was gone. And, as always, he knew the way to her heart. The purple iris was her favorite but the lisianthus wasn't exactly a dog either. Quickly sliding her glasses on, she read the card, "I apologize for everything and I promise – no more secrets. Could I swing a date with you, gorgeous?"

Her smile widened. She really hated fighting with him. Nothing in her life felt right when they argued. Scribbling a note, she wrote their new address then, "Meet me there at seven. We'll give the neighbors something to talk about…" she folded it twice then headed to Hunter's office. She knocked twice, "What did I miss?"

The boss's eyes fired as he volleyed a cautionary glance between her and Ennis. The look demanded the married couple get along or take a corner. Savannah smiled while tucking the note in Ennis's suit jacket.

Everyone except her stared at his pocket. Ennis cocked a brow at her. She winked and he immediately blushed. The man she fell head over heels with was back, literally, in glowing color.

"Anything you want to share with the class?" Josh inquired, apparently still skeptical their spat had ended.

Savannah sheepishly shook her head as Mathis sighed, his shoulders slumping, "Finally. A truce. Maybe there is a God after all. Since you've been out, we've learned our illustrious mayor fell victim to rat poisoning. His Royal Highness spent all his time defending the place and now he's laid up sick from the food."

Much as she hated to admit it, O'Neill deserved it. The dope griped her out for protecting the public and ended up poisoned at his own restaurant. As R.J. put it, sometimes you're the windshield, sometimes you're the bug. It felt nice to be the windshield for once. "I assume O'Neill will recover."

"Some cockroaches you gotta squash, not poison," Mathis said. "He'll be fine."

Josh added, "But he's demanding twenty-four hour protection from his police. Just be thankful he's not asking for you."

Now *that* explained the ruckus at the sergeant's desk. The officers had to wet nurse the mayor and no cop liked guard duty, especially guarding an asshole who resented approving their paychecks. She answered, “He knows I’d be tempted to finish him off. What about the name on the passkey list? Any info?”

Ennis referred to his notes, “Good news and bad news. Good news, Luke Drury was hired by the aquarium to install the security system. From everything to the outside security to the card security used to access the fish tanks.”

The bad news, she guessed, was no one could find Luke Drury. According to Lucy he took off on vacation. Savannah never trusted family to tell the truth. Blood ran thicker than water and no one liked visiting relatives in prison. She’d bet her next paycheck – if the mayor gave her one – that Luke either killed Vaughn or knew who did.

Ennis continued, “The bad news is according to his job application and city records, he lived at the same address his sister is living at now.”

Her brain ground to a halt on one word, “Wait, you said *lived* at the address. Those magazines listed him as living there as late as last month.”

“That’s why it’s bad news. Mathis and I have searched for Luke in every database. The DMV and city have records of him up to last year then he vanishes.”

How conveniently perfect. “But Lucy said he was on vacation. Vanishing from society is a hell of a sabbatical.”

“Unless he’s dead too.”

She turned to John Mathis, regretful that he now resided on her "men I'd love to strangle before bedtime" list. If he kept yammering, he'd jump ahead of Ben Olson. Mathis was a good cop but a sorely negative one. Sure, there was a possibility of Luke's demise but hey, let's not overtax an already complicated case with more bodies yet. She let her expression relay that message.

Oblivious to her evil eye, Mathis expounded, "Ain't you heard of those crazies who kill and keep collecting the dead guy's disability checks?"

Her right eye twitched – and kept twitching until she rubbed it. Why, oh why, did everyone insist on adding more problems? She turned to one of the last sane minds in the room – her husband, "Did Luke rent or own?"

"Owned. It's in Luke's name until last year then magically transferred to Lucy."

"Why would he sign over the house if they don't get along? Revenge because the plumbing's bad?"

"Who knows? Tired of the responsibility, maybe he wanted to move –"

"Or guilt," Mathis added.

Twitch, twitch, twitch… Savannah firmly massaged her eye while addressing John, "Guilt?"

"Sure. Families are famous for it. Jeez, Prince, you should know that best of all." He shrugged, "Okay, families and ex-wives. Lucy's obviously sick with all those pills you saw. She probably hit hard times and their mother or some do-gooder sibling guilted Luke into housing her."

"But signing over the house? If she's sick, how could she afford that?"

"Hey, it was speculation. I never said I was right."

Back to basics, please, before my head explodes and I go cross-eyed. "Luke was in charge of security. Why wouldn't he keep a passkey for himself? Computer programmers leave wormholes in software for emergency access. Keeping a passkey makes sense."

"You think Luke killed Vaughn?" Ennis asked.

"One problem," Mathis argued. "Most of the witnesses said a woman shoved Vaughn into the tank."

Savannah rolled her eyes with hopes Mathis might stop playing the thorn in her side, "Then why did the killer's blood come back male, not female? Georgia's book had a brother and sister team. Reckon Luke and Lucy killed Vaughn then Luke goes into hiding?"

"I hope it wasn't permanent hiding, like under her new geraniums," Mathis grumbled. "Where are your notes? I'll run down a couple of things for you while you have a chat with Lucy."

"They're on my desk. I finally got them back from Ben."

Josh opened a desk drawer, tossed a folder on top. She saw Ben's name on it. Hunter proceeded, "I'm having Olson reassigned to another precinct. As of right now," he pointed to Ennis and Savannah, "if you can get along, you are unofficial partners."

"Thank you," the three detectives said in unison.

Mathis gestured to Ennis, "No offense, but he ain't no party to partner with."

Josh opened the folder, leafed through it, "I've kept track of Ben's progress – and lack thereof. Since he's got time to preen in the locker room and ask officers out on dates, I told the chief he needs a more active precinct. He's in Zone 3 now."

God help her, she couldn't stop herself. She smiled. If Ben thought their precinct lacked excitement, he'd soon learn some places in Atlanta never slept. Instead of female officers finessing their way around him, the ladies in Zone 3 might actually haul off and slap him hard enough his head spun around and his eyes read *Tilt*.

John Mathis smirked, "It's your lucky day, Prince. Your newly adopted son found a new home."

31

In Savannah's opinion, lying was acceptable in very few situations. At Christmas when Georgia asked who ate the last piece of peach pie and looked directly at Savannah, with well-practiced wide-eyed innocence, Savannah always answered, "Not me."

Creating excuses to avoid a highfalutin formal occasion was another example. It wasn't really lying, she told herself. It was an exercise in creativity.

When Lindsey asked where babies came from, Savannah employed a strategy any sane human would. She pointed directly at the girl's mother, "Ask Mama." Denying knowledge or playing dumb worked most times. When it involved explaining procreation to another person's kid, she chickened out and put the onus on the parents. After all, she was about to embark on the murky trail of parenthood and no doubt her own kids would torture her with those uncomfortable inquiries. She prayed by then she'd feel more secure talking about it with them.

While there were acceptable times to lie in life, there was one unquestionable time to always tell the truth – when in the presence of a police officer. Evidently Lucy Driscoll missed that memo and Savannah and Ennis meant to set her straight about it.

"You lied to us," Savannah said the moment Lucy opened the front door.

The woman's jaw plummeted at the accusation. Savannah wondered whether the woman's reaction stemmed from being confronted or surprise that they uncovered the truth. People often thought secreting a detail or two wasn't a problem. It was, of course, especially when it could prove pivotal to an investigation. Some people truly forgot certain details but those folks normally contacted police once they remembered. Difference was, Lucy remembered and purposefully hid something.

"I did not," Lucy replied once regaining her composure.

Ennis bristled at the lie. He turned to confer with his wife, "Wanna just drag her in for impeding an investigation? We've got plenty of room at the inn."

It amused Savannah that the most patient person she knew aside of her mother uttered those words. "Let's give her one last chance to tell us the truth." She stepped forward as a silent request for entry into the house. Lucy moved aside to let them pass. Savannah asked, "Where's your brother? And before you say you don't know, you're taking his mail so you have an idea where he is."

Savannah could tolerate a lot, but nothing pissed her off more than being lied to, especially to her face. "What we need," Savannah enunciated, "is his location right now."

"What for?" Lucy asked.

Did she detect a defensive posture and tone? Yes, she did. Savannah crossed her arms, asking Ennis, "You bring your cuffs? 'Cause it looks like we're having a communication error and it's by choice."

Ennis dragged out the bracelets and Lucy reacted as if he'd whipped a rattlesnake from behind his back.

Savannah tried again, "Luke installed the security system at the aquarium which means he had access to the feeding areas. Take my advice. It's easier to tell us where he is. If you don't, we'll get crankier and you'll head for the slammer on obstruction charges since you delayed the process. Get it?"

Lucy wrung her hands, her vision drifted to the TV, "I really don't know where he is."

Totally fed up with the verbal tennis game, Ennis stepped forward, brandished the handcuffs, "Turn around."

Lucy stepped back, stammering, "But I don't know."

Savannah moved closer, "When you lie, we look harder at you and Luke."

The nearness unnerved Lucy. She backed toward the kitchen, her vision trained on the handcuffs, "Luke wouldn't kill anyone."

"Your brother had a passkey," Savannah reminded. "Barry Vaughn was stabbed with a weapon fitting the description of that spiffy letter opener on your desk. Now Luke's suddenly left town? That bothers us, Lucy. A lot."

"That doesn't mean he killed Barry."

"No," Savannah agreed, "it could mean *you* did it if you had access to the passkey and I'm guessing Luke left that with the house."

Terror clouded Lucy's face, "That's preposterous. You think I did it?"

"I think Luke did. Our evidence puts a man at the scene despite the fact witnesses say a woman gave him the heave ho."

Savannah's cell phone rang. Normally she stepped away to answer but today, she rooted herself, retrieved the phone from her belt. It was Mathis, "I checked out those doctors you wrote down. Lucy's taking antibiotics and estrogen and couple other things, right? The antibiotics are self-explanatory but the rest of the stuff prescribed by Dr. Alan Burch isn't so obvious."

"Mathis, riddles give me hives. Just spill it."

"Spoilsport. Does the term transgender mean anything to you? Burch's specialty is sex change operations."

Savannah's tongue seized up like a dry log in her mouth, unable and unwilling to release. Disbelief stripped the gears in her brain, leaving her to question, "Mathis, are you jerking me around?"

"Take a gander down south if you don't believe me. What do you see?"

Savannah visually roamed Lucy's body. Her frame could be described as sturdy for a female but Savannah saw plenty of those watching the Olympics.

Signs of Lucy's previous gender proved nearly impossible to establish above the waist. Lucy's skin was smooth, her face showing no signs of five o'clock shadow and she arched her brows into two thin, precise lines. How could Lucy be a man and Savannah not notice? Her years in uniform introduced her to a plethora of Atlanta's "colorful" types. She'd seen her share of drag queens and transgender men and most demonstrated why God's plan was better. Before accusing John Mathis of suffering from delusions or fever, Savannah watched closer. While Ennis spoke to Lucy, Savannah noticed her effeminate behavior, right down to the quirk of curling her hair behind her ear and when she crossed her arms, it was a dainty move that read "female" all over it.

Savannah wondered if her experience with Holland and Jordan knocked her detective skills cockeyed. She could tell if a woman used to be a man and still kinda was, right? It should have been obvious. There were two telltale methods to solve the mystery. One she'd rather not entertain the thought of, the other was easy enough to see. She looked at Lucy's throat.

As Lucy voiced another denial to Ennis, Savannah expected to see an Adam's apple bobbing as she spoke. Lucy's throat, however, looked smooth with every syllable.

"Prince, you still there?" Mathis asked.

"Yeah," she said, rubbing the twitch from her eye again. The day would never end at this rate. "Are you sure about this?"

"Just tellin' ya the doc's specialty. According to his office, Lucy is due for an upstairs remodel in two months and she's still got the franks-and-beans. If you want verification, just give her package a little squeeze. If you hit pay dirt, you'll know."

Savannah literally choked on the suggestion. Mathis laughed, "Seriously, check her out. She got a bump in the wrong spot?"

She decided the conversation was best continued in semi-privacy. She moved a few feet away, leaving Ennis talking to Lucy. She lowered her voice to a whisper, "Mathis, if I did that, it'd be assault and I've been in enough hot water lately. Plus, I've heard guys have a way of tucking things so they don't show."

He chuckled, "You've heard that, eh?"

She turned to watch Lucy and Ennis. Her vision migrated south until settling on the crotch area. "I hope she doesn't catch me looking," she whispered to Mathis.

"If she does, just wink at her."

"John, you're killing me," she said. Lucy turned, giving Savannah a side view perspective. The detective's jaw slackened at the distinct bulge. The unmistakable bump that told her Lucy hadn't expected company, and obviously had not prepared for visitors. "My God," she said.

"Franks-and-beans?"

"John, I hope you don't talk like that around your kids."

"Eh, that's probably why my ex got custody. Was I right about Lucy?"

"On the money. Thanks." She placed the phone back on her belt. Ennis looked to her for an update. This situation presented a unique challenge. How the hell could she tell Ennis that Lucy hadn't just changed her name but her whole sexual identity? Then an idea popped into her head. *Let's see how Lucy reacts when I say,* "We found Luke."

Lucy's wide eyes zeroed in on Savannah. The cop felt her appraising her expression. Did she know or was she bluffing, it asked. Savannah wasn't a card shark but she had a decent poker face and she wanted Lucy to sweat a minute before she dropped the bomb.

"Here in town?" Ennis sounded relieved and excited.

He wanted this case solved too but Savannah wasn't finished with their transgender liar, "Yep and he's closer than we thought. Isn't he, Lucy?"

Unable to read Savannah's expression, Lucy opted for denial, "I don't know what you mean."

"Sure you do. I should have realized something was amiss when my partner spoke to you the first time. He's a charming fella. In fact, he could talk the dogs off a meat truck but you kept a distance. Nothing affected you except when you mentioned Barry's sexual advances. I thought it was because of his overbearing nature but it was something else that scared you."

Ennis switched between the two, finally settling on Savannah, "Like to enlighten me?"

Savannah asked Lucy, "You're really gonna force me to explain Dr. Alan Burch's specialty? My partner's patience is already running on rims so how do you think he'll react to finding out Luke is right here with us?"

"Where?" Ennis's vision scoured the room then fixed on the hallway. His hand moved to his gun.

Lucy stepped back, accidentally bumping the antique desk, "Luke is dead."

Savannah wagged her finger at the defensive woman, "Not... quite..." she lowered her finger to Lucy's crotch.

Ennis followed the line of the pointing finger. His eyes flared wide, "You're kiddin'. *This* is Luke Drury?"

"What's left of him." Savannah addressed Lucy, "What happened? Did Barry attack you after he discovered your secret?"

Lucy scowled, "You don't understand what he put me through. When he tore off my clothes and saw me, he started laughing. He called me horrible names."

"Still no reason to kill him." Savannah said. "Maim him real good but not kill him."

Lucy took a step back, "He was a monster and I know there were plenty of people wanting him dead."

"But you were the one who killed him. How'd you get Barry to the aquarium anyway?"

Lucy snorted, her stance and voice more arrogant, "He used two dating sites. Hotlanta and ATL Hookup. I opened an online account on ATL Hookup posing as a woman interested in casual sex. Asked him if he'd ever had sex with sharks swimming around him. I knew he'd fall for it because he loved risk."

Everything added up except one important detail, "But we didn't find dating websites on his computer."

"He always used his phone for that. Quick access to messages." Lucy rolled her eyes, "He'd check it constantly."

And since Barry's phone drowned with him, they never stood a chance of discovering that. If they had, the whole mayor fiasco could have been avoided and Barry's sister would have had a degree of closure.

Savannah tried judging Lucy's reaction. Her hands gripped the desk behind her, only inches away from what Savannah assumed to be the murder weapon. Instinct demanded she draw her gun but by the time she did, Lucy bolted toward the kitchen.

Savannah charged behind her with Ennis right behind. Lucy raced by a cabinet with a cutting board with chopped onion on it. Beside it was an eight inch Trizor chef's knife exactly like the one Savannah had seen at Georgia's. Her sister only bought the best for her kitchen and Savannah knew how sharp and durable her cutlery was. Lucy grabbed the knife and turned. The sight of Lucy brandishing the knife brought Savannah up short.

Ennis slammed into her back, forcing her forward a step as Lucy swung the knife. A brief flash of razor sharp metal caused Savannah to frantically backpedal to dodge the blade. Minutes seemed to pass as she braced herself against Ennis's chest, forcibly pushing him backward to gain precious space between her and the knife slashing within a whisper of her belly.

Sheer fright swept over her. She waited for the pain, the warm sensation of blood. She instinctively covered her belly with her hand in a feeble effort to protect herself and the baby but her reaction had been delayed by a mere second. She dreaded looking, dreaded checking herself for the wound she knew should be there.

Savannah glanced down at her hand and barely restrained her tears. There was no blood, no wound and no worry about losing her child. She inhaled long and deep, relieved that she'd escaped the vicious attack. Then anger set in. How dare Lucy or Luke or whoever the hell that was – *how dare* he try to hurt her child.

The clank of the knife hitting tile focused her attention across the kitchen. The wide-bladed knife skidded across the floor, the handle coming to rest against her foot. Scuffling and groaning filled the kitchen. She panicked, realizing she'd left Ennis vulnerable to Lucy's attack. In a brief few seconds, she'd managed to fail her baby, her husband and herself.

She lifted her gun and turned, aiming toward the sounds of grunts and thuds of fists connecting with flesh and bone. She doubted Ennis suffered the savage beating but crazier things had happened lately. Ennis and Lucy brawled in the corner next to the stove. From her vantage point, Savannah saw Lucy – or Luke – balled in the fetal position, trying to shield himself from Ennis's punishing blows.

Ennis's large fists buried into the killer's stomach, repeatedly pounding away as Luke's now suddenly manly voice pleaded for him to stop.

Savannah holstered her gun, rushed toward her husband, "Ennis, stop. Stop hitting him."

Whether it was selective hearing or the haze of rage, Savannah realized Ennis wasn't about to stop beating Luke. She risked touching her furious mate, hoping it might splinter his fury. It didn't. She grabbed his arm only for him to thrust it forward with another roundhouse on Luke.

"*Ennis, please stop!*" Savannah cried. He'd lost all reason upon seeing Luke swing the knife at her. Ennis jumped him and started swinging. Her panic mixed with his rage failed to shatter his rampage so she scrambled to find another solution.

She cupped his face in her palms, forced his vision to hers instead of Luke who was cowering and writhing on the floor. "Look at me," she ordered in a voice much calmer than she felt. "Ennis, look at me."

When he did an icy shiver ran down her back. His murderous expression reminded her of the night of their fight – only this was ten times worse. The heat from his flushed cheeks nearly burned her palms. She'd literally never seen him so angry. "Stop," she pleaded. "You are going to kill him at this rate and I'm alright."

Those last two words lessened the ferocity obscuring his handsome features. The hardness melted from his coffee colored eyes, "You're okay? Really?"

She saw his vision drop to her belly and she assured, "Really. We're both alright."

"Speak for yourself, bitch," Luke's baritone voice accused with a groan.

She felt Ennis's muscles tighten and saw his fist draw back again. "Don't," she said, reaching for his clenched hand. "Let's get him to the station and go home." Savannah drew her gun just in case Luke Drury had any thoughts of expounding on his statement. Leveling her aim at Barry's killer, she warned, "Give my partner any trouble and you'll be going to the morgue, not the police station."

32

The day after Lucy Driscoll's arrest, Savannah met the work day with a smile. Finally she and Ennis could work together without interference from the mayor. With the Vaughn case resolved, His Highness could go back to delegating and ordering his own people around instead of the cops. The week was looking better, she thought. Way better.

At least it was until, "You puttin' in for desk duty?"

Ennis's remark dispatched her hopeful, relaxed smile as effectively as Lucy cured Barry of breathing. Unless he enjoyed sleeping alone, she nearly said, smart money was on shutting up about desk duty. The veritable bane of every cop's existence resided in planting their behind in a chair only to take and make calls or do paperwork. Brains, along with the body, went soft. She understood why Ennis wanted her behind a desk. It was safer and stood more chance of normal hours but the mere thought of it shredded her last nerve. Still, she attempted to retain her calm – and good mood, "Ennis, can we talk about this when I'm eight months pregnant, not eight weeks?"

He straightened in the chair, stared at her. Oh great. Georgia's tactic. Stare Savannah into submission. It succeeded with her sister but Ennis failed to quite get the hang of it. So she stared back, waiting for affirmation or at least acknowledgment of her request.

The face-off ended moments later as he began chewing his nails, "Hunter hasn't already asked you about it?"

Sweet. He already recruited their boss in his mission to sideline her. "Have you asked him to?"

"What makes you think that?"

My dear, thoughtful vigilant husband. You tend to forget what I do for a living. "You're biting your nails and you answered my question with another question. Why did you go behind my back and ask Josh?"

Ennis rolled his eyes, sighed, "Because you won't."

"I'm new at this too, Ennis. I've never been pregnant, much less pregnant on the job. I'm not stupid but I'm not asking for that wretched duty until I have to."

Ennis's jaw clenched, "What's wrong with now? You'll still be working and you won't be in danger like yesterday."

So this was how it would be for the next few months. The overprotective rancher's son handing out guidelines and commands while using guilt as a weapon. *Oh boy, this'll be a real party…* Their children stood no chance of being reasonable either. The Princes were domineering. The Rutherfords verged on possessive. The two together? Impossible. "Ennis, yesterday was a fluke. Most people don't attack the police."

As she spoke, his frustration escalated, "You are carrying a baby. If that knife had come any closer or you hadn't stopped when you did…"

The memory sent a chill clambering up her spine. Just that close… Ennis had a valid point but caving into desk duty so soon? Her mind would go numb. "I'm painfully aware I'm carrying a baby. My whole body continually reminds me but I'm not changing because of it. However, if you'll give me some breathing room, I'll consider desk duty in the near future."

His shoulders instantly relaxed as his boyish grin returned, brightening his features, "Thanks, babe."

"You'd think I'd be used to all the change anyway. My feet and boobs keep growing, my clothes feel like they belong on Barbie, and the bathroom sees more of me than you do. At least desk duty will put me closer to the bathroom. On the upside," Savannah offered him the morning paper, "did you see the headlines this morning?"

He reached for it, "I was running late. What does it say?"

"See if you recognize anyone." The article above the fold had a brief but bold headline reading, "Aquarium Killer Caught". The piece sang the praises of the Atlanta Police Department and the investigating detectives. The mayor went only so far as to say the detectives "did a good job". Phenomenal was more like it, she thought, considering the crap he put them through.

The police chief referred to them by name which she appreciated. At least someone in the hierarchy valued their efforts. Evidently Ennis felt the same, "Our names are in print – in a favorable light this time. Nice." His chest swelled with pride, "Oughta send this to Ma."

"You *should* send it home. She'll love bragging about you." Then she winked, "As if she doesn't already."

Ennis gave the paper a studious gaze. Savannah could tell he deliberated over sending it. Then he carefully folded it, tucked it under his arm, "Gonna go put it in my locker. Be right back."

Watching him walk out, she smiled. After his run-in as a deputy in Texas, it would do him good to show his family a headline they could rave about. She was glad he decided to send it.

"Detective Prince, do you have a minute?"

The question came from the hallway. She recognized the voice and realized why he put a barrier between them. Their acquaintanceship proved less than harmonious but not even the red-headed wrecking ball could destroy her good mood. "Come on in," she replied with more serenity than she'd felt in over a week.

Rusty O'Neill cautiously leaned in, "You're not gonna throw anything at me, are you?"

"Nah, that was yesterday," she joked. "You're safe today."

He entered with hands behind him and she heard the distinct rattle of a paper sack. Savannah tried to peek behind him, "What's up, Junior?"

"I, uh, wanted to apologize for all the trouble me and my father caused you and Detective Rutherford." He brought the mystery package from behind his back. A white paper sack filled with...

Was that a whiff of pastry? Since getting pregnant, her nose finely tuned itself to sniff out any hint of baked delicacy, most especially chocolate. Her schnoz discerned everything from donuts, cookies, pies and cakes all the way to cream puffs and éclairs. It was better than a bloodhound tracking a scent. This pregnancy thing had real advantages. It gifted her with a bionic beak.

Savannah stared at the bag. Invisible waves of heavenly chocolate wafted past her, rekindling that chocolate daze she floated in every morning with her Cocoa Puffs. Only this aroma smelled sinful. The kind of temptation a pregnant woman with a chocolate habit wallowed in but only in absolute privacy. Without drawing her gaze from the sack she replied, "All forgotten. What's in the sack?"

Rusty seemed amused at her catatonic stare, "I also dropped by to give you these. They're not as good as your sister's but I thought they'd serve as a decent replacement." He gingerly placed the white sack on her desk then retreated a step, "They're called Chocolate Paradise. The saleswoman said it's like German chocolate cake with dark chocolate chips and hazelnuts. Sorry about the Chips Ahoy fiasco."

Savannah greedily – but still with a shred of self-restraint – opened the bag and inhaled. If her pupils weren't dilated, she'd have been surprised. They smelled blissful with the rich chocolate aroma drifting into her senses like a drug. *Chocolate Paradise indeed…* "Junior, this is one of the best apologies I've ever received. Thank you." Unable to resist, she thrust her hand in and withdrew a pillow soft cookie the size of a teacup saucer. She sank her teeth into it and simply melted with joy. They weren't as good as Georgia's but they were damn close. She'd heard of women experiencing orgasms over chocolate and waved it off as urban legend or lunacy. But as she chewed the soft sweet cookie bursting with chunks of silky chocolate, her eyes rolled back in her head. Maybe the whole orgasm thing had merit – but she needed another bite to prove it.

Pleased at her reaction, Rusty extended his hand to her, "It really has been a pleasure working with you, Detective. Even when we clashed."

Smiling, Savannah shook his hand, "It's been an adventure, Rusty. Thanks for the cookies."

"Sure," he headed for the door then stopped, turned. "I meant to tell you I bought Killer Instinct. I'm surprised you let Georgia disclose your acrophobia. I've heard therapy can do wonders for that condition..."

33

The instant Rusty O'Neill stepped from her sight, she plowed into the cookies like Sherman marching through Atlanta. And, like the Civil War general, she left nothing in her wake.

The whole scene was disgraceful and embarrassing. Her gluttony extended to tilting the empty sack into her hand for any crumbs left behind. If witnessed by any unsuspecting soul, the sight would have tarnished her reputation forever yet she plunged herself into the lustful affair with abandon. Savannah swept the cookie crumbs from her blouse, checked herself for errant crumbs on her face then leaned back and sighed. She'd consumed the entire bag of Chocolate Paradise cookies with such unabashed passion, the only thing left was her shame.

To hide her overindulgence, she wadded the paper sack into a tiny ball and tossed it in the trash. Guilt set in that she neglected to save a few for Ennis. Then she remembered him scarfing down Katherine's blueberry muffins, leaving her with zilch.

Fifteen minutes into digesting, her cell phone rang. Awash in the ecstasy only chocolate provided, Savannah decided to forgo the usual screening of Caller ID and answered in a cheery, "Savannah Prince. How may I help you today?"

A reluctant Georgia ignored the greeting, "Savannah, I – I need to tell you something and I'm not sure how."

She rose to her feet. Something was wrong. Dreadfully wrong. Always the voice of common sense and absolute calm, Georgia now sounded close to weeping. For some reason Savannah's first thought was of their father, "What's wrong? Is it Daddy?"

"No, Daddy's fine. I… I don't know how to say this. When I got today's mail there was a video…"

Cold fear closed around her heart like a fist. Blood pounded in her temples. The video. The past few days she'd forgotten about it, forgotten about Jeffrey and Cole. Thanks to her carelessness, her family saw the horrific images of Jeffrey's brutality. Her sister's unspoken truth shook her to the core. She forced herself to ask, "Of me?"

"Yes, but only I saw it. Dane wasn't here."

Savannah exhaled an unsteady breath. To have Georgia see the brutality was bad enough but if Dane had seen it, Savannah wasn't sure she could cope knowing he'd heard the screams tearing her throat, seen the blood spray when the cane slammed against already open wounds and seen her writhe against the pain. He would have heard her crying as sweat trickled into wounds, eating like acid into the raw nerves and flesh.

Georgia continued, "Hon, that's not all. Leah called me and –"

"Not Seth too," she groaned, tears trembling in her eyes. The delicious cookies now swirled into a tumultuous storm inside her. The restroom seemed a mile away and as a tide of dizziness swept in, Savannah struggled to find her balance. She eased into her chair and pulled the trash can closer just in case.

Her brother saw the video, heard those screams and saw her straining against her bonds like a wild animal caught in a trap. He and his wife Leah watched as Jeffrey Holland reduced her to such a depth of despair and misery that she pleaded to God to end the pain. She begged God, not Jeffrey, but now it seemed like a hollow consolation. The whole world was seeing her suffer and Cole Jordan and Jeffrey sat back laughing.

Tears blinded her, choked her voice, "This is never going to end. Cole and Jeffrey are going to destroy me any way they can."

"Savannah, calm down." In those few seconds, Georgia shored up her emotions and her maternal traits shined through. Her voice regained the strength and composure Savannah so often relied on, "Only Leah saw it. The kids were gone and Seth was at work."

She swiped away tears, "But I didn't want *anyone* seeing it and now my family has, my colleagues have…" Another icy shiver raked her spine, "Oh God. Ennis. Georgia, I have to go."

"Don't hang up," Georgia pleaded.

She'd already retrieved her purse and was rushing down the hall, weaving between officers and citizens, "Cole probably sent one to our house too. I have to get the mail before Ennis does."

"*Savannah*, listen to me –"

"I have to get home before he does." Out the door now, she bolted to the Camaro, threw open the door, oblivious to the scorching waves of heat rolling out.

"*Hon, he's already seen it.*"

It took a moment for the words to sink in. Ennis had seen it? For the first time, she noticed the heat but only because she flushed with humiliation. Her skin felt feverish beneath her touch as she patted away perspiration. She'd worried that Dane saw the horrific images and heard her screams. She never imagined Ennis had. "When?"

Her sister delicately continued, "Around the time you started seeing the therapist. It came in the mail. He didn't want you to know."

Four months. He'd kept it secret for four long months and she'd never suspected a thing. He'd seen Jeffrey beat her. He'd seen her at her most vulnerable and at the lowest possible point in her life. The concept of Ennis witnessing the brutality and degradation made her physically ill. She flung open the car door, leaned out in preparation of purging the growing sickness. "He's known for four months," she said. "And he kept *that* from me too?" Not just his past but the postcards and now videos. The bitterness from their ugly fight returned. It, along with resentment toward him and Georgia, had her shaking with anger. Her sister had known for four months too. And not said a word.

"Savannah, if he'd told you, it would have set you back. We all agreed it was best you didn't find out."

"You *all*?" She forced the words between clenched teeth. The treachery spread like a wildfire in her family. Her jaw ached, her body rioted with nausea and disbelief. The whole world appeared to be against her.

Georgia sighed. "Yes. All of us. So if you're mad at Ennis, be mad at me, Dane, Seth and Leah. You have to agree it would have done more damage than good."

Humiliation darkened to raw fury. Yes, she would agree. But damn it, she also thought she deserved the courtesy of being told her naked, beaten body was on display for the masses.

She wasn't sure whether to yell at Georgia or succumb to the tears she'd fought to control. Her stomach made the decision and she leaned out the door and with great effort, barely held her dignity intact.

She couldn't change anything, she finally decided. Nothing except her pride suffered damage. Georgia was right, she told herself while trying to calm down. At the time, she'd have been devastated if she'd learned Ennis saw the video. Even now she felt stripped of her privacy and sense of self. But he'd treated her no differently. No one had. Her family went about their business with no indication of a problem. In retrospect, they'd probably done her a favor by doing so. Savannah sighed, "If he's seen it then getting the mail is a waste of time."

"Hon, please approach this logically. We were trying to help. Cole sends these videos to torture you. We didn't want you hurt any more than you were."

Again, Georgia was right and she said as much. Cole sent reminders of her abuse to keep it fresh in her mind. She knew she battled an invisible force. From God knew where, Cole continued inflicting pain and wreaking havoc in her life. No one could successfully prevail over an invisible force. She had to find him. Find him and lock him in a cage like Jeffrey Holland. Keep him confined to that small, lonely room and prevent him from causing more harm – to her or anyone else.

Think logically, Georgia said. Cole wasn't smart enough to act on his own. He needed guidance. She learned that at the cabin. Jeffrey gave orders, Cole followed them. The leader sat in that small, lonely room, instructing his gofer on the next move. But how? How were they communicating? In person? Doubtful but not out of the question. By phone? Maybe. By mail? "I gotta go," she told Georgia.

"What are you doing?" Her sister's soothing voice switched to her Mama one. The one saying *don't do anything stupid.* Georgia followed it with, "You're not going to see Jeffrey again, are you?"

"No. But I need to find out how he's communicating with Cole. For my own sanity I have to." She said her goodbyes and headed out to Norcross Maximum Security Prison.

34

Savannah called ahead to the prison, asking that Jeffrey's mail be collected and brought to the warden's office. Warden Raymond Strauss initially balked with a demand to know why. She explained the reason but stopped short of details. To her trained ear, the warden sounded a shade defensive of Holland, falling just short of accusing her of violating a prisoner's civil rights. By the end of their short conversation, Strauss agreed to have the mail gathered and brought in.

Savannah hung up then turned off her phone. Georgia's mad spell was destined for Ennis's ears which meant he'd be calling her. Tell it to voicemail, she thought, because I'm off the radar.

Light traffic on I-85 pressed her foot harder on the gas and for the first time in a long time, she drove like Ennis. The Camaro weaved between cars, passing the slower ones as if the red beast sensed the importance and urgency of the trip. The exit for the prison quickly approached. She eased off the accelerator for the hard, winding curve that corkscrewed its way onto another thoroughfare heading to Norcross.

The buildings loomed on the horizon and as she approached, the complex seemed to rise from the ground like a giant. There were no trees within three or so miles of the prison. It stood by itself like a concrete island in an ocean of razor-wire fences and guard towers.

This visit to Norcross was different. No anxiety or fear laced her blood. Her heart had settled into a slower rhythm during the drive. The cold air blasting from the air conditioner cooled and calmed her. She treated it the way she treated any investigation. A journey to a prison for clues. Keeping her self-control meant as much as keeping her distance from the emotions. Look at it like a cop, not a victim, she told herself.

The road angled down for a couple of miles then rose sharply, leaving Norcross on a steep hill. Savannah gunned the engine to ascend the abrupt slope then hung a sharp right into the parking lot. Once parked, she cut the engine, leaned over to open the glove compartment. She removed two photos that she slid into her suit jacket.

She jogged to the first gate, showed her ID and began another journey, this one inside Jeffrey Holland's new residence.

Air conditioning embraced her the second she stepped inside the building. She pulled her jacket tighter around her, glanced at her watch. The meeting with the warden wasn't scheduled for another thirty minutes so she checked the visitor's log. Explore every possibility, even the most unlikely because there was always that small exception to the rule.

But Jeffrey's visitors, she discovered, were few and far between and none of them came close to Cole Jordan. She removed the pictures in her jacket, showed them to the guards. Each one shook his head after seeing Cole's image, saying they hadn't seen him.

By then it was time to meet with Warden Strauss. A guard

escorted her down long hallways, past other offices until stopping at one. She took a minute to strategize. Strauss regarded himself as his prisoners' advocate. She'd heard about Raymond Strauss when he was appointed warden of the new prison. Late forties, built like a brick wall and just as unyielding. He worked his way up the ladder from guard to supervisor at Coastal State Prison then got promoted to warden of Norcross. Coastal – ironically located in Savannah – was built in 1981 and housed nearly sixteen hundred adult male prisoners. In comparison, Norcross was two years old and only housed five hundred but those five hundred were categorized as the most dangerous in the state.

And Raymond Strauss, the once friendly guard turned ill-tempered gatekeeper, stood between her and eventual peace from one of those five hundred prisoners.

Before facing Strauss, she straightened, adjusted her jacket and took a deep, calming breath. *This may be his facility, but this is my life and Jeffrey will not intrude in it anymore.*

The guard opened the door and Savannah marched in, hand extended. Strauss filled out his grey suit a little too well. The unbuttoned coat revealed his girth straining at the buttons on his white shirt. The black leather belt holding up his drawers appeared to struggle with the task. This was not how she pictured big Raymond Strauss. Tall, wide shoulders and so overweight he barely fit his suit. Clearing up some of the confusion: a long jagged scar across his left cheek. Despite his weight, the man held his own in battle and his stiff, impatient handshake expressed his displeasure of her presence. Not a good start to the meeting. "Holland's mail," he pointed to a table across the room. "I don't like this, Detective. Prisoner Holland has done nothing to warrant this invasion of privacy."

"I appreciate the indulgence, Warden, but Jeffrey Holland is sneaky if you remember. He did manage to kill several women in two states before being caught."

"He only pled guilty to assault on a police officer," he quickly corrected. "He hasn't been convicted of murder yet, Detective."

This would be a challenge, she told herself. Winning over the warden who'd already decided Jeffrey was a decent fella. Yes, Jeffrey pled guilty to assault on a cop. She dreaded the upcoming trial for the nine murders since she and Georgia were slated as witnesses for the prosecution. Their testimony may not gift Holland with the needle but it would show that the bastard's brutal streak sank to the bone.

Strauss glanced at his watch, "As you can see, this will take a while and I've got an appointment in less than an hour."

When she turned to the table with Jeffrey's mail, her heart sank. A while? The large canvas bag practically burst at the seams. It would take days to go through it all. "That is Holland's mail?" she asked in disbelief.

"That's just the last two weeks. The letters he kept are in another bag. It's considerably smaller so why don't you start there?"

Thanks for the tip, she yearned to say. "Where are they?"

The warden lifted a clear plastic bag from his own desk, handed it to her. Jeffrey had opened every letter by precisely slicing the top seam along the fold. Dear God, she thought, he's anal in all respects. Even his mail is handled meticulously.

Savannah opened the bag, sorted the letters. Most were from women, a few from men. She looked them over for familiar names but found none.

She opened one from a woman. The letter showered Jeffrey in compliments, notably his good looks and his charming wink. Savannah scowled at the writer's ignorance. What a nitwit. *He winks at the camera because he's taunting authority, not because he wants adoration.*

It was hard to sift through such bullshit. Yes, he was nice looking but he was also a murderer. Her question: What kind of woman wants a killer to fall in love with her? The revulsion of actually reading Jeffrey's fan mail sickened her. He'd read these words and they fueled his ego with the fact some women were as stupid as he imagined. In this case Savannah agreed. When a woman "dreamed" of his hands "caressing" her body, that woman needed the good ol' seventy-two hour supervised vacation in the psych ward.

Savannah forced herself to remember why she came. *You're a cop right now, not a victim.* Investigate, dig for clues and ask questions. *Focus...* "Do you censor mail or screen it before delivering it to prisoners?"

Strauss checked his watch, pursed his lips. His impatience surfaced as a loud sigh as he realized the meeting would take longer than the allotted fifteen minutes. "We have the authority to, depending on the type of mail. Guards are only allowed to search for contraband inside letters from lawyers or any mail deemed classified. They don't read that mail. They are allowed to read non-classified mail. That comes from friends, family," he nodded to the letter in her hand, "or fans or pen pals."

"Pen pals." A chilling notion occurred to her. What if Jeffrey's manipulation reached beyond Cole? What if Jeffrey acquired a new friend too?

"Detective, most of that mail comes from lonely, naïve women –"

"Yeah," Savannah said, appalled, "women who didn't watch the *news* when Holland was butchering all these *other* women."

"He's not been convicted yet," he gruffly reminded. "Prisoners with his notoriety get requests for autographs and personal effects and frankly, the prisoners get lonely too and they develop pen pal relationships."

Well, boo-friggin'-hoo. They did the crime, they can do the time, lonely or not. Despite her bluster, Savannah curbed a groan. Men and women were contacting Holland and she recognized none of their names or their handwriting. She shook her head at the endless possibilities. Her shoulder and back ached, a harsh reminder that others took joy in her pain, just as Holland did.

"As for reading and censoring his mail, he's given us no reason to, not caused any trouble so we try to respect his privacy."

Why not? Of all the prisoners, the serial killer's correspondence sails past security. Meanwhile Jeffrey recruits his own version of the Manson family… But he's not been convicted of *murder* yet, Strauss would gladly say. "Right," she said bitterly. "He's a model prisoner."

"He isn't high on our list of concerns, Detective. He behaves himself, that's all I ask from a prisoner." His tone grew defensive, "We don't have time or manpower to read or censor each piece of mail. This is a large facility."

"I realize that, Warden. My concern is he's communicating with his stepbrother Cole Jordan. If it's not by phone, it's by mail. Holland isn't stupid. He's keeping it low key. He's in contact with Cole and utilizing the guards as his messengers."

The warden's eyes narrowed, giving him the appearance of a life-size bulldog about to attack, "What are you talking about? Guards as messengers?"

"I got a visit from a guard named Mike Baldwin. According to him, Holland sent him on a mission to speak with me and offer me a deal about finding Jordan."

Strauss was already on the phone, stabbing buttons and barking orders for Baldwin to appear front and center in his office. To Savannah he said, "He's got some explaining to do and I apologize for his behavior. Officer Baldwin knows better."

Five minutes later, Baldwin walked in the office and upon sight of Savannah he automatically shrank back, swallowed hard. Strauss motioned for him to shut the door then folded his arms across his chest, "Officer Baldwin, I hear you've already met Detective Prince."

Mike's hand nervously smoothed his tie, "Yessir, we've met." He nodded to Savannah, "Ma'am."

"The detective has some questions for you and when she's finished, I'll take over." He handed the conversation off to Savannah.

Finally. Maybe the warden discovered his house wasn't entirely in order. His confidence, while not completely shaken, certainly wobbled. She started off with, "When Jeffrey Holland has a visitor, are you the guard that accompanies him to the visitation room?"

His wide eyes shifted between her and Strauss to gauge his situation but the warden's expression remained unreadable past just plain angry. Baldwin cleared his throat, "Most usually, ma'am."

She reached in her suit jacket to retrieve the pictures of Cole. "Have you seen this man?" The first picture was of Cole Jordan in civilian clothes. Dressed in a sweater and jeans, he stood on a dock holding a fishing rod. She'd copied the picture from one found in his house after the police discovered Cole's wife, Janine Faulkner Jordan, murdered and stuffed in a chest freezer. Savannah chose the casual photo to give Cole an average appearance.

Mike studied the picture then shook his head, "No, ma'am. Never seen him before."

"You haven't been in contact with him on Holland's behalf? Like you have me?"

Guilt shadowed Baldwin's face, "No, ma'am. I haven't seen him before in my life."

"You're sure?" She handed him another photo of Cole Jordan. This one in his Atlanta police uniform. He appeared more muscular in the photo. The photo unsettled her because that was how she remembered him. Buff and arrogant with a wicked slant to his smile. He looked confident in his police uniform, his piercing blue eyes focused on the lens. "Tell me if you've seen him or if he's been here. If he didn't find a way inside, he may have loitered in the parking lot, waiting to talk to you. Think hard. It's important."

Mike's jaw dropped in disbelief, "The guy's a cop?"

Was a cop, she silently corrected. "*Has he been here*?"

He met her vision, "No, ma'am. Mr. Holland only has visits from his lawyers." He pointed to the picture, "And that ain't either of them."

"Okay, so that leaves mail. How good a friend are you to Holland?"

Baldwin's eyes darted around the room as if searching for the easiest way out – the door or the window. He glanced at Strauss for help but the warden only nodded to Savannah. The guard sighed, "We're not really friends, ma'am, I swear."

"You're cozy enough to personally deliver his message to me."

"But that was a favor. It didn't seem harmful at the time. It was like Mr. Holland was making amends with the folks he'd mistreated."

What he did to my sister and me is considered torture, not mistreatment. He tried to kill my sister. As for me, every scar on my body describes my suffering. I wake up in cold sweats, nearly screaming because of your pal Jeffrey. My body bears a number he carved into me. I will live with it forever, stare at it every day of my life because of your pal Jeffrey Holland. This isn't mistreated, asshole. It's torture. Get it right.

Savannah's jaw set hard enough to shatter her teeth. She trapped the words behind them but their intent emerged in her expression.

Baldwin swallowed hard, looked at the warden. Before she

launched herself at the guard, she relaxed her jaw, rolled her shoulder to loosen it as well, "Tell me how he made amends to the dead women. A séance?"

"I'm sorry, ma'am," he shied from her temper. "That came out wrong. When I'm nervous, I stumble for words."

She willed herself to calm down. The victim inside her scratched her way past the cop and bared her claws. If she continued losing her poise, Baldwin would shut down and she needed answers. She tried to smooth it over, "Sorry. I shouldn't have lashed out at you." She redirected the conversation back, "By his mail it's obvious Holland is popular. Does he tell you about his admirers and pen pals?"

Her change in demeanor seemed to help. Baldwin's apprehension disappeared as he explained, "Only a few of them. Calls one of 'em," he stopped to remember, "an amusing flake. 'Bout a month ago she sent him a letter with the usual compliments but she also put lottery numbers in it. She tells him her lucky numbers and even tells him what his lucky numbers are too."

Lottery numbers? It was official, she thought. Nothing about Jeffrey made sense, not even his crazy fans. "What for? Inmates are forbidden to play the lottery."

"She offers to play for him."

I'll bet he's truly moved by the gesture. "Does he write her back?"

"Yes, ma'am, but he laughs about it. Says it's a game to him. Told me it keeps him busy to write her. I think he's found a good friend in her. He seems happier these days. They talk frequently about the Bible and study it."

Savannah nearly choked. The Bible? The concept of Jeffrey Holland reading a Holy Bible – even for a "game" – temporarily stunned her into silence. He hadn't struck her as a man who catered to women on any level. Prison changed people to an extent but Jeffrey reading the Bible classified as a total makeover. "What?" was all she managed.

"Oh yes, ma'am. He's an honest to goodness God fearing man. I figured he'd be an atheist, him being a doctor and all. Most doctors I've met think *they're* God –"

"He *is* an atheist," she argued. Anger and bitterness laced her voice. Holland everyone fooled. He used his charm to beguile women and now used it to enthrall his jailers. He persuaded a guard to break the rules and beg her to the prison. He deceived the warden into believing he was a model prisoner. If she didn't stop the madness, the courts would let him dance out the door – to kill her and Georgia.

"Maybe he was an atheist but he's not now," Baldwin said. "He's really trying to make amends."

Mark Twain once said, "When angry, count to four. When very angry, swear." Savannah literally boiled and couldn't do either. The oaf in the uniform refused to understand the gravity of Holland's depravity. Amends meant he felt remorse for his actions. Jeffrey was incapable of remorse. She flashed Baldwin a look of disdain, "Boy, that gallbladder must have really meant a lot."

"Gallbladder?" the warden asked.

She told Baldwin to explain how he promised to visit Savannah in exchange for Holland's advice regarding his sister's medical condition. The longer the guard spoke, the narrower the warden's eyes grew, "Baldwin, your actions reflect on me. Guess how I look right now?" In Savannah's opinion, he was wavering between counting to four and swearing. Strauss settled on disappointment, "We have to interact with law enforcement on a daily basis. It's nice to have cooperation from the badges. Understand?"

The guard just nodded. He pushed his hands in his pockets, looking like a kicked dog, "Ma'am, I'm awful sorry Mr. Holland hurt you. From my personal observations, I can only tell you he seems religious and he knows his Bible. Quotes it to me every day."

Savannah rolled her eyes. How gullible could this guy be? "Even the devil can cite scripture for his purpose."

Baldwin stared, confused. Okay, maybe Shakespeare was over his head so she tried something simpler, "Even an atheist can quote the Bible but he's a *psychotic* atheist who's being held over for trial. Nine women are dead because of him."

Mike shook his head, clearly denying her statement, "I don't know nothing about that, ma'am. All I know is when I'm feeling down, he quotes his favorite verse to me. It goes like this." He closed his eyes, "'The Lord is my light and my salvation, whom shall I fear? The Lord is the stronghold of my life, of whom shall I be afraid?'"

Cold fear shot down her spine until she shivered. *The same verse I used when Holland was beating me.* She struggled to retain her focus as Jeffrey's words flooded back. *Call upon the Lord, Detective. See if He saves you… Does it look like God is in this room?*

Baldwin and Strauss stared at her, waiting, but her mind reeled with Holland's taunts. He'd mocked her faith, asking where God was while she screamed for His mercy.

Savannah closed her eyes, concentrated on banishing his voice, his words from her already weary, overtaxed mind. Steering her thoughts toward the current situation, she tried to understand why Jeffrey began quoting the Bible and that verse in particular. It was no coincidence. Nothing with Jeffrey was by chance. Had he instructed Baldwin to repeat the verse at her office and the guard forgot? Jeffrey purposefully planted seeds in the guard's brain and reiterated them, probably with hopes of reminding Savannah of her place. Conform or suffer the consequences. There are consequences to defying me, he'd said. Officer Baldwin, while a naïve and faithful pal, failed to reinforce Jeffrey's *come see me or else* message with the verse.

When Baldwin neglected his duty, it forced Jeffrey into another route. Pen pals, perhaps. And what better minion than a twisted fan? But this pen pal wouldn't have access to the video from the cabin. Savannah tried making sense of everything. The woman wouldn't bring her any closer to Cole and he was the one sending the videos and postcards. The handwriting on the postcards and envelopes was his. But Jeffrey's new lady could cause her own trouble. One letter instructing her where Savannah worked led the nutcase to their new house and Georgia's residence as well. Just follow the pretty red Camaro… "This friend you mentioned..."

Mike answered cautiously, "You mean his girlfriend? Lottery

girl?"

As if the headache tapping at her temple wasn't enough misery. Or the tightness in her shoulder that refused to give. Now a wave of nausea rose in her stomach. Clearly the baby didn't buy it either. Jeffrey had a girlfriend? He had no use for women unless they served a purpose but she tried accepting the news casually, "Okay, his girlfriend. What's her name?"

Mike looked at the large canvas bag holding most of Jeffrey's mail, "It's in there, I'm sure. She writes him all the time and he keeps her letters. She even bought him a Bible. The New International Version so he could understand it better."

Savannah reached for the smaller bag of saved mail. She plunged her hand inside, pulled out the stack of letters, "Find her."

He still regarded her warily, like she'd slap him for saying the wrong thing. She considered it, at least slapping him hard enough to knock some sense into him. Mike sifted through a couple of letters then stopped on one, "That's her. Jean Furkin."

Savannah snatched it from his grasp. Jean Elan Furkin, the envelope read. She stared at the name, running it through a mental Rolodex of names associated with the Holland and Jordan case but came up empty.

She opened the letter from Ms. Furkin and noted the religious overtones of the writing. It had biblical references to it, most notably a reference to the ten plagues. "The ten plagues of Egypt," she whispered. Why would Jeffrey care about that? What significance could the subject hold with him? She checked them off in her mind. Water to blood, frogs, lice, flies, diseased livestock, boils, thunder and hail, locusts, darkness, death of the firstborn. God's judgment upon Egypt. Still not catching the connection to Jeffrey, she told herself. Read it again.

She started from the beginning, reading silently, slowly. *As Pharaoh ignored Moses and paid the price, so will those who ignore you. Your voice will be heard. I promise those defying you will listen.* Uh-huh, time to grab the butterfly net and chase down the loony before she invades my home and family, Savannah thought. She skipped to the last paragraph. *What do you think of these numbers?* Great. A loony with the attention span of a goldfish.

Savannah analyzed the writing. The content, when not threatening was disjointed and the writing resembled a shaky mess. How could Jeffrey be drawn to such a total whack job? What purpose could this person – Jean Furkin – serve with such disorganized thoughts? Savannah skipped down to a list of numbers written at the bottom. They were written in rows, the first one being 5-2-33-5. Below it was a second series, 1-16-5-4, and a third: 35-2-1-8. Jean concluded the letter by saying, "These numbers hold promise today."

Baldwin cleared his throat, awkwardly broached the subject, "Ma'am, Mr. Holland feels really bad about what he did. I think that's why he wanted to see you. To apologize."

In a pig's eye, she nearly spat. The only apology Jeffrey might offer was that he hadn't finished the job. The rage she'd barely managed to contain finally boiled to the surface. How did Baldwin pass an IQ test? How could he be that ignorant to believe a serial killer felt remorse, especially one that smiled during his arraignment hearing – for assaulting a cop the warden would add. How could he maintain Jeffrey felt shame when he chuckled that "they missed two" when tallying the count of murdered women in two states? The same serial killer who vowed in his private perverse code to achieve the goal of "Number Ten" then turned to Savannah and winked. Jeffrey Holland was a monster and Mike Baldwin was an idiot. "How often does he get mail from this woman?" she asked.

"About twice a week and he responds in kind."

Savannah turned to the warden, "I want copies of all the letters from anyone he corresponds with, especially Jean Furkin." Then she turned to the idiot in the uniform, "You might believe Holland's changed and he's a swell guy but you're underestimating him. Nearly everyone who does ends up dead."

35

Supper had been abnormally quiet. She arrived home, changed into a tank top and shorts then whipped together a quick meal of chicken cutlets with pecan sauce. At the time Ennis seemed excited about supper – until setting eyes on the thick manilla envelope on the table. One look inside set his temper on edge. While she wolfed down the meal, her husband sat, staring at the envelope like a bad relative barging in at the holidays. She'd eaten half her chicken and Ennis barely touched his – and hadn't uttered a word. "What's wrong?" she asked. "Too much brown sugar in the sauce?"

"It's fine," he replied, picking at the coarsely chopped pecans on his cutlet. "Everything's… just… fine."

She let it drop, figuring he'd eventually turn loose with a scathing speech about visiting the prison and trolling Jeffrey's mail. Diving back into the chicken, she broke into a pleased smile. She'd actually done a pretty good job on the meal. Tender fried chicken cooked perfectly and the sauce had just right amount of chicken broth, vinegar, brown sugar and thyme. This cooking gig looked promising and best of all, she loved doing it.

Ennis washed the dishes while she relaxed at the table. Since he pouted about her trip to the prison and the resulting package on the table, she tackled it while he went about watching the Braves game on TV. She spread out the half dozen letters on the table, arranging them in order of postmark. After an hour of studying them and highlighting portions with a pen, they still made no sense.

For his part, Ennis sneered at the letters from the couch. As expected, he'd lectured her about going to the prison, getting Jeffrey's mail, calling it unhealthy for her and the baby. Well, having a crackpot loose and gunning for her wasn't exactly healthy for her or the baby either.

Each letter from Jean Furkin contained references to the number ten in the Bible. Besides the letter with the ten plagues she'd read at the prison, there were letters listing the ten rebellions of Israel, the ten times fire rained down from Heaven, Abraham's ten trials, the ten people who stated "I have sinned". "This woman's obsessed with the number ten," she said.

"Like someone else we know?" her husband snapped.

Oww, Ennis, that hurt. "Please don't be upset," she said.

He rose from the couch, stomped to the table. His jaw clenched and released as he debated his reply. The words squeezed through gnashed teeth, "They have references to the number ten because Jeffrey kept yapping about 'Number Ten' on TV every chance he got." He reached toward her right shoulder, his fingertip tracing the scar beneath the collarbone. Slowly, methodically, he traced the "1" then the "0". "He was talking about you, Savannah. Number Ten. What if this whacko writing to him takes on his fixation about you?

"That's why I want to stop her. I don't want me or Georgia in danger."

"Georgia's not in danger," he growled, balling his fists. "Holland never mentioned her. He wants Number Ten. That's you."

Ennis's temper flared hotter than she expected. He expressed his displeasure with silence first. Then came the clipped replies. An all-out tantrum currently simmered just under a boil and she wanted to avoid the explosion. She placed the letter on the table, made firm eye contact, "Ennis, I realize what he wants – and who. But wouldn't it be better to prevent trouble than wait for it?"

From the corner of her eye, she watched his fists gradually relax, his frown lines smooth. Her argument hit its target and he stepped behind her, his hands falling gently on her shoulders as they rubbed, "Then let Mathis read these letters. Let him find the evidence this woman is a threat."

Savannah covered his hand with hers, "Mathis doesn't know Jeffrey like I do. He might miss a subtle message or a word that I wouldn't." When he went silent again, she tightened her grasp a degree, "Ennis, please understand. I have to do this."

It was a full minute before he spoke, "What can I do? Quicker we get rid of these things, the better I'll feel."

"That massage sure felt good," she hinted. Before she finished, he began kneading the tense muscles again. She let her head fall forward into her hands, groaning, "That really feels good." Keeping her husband from blowing his stack rose to the top of her list. That decision was made the second she walked in the door. The letters provided enough kindling for a fight, so mentioning the fact he'd already seen that atrocious video was out of the question. He realized she knew the truth. No sense in hammering it in like a nail.

That choice paid off when he swept her hair aside and warm lips pressed a kiss to her nape, "I got something else that might feel good. No rule says you can't take a break and soak in a steamy, hot bubble bath."

The idea struck a nerve but so did the description. Steamy. Word association led to *McSteamy* which brought an image of Jeffrey Holland. The two men were practically twins and until they were both out of her life, she'd never relax. "Let me work another thirty minutes."

Ennis diligently massaged the knots then glanced over her shoulder, "You mentioned she's obsessed with the number ten. What does she mention?"

"The references are all from the Bible. So far, the ten plagues, Israel's ten rebellions, fire from Heaven ten times, Abraham's ten trials, and the ten people who said *I have sinned.*"

His grasp tightened a little too hard. As if he realized it, he lightened the pressure, "Those sound ominous. To me, it sounds like she's planning to make someone pay."

She opted to leave out the part where Jean basically promised Jeffrey she'd make "those who ignore you" pay the price. Savannah was tired of seeing Mad Ennis.

He went to the kitchen, brought back a Yoo-Hoo for her then resumed the shoulder rub, "What are those numbers?"

"Lottery numbers."

His fingers momentarily stopped, "Lottery numbers? But Jeffrey's not –"

"No, Jeffrey's not allowed to play the lottery. That's just another reason none of these letters make sense."

"Another reason, huh?" His fingers dug into one particularly stubborn knot, tenaciously battling her body's tension until she winced.

She couldn't be certain but something kept and held her attention about the name. "Look at that name. Jean Elan Furkin. Mathis checked with the DMV and there's no Jean Elan Furkin listed in the city – or state for that matter."

"Coulda moved here recently to be close to Holland. It hit the national news so anyone could have seen it. Or maybe she doesn't drive."

Whatever the reason, Jean Furkin was quite a mystery. She latched onto Jeffrey for whatever reason and he'd answered in kind. He found a friend in Jean – question was how good a friend was she? Staring at the name, Savannah wondered aloud, "Why does she address it with her whole name? Doesn't make sense. Hardly anyone does that."

"Maybe she's different." Ennis peered over her shoulder at the envelope. "'Course her elevator don't go to the top if she's writing a serial killer anyway. What's got you puzzled?"

"Besides the fact the initials spell JEF? I'm not sure." She indulged in a swallow of Yoo-Hoo while Ennis studied the name.

He sat next to her, pointed to the letter on the far left, "Is that the first one she sent?"

Savannah nodded, handed it to him, "As far as I know."

He cleared his throat, read aloud, "Hello, Jeffrey. I hope this finds you well –"

"What are you doing?" She'd read all the letters until her brain threatened to explode. She really didn't require – or want – a vocal recounting of them.

"Maybe we missed something. The woman's kinda spacey but if he's writing her back, there's more to her than we're seeing."

Didn't she just basically say that? Instead of voicing the thought, she wisely grabbed the Yoo-Hoo and took another healthy swallow. Better to use it to engage her mouth in something other than condescension.

"…for me. How long has it been since you found the Lord?"

She stood up to stretch her legs, "That woman's really misguided if she thinks Jeffrey believes in God, much less worships Him." The muscles in her thighs and calves cramped from sitting so long. This situation tested her emotions and now her physical capabilities. She never sat that long without walking or moving around but keeping Jeffrey at bay and finding Cole became an obsession. She rubbed her calf, wondering if the pregnancy caused leg cramps that insanely severe. If so, God help her.

Ennis patted his knee, "Need a good rub?"

The suggestion sounded like heaven, "You mean all over?"

He winked, "That comes later. Let me work on your legs and feet for now."

She plopped down and placed her cramping leg across his thighs.

At first touch she cringed. The bunched muscles clamped down like a fist in her calf.

Ennis tenderly rubbed and kneaded the muscles, wincing in sympathy with her. Pain impulsively made her pull back but his fingers closed around her ankle to keep her still, "I'm not rubbin' the knot, I'm rubbin' around it."

"It still hurts."

"If you'd take an occasional break, you wouldn't cramp up. Your body is telling you to stop." He punctuated the statement by sliding his knuckles along her calf a little too firmly.

She whimpered more for effect but it still hurt, "There's no call for malicious behavior, Ennis. Stop torturing me."

"I'm helping, not torturing."

"It's helping if I can walk after you're finished."

He sighed with disgust, "Why don't you stop for a while?"

"If I stop, Jeffrey wins." The instant she said it, she regretted it as the massage turned even more vigorous. She recoiled, trying to reclaim her leg. Ennis caught it and offered an apology, "I'm sorry. It's just… He's not losing right now either. You're obsessing over these letters. He's on your mind. He wins that way too. But if we figure this out, maybe I can get my wife back." Ennis pulled the letter closer while he worked and read aloud, "Exodus describes how the Lord brought ten plagues upon Pharaoh..."

Savannah listened, her eyes closing as his fingers settled into a gentler motion. Finally a true, relaxing massage. She let him continue, "'Remember to keep the faith. There are those who pray for you.' Then she signs it and postscripts a paragraph on the lottery."

He extended the letter to her. She glanced over the postscript. "'I know a religious soul shouldn't be tempted but I think I'll get lucky.'" She frowned, "I told you. Certifiably cuckoo. Religion and lotto in the same letter? That's like mixing milk and beer."

"Actually I've done that but it was an accident and you're right. It wasn't a great combo."

She let that slide because bathrooms saw enough of her lately. No reason to puke unnecessarily. "She's fanatical about both God and her numbers." Savannah scooped up Jean's second and third letters, handed them to Ennis, "She's the first person I've seen that shares her lotto numbers. Most people protect those. I've seen them hunkered over the cabinet at Kroger like kids shielding homework from cheaters. Why would Jean just hand him those numbers? If he's corresponding with other people, he might decide to share them."

Ennis's massage moved from her calf to her foot, "They look like numbers for the Georgia FIVE and Fantasy 5 but there are duplicate numbers in the first group. 5-2-33-5 then 1-16-5-4, 35-2-1-8."

She scanned over the other letters. Jean arranged numbers in rows then stacked them atop each other. Except one. Savannah picked up that letter, "Look at these numbers. They're not written the same way. This one is a single line of numbers. 48-86-30-33-8. And why aren't *any* of these numbers in sequence?"

"She's disorganized for one. Stupid for another 'cause only a fool writes a serial killer."

Was the woman as stupid as she appeared? She was off her rocker in one way, sure. As Ennis pointed out, what stable person wrote a serial killer? But stupid? Her gut told her no. Because as crazy as Jean Furkin was, why did Jeffrey write her back? "I don't think so. I think there's a connection Jeffrey made with her but I can't figure out what." Her muscles still ached as they surrendered to Ennis's tender manipulations. He'd succeeded in eliminating nearly every ounce of tension in her body. She much that she yawned, "That bubble bath sounds heavenly."

Ennis dropped the letters like they were on fire and winked, "I'll get on it."

"After I soak a while, I'll find a way to properly thank you."

O O O

She awoke with a start. Not from a nightmare or Ennis's ripsaw snoring. The letters on the dining table continued bothering her. Yes, they contained duplicate numbers and none of the numbers were sequenced. The letters made absolutely no sense but it was another reason that brought her wide awake. Some of the numbers sounded familiar.

Ennis continued to snore beside her, unaware that she'd basically bolted upright in bed. A quick glance at the clock revealed the ridiculous hour of three in the morning. Since sleep seemed implausible, Savannah carefully and quietly rolled out of bed, shrugged on her robe and trudged back to the dining room. She fished through all the letters until finding the one that refused to let her sleep. At the bottom it read, "Your lucky numbers are 48-86-30-33-8."

She rubbed her eyes to clear them then slid on her glasses to closely examine the numbers. Thunder rumbled in the distance and the wind began churning outside. The longer she stared at Jean's correspondence, she wondered if the storm, not the letter, had awakened her. Atlanta's weather had a habit of turning a regular thunderstorm into a wild ride that shook rafters, whipped trees to the ground and occasionally it even scared the hell out of Ennis. Considering the unrelenting heat and now an unexpected ferocious storm, she decided to stay up and work instead of fight the bed for sleep.

The house creaked and she turned, thinking perhaps Ennis woke up and sought her out. The doorway stood dark and empty. A gust of wind buffeted the house, causing the rafters to pop and groan and tree limbs to scrape the windows. The new house's strange, distinctive noises unnerved her more lately. Until she resolved the issue of Jeffrey and Cole, she'd continually be on edge.

She thought about brewing coffee and staying up but her eyelids reminded her of the absurd time. Three o'clock was too early for coffee. She closed the coffee pot's lid and her vision dropped to the cabinet with the day's mail. Sorting through it took only a minute since their cars didn't require an oil change, their lawn had already been mowed and they sure as hell weren't selling their house. Been there, done that, and never doing it again – despite the fact their new abode snapped, crackled and popped. To show her discontent at the real estate company, she ripped the flyer in half then half again. *There. Stick your offer where the sun don't...*

Savannah stopped cold as she stared at the torn bits in her hands. What she saw trumped any cup of coffee as adrenaline shot through every vein, her heart slammed against her ribs.

The scrap atop the heap read "4886." Their house number. Maybe the early signs of paranoia surfaced but she stepped back to Jean's letter to read: *Your lucky numbers are 48-86-30-33-8.* Savannah stared at the pieces in her hand, "4886." She quickly sorted the pieces until coming across their zip code – 30338. Jean's final numbers: *30-33-8.* The gravity of Jean Furkin's letter robbed her stability, and she sank into the dining chair before her knees gave out. "They're not lottery numbers. They're code. And this one told Jeffrey our new address and zip code." Not the entire address but the house number and zip code. Where was the rest of the address? Buried in more code? Sent in another letter? No, Jean Furkin wasn't stupid after all. She was dangerously clever.

Savannah tried to quell her frantic heart. She felt faint. She felt enraged. But most of all she felt terrified to the bone. This woman who regularly wrote Jeffrey *knew where she and Ennis lived.* Somewhere in those letters she hid the address, Savannah would bet money on it. The trick was finding it.

Pressing a hand to her heart, she reminded herself. Cop, not victim. Look at the correspondence with fresh eyes. Fresh eyes at three in the morning during a violent, crashing storm, yeah, right... She read it once then twice then slammed the pen down in frustration. She needed peace and quiet. She needed sleep and rest and none of them appeared promising.

The language in the letters rambled and Jeffrey hated rambling.

For him to tolerate such nonsense meant the woman provided a significant service. Whatever message Jeffrey and Jean shared, it was still in the letters – in code. More damn code, she guessed. I like puzzles, she thought, but not when they screw with my life...

She glanced down at the letter, reached to move the pen then stopped. Focusing on the pen's position on the page, she noticed that it aligned perfectly down the page, isolating the first word of every paragraph. As she read each word, it didn't reveal a code – but the first *letter* of those words did.

Savannah circled the letter *T*. Moving to the next paragraph, she circled the *I*, then the next paragraph began with *L*, the next another *L* and so on until she read the startling truth aloud, "Tilly Mill Road. The 'lottery numbers' gave him the house number and zip code. The rest of the letter spelled out the street name." She shuddered all the way to her toes. Jean Furkin found a way to tell Jeffrey their address without raising a single eyebrow at Norcross.

She stared at the simplicity of the code, wondering how it escaped her. *I'm the idiot, not Jean or Jeffrey, but me. She hid the code in plain sight and allowed the numbers to distract anyone reading the letters.*

A crack of thunder split the silence and rattled the windows. The storm moved in fast, promising torrential rains and jarring peals from the heavens. From calm to violent, that seemed to be the story of her life lately.

She shuffled through the other letters, beginning with the first. She circled the beginning letter of each paragraph as she'd done before.

The *H* in "Hello, Jeffrey." The *I* in "I hope this finds you well." Next the *B* in "Begin with Genesis…" The *R* in "Rather than reading…" She kept circling – *O, T, H, E,* and finally the *R* in "Remember to keep the faith."

Savannah read the message from top to bottom, "*HI BROTHER.*" A sudden churning sickness propelled her from the seat and sent her racing for the bathroom. Violent heaving spasms racked her until her head and back ached. She braced her hand on the cabinet to steady herself. Not only her balance but her life went askew with Jean Furkin's real identity. Jean was Cole Jordan and he told Jeffrey where Savannah lived. The monster finally stepped from the shadows and she had to stop him any way possible.

The rain cascaded in sheets and lightning strobed through the bedroom and bathroom. She doubled over again as a gentle touch settled on her shoulders. There was nothing left, she groaned to herself. Nothing left to purge except the evil of Cole and Jeffrey.

"You okay, sugar? That sounded pretty bad."

You should've been on my end of it. Before she answered, the urge overwhelmed her again, leaving her stomach sore and her back now throbbed.

She heard water running, then Ennis pressed a cold wet washcloth to her throat. Savannah welcomed the chill. It settled her rioting stomach and focused her mind on Ennis. He would protect her. He was her knight in shining armor. He wouldn't let anything harm her or their baby but she had to do her part. That meant finding Cole.

"Have you made an appointment with Dr. Boulton yet?" Ennis's soft tone and delicate touch soothed her. He swept her hair aside and added another cold cloth to help ease the sickness. Poor Ennis. He blamed the baby and the deceptively named "morning sickness" for her spectacle when in reality, it was pure terror ripping her guts out.

She nodded, giving herself time to gather her wits and regain her composure. She'd made the appointment with her OB-Gyn earlier and surprisingly, he had an opening later the next week.

Another round of thunder shook the house. Savannah cringed at the noise while testing her sea legs. She steadied herself with a hand on Ennis's arm, answering, "My appointment is next Thursday but that's not the problem."

Ennis slid his arm around her for support. "What is?"

Once she felt confident enough to exit the bathroom-with the cold cloth in hand, she replied, "I'll show you." Lightning flashed followed by tearing thunder. She led him to the dining room, pointed to the letters.

Ennis's shoulders slumped, "Jeffrey's mail. Of course."

His disgust hurt her. Jeffrey remained a legitimate threat. God knew who else might contact him and take up his cause to kill her. Cole was the immediate danger but others could follow. And Ennis acted as if she'd yanked him out of bed to show him a flyer for a new vacuum... That, she safely bet, was about to change.

She handed him the letter spelling out Jean's identity. His sleepy vision roamed the letter – to placate her, no doubt. He rubbed his eyes, "What are these marks?"

"Read the circled letters."

A few moments later, his eyes grew wide. Now he was awake. "Jean is Cole?" Suddenly his temper flared, "Why that sneaky…" he added an expletive so fiery, she nearly held her hands over her belly. Who knew when the kid's hearing kicked in? And *she* sure didn't fancy hearing that word either.

Now that she had his undivided attention… "There's more," she said, handing him the letter with their address.

Ennis perused the page then blew out a breath, "Jeffrey knows."

"Jeffrey knows. The lotto numbers are our address and zip code." Another little wave of nausea bubbled up, forcing her to hold the cold cloth to her throat. *Jeffrey knows.*

"Then what are the numbers in the other letters?" Ennis asked.

She swallowed hard, wiped the cloth across her neck and cheeks and shrugged. The other numbers hadn't struck a chord with her and the thought of breaking another code about finished her off. She'd dumbed into the others and luck only held out for so long.

Ennis scrubbed a hand through his hair and headed to the coffee pot, "If we're decoding things, we might as well have some caffeine to sustain us. Doesn't look like the storm is letting up anyway."

Savannah looked over another letter using the same strategy. But when she read from top to bottom, the message made no sense. Cole used the same code for the first few letters. She examined the postmarks on the envelopes. The first two letters had the code then it stopped. Twice a week, Baldwin said. Jean wrote twice a week. According to the postmarks Tuesdays and Fridays were the days Cole mailed them. At least two letters were missing. She groaned.

Ennis sat the carafe down, "What's wrong?"

"There are missing letters. Two or more. Jeffrey either threw them away or the staff didn't copy them all."

"Well, let's work with what we've got."

The smell of brewing coffee wafted to her, bringing her senses alive. Her body needed an infusion of java, a jolt to rouse her brain and get her intuition into gear. If she'd brewed it, they'd both get some work done but with Ennis's coffee, she'd be glad to keep her eyelids open.

Coffee cups clinked onto the counter but Ennis held off pouring her coffee, "Your stomach better yet?"

"Yeah," she replied, still distracted by the cryptic correspondence.

He brought the two cups to the table, sat down beside her. He studied a letter with a later postmark, "This doesn't have the funky paragraph code."

"I noticed." Savannah rubbed her eyes, trying to clear them. "Back to square one. There's a code and no obvious key."

Ennis sipped his coffee, studied the letter again. "Reckon it's the name? Could that be part of the code? Jean Furkin? You said Mathis couldn't find a record for the name anywhere."

That was true. Savannah turned her attention to the name Jean Elan Furkin. Where *had* Cole found that name with no record of it anywhere? Practically everyone left a trail if they were alive – or deceased for that matter. The distinctive name should have popped up somewhere, right? If it too was a code, it served a purpose and judging from Cole's capabilities, he embedded puzzles throughout the letters. Never take anything for granted, especially a nutjob with a grudge.

With Cole's ego, she considered the fact he might use a victim's name but when she mentally ran down the list of nine victims in Atlanta, she came up empty. They'd killed twenty women in Washington State. Savannah didn't know the names but Ennis had seen them. "Any of the Washington State victims match the name?"

Ennis shook his head. So where did that leave them? Nowhere. Unless he invented the name, "What if Jean Furkin isn't alive?"

Ennis shrugged, "Then she would be dead and with Cole she didn't get there fast."

"What if she's not dead either?"

"Then she's got more problems than Cole Jordan and Jeffrey Holland."

"Ennis, listen."

"I'm trying but you're not making sense. There's only dead or alive. There ain't no in between, no matter what those transcenmentalists think."

No, no, no, "What if *she never existed*? Maybe he simply created the name."

The wheels behind his bleary eyes locked down. Incredulous, he asked, "Jean Elan Furkin? That goes beyond creative. That's purt-near insane."

A particular nuance in Ennis's enunciation caught her attention. "Say that again."

"It's purt-near insane. 'Course Jordan's always been left of center–"

"No," she impatiently corrected, "her name. Say her name again."

Ennis slanted her a look suggesting she'd lost a few marbles but he repeated the name to appease her.

And there it was. Thanks to his Texas drawl dragging out the names Jean and Elan, she figured out the significance of the whole name. Cole hadn't created the name but toyed with the original. "Ennis, she *did* exist."

He returned to the coffee pot for a refill, mumbling, "I hope this pregnancy thing doesn't affect a woman's reasoning abilities for long because you are concernin' me."

"I'm fine. I was wrong a minute ago but I'm fine," she assured while feverishly scribbling the name Jean Elan Furkin. "Do you remember Cole's wife's name?"

"It wasn't Jean or Furkin."

Again she scribbled, this time a different name, the one she asked Ennis about, "But what was it?"

"Savannah," he finally groaned, "this is ridiculous. After what we've been through, how am I supposed to remember something nearly five months ago?"

Systematically she checked off letters in Jean's name then stood up, proud of her accomplishment. Her husband, bless his heart, suffered from sleep deprivation and he tended to be a bear at those times. However once he saw the results of her work, he'd understand her persistence.

She met him in the kitchen, held the paper so he could read it. Ennis sighed, glanced at what she'd done – to appease her, she assumed. He sat his coffee cup down. By his expression, he still didn't quite get it. "Janine Faulkner. Okay, your memory's better than mine. But what does that have to do with –"

"Ennis, look at the name," she stressed. "Jean Elan Furkin is an anagram of Janine Faulkner. Cole killed his wife and decided to use her name to alert Jeffrey to his letters. Once Jeffrey read 'Hi Brother', every time he received a letter from Jean, he knew it was Cole."

"You're giving them both a lot of credit. Especially Cole."

"Jeffrey only has time on his hands. He loves playing head games. And Cole may be dense in some cases but he's not that stupid. He managed to kill Janine then help Jeffrey kidnap and kill nine other women and stay under the radar. And don't forget, he's eluded capture for nearly five months. That's definitely not the description of an idiot."

36

Savannah despised the word *no*. People around her used it frequently and emphatically to drive home their feelings. Her parents used it as most parents did, sometimes a little too liberally, in her opinion. Georgia ran it on rims as a teenager, telling her sister *no*, she may not borrow her favorite sweater for her date or *no*, she may not use the new blush she just bought. Ennis rarely uttered the word, probably for fear of repercussions but when he felt it was important, he too exercised his veto power.

Josh Hunter had grown a thick skin over the years. Thick enough to say no to her and stand back and wait out her temper. After graduating from the academy, they assigned rookie officer Prince to that very precinct, under the authority of Captain William McClelland and Lieutenant Josh Hunter. Hunter served as intermediary between officers and the captain and because of it, his job became more that of referee. Savannah tried not to rock the boat her first year but managed – as she always did – to get under someone's skin. Her biggest challenge: Overcoming the nickname her training officer Riley Murphy pegged her with. PITA – or "Pain In The Ass". Murphy still referred to her as PITA as a joke – probably because she wasn't his personal PITA anymore.

Today she had been Captain Josh Hunter's PITA. She spent the better part of an hour in his office, asking, demanding then pleading to be part of the undercover team staking out the post office box Cole Jordan appeared to be using for mail.

Without intending to, she managed to gift Hunter with a headache, be called Pain In The Ass for old time's sake, and be warned if she screwed up or interfered, PITA would be UE, or unemployed.

By afternoon, she sat in a sun baked unmarked police car with Lieutenant Charles Selby who showed as much enthusiasm about her presence as Josh Hunter had. He'd parked the sedan across the intersection from an Express Mail store. The P.O. Box was registered to a Denise Colbert who rented the box two years ago but hadn't been seen in several weeks.

Selby sat patiently in the car, impervious to the heat and her suffering. His dark skin shined with perspiration that he didn't seem to notice while she kept a vigilant effort to wipe hers away.

I asked for this – actually demanded it, she reminded herself. The last thing she intended to do was complain about the heat, despite the fact she felt her body swelling by the second. And why didn't men require air conditioning anyway? Let a man sit in the heat and all they needed was a beer. Let a woman sit in the heat and after an impassioned crusade of complaining, she'd write SOS in her own sweat just before she passed out.

Located in a lower income area of the city, the Express Mail might as well have sat at the corner of Smith and Wesson. Residents there kept guns closer than their phones because bullets traveled faster than police cruisers. In these parts, no one wanted the cops around.

Half the residents considered them the enemy, the others felt forgotten.

The broad-shouldered black lieutenant fit right in with the neighborhood. Dressed in jeans and worn Atlanta Hawks t-shirt, his muscular physique and rough features gave the impression of a man who knew the streets and owned them. In comparison, the white girl in the dark blue suit (a decision she'd been regretting for the last hour), stood out like a sore thumb and passers-by let her know it.

Once upon a time the little strip mall across the way held promise. The building had housed everything from a neighborhood grocery, to a bookstore and electronics store. Over the years, businesses fell victim to enough crime they either closed or moved to safer locations. Only a liquor store remained next to the Express Mail. The liquor store was more popular than the Express Mail, Savannah assumed, because of the general economic misery of the neighborhood and probably somewhat due to the heat. She remembered how R.J. guzzled beer and scotch during the summer months. Even in ninety degree heat, he'd extricate himself from a nice cool house to fetch more booze and replenish his stock. It made no sense to her and watching the same scenario unfold with total strangers, it still didn't.

The heat became nearly unbearable as they sat waiting for Cole to arrive for his mail. She shrugged out of her suit jacket and fanned herself. Lieutenant Selby just looked at her. *Women*, his expression seemed to say. For some reason, she felt the need to apologize. Being knocked up and all the raging hormones certainly didn't help her plight but Selby knew nothing of her condition so she uttered a quiet apology, rolled the window down a little further and resumed suffering.

Selby frowned at the window action. Safety issues, she figured. But unless he enjoyed reviving newly expectant mothers, he'd have to cope with a meager breach of security. Everyone in the neighborhood could spot an unmarked cop car from a mile away and lately there'd been plenty of violence on those streets lately, a lot of it directed at police.

Savannah came prepared for that event. The .38 nestled at her hip gave her more security than the big lieutenant sitting next to her. She'd promised the no-nonsense Selby that she'd keep the weapon holstered unless absolutely necessary – and he'd reminded that merely *seeing* Cole Jordan did *not* signify an emergency.

Maybe not, she thought, but all the gang members roaming the streets did. The sight had her pulling her elbow closer to her side, the feel of the gun comforting her. And as for the window, it was staying open whether the lieutenant liked it or not. Better to have sweaty backup than the comatose kind.

A group of young black men crossed the street in front of them, eyed their car then moved along. "It figures Cole would choose this part of town," she said. "No one knows him and no one cares."

Selby didn't comment, choosing to ignore her instead. Okay, she'd pulled every string within reach to be there and she damn sure knew Selby hated that fact. However, since they were spending the afternoon together, why not lower the level of misery by *trying* to hold a conversation?

She dabbed the shine from her forehead, praying Cole showed soon or she'd melt. That or go crazy from the silence. In retrospect, she finally decided Lieutenant Selby was naturally quiet. Even when communicating with his team he barely spoke a word. He'd assigned one officer to work the counter inside and stationed three others along the street on foot. She gave Selby credit. He'd put enough manpower on the stakeout that Cole Jordan had to be Houdini to slip through the cracks. Savannah wouldn't dismiss that idea either. Anyone who could evade capture for nearly five months wasn't exactly an idiot.

"This goes down and you stay in the car," he ordered.

Savannah swiveled to him. No one said anything about sequestering the sweaty girl with the agenda. She agreed to watch the arrest but not from the nosebleed section.

When Selby met her gaze, her stomach tightened and she swallowed hard. There was an edge to the lieutenant's voice, "Detective, this is probably the only solid lead we'll get on Jordan. You jump out of this car and you could start swinging 'cause I've seen it happen on this job. You do that and we're screwed. No matter who shows up to this place, you sit your ass in this car because I said so."

After a heated argument in Josh Hunter's office about "keeping her on the sidelines", the lieutenant emerged disgruntled and fuming. He'd lost the argument to the captain but he was still her senior officer and reminded her of it. Selby left no question that disobeying him guaranteed serious repercussions. To reinforce that, he asked, "Do we understand each other?"

She nodded an acknowledgement, "Understood."

He returned to surveying the store across the way, "It's not smart, you being here. Too much temptation. I give you credit for finding Jordan but you should have let us handle the arrest."

How did she reply to that? No one except her and Georgia realized the hell Cole and Jeffrey put her through – at the cabin, at her own house and now. She'd promised no interference but she did deserve to be there for the arrest.

Selby checked his watch, resumed watching the store, "I guess what I'm saying is you've done your part, now it's time we did ours."

The softened postscript helped ease the hurt. He wasn't a jerk and she'd known that. He continued, "The clerk said Colbert stopped picking up mail around two months ago or so. A guy comes in for it now." The lieutenant reached in his back pocket and handed her a folded piece of paper. "This is who's been coming and going from the apartment."

Savannah unfolded the paper. It was a picture from a computer printer. The man on the page wore jeans and a white t-shirt. He stood tall, his broad shoulders pushed back proud and strong. His dark brown hair curled below his collar to match the thick mustache and goatee ringing his lips. He wore sunglasses but Savannah still recognized his face. "It's Cole."

"You're sure?" He backed off at her frown, "Just checking, not doubting. They say he comes here around three to get the mail." Selby checked his watch again, "And he's late."

"He'll be here." Cole was a lazy, arrogant, chauvinist bastard but he wasn't too lazy to pass up a prime opportunity to torment her. Between him and Jeffrey, they constructed what they considered a foolproof trap. They orchestrated it as well as their abductions and killings. The only difference: Savannah's experience gave her an advantage. It schooled her on their personalities. Jeffrey was the composed leader, relying on strategy rather than brute strength. Cole was the loyal follower, the dutiful enforcer. His lack of punctuality signaled confidence, not laziness.

Lieutenant Selby reached for his radio and pointed across the street, "That Jordan?"

Savannah sat straighter in her seat, leaned forward. Sauntering along the sidewalk in sunglasses, jeans and a light blue t-shirt was a man she'd not seen in nearly five months. The last time they interacted, she shot him twice – in the knee and thigh. Thanks to her, Cole now walked with a noticeable limp. The hitch in his gait, however, didn't lessen his bruising, muscular physique or the intensity of his expression. She remembered his piercing gaze, the one that flashed from friendly to cruel in an instant. His strong arms effortlessly lifting and carrying her. The brutal power behind his fist.

"Detective," Selby prompted, "is that Jordan?"

Her heart slammed against her ribs so hard she pressed a hand to it, "That's him." Mere moments separated her from ending the nightmares, paranoia and sleepless nights. Not months or weeks. Moments. No more looking over her shoulder, worrying about the day's mail or who saw the abhorrent videos of her beating. Her body tensed, her vision darting around the immediate vicinity, afraid someone might act too quickly and scare Cole off. Being an ex-cop gave him instincts. If he sensed their presence or worse *saw* them, he would have a considerable head start on yet another escape.

Cole made his way toward the Express Mail without surveying his surroundings. He was too focused on his mission to care. Before entering the store, he unexpectedly stopped and turned. Savannah watched him glance over his shoulder and stare in her direction.

Fear paralyzed her. Had he seen her? Sensed her presence? Her initial reaction was to flee – to get as far away from Cole Jordan as possible. The irony of it, she thought. Everyone including her assumed she'd charge the bastard… Instead she cowered from him. Great. She sank back in the seat, "Does he see me? He's not moving."

Selby cut his vision to her, his expression making her feel like a whiny little brat, "He's probably just scouting things out." He radioed his officers, alerting them to Cole's arrival.

Savannah glanced down at her hands. They were shaking. She tried to gain control of the base fear coursing through her. Something wasn't right. Cole should've gone inside by now. Should've already accessed the mailbox. Should've already been handcuffed and read his rights. But he stood, staring in her direction. He knows, she told herself. *He knows I'm here and he's going to run and he'll get away again.*

"Detective, relax," the lieutenant said.

She swallowed hard, her vision riveted to Cole Jordan as she silently pleaded *go inside. Check your mail so I can live in peace. Just check it one last time.*

Seconds ticked by, feeling more like hours. Cole finally reached for the door and walked inside. Savannah released shaky pent-up breath.

Her body still remained tense, waiting. Waiting for the undercover officer inside to give the word. The one saying Cole opened the mailbox registered to a woman Savannah knew was dead.

She listened for the officer to say the word. Nothing. The radio remained stubbornly silent. She looked at her watch. Only a minute passed but it felt like a lifetime. Waiting. Another minute gone. Then another. "What's taking him so long?" she asked.

Selby didn't answer. His vision narrowed and trained on the door as if wondering the same thing.

The waiting gradually drove her crazy. It was their only opportunity to catch Cole. If he slipped through their fingers this time, he'd never be caught. She and Georgia would live their whole lives in fear, looking over their shoulders, dreading the mail and wondering who got the next video showing their horrific suffering.

The undercover officer inside the store gave the signal to move in. Lieutenant Selby opened the car door with a single warning, "Stay in position, Detective. Don't move."

Savannah's reply was met with a slamming door. She leaned forward in the seat, waiting to see Cole dragged out in handcuffs. Seconds passed when another voice crackled over the radio, "Suspect ran out the back door and is headed toward Dorsey Avenue. Need backup now."

The officer's request sent her heart into her stomach. Cole was getting away. Again. And she couldn't do anything – if she followed orders, that was.

The repercussions of disobeying a direct order paled in comparison to living in fear every day of her life. Hell, there were other jobs though none she'd love as much. Whether Josh suspended or dismissed her, her future appeared irrefutably crappy if Cole escaped. Hiding in fear, searching for strange cars, looking for his face. Trying to protect her baby from the evil of Cole Jordan, and trying to raise the infant in a normal environment without transferring her paranoia to her son or daughter.

Bile rose in her throat. She couldn't live like that and she couldn't ask Ennis to either. Most of all, she refused to let their child grow up with the same crippling fear that haunted her.

Savannah pushed the car door open and rounded the driver's side. Settling behind the wheel, she cranked the engine, threw it in drive and floored the accelerator. She sped across the intersection, turning left onto Riverside and headed toward Dorsey Avenue as an officer gave another update, "He's runnin' down the alley on Dorsey. Coming up on Riverside."

Well, she'd see about that. Racing down the street, Savannah steered the car along the front of the meagerly populated strip mall. The alley quickly approached and she slowed for the turn. The car bucked through the entrance to the parking lot and she punched the accelerator again.

"Suspect is headed to the mall's Riverside exit," the officer panted into his radio.

Movement from behind the building forced her to hit the brakes. The Ford screeched to a stop as she came face to face with Cole Jordan.

Their eyes locked and he froze.

Panic laced her blood, her heart still hammering in her chest so hard it literally ached. The engine idled, waiting for her next move. She'd driven like a bat out of hell just to stop short of running Jordan over. The engine sped up slightly, probably voicing its displeasure of being driven so hard. But its impatience evoked images of mashing the accelerator and ending the bastard once and for all. The space between the passenger side and the brick wall left enough running room if he bolted. She couldn't stop him if he did. Cole wasn't stupid enough to run past the driver's side. She'd slam open the door and knock him down. His only escape was around the passenger side or over the car.

Savannah slammed the car into park, threw open the door and slid her gun from its holster, intent on detaining him until the cavalry arrived.

Cole's expression, however, relayed the fact he'd die before being arrested. He would plow her over if need be, just to remain free. He started straight at her, taking one step forward then another.

Savannah tightened her grip on her .38. The familiar weight of it and the security of its power tempted her to squeeze the trigger as she leveled the barrel at his broad chest.

Undaunted, Cole stalked closer, silently daring her to follow through. She stood her ground, "I'll shoot you and you know it," she warned. "Only this time you're going to the morgue."

The words prompted a smile as he neared. Savannah's finger tightened on the trigger. She knew her weapon as well as she knew herself. She knew exactly how much pressure the trigger required before firing and how much play it had. In those brief moments, she bore down on the trigger as various thoughts swirled in her mind. The relief of not looking over her shoulder forever. The joy of raising a child in peace. Hers and Georgia's lives returning to normal because Cole Jordan was dead. Just one more tiny ounce of pressure fulfilled those desires and dreams.

Cole lunged forward but not of his own accord. His muscular form crumpled across the Ford's hood as two undercover officers tackled him into it. Lieutenant Selby appeared shortly after, his chest heaving to catch his breath. His vision locked on her weapon then switched to her. He offered no command to holster the gun, no berating about disobeying, nothing except a concerned frown questioning her intent.

The officers handcuffed Cole while Savannah maintained a steady aim, battling the inner cry to pull the trigger.

"You weren't that cocky on the video were you?" Cole taunted, "How did your buddies enjoy watching it?"

The arresting officers yanked him to a standing position with a stern warning to shut up. Cole merely chuckled, "Between them and your family, I'll bet they were all surprised to see what a weak, sniveling bitch you are."

The mention of family struck her like a brisk slap. Killing Cole Jordan, as appealing as it sounded, wouldn't bring peace of mind. Adding a few more holes to the ones she gifted him with five months ago would not make life easier. If anything it complicated it. An Internal Affairs investigation, a probable trial and the knowledge and guilt that revenge, not self defense, provoked the shooting. No, she needed to concentrate on enjoying life with Ennis and their baby.

To the lieutenant's relief, her finger released the trigger and she eased the .38 back into its holster. She nodded to the two officers, "Take this animal and put him in a cage."

Cole lunged at her, forcing her back a step, her hand instinctively returning to her gun. He laughed, "You really are that scared little bitch from the cabin. The one that cried and screamed for God to save her."

She stared at him, listening to the condescension and patronizing tone. No, she *wasn't* the same person he remembered at the cabin. She was stronger now. With help and intense work, she found the self-assured woman she was before Cole and Jeffrey entered her life. Thanks to her family, friends and God Himself, she'd returned from the abyss of the two killers. Through it all, she faithfully read her Bible, prayed to the Lord, listened to her family and emerged from the experience bent but not broken. No matter how Cole or Jeffrey mocked her religion, she put her faith in God and family and always would.

Fury darkened his features as though he realized the finality of his position, "You think this is it, that you're rid of me and Jeffrey?"

Savannah stood without uttering a word. The beast haunting her nightmares resided behind bars. The beast haunting the shadows now wore handcuffs and was finally headed to jail. No words came to mind for a reply to his question. Yes, she felt secure knowing neither he nor Jeffrey roamed the streets anymore. But no, she'd never feel entirely "rid" of either one.

Her stoic silence escalated his anger, "We'll be seeing each other again and when we do, no one can save you. Not your husband, not your sister, not even God."

Still she said nothing which outraged him. For some reason, he wanted her to speak and she refused to give him the satisfaction.

He strained against the officers' hold, "You're so sanctimonious standing there with your chin up high. I remember you another way. The bitch who hung her head, *praying* for God's mercy, the bitch *crying* for it. The bitch quoting from that precious Bible of hers. That book is a gimmick for fools like you. You read it, learn it, quote it, and it gets you nothing 'cause it's fiction. It's just a tool. Here's a newsflash. God didn't save you, Savannah. Luck did and luck runs out."

It should have provoked a blistering response. Lord knew it deserved one. But Savannah stood as he spewed the venomous words, her mind cranking while he struggled against the officers. Then it dawned on her. The answer to the mysterious letters stood right in front of her, his anger overriding his better sense as he revealed how to decode his and Jeffrey's correspondence.

A genuine smile curved her lips. A shrewd one that gave Cole pause as she simply said, "Thank you."

Confused, he asked, "For what?"

"For giving me the key to yours and Jeffrey's code."

37

She looked too sexy to pass up, sitting at the table with bare feet and dressed in her bright pink tank top and matching shorts. Ennis had never possessed an attraction for feet but Savannah's slender size ten feet fascinated him. The sounds she made when he massaged them, the way the toes curled during lovemaking... She hated her feet, saying they were limousines but Ennis found himself staring at them, his gaze sliding up her long, shapely legs to the objects of his continued obsession. Her breasts. They always seemed perfect to him, in size, weight and shape. They truly fit perfectly in his hands. Now with the pregnancy, they filled out more, gaining heft and size.

Ennis swallowed hard. Those breasts called to him. He could spend weeks with those breasts just with his mouth and according to Savannah's reaction lately, those big beautiful babies also gained considerable sensitivity to his touch. The sight tormented him while he reached down, adjusted his growing erection. *I need those breasts now.* "I thought you were celebrating Cole's arrest," Ennis said, trying to clear the roughness from his voice. "I had a specific activity in mind for that occasion."

His suggestion unfurled a smile. At least she hadn't refused him, he thought. But she hadn't exactly leapt into his arms either. No, she remained seated at the dining table toiling over those damn letters again. His wife drove him crazy. She was headstrong and semi-deaf when it suited her and capable of creating hard-ons with the half-life of plutonium. His boner was ready, willing and able to deliver a celebration for the ages and she'd rather stare at a killer's mail. Something really wasn't right about that.

"Sex, Savannah," he said outright. "I wanted sex and I was hoping you might too. Otherwise my body's pitching a painful and unwanted tent in bed."

"Sex," she repeated distantly. "Sure, babe. Just give me another thirty minutes."

Ennis glanced down at his hopeful arousal. Should he be insulted at the delay? Lately she beat him to the bed for a good, lengthy romp. Now she treated it as though it rated with washing dishes. Her breasts wanted him, he was quite sure of that. So why didn't she act as eager? Incredulous at her response, he asked, "Seriously?" She either failed to realize the improbability of a thirty minute wait or she tested his longevity. Neither scenario suited him. His idea: Jump in bed, make love, sleep, make love again, "Thirty minutes?"

She began feverishly writing then amended the time, "Twenty minutes then."

Not much better, he frowned. He approached the table, intent on discovering what delayed their sex. Plopping his hands on her shoulders, he began what he hoped was a sensual massage. Surely he hadn't lost his touch with foreplay.

Savannah continued writing then flipping pages in the Bible then writing again. Okay, on to step two. Ennis swept her long tresses aside, pressed a lingering kiss to her nape. That always worked. He kissed beneath her ear – that never failed either – especially when he whispered, "I want you now."

Indeed, her hand slowed its pace and her eyes closed when he added another slow kiss to her nape. His ego and erection regained strength. He slowly broke that stubborn side of hers. He continued whispering exactly what he intended to do with his hands, his tongue and his lips – once she hit the sheets.

As he kissed, her body warmed with his touch, relaxed with his kisses. She laid the pen down, stood up. When she turned, the hunger in her eyes described how successful his efforts were. She was ready for him to follow through on his promise. She rose to tiptoe to kiss him, "You win, cowboy."

His hands settled at her hips, brought her against him, "I'll make it worth the ride."

"I know you will. That ol' paperwork can wait till tomorrow. I'll finish it before I go to the prison."

The wheels in his libido ground to a halt. Did she say *prison*? Irritation surfaced and his grasp on her hips firmed, "The prison? Why the hell are you going there?"

Her face split into a radiant smile. She pecked another kiss to his pursed lips, "Now don't get riled. You get to come with me. You'll *want* to see this…"

O O O

They currently stood right outside the visitation room. They'd been relieved of their weapons, temporarily stripped of their shoes and watches and run through God knew how many detectors and checkpoints. All this to see Jeffrey Holland.

Ennis glanced at his wife. Savannah smiled at him. He'd seen this smile plenty of times, mostly before Jeffrey, before her cancer. In classic Rita Hayworth splendor, his wife beamed with carefree joy, its wattage so dazzling that people naturally returned the favor. It was the very smile that brought him to his knees and doomed him from day one.

"Are you ready?" she asked, reaching in her suit jacket. She retrieved a piece of paper that she left folded. "It won't take too long so get ready to leave."

Now that sounded ominous and judging from her cheerful demeanor, she would enjoy every minute of this visit. The weird part: it appeared she looked forward to seeing Jeffrey, at least in some way. Ennis wished she'd let him in on the joke. She hadn't even revealed why the letters preoccupied her. Instead, she sat at the dining table that morning, scribbling on a sheet of paper like a kid late with their homework. She thumbed through her Bible now and again then scribbled then repeated the task a few more times. Once finished, she reverently closed the Good Book while that same shrewd smile brightened her face.

"Well," he motioned to the door, "let's get this over with."

Savannah took a deep breath and reached to open the door. Then she hesitated. That relieved Ennis. At least she hadn't totally lost her mind. The man behind that door craved to inflict pain any way possible. He manipulated and cajoled for his own pleasure. And his sights aimed directly on Savannah. For her to stop for that instant told Ennis she wasn't as completely detached or relaxed as she appeared.

She closed her eyes and he heard her whisper under her breath. A prayer. Then just as quick she squared her shoulders and thrust the door open. Her confident stride impressed Ennis. What a dramatic change from months earlier when she cowered against him at the mere sound of a phone ringing.

"Good morning, Jeffrey," she greeted with the Rita Hayworth smile. Ennis harrumphed. Jeffrey didn't deserve that smile. She reserved that smile for people who mattered and Jeffrey Holland certainly did not matter.

But the smile disarmed Jeffrey. He'd not seen her so happy or self-assured. "To you as well, Savannah. To be honest, I'm rather surprised you're here."

She sat down directly across from him, crossed her legs, "Oh, I wouldn't miss this visit for the world."

Jeffrey found that remark humorous, Ennis noticed. Until the asshole looked up and saw *him*, of course. Then Holland's smile faded, "I see you brought your watchdog too."

Savannah waved off the comment, "Don't mind him. He's along for the ride today."

Where the hell did that accent come from? She sounded so much like Georgia with her thick Southern brogue that Ennis did a doubletake. When she looked up, he realized she wanted confirmation of the fact. So he agreed, "That's right. I'm only along for the ride. Unless you try something then I get to follow through on that promise from our last meeting."

Jeffrey ignored the comment, instead turning his attention to Savannah, "So tell me, how's the young 'un treating Mama this week?"

Ennis bristled at the question. How did Holland know about the baby? He couldn't see Savannah sharing that information with the man who tried to kill her. However the bastard found out, Ennis was about to cure him of his curiosity. He started around the table when Savannah put a hand to his arm as a sign to stop.

Jeffrey puffed up at Ennis, "Now hold on, Detective. I was merely inquiring how she's faring with her pregnancy."

Ennis leaned across the table, "My wife is none of your damn business. Keep your mouth shut and listen to her."

Savannah took that opportunity to fan Jean Furkin's letters onto the table, "You've got an admirer."

Jeffrey smiled. It set Ennis on edge. It resembled a predator before it pounced on its prey. Holland singsonged, "Shame on you, Savannah. Stealing a person's mail is illegal. You could be my bunkmate if you're not careful. Now, wouldn't that be fun?"

An amazing yet essential detail suddenly dawned on Ennis. Not only had Savannah's confidence returned, but for some reason the tiny room didn't produce the usual signs of claustrophobia. She flushed somewhat and he noticed a fine sheen of perspiration on her forehead but her hands generally remained steady, and her breathing was slower and easier than he'd ever seen it. Ennis stared at her, marveling at her composure.

Her charming grin appeared again. She tilted her head and Ennis swore she looked positively luminous. If they weren't stuck in a lousy prison, Ennis would've jumped her on the spot. Problem was her gesture aroused Holland too. The mouse toying with the cat. Ennis watched him carefully, the gleam in his eyes, the way they roamed her body. *Hurry up, Savannah. Let's get outta here…*

"'Fraid you'll have to wait to bunk with me, Jeffrey," she said. "I don't want to compete with Jean. She's a little too kooky for my taste. In fact, she might be crazier than you are."

Holland feigned injury, "Just when I think our relationship is on track you cut me to the bone. Why does this woman concern you? I've already explained you're my one and only."

Ennis's blood pressure flirted with its threshold. By now most husbands would've beaten the presumptuous bastard into a coma. But most husbands weren't protecting their spouse from a serial killer. And most husbands wouldn't have promised to stand back and give her the time she required to face Jeffrey. Regret set in, making him wish he hadn't bargained so carelessly.

Savannah clearly felt the heat emanating from his temper since her hand returned to his arm, this time with a gentle squeeze. She shrugged a shoulder at Jeffrey, "I don't understand why you want me.

Your pen pal seems more attuned to you. She's obsessed with the number ten, like you are." She sounded a bit skeptical, "Although she *is* a Bible thumper. It really surprised me that you developed such a rapport with a devout individual."

Now Jeffrey shrugged, "I do what I can to appease my fans." He started to lean across the table, saw Ennis's brow sink then sat back again. His eyes darkened, sending a violent chill through Ennis. In one instant, Jeffrey's eyes appeared to blacken to an abyss when he spoke to Savannah, "That's why you're so special to me. You know me better than anyone. You're certainly privy to my feelings about God. We had a *long*, extensive discussion about Him that day in the cabin, didn't we?"

Ennis expected a reaction. Anger, fear, anything corresponding to her nature. She fought both emotions for months. When the time came to face the monster again, Ennis only felt a slight shiver. He, on the other hand, flared, "This meeting is done. Let's go, Savannah." To his frustration, she remained seated. His wife infuriated him when her mulish streak kicked in. Was she willing to sacrifice numerous hours of therapy, her struggle to abstain from alcohol and all the huge emotional strides she made the past few months? Just to stare Jeffrey down?

Whatever her mindset, Ennis centered his own just fine, "It's not worth listening to him." He tugged on her arm, "Let's go."

Savannah tensed beneath his hold, her jaw set in refusal. Reinforcing her intent, she resumed her conversation with Holland, "I'm special to you because I'm Number Ten, isn't that right?"

Holland's eyes sparkled as they wandered to her breasts then up again, "It's much more than that. Number Ten is significant to me, yes.

But you remind me of Eva." His eyes slid closed, his expression transforming to unmistakable sexual arousal, "Five days, Savannah. I had her five days."

Ennis glanced down at Jeffrey's hands clasped on the table. They trembled as he clearly revisited his time with the woman. Ennis watched those hands closely. Cuffed or not, Jeffrey was a credible threat.

Holland's eyes opened, settled on her again, "Would you last five days?"

Ennis was literally appalled at the casual nature of the inquiry. Holland presented it as quiet and benign as offering her a glass of water or tea.

With surprising calm, she redirected their discussion, "You and Jean wrote a lot about the number ten, especially from the Bible. The ten cubits, the ten loaves –"

"I think you might," Jeffrey countered confidently. "Eva's strength was different from yours –"

"The ten plagues, the ten horns –"

"You're physically strong but," he tapped his temple, "it's mostly up here. The more your father beat you, the deeper your defiance grew, the stronger you became. You were determined to show him he'd never conquer you. I've seen that defiance in you and with it, you gave me something to live for. If I can do what your father couldn't –"

"The ten lepers," she proceeded after a brief hesitation. Ennis noticed the talk of R.J. rattled her but she quickly regrouped, "the ten virgins –"

A tiny smile crossed Jeffrey's face, "Okay, Savannah, we'll talk about your Bible's list of tens."

Ennis recalled the intense studying she'd done through the evening and that morning. Maybe that's what she was doing, he thought. Brushing up on that list.

"I stayed up late last night, Jeffrey. Reading my Bible. The one book you've been studying as well. I discovered what the number ten signifies. It signifies completion."

Jeffrey countered, "It also signifies perfection."

"But completion is more your style. You want Number Ten, you said, and you'd do anything to get it. Even write a person who could help you with that task."

The smile turned sour. Ennis watched Jeffrey's arms tense, his fingers curl into fists. Ennis stepped toward the table, purposefully insinuating himself between the two, "Careful what you're thinking, Holland. You make one move and you'll make my day."

Savannah never broke visual contact with Jeffrey, "You and Jean devised a code for your correspondence. A code that had me buffaloed as my husband would say. I worked a long time to crack it. I think you chose the Bible because it was a backhanded insult to me. You mocked my faith when you were beating me. You taunted me with God and the Bible verses I recited. It shouldn't have surprised me that you chose the Bible as a means to taunt me again. You and your 'new friend' created a clever code to communicate with each other. It took me a while but this is what I came up with." She held up the folded piece of paper. "Take a look and tell me if I'm right." She slid the folded paper across to Jeffrey.

The temperature plummeted between the two. Ennis heard the arrogance in her voice. She sat straighter in the chair, her posture more aggressive as she leaned slightly nearer to the monster. Such a diverse change from months earlier but the show of assertiveness concerned Ennis. Jeffrey's dark eyes narrowed at her. He assumed he retained the upper hand, held her fear in his grasp to toy with it as he pleased. Savannah's poise pricked that assumption and most assuredly his ego.

The killer's stare drilled her as she slid the paper across the table. Something wasn't right. Ennis failed to put his finger on it but that paper was bound to disturb Jeffrey or she wouldn't have poked it at him.

Ennis motioned to the guard. Savannah felt sure she'd cracked the code and if she had, besides Ennis, that guard was her only protection against an enraged Jeffrey Holland.

The guard moved in behind Jeffrey who slowly unfolded the paper. His eyes shifted down to the page and Ennis saw a subtle change in his expression. One that telegraphed imminent violence. The more Holland read, the angrier he grew.

Ennis took Savannah by the arm and was surprised when she voluntarily rose from her seat. She nodded to him, silently agreeing it was time to go. She wasted no time heading to the door. Ennis expedited their departure with a gentle hand at her back. He heard the chair scrape the concrete. Jeffrey was on his feet. The sound of those feet scrambled toward them, forcing Ennis to nudge harder at the small of her back. The second they were clear of the room, he slammed the door behind them. A loud report echoed like gunfire when Holland pounded on the metal door, "Savannah! Get back in here! Don't walk away from me, you bitch! If I ever see you again I'll –"

"Let's go home," was all she said, overriding Jeffrey's vicious tirade and vile, cruel acts he vowed to inflict upon her.

Ennis hurried her along, allowing their escort to lead the way. He wanted out of the prison before he collapsed or worse, Holland broke free from the guards.

Jeffrey's threats echoed down the hallway, leaving Ennis's heart deciding to either leap from his throat or just plain attack him. Savannah, however, seemed surprisingly at ease. In fact, he noticed quite a smug grin curving her lips. "What just happened?" he asked.

"I'll tell you in the car."

So there. Normally waiting wasn't a problem. Today, he practically busted a gut with anticipation as they collected their weapons and passed through the series of electronic gates. She headed to the Camaro and once they climbed inside, Ennis sighed then slumped against the seat, grateful the encounter was over. Savannah cranked the engine, flipped on the AC and waited patiently for him to regroup his poise. "You okay?" she finally asked.

"I should be asking you that question. But yeah, I'm better now. What the hell was on that paper?"

"Remember the letters without the paragraph code? The ones with the lottery numbers?"

A test. Just what he needed. He was on the verge of a nervous breakdown and she fired questions at him. Great. He nodded to move her along.

"I mentioned the fact either the staff neglected to copy all the mail or Jeffrey threw away the key to those mysteriously coded letters and he did. Cole sent him a Bible for a reason. Used the letters to cover why he'd sent it by preaching religion and so forth."

Yeah, yeah, yeah, "But what caused Jeffrey's explosion?" He pushed her, he realized it but frankly he was dying by degrees. He asked the time and she explained how to build a watch.

She relented with a easy shrug, "Okay. You'll figure it out once you see it." She reached in her suit jacket again, handed him a folded paper just like she'd done with Jeffrey.

Ennis's hands still shook. Holding the paper steady was hopeless. He'd never be able to read it at this rate. And her calm disposition baffled the shit out of him. Jeffrey's fury and horrific promises sent his stomach into such a storm, he barely kept his breakfast down. For Savannah to smile after Jeffrey pledged to slice her to pieces made Ennis question her sanity. Jeffrey's words scared *him*, so how the hell could she *smile* after hearing the monster vow such brutality?

He unfolded the page, self-conscious of his shaking hands. Savannah's warm hand covered his, "Babe, calm down."

Oh sure. Easy for her to say – evidently. He gifted her with a nod while turning his attention to the page he held. On it Savannah wrote the "lottery numbers" then below filled in the blanks and underlined particular words:

5-2-33-5

Deuteronomy *2:33*

*The LORD our God **delivered** him over to us and we struck him down, together with his sons and his whole army.*

1-16-5-4

Genesis *16:5*

*Then Sarai said **to** Abram, "You are responsible for the wrong I am suffering. I put my servant in your arms, and now that she knows she is pregnant, she despises me. May the LORD judge between you and me."*

35-2-1-8

Habakkuk 2:1

*I will stand at my watch and **station** myself on the ramparts.*

Further down the page was another message, this one from the last letter Cole sent Jeffrey. Again, Savannah wrote the supposed lottery numbers above the book, chapter, verse and word they represented. The verses, from Judges, Deuteronomy, and two from Genesis read "Delivered to sister and brother."

Somehow Ennis's stomach wasn't feeling any better with the knowledge the two killers conversed so easily. "Oh my God," he groaned. He rubbed his head since it decided to join the chorus with his stomach. "There's no telling what they could have done if you hadn't stayed with these damn letters. And I kept trying to pry you off them."

"I understood why you wanted me to stop."

She sounded nearly apologetic and that made him angry. Angry at himself. If she hadn't cracked the code, Jeffrey and Cole could have gone merrily along with their plans to kill Savannah and probably Georgia too. She'd likely saved her own life and her sister's too – again.

She handed him another folded page, "This caused Jeffrey's meltdown."

His wasn't entirely sure his heart could take anymore. They'd escaped Jeffrey's fury by two measly seconds. Now he was about to see what incited the monster's rage. So, as Jeffrey had minutes prior, he unfolded the paper, curious what provoked such a dramatic reaction from the usually composed killer. The page read:

1-20-16-8-9-16

*Genesis 20:16. To Sarah he said, "I am giving **your brother** a thousand shekels of silver. This **is** to cover the offense against you before all who are with you; you are completely vindicated."*

44-5-18-8-11

*Acts 5:18 They arrested the apostles and put them **in** the public **jail**.*

1-1-22-11

*Genesis 1:22. God blessed them and said, "Be fruitful and increase in **number** and fill the water in the seas, and let the birds increase on the earth."*

1-16-3-9

Genesis 16:3. So after Abram had been living in Canaan ***ten*** *years, Sarai his wife took her Egyptian maidservant Hagar and gave her to her husband to be his wife.*

20-11-30-14

Proverbs 11:30. The fruit of the righteous is a tree of life, and he who ***wins*** *souls is wise.*

7-18-25-17-22

Judges 18:25. The Danites answered, "Don't argue with us, or some hot-tempered men will attack you, and ***you*** *and your family will* ***lose*** *your lives."*

He really needed Mylanta. Maybe even a fire extinguisher to put out the inferno in his gut. If he'd known what the paper said before they ventured into the visitation room, they wouldn't have gone in. Of course Jeffrey went berserk after reading the last passage. Savannah not only cracked his code but rubbed his nose in the fact. Ennis cringed at the scenarios shadowing his panicked brain. Savannah barely escaped with her life in that prison. Holland's fists pounded the door with such force Ennis feared he'd break through. The killer raged against her with threats that turned Ennis's blood cold. What he promised to do before letting her die made Ennis literally nauseous.

As if sensing his turmoil, Savannah took his hand, clasped it her warm one, “It’s okay, babe. It’s over. It’s really over.”

Oh yeah? Tell his stomach. And his heart. And don’t forget his brain that still ran rampant with horrible scenes of Holland’s promises. When he turned to her, he noticed the genuine smile curving her lips. The same Rita Hayworth smile reminiscent of a year earlier when their lives were serene with no breast cancer, no Jeffrey or Cole. Ennis fell in love with that smile and now here it was, back in its full glory. How could he argue with that? He returned the smile with hopes, “It’s really over.”

38

At forty, Leah Prince looked remarkably young for her age, especially after marrying a moody, fractious Army Ranger and giving birth to two kids. Savannah always believed only an exceedingly patient woman could or would tolerate Seth. A woman who could hold her own against such pigheadedness, and could oppose him when necessary and teach him his way wasn't always the best way. Turned out Leah Sutton was just the woman. She stood around Georgia's height, and kept herself trim and fit. At work she wore her golden brown hair in a bun but on her days off let it drape down her back.

Nature gifted Leah with soft, friendly features that naturally comforted people and in her profession of trauma nurse, seeing a calm face among the chaos was priceless. Over the years she'd fielded family emergencies with her expertise and earlier that week Savannah relied on her sister-in-law's knowledge for far more than a simple cut or bruise. When Savannah drove to Seth's the night of hers and Ennis's argument, it was Leah who quieted her worst fears and asked questions in a manner that resulted in answers without escalating her panic. With a few questions and an assuring embrace, Leah alleviated her worries of a miscarriage.

For all her professional expertise and general everyday aplomb, it surprised Savannah when Leah's composure cracked over one triviality – the line of thick dark hair that proliferated beneath Seth's nose.

After Lindsey's play concluded, Savannah felt Leah's temperature rise when the mustache set off mooneyes and fluttering hearts among the younger girls and sent the older ones on a nostalgic trip. Sweet, mild-mannered Leah Prince bowed up at the overt female interest while her husband lapped it up like a starved alley cat finishing off a bowl of milk.

Before Leah plucked the mustache out with her bare hands, Savannah hurried her brother along on the pretext of time. She'd rounded Seth up and reminded him of Leah's early morning shift at the hospital.

She'd never considered her brother stupid but he sure presented a fine impression of it sometimes. Any married man who encouraged swooning females only invited violence, she nearly told him. And it wasn't really smart to provoke a spouse who worked with needles and scalpels and other sharp, pointy objects.

Since arriving back at their new house, her brother migrated to the coffee pot. Not to brew coffee as any normal person might but to stare at his reflection in the carafe. Savannah really needed a shot of caffeine and her brother blocked the whole area with his tall, muscular form.

He combed his mustache with his fingers and grinned into the curved glass. The face staring back looked like a funhouse mirror, fat and distorted. At first Savannah watched in amusement as her brother primped. It proved he was human but it also interfered with her need for caffeine and that wasn't so funny.

He asked, "You really think I look like him?"

Savannah wasn't sure who he'd asked. Leah crossed her arms as he admired the thick, slightly graying mustache. Seth's ego leaned toward the hefty side anyway but when the ladies at Lindsey's play fawned over him and lavished him with compliments on his Magnum-esque looks, Savannah knew Leah was in for a long night – and if he didn't shut up soon, Leah would probably pin him to the floor and personally demonstrate her nurse's proficiency with a razor.

"He's talking to you," Leah nodded to Savannah. "'Cause he already knows my stance on that hairball growing on his lip."

Uh-oh. How did she answer? If she said no, she'd hurt Seth's feelings. If she said yes, she'd make Leah mad and after seeing her seethe earlier, Savannah really hated to stoke that fire. She cut her vision to Ennis who opted to go the Switzerland route. Thanks, she wanted to say. Thanks a lot.

Even Lindsey and her younger brother Dylan awaited Aunt Savannah's answer. Aunt Savannah prayed she didn't make an instant enemy out of either Seth or Leah. She also prayed that she didn't sound cheesy when she said, "I do see a resemblance but I also wouldn't want to kiss a caterpillar if Ennis grew one."

Seth straightened, turned to face her. She'd managed to aggravate him, she thought. Well, it figured. If any family had a no-win policy, the Princes wrote and copyrighted it. Her brother frowned which gave him an uncanny resemblance to a frustrated Magnum. "Well," he sighed in defeat, "it does itch."

He ambled toward the living room where Ennis switched on the baseball game. Savannah silently thanked her husband. Get Seth involved with baseball. He'd gripe at the Braves instead of how the women in his life ganged up on him.

Leah leaned closer to Savannah with a sincere, "Thank you. That bush has made our lives hell lately."

"Mama," Lindsey scolded. "Don't cuss."

Leah lifted a brow at her sister-in-law. It seemed to question who the mother was. "Yes, ma'am," she finally replied to her daughter. Then to Savannah, "Kids. You try to teach them and it comes back to haunt you."

Oh, Savannah could only imagine. If calling parents down for cussing was considered payback, their child would have a field day with her. Just another thing to change about herself. Her language.

Lindsey bear-hugged her, "Can I stay here this weekend, Aunt Vanna?"

Sure, why not? After all, no time like the present to start sweeping her vocabulary clean. The request didn't come as a complete surprise since Lindsey loved their new house and practically deemed the guest room her own. "It's fine with me," Savannah said, "but you'd better get approval from Mama and Daddy first."

Seth nodded and Leah shrugged, "If you and Ennis are okay with it, so are we." She addressed her daughter, "Mind Aunt Vanna and Uncle Ennis and don't go out without their permission. It's a new neighborhood and you don't know anyone. Daddy'll pick you up tomorrow evening so we can get to church early Sunday."

Sliding her arm across Lindsey's shoulders, Savannah drew her closer, "We'll have fun tomorrow. I recall something about breaking in the oven. Chocolate chip cookies, wasn't it?"

"*Double* chocolate chip," Lindsey corrected.

"Double chocolate chip it is," her aunt acknowledged. She winked at Leah, "So who was that boy mooning over my niece tonight?"

Lindsey's mother rolled her eyes, "Oh, that's *Bennett*."

"The boyfriend," Seth disdainfully added.

Savannah feigned shock, "A boyfriend at your age? I'm not sure I'm comfortable with this. I'd better run Bennett the Boyfriend for outstanding warrants before you get too serious."

Temporarily stunned, Lindsey's eyes popped wide, "Aunt Vanna, he's nice..."

"But run his parents just to be sure," Seth suggested from the couch.

"Daddy, stop it!" the girl cried.

Savannah chuckled at the girl's reaction. It may have been fun teasing around with her niece but if she threatened the same thing with her own kid, there'd be hell to pay, especially if their child possessed Mama's temper. Her smile wilted with that image. Best to change the subject. "So does Bennett the Boyfriend rate any cookies?"

Lindsey's mad spell faded and she blushed. Savannah took that as a yes, "Looks like a double batch then."

Leah shook her head, amused, "You're so good with our kids.

It'll be nice to spoil *your* children for once."

"Let's avoid using the plural of the word. One is enough for about eighteen years. It'll take me that long to hone my mothering skills to rival Ennis."

Leah whispered, "He's the kind that'll want a dozen kids."

Savannah nodded knowingly, "And people in you-know-where want cold water too. Mama raised Seth and Georgia then she got me. By the time I hit my teens, she told me I could've brought Job to his knees. I don't want a dozen potential mini mes running around."

Her sister-in-law laughed. Somehow Savannah neglected to find the humor but smiled anyway. She supposed from the outside looking in, it was comical. But for Charlene, she probably stayed awake nights wondering what sin she committed to be cursed with such a rebellious urchin.

"I'd swear something's up with Dane and Georgia," Leah said. "He looked plum wily tonight before they left. And don't think I missed that wink he gave you."

Dane hadn't exactly sworn her to secrecy, she told herself. Once she realized Seth and Ennis cared more about the Braves' five to one deficit, she waved Leah closer then covered Lindsey's ears, "He's going to propose to her this weekend. That's why he was so eager to hit the road."

Lindsey squirmed away, "I wanna hear the secret."

"You'll hear all about it later, sweetheart," she told her niece.

The girl huffed up, crossed her arms and stomped off pouting. Oh boy, Savannah winced. *I'm really in trouble when* that *girl gets mad at me.*

Leah waved off her daughter's drama, "She'll be fine. You know how kids are."

"I'll need you on speed dial for emergency parenting advice. Being the aunt is so much easier than being the mom."

Seth's wife beamed, "I finally get to find out." She visually rounded up her daughter, found her sitting next to Seth on the couch. "Don't you think Dane's pushing it? I mean, Georgia was devastated after the divorce and they haven't known each other that long."

That was the beauty of Rutherford men, Savannah wanted to say. No matter how hardcore against marriage a woman might be, insert a Rutherford and their whole attitude changed. The second she met Ennis, fascination set in about this gentle, thoughtful man. Then denial followed. Fictional characters are sweet and protective, not flesh and blood ones who hit and demean women for their own pleasure. Then reality dawned. Ennis was different. Ennis truly cared for her and loved her and the biggest bonus of all – she loved him right back. "Oh," Savannah smiled a little, "I'm bettin' things work out for them. Unless Dane flat-out faints before he asks her, which is a distinct possibility." She grimaced as her bladder pinged for a pit-stop. It nagged at her for an hour and she'd been able to delay the trip but not anymore it said, not unless she handed her guests some oars… "I'll be right back."

Leah shook her head, "I remember those days. The bathroom as a second home."

Yeah, "Tell me about it." She headed off to appease her pea-sized bladder. Their new home was big and beautiful but the bathroom felt like a mile long hike when nature's urge hit.

If her bladder didn't ease up soon, she'd have to create a map of toilets around the city just for emergency peeing. Washing her hands, she stared at her belly, "Listen, kid, I'm peeing for two now. Can't you hold it a little longer for me?"

She returned to the living room, met with Leah who appeared as interested in the Braves' miserable losing streak as she was. Savannah stretched her back, "How did you cope with all these changes? I'm just hoping I *survive* this kid. He or she has a bladder the size of a gnat and if my feet get any bigger, I'll have to shop at Barnum & Bailey for new shoes. I've already had to buy new blouses 'cause I'm starting to blossom like Dolly Parton."

Leah chuckled, "I'll bet Ennis loves that part."

"Let's just say he has a new hobby and that's losing himself in them."

"What are you talking about?" Lindsey asked.

Savannah immediately shut her mouth. It was worse than the time when the girl asked where babies came from. She hoped between her and Leah they could deflect the comment onto something more suitable. Like cookies. Lots and lots of cookies.

Judging from Lindsey's upturned, eager features, neither of them stood a chance. Savannah would leap into a vat of acid before actually *repeating* her last statement and explaining the meaning behind it. Little girls Lindsey's age didn't need *that* particular education yet.

Leah glanced at Savannah's belly, "You mind if I tell her

about..."

She just shrugged. Hell, the entire universe would know before sundown anyway.

Seth's wife bent to whisper the news and the second it registered, Lindsey threw her arms around Savannah, "A baby! Yay! I hope it's a girl!"

Smiling, Savannah embraced the youngster who gripped her like a bear hugging a tree, "I just pray the kid is my exact opposite in some ways *and* I hope my bladder returns to normal."

"What if you have twins?" the girl wanted to know. Her enthusiasm returned full force, "Two girls!"

Fear struck Savannah's heart. Two girls or two boys or one of each. The mere notion of raising two babies at once made her head ache. "Please don't say such things, sweetheart. One is hard enough, two would be insanity."

39

Excluding the sweltering weather, it was a nice Saturday evening. She and Lindsey spent the afternoon baking cookies and Savannah noticed that somehow Bennett the Boyfriend missed out. Once her niece sank her teeth into the soft chewy treasures, no mention of Bennett fell out of the kid's mouth. Yes, Savannah thought proudly. Lindsey was a bona fide, card-carrying Prince. Never surrender the chocolate except under threat of death.

Seth dropped by around six to pick up his daughter for church the next day. After they left, Savannah and Ennis unpacked a few more boxes to make the place seem more like home. Then they piled up in bed to watch the Braves lose yet again. Savannah changed the channel to a repeat of a Falcons game. Much better.

Ennis leaned closer, reached for the remote. She lightly slapped his hand with a mild scolding, "Hands off, bad boy. No toying with my Falcons, even on reruns."

He pressed a kiss to her shoulder, "Who's more fun? Me or the Falcons?"

"You know the answer to that. The Falcons can be disappointing. You never are."

He tugged at her nightshirt, "Isn't this too warm to wear? Lindsey's gone. Take it off."

"You're not subtle tonight, are you?" She barely got the words out before he stripped the shirt over her head and tossed it to the chair across the room.

"No, not when I want something." He snuggled closer, his hand caressing her bare thigh.

She stared at his hand while a partial smile emerged, "That's a penalty for encroachment."

He slid his hand beneath the covers, "As I recall that penalty isn't so stiff – unlike me, that is." He touched her inner thigh, the fingers slipping between them to ease her legs apart. He continued, "The trick is, after getting penalized, can the player still score a touchdown? That," he leaned in, his lips touching hers like a whisper, "is my specialty."

She smiled, "You're pretty good at that, I'll agree."

In one deft move, he rolled atop her, letting his weight pin her, "My playbook has two options. I can bull my way for a touchdown." He dipped his head for another kiss and worked his way down her throat, "or finesse my way there."

Savannah opened her mouth to answer when his lips met hers in a deep, demanding kiss. His warm hand covered her right breast, squeezing it tenderly. She held to him as the rough pad of his thumb grazed the nipple. She separated from the kiss long enough to ask, "Is this bulling or finessing because it feels like both."

"No talking," he said, his mouth capturing hers once more. His hand glided from her breast to her belly then slipped into her panties.

When his fingers pressed against her, she moaned against his lips.

Taking that cue, his fingers curled into the panties, eased them down her legs. He disappeared under the covers and Savannah saw him sling the panties from beneath the covers.

She suddenly gasped as his hot, wet tongue dipped into her navel then slid further down. Now *this* was how hot nights were intended to be spent, she reflected at the very same time the phone rang. The incessant – now irritating – tune "A Little Less Conversation" shattered her focus on all the delightful sensations Ennis created. "Ennis," she called only for him to ignore her. She reached to the nightstand, "The phone. Let me answer the phone…"

"No," was all he said.

She strained toward the nightstand but Ennis grasped her hips, pulled her back down. "*Ennis*, please," she begged.

"I'm trying, babe," was the muffled reply.

"No, I mean stop. *No*," she couldn't think straight because his efforts were more than succeeding, "I mean *pause*." Savannah strained to reach her cell phone. Through the fog of pleasure, a scrap of clarity floated to the forefront. Dane was proposing to Georgia that night. The caller – despite their bad timing – might have been her sister to announce her acceptance. Or, she thought dismally, Dane calling to cry on her shoulder.

"God made voicemail for a reason," her husband hinted from under the covers.

She couldn't let Georgia leave a message on voicemail, for

Heaven's sake. Or Dane either. Not with something that important.

She struggled to close her thighs but that only complicated matters as his five o'clock shadow scraped along her sensitive inner thighs.

Sensing her urgency, Ennis locked his arms around her legs, effectively leaving her at his mercy. Now she *really* couldn't move. To tilt the situation to his favor, he dove back in, doubling his efforts until she wriggled in his grasp. It only intensified his objective and reinforced his hold.

Finally, she threw back the covers, praying he'd listen, "The phone..." Her breath caught in her throat as the sensations built at lightning speed now, "Oh God, Ennis, stop, *please*... The phone..." Her eyes closed tight and she earnestly pushed at him, "Ennis..." With the blood rushing in her head – and everywhere else – she wasn't sure if she shouted it and really didn't care. The last thing she wanted to do was answer the phone during a climax.

He heeded her tone and suspended his efforts. His frustration showed in his expression and voice, "Since when does the phone override our sex life?"

She inhaled sharply, willing the sensations to ebb, at least for the time being. She stared down at his head, his hair flaring out in every direction. His flushed face no doubt matched the flaming red of her own and while trying to catch her breath, she explained, "Since your brother is proposing to my sister. Tonight's the night."

Ennis groaned, rested his chin below her navel, "That boy has the worst timing." He gestured to her, "Go ahead, I promise to play nice.

But I'm not letting you go."

And he didn't. She felt embarrassed at her awkward position as she answered the phone. Ennis had her knees flung over his shoulders, and his chin rested at the apex of her thighs as he stared back at her.

To ease her conscience, she closed her eyes while greeting the caller. It was Georgia. "Guess what?" the older sister sounded like a giddy fifteen year-old.

Savannah played along, "What?"

After a dramatic pause, Georgia exclaimed, "Dane and I are getting married!"

"Oh, Georgia! I'm so happy for you both –" her statement was cut considerably short when Ennis dove in for a momentary second try. She strained against him, covered the receiver, whispering, "You promised." To punctuate her warning, she swatted the top of his head, gave him a good-natured but somewhat serious glare.

He backed off with a smile while she asked Georgia, "So when did Dane pop the question?"

"A little while ago. We had supper and –" Georgia squealed loud enough Savannah pulled the phone from her ear, grimacing. Georgia giggled, "Stop that."

Savannah guessed she wasn't exactly talking to her. Then Ennis tossed in his two cents, "Georgia, tell Dane to behave himself."

Look who's talking, Savannah's expression said.

He shrugged then kissed her stomach. She expected him to move lower – just to exact a little vengeance for her glare but he pressed a long lingering kiss to her belly then placed his ear just below her navel, listening.

Savannah couldn't help but smile. She covered the receiver, whispering, "I think it's kinda early for her to speak to you."

"You mean it's too early for *him* to speak. We're having a boy, I can feel it."

Men and their boys, she thought. It honestly didn't matter to her – boy or girl – as long as the baby was healthy – and their temper wasn't reminiscent of The Exorcist. "So when's the wedding?" she asked Georgia. She figured her sister might hem and haw with "not sure" or "don't know yet".

"We're thinking August. That way you'll be able to travel with the baby by then."

Wow, she thought. That was faster than green grass through a goose. It took her and Ennis at least a whole *day* to figure out their wedding month. Dane and Georgia decided to sprint their way to the matrimonial finish line. Savannah wondered if her sister had already chosen colors, her dress and the cake. But first things first, "Where is this wedding taking place?" *As if I don't know.* But it was fun to finally hear her sister so blissfully happy. Might as well feed the joy. Meanwhile she heard Ennis mumbling to her navel. He was prepping their child for the future – and probably forewarning their little one of the hazards of being a Prince/Rutherford mix.

"At the ranch," Georgia replied. "It worked for you and Ennis so we'll stay with tradition. Do you think August is okay for you?"

Good grief. "Stop worrying about me. This is your moment, not mine."

"But you're my matron of honor. You have to be there."

"I will be. It's a baby, not a brain transplant. Go ahead and plan your big day, sis. I wouldn't miss it."

Ennis continued the baby talk. He sounded absolutely adorable as he spoke to her stomach, "...football and baseball and maybe even golf if you get your mama's hankering for it. Then you'll go to college and be a doctor or lawyer –"

"Whoa there, cowboy," she cut in. "No lawyers. And the doctor is in question too."

"What?" Georgia asked.

"Sorry. Ennis is planning our child's future."

Ennis smiled at her belly, "These little babies are going to be so beautiful and successful –"

"Wait," Savannah interrupted again. The phone call from her sister took a back seat to his odd – and alarming – declaration. Threading her fingers through his thick mass of hair, she lifted his head until their vision met. "You just said *babies*, not baby."

He nodded. She forced herself to ask, "What did you mean by that?" And please don't say what I think you meant...

"It's Ma's family. We've got two sets of 'em."

Her mouth went dry as reality hit, "Sets. Ennis, *sets* could mean anything. Furniture comes in sets. So do encyclopedias, tools, golf clubs. My God, there are *fourteen* golf clubs in a set." Her hand migrated to her belly. The world began spinning. Sets. How many little ones currently resided below her rapidly expanding breasts?

Savannah suddenly squeezed her thighs together, trapping his smiling face between them. A smile he'd likely ditch if the wrong answer fell from his lips. She tightened her hold on his neck like a vise until his grin wavered and his face flushed from the pressure. She tried not to sound gruff, "What does the word *set* mean in your family?"

"Savannah, what's going on?" Georgia wanted to know.

She was nearly afraid to find out. "I'm nearly afraid to find out."

Ennis's smile now widened to one of a man who wasn't destined for nine months of leg cramps, swollen ankles, Baby's feet in his ribs or any of the thousands of disagreeable aspects associated with just one single child. He kissed her again, "Ma's family has the twin gene."

Savannah swallowed hard. Two at one time. *Oh... My... God...* "Georgia," she said weakly.

"Honey, it'll be okay," her sister assured. "Chances are it's not twins. Just because they have the twin gene doesn't mean you'll have twins."

Savannah heard it. By the conclusion of her sister's pep talk, her voice developed a smile, probably as big as Ennis's. "You think this is funny," Savannah accused. "How in the world can you possibly find this amusing? You're about to marry a guy who has the same gene."

Silence trailed into a full ten seconds when Georgia finally answered, "Hmm. You're right, I am. Well, I guess there's only one thing you can do at this point."

"Pray?"

"That and be grateful you're having babies and not golf clubs."

Savannah never credited her father with being a poet. Besides his swinging fists and storming temper, she knew him as boorish and terse. On occasion, however, he exhibited a rare wisdom, expressed in a way only R.J. Prince could. Her father's words to her mother floated back to Savannah's overloaded mind. *If she was twins that kid'd be an everlastin' riot. If she was triplets, she'd be an insurrection.*

Savannah fell back on her pillow with a sigh. From zero to two children. The world would never be the same…

40

One Week Later

For the first time in weeks, Savannah successfully overlooked the sultry weather. Well, semi-successfully. She supposed it revolved around less stress in her life. No murder case looming over her, no mayor breathing down her neck and most importantly, no Cole or Jeffrey to worry about.

She closed her eyes, tilted her chin toward the Sunday morning sky and inhaled long and deep. Georgia pine mixed with blooming gardenias and fresh cut grass drifted past with the breeze. Sounds of chirping and singing birds brought a smile to her face. Even the warmth of the sun felt comforting.

"Seven, eight or nine?" Ennis asked.

His question, along with a muted metallic clang temporarily suspended her reverie. She turned to him, watching as he trolled the clubs in her golf bag.

"Isn't it beautiful this morning?" she inquired, still admiring nature's splendor.

"Yeah," he deadpanned. "We're standing on a giant lawn in the heat and I can't tell an eight iron from a clothes iron."

She leaned down, placed the ball on the tee, "I want the pitching wedge, not an iron."

Ennis stared at her as if she spoke an entirely different language, "The what?" He stared into the golf bag like it was a giant Rubik's Cube then scratched his head.

"Pitching wedge," she reached over, slid the club out. Ennis just sighed, "Hey, at least I know the driver and putter."

U-huh, she thought. Because they're the biggest and smallest – well, *narrowest* – clubs in the set. She took time to offer a lesson because she'd hoped to encourage him to try the sport. Granted, it took some learning. Distance, which club, wind direction and speed, not to mention fairways, roughs and reading the greens. So many things to analyze and consider but her husband was a fast learner. He could do it. "The pitching wedge," she explained. "It's used for shorter distance holes from around eighty to one hundred thirty yards. They're great for some par three holes because the ball flies high and not too far and when it hits the green it 'bites', meaning little to no rolling. It's a very versatile club. They're great for approach shots when you need precision, not power." She stopped there since his eyes glazed over from information overload.

Savannah approached the tee, gave a test swing then backed away with a thought, "You want to try?"

He snorted, "You want to find your ball in the next year?"

She waved him over while he vehemently shook his head. "Come on, scaredy cat," she teased. "Try it once."

"Babe, seriously, it's not my thing. I'm a football guy and I ain't slapping pads and a helmet on you, am I?"

Okay, she thought. She'd give up for the day. Yes, she loved football too but not enough to actually play it. She took another practice swing, judging the power and distance. The breeze was negligible so it presented little effect on the ball. She stepped to the tee, lined up her shot, adjusted her stance. Then she stopped, the feeling of being watched tickling at her brain. "Ennis, are you staring at my ass?"

"M-hmm."

She'd felt the same nagging feeling for the last six holes. Someone staring at her. Now she knew the culprit. "In a few months you won't have to stare. It'll be so big you can see it from space."

"Are you sure it's safe to do this? I mean, the baby and all. With all these twisty, turny gyrations…"

She stepped back from the ball again. It took less than a week for him to swoop into his protective husband – and now father – persona. Her hubby, while supportive, really hadn't cottoned to the idea of her golfing while pregnant but before getting upset, she reminded, "I asked the doctor and he said it's okay. Baby and I will be fine." One baby. Whew. Not a whole daycare class at once. She wanted to try out motherhood by dipping a toe in, not plunging head first into the deep end and thankfully, for once, she'd satisfied everyone in her life. She'd seen the doctor about the baby and ensured his or her health then gone to Dr. Wyatt for her breast cancer checkup. All was well with mother and child.

Trying again, she approached the ball, lined up the shot. She swung back and on the downswing, felt the club head strike the ball perfectly. A giddy, warm joy spread through her at the sight of the ball sailing right toward the hole. Savannah was in her element again – and sober while playing. She drank her way through her senior year in high school. Drank her way through tournaments and lost. Drank her way out of full scholarships and because of it, she lost the passion for golf.

Shielding her eyes against the sun, she giggled as the ball landed on the green a few feet from the hole. One trip to the golf course and her passion and love for golf rekindled with the new clubs, the manicured course and her handsome caddy from Texas. She had her life back and in the spring, she'd share that new peaceful existence with their newborn child. Yes, it was a beautiful day and finally, a beautiful life.

J.L. Lemon lives in Texas surrounded by a loving and supportive family, two adorable and devoted puppies, and hordes of garden gnomes.

Before 2002, J.L. Lemon wrote opinions and product reviews for an online consumer guide. When fellow reviewers cited the author's knack for humor, she decided to return to writing fiction. Along with the standalone title Second Chances, she's published 8 books in the Savannah Stories Series.

www.ingramcontent.com/pod-product-compliance
Lightning Source LLC
Chambersburg PA
CBHW030922020726
47498CB00001B/68

* 9 7 8 0 9 7 9 6 1 1 7 8 0 *